DEBORAH SLAYING

A Novel

Book of Deborah 3

Avraham Azrieli

ISBN: 978-1-953648-07-5

ALSO BY AVRAHAM AZRIELI

Fiction:

The Masada Complex
The Jerusalem Inception
The Jerusalem Assassin
Christmas for Joshua
The Mormon Candidate
The Bootstrap Ultimatum
. Thump
The Elixirist
Deborah Rising
Deborah Calling
Deborah Slaying
Deborah Striking

Nonfiction:

Your Lawyer on a Short Leash – A Guide to Dealing with Lawyers
One Step Ahead – A Mother of Seven Escaping Hitler's Claws

Author Website:
www.AzrieliBooks.com

For Sarai Azrieli, with love.

DEBORAH SLAYING

1

The moment Deborah and Sallan dismounted the horses outside his family home, loud drumming erupted. The sound came from the top of the hill, where the king's palace dominated the city. They tied the horses and entered through the tall hedges into the front garden, where his whole family was gathered around a table for a meal. The drumming rattled the air, and a flock of birds bolted from the canopy of the jujube tree above the table. The children pointed at the fleeing birds.

At the head of the table was Sallan's mother, whose black dress contrasted with the colorful dresses of the other women — her daughters and granddaughters — as well as the white robes of the newlywed couple at the opposite end of the table. The matriarch rose slowly, her eyes gleaming, and opened her arms. Sallan limped over and kissed her on both cheeks.

Deborah stayed back, her shorn head covered with the hood of her plain travel robe. The hood did little to muffle the drumming, which was ponderous, unlike the light patter of the priests' small drums she had heard at the Hebrew temple in Shiloh.

"Blessed be Qoz." Umm-Sallan caressed her son's cheek as if he were a child, not a gray-haired man, scarred by a life of calamities. "And blessed by all the Gods of Edom."

Sallan took her hand and pressed it to his chest. "Please forgive my short absence. I had no desire to take an overnight trip so soon after returning home from foreign captivity, but my old friend Kassite was eager to return to his family homestead in the red hills." He gestured at Deborah. "Fortunately, my young companion is still with us."

Everyone turned to her, standing at the edge of the garden.

"Don't let Borah's youth mislead you." Sallan helped his mother sit and settled in a vacant chair beside her. "This boy's courage and cleverness saved us repeatedly during our escape to freedom. If not for

Borah, my long years of captivity would not have ended."

Deborah felt her cheeks flush, not because of his praise, which was justified, but because he was lying about everything else with such blatant ease. She kept her expression blank and bowed in a way she imagined a young man would acknowledge praise from his elder patron. She noticed dried mud on her travel robe from the mucky bottom of the dormant copper mine, where Sallan and Kassite had trapped her overnight.

A servant placed another chair by Umm-Sallan. She beckoned Deborah, who came over and sat down, keeping her head bowed. The drums' reverberations penetrated her chest, which tightened with anxiety.

Sallan raised his goblet. "To our monarch, King Esau the Twentieth."

The men held up their goblets.

"And to the king's abducted sister – may she return home safely."

Leaning over, Deborah whispered in Umm-Sallan's ear. "What is this drumming?"

"Qoz is hungry."

"For what?"

The matriarch glanced warily in the uphill direction.

"And to family." Sallan's hand shook, and wine dripped from the goblet. "After so many years, I'm reunited with you, at last."

The women started clapping in sync with the drums and encouraged the children to join. The men sat back, heads bobbing with the rhythm, lips curled in forced smiles. Deborah lounged back and bobbed her head, imitating the men's facade of masculine nonchalance. The women sped up the clapping, and the children tried to keep up, faster and faster, until laughter erupted around the table.

Holding up the goblet, Sallan said, "And to our ancient nation – Edom!"

The men tipped their goblets and drank. Deborah pretended to do the same, but she swallowed none of the wine.

Several servants appeared with trays of roasted meat, steaming barley, and freshly baked bread. Deborah stared at the food, her mouth watering. Umm-Sallan snapped her fingers and pointed to instruct them where to put the trays and bowls down on the table.

Deborah reached for a leg of goat, but paused when no one else touched the food.

Sallan filled a plate with samples from each dish and placed it before a copper effigy that held a thunderbolt in its hand. "Thank you, Qoz, supreme master of the world, for the food that you deigned to share with us."

The others chorused, "Blessed be Qoz, supreme master of the world."

Deborah covered her mouth and murmured, "Blessed be Yahweh, king of the world, the one true God, for providing this food."

The children collected smaller samples and placed them before effigies of other Gods, which stood on a stone ledge. Deborah recognized Ra, the Sun God, which had a man's body and a hawk's head, crowned with a solar disk and a coiled serpent. She also noticed Sallan's favorite, Kothar-wa-Khasis, God of Craftsmanship, with its hands sculpted to resemble miniature tools.

The family members reached for the food. Deborah took the goat leg she had eyed before and sank her teeth into it. The meat was soft and flavorful. She took a second bite. The drums continued to beat, while noise from the street filtered through the tall hedges upfront, telling of a large number of people on their way uphill. A few tried to peek through the hedges, their chatter penetrating the garden.

"The Elixirist is back!"

"Is he in there?"

"Will he come out?"

The servants went to shoo them away.

"Uncle Sallan," Leola, the newlywed bride, called from the opposite end of the table. "When will you start mixing elixirs again?"

Her young husband hushed her, but the rest of the adults perked up, eager for his answer.

Sallan glanced in the direction of the drumming. "The king hasn't given me permission yet."

"But he has to." Leola tossed her long golden hair playfully to shoo away her husband. "And then, you'll do it, won't you?"

"Creating elixirs isn't easy to do alone." Sallan glanced at Deborah, who lowered her eyes, hoping no one noticed, and took another bite.

"Mother kept your workshop untouched," one of his sisters said.

"True," Umm-Sallan said. "Since the day of your disappearance, nothing has changed."

"I have changed." Sallan smoothed down his unruly hair, gray with a reddish tinge. "A fresh start requires youth, which I don't have anymore."

He was still looking at her, Deborah knew. She lowered her hand with the leg bone and held it out for one of the dogs.

"But the people expect it." Leola's pretty face contorted petulantly. "They're waiting."

"They've waited for twenty-one years," he said. "They'll wait a little longer."

Deborah picked up a chunk of roasted beef with her fingers and put it in her mouth.

A new sound emerged over the noise of the people and the heavy drumming. It was the rumble of marching soldiers, their weapons clanking. They entered through the tall hedges, led by General Mazabi, the towering, gray-bearded chief of the royal army. His right arm was missing at the shoulder, and in his left hand he carried a long spear – not the common wooden rod, but one forged in copper with a sharp point and a bulging bottom, which he landed on the ground with every step.

"Welcome, General," Umm-Sallan said. "Would you care to join us?"

"Thank you, but not today." His voice was gruff, but his tone was almost apologetic. "I come with a wedding gift."

Leola chirped happily at the opposite end of table. "Another gift!"

He beckoned the soldiers. "It's from the king."

Their steps timed to the heavy drumbeat from uphill, two soldiers carried over a large potted plant and placed it on the ground. The pot was decorated with colorful shapes, but the plant had wilted.

Everyone stared at it, and Leola buried her face in her husband's chest.

Umm-Sallan cleared her throat and motioned at a servant. "Serve wine to our guest."

The servant filled a goblet and handed it to the general, who gave his spear to one of the soldiers, accepted the goblet, and emptied it with a series of noisy gulps.

He smacked his lips, placed the goblet on the table, and looked at Sallan. "The king requires your presence at the temple."

Sallan nodded.

"We'll pray for Princess Needa's release." The general recovered his spear from the soldier and made a stabbing motion. "And death to her Hebrew abductors."

Deborah felt a cold shiver.

The drumbeat went up a notch.

Sallan tugged at his grimy travel robe. "I'll change into my good coat and send for my horse."

"A wagon is waiting." General Mazabi tilted his head in the direction of the street. "For all of you."

The awkward silence was filled with the heavy drumming. No one spoke, their faces reflecting a mix of surprise and wariness.

"Including the newlywed couple." The general's gray eyes surveyed the table, pausing on Deborah. "And your guests."

Sallan hesitated, but his mother said, "We are honored. Please allow us a few moments to prepare."

The general bowed and led the soldiers to the street.

"Go inside," Umm-Sallan said to the family members. "Change into your best clothes, leave the children in the care of the servants, and come back here. Our young king isn't fond of waiting."

They got up and hurried into the house.

The servants carried away the colorful clay pot with the wilted plant.

Deborah scooped another chunk of meat with her fingers, stuffed it in her mouth, and lowered her hand to be licked by the dog. Her heart was beating almost as loudly as the drums. She glanced towards the horse stable at the far side of the garden, wondering whether the servants had already unsaddled Rogez. How long would it take to fetch her few belongings, get the horse ready, and take off? Was there a path behind the neighboring houses, not visible from the street?

The matriarch patted her arm. "Trying to escape is an admission of guilt or cowardice, or both."

Deborah wiped her lips on her sleeve. "Am I a prisoner?"

Umm-Sallan reached over Deborah's head and gently pulled down the hood of the travel robe. Her cool hand rested on Deborah's nape for a moment, then moved up over the short stubble in a slow caress, pausing at the hairline above the forehead before descending to Deborah's left cheek, where it lingered.

"In a land ruled by a king," she said, "we're all his prisoners – and his children."

As cool as the hand was, it felt like hot iron against Deborah's cheek.

"How long has it been since someone touched you with kindness?"

"I need no pity."

"You need a friend." Umm-Sallan rose from her chair. "In a man's world, every woman needs a friend—even a girl who pretends to be a boy."

Fighting back sudden tears, Deborah didn't respond.

"And you also need something for your smooth cheeks."

Deborah touched her chin. "I've put on soot from the fire, but—"

"I'll ask Sallan to mix something that will look natural." She took Deborah's arm. "Come, put on your leather armor, strap on your sword, and assume a soldier's bearing."

"Imitate until you mutate."

"That's clever. Imitate until you mutate. I like it."

"That's what Kassite advised me to do after he cut my hair and gave me the sleeveless shirt of a male slave in the tannery."

"My son's friend is a wise man. I wonder how the king knew about him and you."

"He saw us at the gates. We returned from the hills just as the royal convoy arrived from the west. The king stopped his chariot to greet Sallan and said that Edom needed the great Elixirist now more than ever. Sallan introduced Kassite and told the king about his expertise in making cowhide into fine leather."

"And you? Did the king notice you?"

"Yes." Deborah imitated the king's high-pitched voice. "A boy on a rich man's horse."

Umm-Sallan paused by the front door of the house and glanced uphill in the direction of the drumbeat. "I'm afraid Kassite's absence might be noticed."

The drums stopped beating.

2

The crowd on the street parted to make way for the soldiers and the large military wagon transporting Sallan's family. Deborah stood in the back of the packed wagon in full leather armor, helmet, and boots. Sweat ran down her back. She untied the sling from around her hips, bunched up the straps, and used the pouch to fan her face, before the sweat had a chance to mess up the fake stubble Sallan had pasted on her cheeks and chin.

At the top of the hill, the wagon stopped in the shadow of the king's great palace. General Mazabi dismounted his horse, handed his copper spear to a soldier, and helped Umm-Sallan down from the wagon. He led her through an arched entry in a whitewashed wall and supported her up a long flight of stairs. The family followed, Deborah in the rear behind Leola, who had stuffed her golden hair into the hood of her robe.

The stairs reached a high balcony overlooking a large amphitheater. In the center of the sandy arena, a giant copper statue of Qoz sat on a massive stone throne whose armrests were carved to form a bull and a cow. The deity's head sprouted three short horns, and the bulging eyes watched blankly from above as the people of Bozra, panting from the hike up the hill, filled the tiered benches around the arena. The men and women craned their heads to look up – not at Qoz, but at Sallan, standing at the wooden railing of the high balcony.

Behind Sallan stood his mother and the rest of the family. Deborah planted her leather boots at a wide stance and rested her hand on the bejeweled silver hilt of the sword, sheathed against her right hip. It was an expensive weapon that belonged on the hip of a rich man, rather than a teenage boy who was supposed to have recently escaped from Egyptian captivity. It might have been wiser to leave the sword at Sallan's house, but carrying it made her feel stronger.

General Mazabi stood with a few other dignitaries at the opposite end of the balcony, which was built against the exterior wall of the palace. A pair of tall red doors connected the balcony to the palace. At the center of the balcony was an ornamental throne, guarded by several soldiers in helmets with red-horsehair rooster combs. Down below, an endless stream of people continued to pour into the amphitheater through three entrances and push against those who were already seated on the tiered benches behind the low wall that encircled the arena.

A new arrival pointed up and yelled, "The Elixirist!"

Sallan waved, and the crowd cheered.

Deborah gazed up at the statue of Qoz. Its sheer size awed her. She had never seen an idol of such enormity. Under the three horns, Edom's supreme deity had an almost human face—neither male, nor female. Its exposed breasts bulged beyond masculinity, yet not to the fullness of a nursing mother. The polished copper shone like gold, except for the dark stains on the thunderbolt that, with its three sharp spikes, resembled a pitchfork.

The amphitheater was full, but people kept pushing in through the entrances. General Mazabi signaled to the soldiers, and they rushed onto the tiered benches and pushed people closer together to make room for more on each level, all the way to the top bench.

Looking up at the thunderbolt, Deborah wandered whether someone splashed paint or mud on it. Shielding her eyes to see better, it occurred to her that the stains might be dried blood, trailing dark lines down the spikes and the stem of the thunderbolt, onto Qoz's hand and upturned forearm. Her eyes searched the arena underneath but found no traces of blood in the sand, which showed only thin lines from raking. She gazed up again, confused. How could blood have reached the thunderbolt, higher than any stepladder?

She was sweating under the leather armor over her chest and back, while her scalp itched inside the leather helmet.

Sallan's mother beckoned her closer. "Don't be afraid," she said quietly. "Qoz isn't thirsty for the blood of young men."

The words confused Deborah. Whose blood was their God thirsty for, then?

"Gods expect their fair share," Umm-Sallan said as if answering Deborah's silent question. "Don't you offer every first born to your Hebrew God?"

"Yes. The first born of every cow, goat, or sheep is sacrificed at the altar."

"And baby boys?"

Relieved that she knew the answer, Deborah smiled. "They're supposed to serve in the temple, but most are redeemed with a generous gift to the temple."

"Gifts for a God who cannot be seen, touched, or heard?"

"His priests receive the gifts."

"Do they tell your God about the gifts?"

"Yahweh doesn't need telling. He's everywhere, all the time." Deborah gestured around. "He knows what happens in every corner of the world." She pressed her hand to her chest. "Or in my heart."

"Really?" Umm-Sallan placed her hand over Deborah's hand. "I'd like to know what's in your heart."

"The desire to serve Him."

"Serve? How?"

"My father had a dream shortly before I was born." Deborah closed her eyes, recalling her father's kind face and strong arms. "In his dream, I sat under our palm tree and delivered God's message to our people."

"Must be a special tree."

"It's very old. That's why our family's land became known as Palm Homestead. After that dream, my father named the tree for me." The memory filled her with painful longing. "Deborah's Palm."

A man yelled from below, "Welcome back from Egypt!"

Sallan waved again, and the crowd began clapping at a slow pace, each clap as loud as a roaring thunder.

Umm-Sallan's grip on Deborah's hand tightened.

"What's wrong?"

The matriarch sighed. "Old age is both a blessing and a curse, because each year brings greater joys and deeper worries."

The crowd kept clapping, Sallan kept waving, and his mother's expression grew darker.

"They're happy he's back," Deborah said.

"I'm happy, too, but the king won't be happy to see his subjects' diverted adoration. What happened before might happen again."

Deborah's face must have shown her shock, because Umm-Sallan leaned closer, her lips near Deborah's ears. "I never believed the official story. Why would the Egyptians lock up the famous Elixirist? If they had really abducted my son, they would have done one of two things: hold a show trial and execute him for destroying Pharaoh's army at the gates of Bozra, or put him up in a gilded palace under guard to mix his magical potions and elixirs. Enslaving him in perpetual anonymity for menial labor made no sense, and the Egyptians are, if anything, supremely astute."

Deborah glanced at the gilded doors connecting the balcony to the king's palace.

"Tell me more, child. What happened to your father?"

"My parents were slain while working in the fields." Deborah inhaled deeply, determined not to cry. "We were told that Canaanite marauders did it, but later on, I learned the truth. They were murdered."

"Murdered? Why?"

"Judge Zifron, the ruler of the area, coveted the ancient cistern on our land, because rain comes infrequently in the Samariah Hills."

"Water is precious here, too, even more than copper, but never more than a life."

"The judge sent his son to pressure my father to sell Palm Homestead, but he refused." Deborah took a deep breath. "Seesya slew both my parents in the field where they stood."

Umm-Sallan looked at her sadly. "We have an old saying: Greed and spite dwell like wicked brothers in every man's heart, constantly fighting their good sisters, charity and sympathy."

"Seesya's heart harbors only greed and spite."

"It's a common mistake." She glanced at Sallan. "When my only son was taken away, I hated the old king, who not only lied about it, but used the story of the abduction to enrich himself by confiscating all the copper mines, claiming he must save up to pay a ransom to the Egyptians to free my son. For a long time, I believed the old king's heart was pure evil, but the years have taught me otherwise. I saw how he rebuilt Edom from its ruins, gave the people stability and justice, especially for women, whom he awarded many rights and privileges."

"Because your women had drunk the Male Elixir and defended Bozra, pretending to be men."

"Yes." Umm-Sallan smiled. "The old king always commended our bravery at war and our fortitude in peace – bearing child after child to replenish Edom. So, you see, good and evil always compete for man's heart, which is why even the worst man convinces himself that his evil actions are in actuality good, just, and necessary."

The crowd continued to clap rhythmically, and Sallan kept waving from the balcony.

"Some men know they're evil, but persist."

"Seesya didn't kill you in the field, did he?"

"He would have if I were there, but my older sister and I had taken the sheep for shearing at a neighbor's homestead." Deborah inhaled deeply to ease her heartache. "After our parents' death, the judge took us into his household and betrothed Tamar, who was a year older than I, to his son—"

"The son who had murdered your parents?"

"Yes, though we didn't know it at the time. We felt fortunate to join the judge's family. On their wedding night, however, when there was no blood on the bedcloth, Seesya accused my sister of having whored with another man before the marriage. They put her on trial at the gates of Emanuel, the elders found her guilty, and the judge sentenced her to stoning. I had to watch it."

"Was she innocent?"

"Tamar died a virgin. Seesya later admitted that he could not perform with either of us."

"He married you, too?"

"To inherit my father's land." Deborah recalled the words of Obadiah, the priest in Emanuel. "Under God's law, only men can own land. If a landowner dies with no son but a daughter, the local judge holds the land in trust until the daughter marries, and her husband becomes the owner of the land, provided he is from the same tribe."

A loud screeching noise sounded, and everyone stopped clapping.

"How did you avoid your sister's fate?"

"At first, I ran away." Deborah looked around for the source of the screeching. "A friend told me about a legendary Elixirist who had turned the women of Bozra into men and saved the city from an Egyptian army. I decided to find that Elixirist and convince him to turn me into a boy so that I'd be able to inherit my father directly."

The screeching noise came closer.

"You went to look for my son?"

Deborah didn't have the heart to tell Umm-Sallan that her son had been deceitful, sending her on a dangerous fool's errand across Canaan on the false claim that Kassite was the Elixirist.

"It's a long story," she said. "But yes, in the end, after many terrible setbacks, I helped liberate Sallan and Kassite from slavery, and they helped me discover the truth about my parents' murder and gain freedom from Seesya."

A group of slaves pushed a large wooden box with screeching wheels into the arena. The box was filled with stones to secure an upright tree trunk, very tall and trimmed of all branches.

"Not completely free," Umm-Sallan said. "You still wish to become a young man, don't you?"

"I wish to be as free as a man, but to answer my calling as a woman."

The slaves positioned the box in the center of the arena between the statue of Qoz and the royal balcony. The wooden pole reached higher than both.

"Do the Hebrew tribes have women prophets?"

"Not yet."

"Do you have a claim by lineage, or wealth?"

"Only my faith."

A few slaves entered the arena carrying wood planks and ropes.

"Faith has no force unless it's shared by others," Umm-Sallan said. "Even here, in Edom, a girl would be laughed at for such aspirations."

"My father said that Yahweh, who created the whole world, could easily create a prophet out of a girl."

"Any girl?" Umm-Sallan patted Deborah's armored chest. "Or only a girl who pretends to be a boy?"

Deborah saw no mockery in the matriarch's face, only concern. "I don't know."

"Yet you're determined to pursue it."

"When I'm ready, yes."

"Ready? How?"

"I don't know. God will tell me."

One of the slaves tied the end of a long rope around his waist and scampered up the pole.

"Only a cruel God would send a girl back to Canaan to fight a rich ruler, his son, and his soldiers." Umm-Sallan's gray eyes did not leave

Deborah's face, ignoring the activity in the arena.

"I won't be alone."

"Do you have enough silver to hire soldiers?"

Deborah shook her head.

The slave reached the top of the pole. He used the rope to pull up a thick plank of wood with a wheel attached to one end. He secured the plank to the top of the pole. The plank extended horizontally four or five steps from the top of the pole.

"Even if you win, all the men in Canaan would seek your downfall."

"Why?"

"They have wives and daughters who might find inspiration in your success and seek the right to carry weapons, possess land, and speak for God. The Hebrew men will fight you to defend their privileges."

Deborah gripped the hilt of her sword. "I'll fight them back."

"All of them with one sword?"

"And with stones, if I have to." She touched the sling, tied around her hips.

"Don't be silly, child. A woman cannot win with weapons."

At the top of the wooden pole, the slave stepped onto the horizontal plank and walked out to the end, where the wheel was attached. He seemed unconcerned with the immense height.

"How can I win without weapons?"

Umm-Sallan glanced at General Mazabi, who responded with a quick smile from the opposite end of the balcony. "Have you ever seen a caterpillar emerge from its cocoon as a butterfly?"

Deborah nodded.

She gestured at Deborah's armor. "Under all this, there's a girl ready to emerge as a beautiful woman. Let her out, and attract a husband."

"I don't want a husband."

"But you need one. Even if you don't like him at first, it doesn't matter. A smart girl uses her head to decide whom her heart should fall for. And when you capture a good man's heart, he'll fight for your inheritance and indulge your desire to serve your God."

"It would be wrong," Deborah said.

"Which part?"

"Seduce a man whom I don't feel anything for."

Umm-Sallan smiled. "Have no boys ever touched your heart?"

"I once travelled with a Moabite caravan for a few days, and there was a boy." She sighed, thinking of Zariz. "He was nice, but he won't do. Only a husband of my tribe can inherit my father."

The slave kneeled on the plank, untied the rope from his waist, and threaded it over the attached wheel at the end of the plank. The rope was very long, both ends reaching the ground with plenty to spare. Deborah realized that the contraption was a very tall crane with a pulley for lifting heavy objects.

"Who was the friend who told you about the Elixirist?"

"Barac, son of Abinoam the blacksmith. We were friends in Emanuel."

"He's probably waiting for you there."

"No, he also fled Emanuel."

"Why?"

"He refused to cast a stone at my sister's execution, and Seesya tried to kill him."

"The boy risked his life to impress you. Isn't that a strong sign of a captured heart?"

Deborah blushed.

"Where did Barac go?"

The slave walked back along the plank and climbed down the pole. The others pushed the box closer to Qoz, positioning the pulley high above the bloodstained spikes of the thunderbolt.

"His father said that they'd be going south to join the tribe of Simeon, but Seesya later bragged that he had caught Barac and killed him." Deborah recalled Seesya's gory description of Barac's severed head rolling in the dust, and her eyes welled up.

"Bragging and lying are first cousins," Umm-Sallan said. "Keep your hope alive."

3

The ornate doors in the back of the balcony opened, trumpets sounded, and King Esau the Twentieth appeared. He wore a red coat and a gold crown that seemed heavy for his slight stature. The trumpets blew again, the dignitaries on the balcony bowed, and the crowd stood up and applauded.

"People of Bozra." The king's voice was thin and boyish. "We summoned you to pray for the safe return of Princess Needa, whose absence fills our hearts with sadness. How much longer will our sister continue to suffer at the hands of roving Hebrew outlaws? How much longer will this injury to our ancient nation's heart continue to bleed? How much longer will our music stay silent—"

He paused and looked to the left at Sallan and his family.

"—and our celebrations delayed in lamentation?"

Leola uttered a muffled whimper.

Deborah recalled the wilted plant the king had sent to rebuke the family's celebration of Leola's wedding. Obviously, he was still angry. Was the worse yet to come?

Sallan took his mother's arm. Together, they stepped forward and knelt before the monarch.

King Esau the Twentieth held out his hands, which Sallan and his mother kissed.

The crowd cheered.

The king said in a low voice, "We summoned those who escaped from Egypt with you."

Sallan turned and pointed at Deborah, who took a deep bow, keeping her eyes on the wooden planks of the balcony floor.

"Where is the other one, the leather tanner?"

After a brief hesitation, Sallan said, "He went to look for his family."

The king grunted. "Where?"

"A small homestead in the hills. It's been many years. His family might not be alive anymore."

"Which hills?"

"A few hours to the south." Sallan waved vaguely. "Perhaps a tenth of the way to the Sea of Reeds."

The king turned to an older man who held rolled parchments, ink, and quill. "Do we collect taxes from homesteads in the Red Hills?"

"There are no more homesteads in the Red Hills," the scribe said. "Only the king's copper mines."

The king turned back to Sallan. "Perhaps your friend wasn't aware that our wise grandfather appropriated all the copper mines in Edom in order to accumulate a ransom to pay the Pharaoh for your freedom."

Sallan bowed.

"The Pharaoh, however, always denied having you. I wonder why."

An invisible hand pressed on Deborah's chest. Did the king know there was no truth the story of Sallan's abduction by the Egyptians? Did he know that his grandfather had locked Sallan up at the bottom of Kassite's family's inactive copper mine, with Kassite as his sole jailer? Or that the two of them had fled together to Canaan?

Still mum, Sallan kept his head bowed.

The king placed his left hand on Sallan's head and announced, "We welcome our long-lost servant, the savior of Edom, the Elixirist!"

The arena erupted in applauses.

Deborah heard wooden doors creak below the balcony, and a pig sprinted into the arena. A red harness hugged its plump midriff, and its short legs kicked up a wake of white sand as it ran around Qoz's stone throne. A few slaves gave chase, but the nimble pig avoided its pursuers with quick turnabouts, making the crowd laugh.

The slaves boxed in the pig with its back to the low wall separating the round arena from the tiered benches. A young slave managed to grab the harness, but the pig dashed off, dragging the slave, who bounced on the sand until his sleeveless long shirt tore away, leaving him with only a loincloth. As thousands of men and women pointed and hollered, the slave collected his shirt and ran back to the doors under the balcony.

The other slaves resumed the chase, pursuing the pig around the area once, twice, and a third time, the amphitheater shaking with laughter.

Deborah noticed General Mazabi raising his spear at the opposite end of the balcony. He balanced the spear in his left hand above his shoulder, waited for the pig to run around the arena again, the slaves close behind, and hurled the spear.

The crowd held its collective breath as the copper spear travelled through the air. Deborah was certain it would miss the racing pig, but the spear reached the ground at precisely the right moment to intercept the pig and pin it to the ground on its side. She expected to see blood spreading on the sand while the pig oinked, twisted, and kicked, but there was no blood, because the spear had threaded through the harness without hurting the pig.

The king clapped, the crowd cheered, and General Mazabi smirked.

Deeply impressed, Deborah looked at him and resolved to one day achieve similar mastery and precision.

The slaves grabbed the pig while a soldier ran over, pulled out the spear, and ran to a set of circular stairs that led from the arena up to the balcony, where he handed the spear back to the general.

A tall and muscular man wearing only a red loincloth entered the arena from under the balcony. His hairless head and body were painted the color of copper. Deborah recognized him. It was Qoztobarus, the high priest of Edom, who had officiated at Leola's wedding ceremony three days earlier.

A hush fell over the amphitheater.

Deborah was sweating under the leather armor.

The slaves left the arena, and six boy priests joined Qoztobarus. They looked like him, except for their youth. One of them climbed the pole and walked confidently along the horizontal plank to the end, where he sat down with his legs dangling on each side of the pulley. He made sure the long rope was properly threaded over the wheel of the pulley. Meanwhile, the others tied one end of the rope to the pig's harness and pulled the other end of the rope, causing the pig to rise into the air. It swung from side to side, just under the pulley, oinking miserably.

The crowd was silent, all eyes turned up, focused on the pig, its belly heaving and its stubby legs running in the air. Below, the young priests gave the end of the rope to Qoztobarus and ran back to push the wooden box of stones at the base of the pole. The wheels screeched under the heavy weight. From the plank above, the young priest shouted directions while the others nudged the wheeled box until the pulley was exactly above Qoz's thunderbolt. The movements caused the pig to swing back and forth, and its oinking turned to squealing.

Qoztobarus began to chant a monotonous tone.

The people joined him.

The chanting grew louder, as did the pig's squealing.

Deborah tried to chant along, but her throat was dry and her chest was tight. She glanced at Umm-Sallan, who nodded and smiled.

The chanting stopped, and Qoztobarus looked up over his shoulder at the king.

King Esau the Twentieth raised both hands towards Qoz. "We give you this gift of blood in gratitude for keeping our blood from being spilled during our voyage to the Negev Desert."

Qoztobarus took three steps forward, causing the long rope to loosen between him and the pulley above. The wooden wheel of the pulley screeched as it turned, lowering the pig until the three spikes of the thunderbolt penetrated its belly through the harness.

The pig shrieked, and blood flowed down the thunderbolt and over the smooth copper of Qoz's raised hand, forearm, and elbow, where it disappeared, none dripping to the white sand of the arena below.

Deborah wiped the sweat from her brow. She couldn't look away.

Qoztobarus stepped backwards to pull the rope and raise the pig, detaching it from the spikes. The animal resumed squealing and running in the air.

"We give you this gift of pain," the king continued, "in pleading for an end to the pain our sister is suffering at the hands of her savage abductors."

Again, Qoztobarus stepped forward, and the pig descended onto the sharp spikes of the thunderbolt, uttering sharp, hoarse shrieks while fresh blood flowed down Qoz's arm.

Deborah cringed. She wanted to yell at them to stop.

"Hush," Umm-Sallan whispered. "It'll be over soon."

Stepping backwards, Qoztobarus raised the pig off the spikes and higher up until it was near the pulley. The pig's stubby legs barely moved anymore. The high priest took a few steps aside so that the tight rope passed near the balcony railing before the king.

King Esau drew his sword and held it forward, touching the rope. "We give you this gift of life in prayer for the life of our sister, Princess

Needa, and her return to us."

Bringing his sword back over his shoulder, the king paused for a moment, and swung it across. The blade passed over the railing and slashed the rope. The pig dropped, and the three spikes impaled its belly. The plump body writhed a few times and fell limp.

"That's it," Umm-Sallan whispered. "Qoz drinks the blood and grants the king's wishes."

Deborah looked at her. "And the pain?"

"Don't animals die in your temple, too?"

"With one slice of a sharp knife across the neck, ending the pain before it starts."

Down in the arena, a young priest pulled on the severed end of the rope which, looped over the pulley above, lifted the dead pig from the spikes. He waited for the others to push the wheeled box and let go of the rope. The dead pig dropped to the sand. They removed the harness, which was still tied to the rope, wrapped the carcass in a white sheet, and carried it away.

Qoztobarus walked to the middle of the arena and stopped in front of the massive stone throne. His wrought muscles rippled under his copper-dyed skin.

His face upturned, Qoztobarus began chanting the same tune as before, but now he was reciting words: "Accept this blood, great Qoz. Accept this blood, great Qoz."

The crowd repeated after him. "Accept this blood, great Qoz. Accept this blood, great Qoz."

Crouching, the high priest fell forward, his forehead landing on Qoz's toes.

A loud rumble sounded.

The people got up from the tiered benches and bowed.

On the balcony, everyone also bowed, including the king. Deborah supported Umm-Sallan, but kept looking around the arena, trying to locate the source of the rumble.

"Accept this blood, great Qoz," the crowd chanted. "Accept this blood."

The rumble grew louder, and Deborah realized it came from within the copper statue.

With an edge of urgency, the crowd chanted, "Accept this blood, great Qoz!"

The rumble was augmented by a series of sharp, metallic creaks.

"Accept this blood," the people cried. "Accept this blood, great Qoz!"

The high priest stood up.

Beside Deborah, Umm-Sallan groaned.

The crowd wailed in unison, begging, "Accept this blood, great Qoz!"

The rumble and creaking stopped.

The chanting paused, and many voices cried, "No! No! No!"

Qoztobarus took three steps backwards, looked up, and opened his mouth.

A thin jet of blood shot out from between Qoz's lips, flew in an arch, and came down into the high priest's open mouth.

Many in the audience screamed. Around the amphitheater, women and girls rushed to the exits, but were blocked by guards. Deborah saw some women hide their daughters under their robes.

The jet of blood splattered as it hit Qoztobarus's mouth, overflowing on his bare chest and arms, dripping from his hands to the sand.

Deborah felt Umm-Sallan's fingernails dig into her arm. It hurt, but she ignored it, seeing how the matriarch was shaking.

When Qoz finished spewing out the blood, the high priest turned slowly, showing himself to the people around the amphitheater. His body glistened in the afternoon sun as his feet kneaded the blood-soaked sand. After two full turns, he stopped and faced the royal balcony.

Total silence fell over the amphitheater.

The king looked down at Qoztobarus. "What happened?"

"The great Qoz has rejected our gift of blood."

"Why? Our thanks were sincere."

While this was going on, Umm-Sallan motioned for Leola to leave. The girl seemed paralyzed, but her young husband pulled her towards the enclosed stairwell leading down the street.

Qoztobarus pointed up at the statue of Qoz behind him. "The favor we ask requires a more fitting sacrifice."

The two soldiers guarding the stairwell tilted their spears across, blocking the way. Umm-Sallan stepped out of the group of family members—not towards Leola, but the other way, behind the king's throne, and drew General Mazabi's attention. He peered over everyone's heads, saw what was going on at the opposite end of the balcony, and signaled the soldiers to let Leola and her husband leave. The couple disappearing down the dark stairwell.

The king's hands formed into fists, and he pounded the railing. "What would the great Qoz accept in order to return our sister from the cursed Hebrews?"

Qoztobarus made another slow turnaround, gazing at the countless Edomites pressed together on the tiered benches of the amphitheater. Their faces turned aside to avert the blood-dripping priest in the arena below.

"Tell us," the king demanded.

"We must offer Qoz that which we ask for."

"Yes," the king said. "A young woman of beauty and refinement."

Qoztobarus pressed his hands to his head. "Qoz is not satisfied."

"What, then?"

"We must offer Qoz that which we ask for."

The king's young face twisted with frustration. "Five young woman of beauty and refinement?" His thin voice went to an even higher pitch. "Ten? A hundred?"

Panic erupted in the arena as mothers and daughters tried to leave, pushing and screaming. More soldiers poured in. They didn't draw their swords or raise their spears, but formed impregnable barriers at the ends of the tiered benches of the amphitheater, confining the panicked crowd.

General Mazabi spoke to one of the king's guards, who ran through the ornate doors at the back of the balcony into the palace. A moment later, drums began beating. Deborah couldn't see the drummers, but she could tell they were on the roof of the palace. The pounding noise forced everyone to cover their ears and stop pushing for the exits.

In the arena below, Qoztobarus swiveled around, holding his head, swaying.

The general stuck two fingers in his mouth and whistled.

The drumming stopped.

Kneeling in the sand, Qoztobarus yelled, "Offer Qoz that which you ask for."

Finally, the king understood. "A princess?"

The high priest nodded.

"But we can't," the king cried. "We don't have another sister."

Still holding his head, seemingly in receipt of Qoz's messages, the high priest said, "A young woman of the most noble family in the land."

The king turned to the left, where Sallan's family clustered tightly. "The beautiful Leola," he said. "That's what Qoz wants."

Qoztobarus opened his arms and bowed.

Leola's mother wailed and collapsed.

"Leola," the king said. "Where is the girl?"

Umm-Sallan stepped forward. "Leola became sick and had to leave. Surely Qoz does not want the blood of a sick girl."

The king waved in dismissal. "She can't be too sick, having just celebrated her marriage while we were scouring the harsh Negev Desert in search of our sister." He sat on his throne and clicked his fingers at General Mazabi.

The general glanced at Umm-Sallan, his creased face saddened, and marched off with a group of soldiers.

Murmuring swept through the amphitheater like swarms of bees, and thousands of eyes stared at Sallan's family. In the arena below, Qoztobarus was joined by his young priests and began to chant the same mournful tune without words. Gradually, the crowd joined him, and the chanting grew louder until it engulfed the whole amphitheater.

Deborah stepped close to Sallan and spoke in his ear. "You have to stop this."

Sallan shielded his mouth with his hand. "How?"

"Talk to the king."

"He won't listen."

"Then talk to the people. They'll listen to the great Elixirist."

"Do you want me to lose my head?" Sallan motioned at Qoztobarus in the arena below. "That's what he's hoping for. He hates me."

"Why?"

"There was a girl once." Sallan's eyes glistened. "Lovelier than Leola. She was betrothed to him, but I won her heart."

"When?"

"The last time I was on this balcony. He tore her out of my arms and threw her over." Sallan pounded the railing. "She survived and married me, right here in front of Qoz. Now, he'll take his revenge by killing

Leola."

General Mazabi and his soldiers marched into the arena below. One of the soldiers carried Leola over his shoulder. Her husband followed behind, weeping, and when the soldier lay Leola down on the sand, he rushed forward and fell over her. The soldiers grabbed him and followed General Mazabi, leaving the fainted girl.

The young priests strapped on the bloody harness, which covered Leola from armpits to hips. A new rope was threaded through the pulley and tied to the harness in the middle of Leola's back. They pulled the other end of the rope while walking away from the crane. The rope traveled through the pulley above with a sharp screech that silenced the chanting and raised Leola off the ground.

She came to, saw where she was, and screamed.

Sallan's family pressed together, holding each other, the women sobbing, the men barely holding back their tears. Only Umm-Sallan's gray eyes were dry and clear.

"I'm sorry," Deborah whispered.

"Don't be sorry," the matriarch said. "Sorry is no help."

The young priests kept pulling the rope, raising Leola higher. The harness held her horizontally, facedown. She kicked with her legs and flailed her arms, screaming in terror. Her long hair came out of the hood of her robe and hung down like a golden veil.

Qoztobarus took the rope from the young priests, who ran back to the base of the crane and pushed. The large wheels turned slowly as the crane shifted. The one sitting above the pulley shouted directions until Leola was dangling right above Qoz's three-pronged thunderbolt.

The rope went up from her harness to the pulley, then down diagonally all the way to Qoztobarus, who looped the end around his arm several times to secure it. He adjusted his position to bring the rope closer to the balcony railing above him.

The movements caused Leola to sway and bob. She wailed, her voice lonely in the hushed amphitheater.

Deborah recalled what had happened with the pig and shuddered at the thought of this living, breathing girl, a girl her own age, being impaled by the sharp spikes. It felt unreal, like a nightmare that would soon end with a new sunrise. Leola's agonized cries, however, were real. This wasn't a nightmare. It was happening, and no one could stop it.

"Save me," Leola cried.

"Be brave," Umm-Sallan said.

"Brave?" Deborah voice shook. "How can she be brave?"

The matriarch pressed her arm. "I was talking to you."

Qoztobarus took another step aside, and the rope came within reach of the railing in front of the king.

"Please," Leola cried. "I don't want to die."

Deborah saw Leola's face through the screen of golden hair, and their eyes met.

"Save me!"

The girl, Deborah realized, was begging her to do the saving.

"Be brave," Umm-Sallan said. "As brave as you were in Canaan for my son."

The king stepped up to the railing and drew his sword.

A nervous murmur passed through the crowd.

"Please," Leola cried. "Save me!"

"I can't," Deborah whispered. "No one can."

The girl took a deep breath and wailed, "I don't want to die!"

The king leaned over the railing and looked down at Qoztobarus, who stood below, holding the end of the rope. The high priest nodded. The king raised his sword over the railing and touched the tight rope lightly with the blade.

The crowd stood still, their eyes shifting between the king and the girl.

High up, above the thunderbolt, Leola shrieked.

"Great Qoz," the king said. "We give you this gift of a noble girl's life in prayer that you save the life of our sister, Princess Needa, and bring her back to us."

Unable to watch, Deborah shut her eyes and imagined she was no longer subjected to Leola's pleas, no longer encircled by homicidal Edomites, no longer dwarfed by their blood-thirsty copper deity. She imagined being alone at the bottom of Kassite's abandoned copper mine, the solid door no longer a barrier to escape, but a shield from the outside world. She could smell the musty dampness, feel the cold mist on her skin, and hear the roar of the water hitting the bottom of the shaft. She stared into the dark, where the eagle's yellow eyes glistened. Suddenly, however, she was no longer at the bottom of the mine, but on the shore of the Sea of Salt, where the warm water lapped at her feet, the moon shone on her from above, and the eagle's wings sent soft puffs of air at her flushed face.

"You can fly," the eagle said, her familiar voice deep and comforting. "Fly. Fly. Fly."

"Fly where?"

"Open your eyes, and you will know."

As Deborah opened her eyes, the king swung the sword back and held it briefly, poised for a strike.

Leola screamed.

"Be brave," Umm-Sallan said.

"Fly, Deborah," the eagle said. "Fly now!"

4

Deborah hopped onto the railing and ran. The king's sword cut through the air with an audible swish. She accelerated along the top plank of the railing.

The blade slashed the rope and continued its swing, passing just under the soles of Deborah's boots as she leapt into the air. The sliced end of the rope fluttered upwards while Leola dropped towards the spikes of the thunderbolt. Deborah reached up with both hands and grasped the end of the rope, halting Leola's drop the moment the spikes pricked the harness. Clutching the end of the rope, Deborah flew downwards in half-circle, her weight raising Leola back up to the pulley, and crash-landed on the sand in the arena, rolling over several times.

The crowd roared.

The rope began to drag Deborah towards the crane while Leola descended towards the spikes again. She shrieked, and Deborah got up quickly and pulled the rope in the opposite direction. The pulley screeched, the crane swayed, and the young priest on the thick plank above clung to it with his hands and legs.

The other young priests raced after Deborah. She kept a tight grip on the rope and ran around the statue of Qoz at the center of the arena, coming full circle while the rope looped on the throne. She continued to the base of the crane, climbed onto the wooden box, which was full of stones, and coiled the rope around the pole several times, securing the end just as the young priests caught up with her. One of them grabbed the back of her armor and pulled, hurtling her down from the box. She landed on her back, the air knocked out of her. She tried to get up, but the whole amphitheater started spinning, and she fainted.

Two yellow points of light appeared, and the eagle emerged from the dark, hovering above her. "Nice flying, Deborah, but this is not a good time to dream."

"It's a good time for you to get me out of here."

"What's the rush?"

"Isn't it obvious?"

The eagle chuckled. "The girl is still in danger."

"We both are. I can't fly us out of here. I don't have wings."

The eagle circled above and returned to the same spot above her. "You don't win a fight by fleeing."

"Neither by dying."

"Fear of death has won more battles than greed, honor, and love combined."

"There's no battle here. I'm one against many."

"One?" The eagle shook her head. "You're not alone. There are other girls."

"Girls?" It took a moment for Deborah to understand the eagle was referring to Princess Needa, in addition to Leola. "How can I save them?"

The eagle flapped her broad wings. "The weak can prevail by winning over a powerful ally."

"Who?"

"The one with the most power."

"By what measure?"

"That's a choice you must make wisely, Deborah." The eagle's eyes blinked, glowing kindly. "Men acquire power in different ways: priests and prophets invoke mighty gods, kings and judges proclaim supreme laws, and rebels point out inconvenient truths."

"And when I choose, how do I win him over?"

"Improvise."

"Not funny. Tell me what to do."

"Let me repeat myself," the eagle said. "Open your eyes, and you will know what to do."

Deborah opened her eyes.

Lying on her back, the first thing she saw was Leola, hanging upside down over the thunderbolt, screaming. Deborah put a finger across her lips, and Leola stopped screaming.

Countless faces looked back at Deborah from the tiered benches of the amphitheater. Up on the balcony, the king was still holding his sword while staring down at her, as did the guards around him, the members of Sallan's family on one side, and General Mazabi with other dignitaries at the other end. Below the balcony, Qoztobarus held the sliced tail of the rope in his hand.

The king used his sword to point at her. "Who were you talking to, boy?"

Deborah gazed up at the spot where the eagle had been.

"Tell me," the king said. "Was it Qoz?"

Qoztobarus stepped out from under the balcony and looked up at the king. "The mighty Qoz talks only to me."

Deborah got up and adjusted the sword on her hip, resting her hand on the hilt – not that she had any chance fighting her way out of this situation. Her only hope, she realized, was to follow the eagle's advice: "The weak can prevail by winning over a powerful ally." But whom could she win over?

"The priest is right," she said. "I wasn't talking to Qoz."

Qoztobarus looked at her.

"It was my own God," she said. "Yahweh."

The crowd groaned, and the king leaned over the railing. "A Hebrew!"

Deborah bowed deeply. "I'm from the Hebrew tribe of Ephraim, not the savage tribe of Simeon that has taken your sister."

Qoztobarus tossed the short piece of rope to one of his young priests. "Tie the boy up. We'll feed him to the pigs – a fitting fate for a Hebrew spy."

The crowd laughed.

The young priest with the rope approached her, but stopped when she drew her sword.

"My God sent me here," Deborah said. "He wants me to save the king's sister."

"Qoz needs no help." The high priest sent one of his young priests to the crane. "Untie the rope. Qoz is thirsty for the blood of a noble girl."

Deborah moved in front of the box, blocking the way. "If this girl dies, Princess Needa will die, too."

"Where is this Yahweh?" Qoztobarus stretched out his muscular, copper-painted arms. "Are we going to deprive Qoz of his desired blood because of a Hebrew God who cannot be touched, seen, or heard by anyone?"

The crowd laughed.

The high priest gazed at the sky. "Speak to us, too, Hebrew God, if you can."

Deborah rested the tip of her sword in the sand. "He only speaks to those who listen."

Qoztobarus sneered. "A mute God is no God."

"Yahweh is mightier than all the Gods," Deborah said. "He liberated us from slavery in Egypt, parted the Sea of Reeds, and delivered us back to Canaan. And now, He will liberate Princess Needa and deliver her back home to Edom."

"Lies." The high priest spat in her direction. "This boy is an imposter and a thief, by the look of the sword he's carrying."

"We were wondering about that," the king said. "Tell us, boy, from whom have you stolen this bejeweled sword and the splendid white horse I saw this morning by the gate?"

She didn't hesitate. "Those were gifts from my God."

"And before that," the king said with a hint of a smile. "Surely a man of power and wealth owned those gifts, right?"

"Yes," Deborah said. "A young man of power who refused to believe I was called by God to liberate the great Elixirist and bring him home to Edom."

"Enough." Qoztobarus stomped his foot in the sand. "This boy is making up stories."

"We'll be the judge of that." The king turned to Sallan. "Is it true? Did this boy save you?"

Sallan bowed. "Yes, my king. If not for Borah, my long years of captivity would not have ended."

"God empowered me," Deborah said. "And if you set Leola free, He will empower me to bring home the princess, as I have brought home the Elixirist."

Qoztobarus paced across the arena and stood by Qoz. "Only the mighty Qoz can save Princess Needa, and Qoz wants Leola's blood. He told me so."

Deborah knew she must respond, but her heart was pounding too hard for her mind to formulate a reply.

"Qoz is angry!" Qoztobarus clapped his hands and gestured up at

Qoz's great head. "Very angry!"

From where she stood nearby, Deborah noticed that, even though the high priest's face was turned up as he clapped and gestured at the blank, shining face of Qoz above, his eyes glanced down and his bare foot tapped quickly on Qoz's toes. No one else seemed to have noticed, and Deborah recalled what Kassite had said: "People don't see what's right in front of them when they expect to see something else. It's as if there's a sieve between their eyes and their minds that filters out what doesn't fit their expectations and fills the blanks with what does."

"Angry!" Qoztobarus stepped back. "Qoz is angry!"

In the hush that fell over the crowd, a deep rumble came from inside the statue of Qoz, similar to the noise that had preceded the jet of blood earlier.

Qoztobarus dropped to his knees and prostrated himself on the sand before Qoz.

The crowd shouted in fear. On the balcony, everyone retreated until their backs were pressed to the wall of the palace, except for the king, who remained at the railing, General Mazabi, who stood still with his copper spear, and Umm-Sallan, who looked down at Deborah and mouthed, "Be brave. Be brave. Be brave."

The rumbling stopped.

After a long moment, the king bowed. "Forgive us, Qoz."

Rising to his feet, the high priest sneered at Deborah while brushing the white sand from his chest and thighs. He walked over to the base of the crane and reached up to untie the end of the rope.

On the balcony, the king said, "We give you, mighty Qoz, this gift of life in prayer that you save the life of our sister, Princess Needa, and bring her back to us."

The crowd watched in silence.

Deborah stepped closer to the stone throne. "Qoz doesn't want her blood."

The high priest laughed. "Now this boy can communicate with our great Qoz, as well?"

"Yes, I can," Deborah said. "You misunderstood Qoz's wishes."

The crowd groaned at her audacity.

"Here, let Qoz speak to all of you." Imitating Qoztobarus's earlier show, Deborah stepped up to Qoz's large feet in front of the stone throne, turned her face up, raised her arms, and clapped in the direction of Qoz's face high above while surreptitiously tapping the copper toes with her boot. "Qoz says, enough blood for today!" Nothing happened, and she continued clapping above her head while tapping the other copper toes with her boot by feel alone. "Be heard, Qoz, tell them to free Leola so that Princess Needa will be freed, too!" Deborah felt one of the toes give in with a click. Without looking down, she pressed it down firmly. "Is that right, Qoz? Make a sound!"

A rumble came from Qoz's belly.

The crowd's fearful cries snapped all the tension that had built up inside Deborah, who barely managed to hide her laughter while bowing before Qoz.

"It's another trick," Qoztobarus yelled, barely audible over Qoz's rumblings and the crowd's yelling. "The boy made Qoz angry!" He untied the knot and started unwinding the rope from around the pole. "Qoz wants this girl's blood!" With the rope almost detached from the pole, Qoztobarus grabbed it and pulled impatiently, which caused the whole structure to sway.

High above, Leola screamed.

Qoztobarus shook the rope to loosen it from around the stone throne.

"Wait!" The King looked from the high priest to Deborah, up at Leola, and back to Deborah. "Why would the Hebrew God care to save an Edomite princess from Hebrew tribesmen?"

The clever question surprised Deborah. Why, indeed, would Yahweh help the Edomites against His chosen people? He surely cared more about the tribe of Simeon, the descendants of Jacob, Isaac, and Abraham, than about these idol worshippers who killed their own girls to feed a false deity.

Qoztobarus kicked sand in her direction. "Ask your God, boy."

Deborah felt small and weak before the strapping high priest with his bulging muscles and regal posture. Something Sallan had once told her came to her mind: "With dogs and with men, if you cower and show weakness, they will abuse you, but if you stand proud and exude confidence, they will seek your approval." She pulled back her right leg and kicked, showering the high priest with double the amount of sand he had kicked at her.

Some in the crowd laughed, and even the king smiled.

"It is a wise question," Deborah said as loudly and as confidently as she could while sheathing her sword. "Yahweh wishes to prevent war between all men that He created in His image." She threw her hand around, gesturing at the whole amphitheater. "And he wants to save the men of Simeon from certain defeat by the powerful king of Edom."

General Mazabi pounded the bottom of his spear on the balcony and grumbled, "He's right about that."

Qoztobarus's face twisted in rage. "The Hebrews are known for their oily tongues. This boy spits lies out of his mouth quicker than a snake spits its venom."

He let go of the rope, which began to slither away, slowed by the friction of the stone throne it was circling. Leola began to descend towards the spikes, and Deborah sprinted over and fell onto the rope, grasping it with both hands. She got up and pulled, stepping backwards towards the base of the crane. The same friction that had slowed the rope from running away now slowed Deborah down.

Qoztobarus put out his foot, tripping her, and she fell, barely holding on to the rope.

The crowd laughed.

"Secure the rope," the king said.

General Mazabi signaled, and two soldiers ran into the arena, took the rope from Deborah, and tied it back to the pole of the crane.

High above, Leola moaned.

"Qoz is angry," Qoztobarus protested. "He wants the girl's blood. And the Hebrew boy's blood, too."

The crowd cheered.

The king raised his hand, restoring silence. "Who are we to doubt the High Priest?" He looked down at Qoztobarus. "Go ahead and kill the Hebrew boy."

The high priest grinned, rubbing his hands.

"But if you fail," the king continued, "we'll know that the boy speaks the truth."

5

The whole amphitheater was frozen in tense anticipation. Deborah looked at the hulk of a man, twice her size, all muscle and malice, and knew that he would enjoy killing her with his bare hands. She looked around at the low wall, about waist-high, that surrounded the sandy arena. Behind it, the tiered benches were filled to capacity with Edomites, thirsty for her blood. The three exits were guarded by armed soldiers. She stepped backwards and bumped against Qoz's stone throne at the center of the arena. Her knees weakened, and she had to lean against the deity's copper leg to stay upright.

The high priest paused about ten steps away, his white teeth glinting in his copper painted face. He punched the air in her direction and yelled, "Boo!"

Startled, Deborah jumped aside and tripped over Qoz's feet.

The amphitheater exploded with laughter.

Staying down made her much more vulnerable, Deborah knew, but she couldn't find the strength to get up. She put her head down, her face in the crook of her arm, and felt tears well up. Was this the end?

For a fleeting moment, she was riding on the back of the eagle obove Palm Homestead and the throngs of Hebrews on the adjacent slopes, listening to her as she delivered God's message. It was her True Calling, but she would never succeed in answering it. Sadness washed over her, a wave of grief as thick as the water of the Sea of Salt, followed by a flash of anger. Where was God now, when she needed Him more than ever? After all she had gone through, how could He abandon her now? Her anger heated into fury, and a voice sounded in her ears – not the eagle, but Kassite, repeating what he had told her at a similar moment of despair: "Rage is like a mighty stallion, an explosive force of nature. If you fail to tame it, the result could be deadly, but if you harness it wisely, it will carry you over the highest peaks, trample your enemies to oblivion, and deliver you through the toughest battles, all the way to the ultimate victory your heart desires."

Leaping to her feet, Deborah drew her sword, gripped the hilt with both hands, and swung the blade at Qoztobarus.

The crowd yelped in surprise.

Qoztobarus turned to the balcony. "Fairness requires that opponents are equally armed, or unarmed."

"Fairness?" The sword was heavy, but Deborah kept the blade up. "I'm a stranger in your land, my God is invisible before your mighty Qoz, and my strength is but a tenth of my opponent. How could there be fairness here?"

The king seemed amused by this turn of events. He gestured up at the thunderbolt. "Qoz is holding a weapon. His high priest should also have one – a weapon of his choice."

The wisdom of their monarch pleased many of the people, who shouted their approval.

"I choose this one." Qoztobarus swiveled around and pointed at Deborah's sword.

Deborah took a few steps aside, moving away from the stone throne into the open arena. "That's my sword."

General Mazabi signaled with his hand, and soldiers stepped into the arena from all sides, their spears aimed at her.

She looked up at the king. "Is this Edom's fairness?"

The audience did not voice support for her.

"You can choose a weapon, too," the king said.

The soldiers looked at General Mazabi, who used his copper spear to signal them to move in on her.

"I choose his spear." Deborah pointed at the general.

The audience burst out laughing, and the king did, too.

His face sour, General Mazabi raised his spear and hurled it at her. The spear flew through the air, its flared arrowhead spinning, the sharp point aimed at her head, then at her abdomen, and further down, until the spear completed its arched journey and hit the ground between her boots, stabbing through the sand with a thud that travelled up through her legs and spine.

A burst of applause came from the crowd.

By now, the weight of the sword had exhausted Deborah's arms, and she knew there was little chance she could use the weapon effectively even if she kept it. She tossed the sword to the sand, grabbed General Mazabi's spear, and pulled. It didn't move.

Qoztobarus sneered.

His mockery fueled the fire of her rage, and she kicked the spear. Still, it didn't budge.

He cradled his cheek in his hand, making the people laugh.

Her face flushed, Deborah stepped around the spear, grasped the bulging butt of the spear, and pushed it back and forth, throwing her weight into it. The crowd pelted her with pits, fruit, and even a sandal, which hit her shoulder as the spear finally gave way. She pulled it out of the ground, and was immediately shocked by its weight. How could the old general hurl this thing though the air with one hand?

She turned to face Qoztobarus, rotated the spear, and pounded the bulging end on the ground the way she had seen General Mazabi do.

The high priest leaned forward, placing his hands on his thighs, and peered at her the way one examined a lizard or a turtle that happened on the road.

The crowd quieted down.

His dark eyes focused on her sword, resting on the ground by her feet.

Sensing he was about to sprint in her direction, Deborah knew she had to get ready with the spear, but she had only thrown wooden spears a few times, and never one as heavy as this. Nevertheless, it was all she knew how to do. Taking a step back with her right foot, Deborah positioned her body sideways, and raised the general's spear. It tilted back over her right shoulder, the weight pulled her backwards, and she stumbled, dropping it.

The crowd laughed harder than before.

Deborah regained her balance. Qoztobarus was still in the same position, hands resting on his thighs, peering at her. Unlike before, though, he did not bother to mock her or partake in the crowd's glee. She realized he was about to attack.

As he took the first step, she bent down and picked the spear up with both hands. When she straightened up, he was already halfway to her, his arms pumping, his fists clenched, his dark eyes murderous. She had no time to think. Using both hands, she threw the spear horizontally as one would throw a wooden log. It collided with both his knees like a low railing and knocked his legs from under him. He fell forward and slammed into the ground facedown.

Her first impulse was to run away before he got up and killed her, but instead, she lifted her leg and landed her boot hard on the back of his head – once, twice, and a third time as hard as she could.

The silver hilt glistened from the ground beside her. She picked up her sword and rested the point of the blade at Qoztobarus's neck.

The amphitheater became silent, every eye on the sword in her hands.

Qoztobarus groaned and started to move.

Deborah pushed lightly on the sword, the tip poking the side of his neck.

He froze in place.

A memory flashed through Deborah's mind of Seesya's soldier, Hashkem, glaring at her from under the water in Ein Gedi, his mouth open, blood clouding the stream while she pushed her sword deeper under his chin, up into his head, until the point of the blade would go no further.

She looked up at the king. "Yahweh commanded us: Do not kill!"

The king watched her, not responding.

An angry hiss came from the high priest, but he didn't dare to move.

She held the sword firmly and pleaded with the king, "Declare me winner. I don't want to kill him."

The king held out his hand, his thumb pointing sideways.

The crowd was completely still.

The royal thumb turned downward.

The crowd roared, and Deborah knew she must run the blade through the man lying at her feet before he made a move to attack her. Would Yahweh punish her for violating His Sixth Commandment? Would the dead Qoztobarus return to haunt her every night, as Hashkem had done until the eagle told her that the commandment, "Do not kill!" was not absolute: "When a person rises to kill you, rise first and kill him." But the high priest was not attacking her, not yet, anyway. How could she stab a man lying on the ground?

Qoztobarus moved his hand slowly towards her leg.

She had to decide: To kill, or not to kill?

Unable to bring herself to do it, Deborah stepped back and stabbed the blade into the ground. "I spare his life. No more bloodshed!"

The crowd booed, the king shook his head, and the high priest laughed, rising from the ground.

Deborah ran.

A quarter of the way around the arena, she saw an exit and headed for it, hoping that Qoztobarus would chase after her, leaving the temple behind, which might cause the crowd to break up and end the sacrifice ceremony. When she reached the exit, however, the soldiers blocked her way. She tried to push them, but they were large, heavy, and firm. She ran around to the next exit where, once again, the soldiers barred her. The audience cursed and threw litter at her. Stepping back, she feigned going to the left, then leapt right and around the soldiers. Her agility got her through, but another soldier came from the side and tackled her.

Cheers broke out, and Deborah saw Qoztobarus walk around the statue of Qoz. His face and chest were covered with white sand, and he carried both her sword and the general's spear, one in each hand. Two of his young priests hurried after him with a bucket and rinsed his face, which became pale without the copper paint. The water ran down his chest, covering it with a wet mix of white sand, copper dust, and lumps of congealed pig blood.

He continued towards her, and as he got closer, she could see his enraged expression. She tried again to get through the soldiers, but they shoved her towards the approaching high priest.

He stopped about ten steps away.

The crowd quieted down.

Raising the copper spear, Qoztobarus suspended it above his shoulder.

The crowd began to chant. "Kill the boy! Kill the boy!"

Deborah considered running, but knew the spear would be faster than her. If she had to die, it shouldn't happen while she fled. Let all these hateful Edomites remember her as a brave Hebrew boy who fought to the end.

The high priest tilted the spear back, ready to throw it.

Leaning forward, Deborah placed her hands on the armor pieces over the front of her legs, imitating his earlier posture, which turned her into a smaller target while the bent knees made her ready to jump or run.

"Kill the boy! Kill the boy!"

Deborah watched his face. When she saw his lips purse, his nostrils flare, and his eyes narrow, she jumped to the right just as he hurled the spear. The arrowhead nicked the outer edge of her upper left arm and ended its brief flight with a heavy thump. One of the soldiers cried and fell backwards with the spear in his chest. His legs twitched, and blood pulsated from his mouth.

The whole amphitheater exploded with cries of shock, but Deborah knew that Qoztobarus wouldn't wallow in remorse. Sure enough, he lunged forward while passing the sword from his left hand to his right. He was upon her before she could run, and as he thrust forward, she twisted sideways and managed to dodge the blade, but he caught her with a left hook, his fist thumping her squarely on the forehead. The blow felt as if a heavy rock had struck her head. Her legs folded, and she collapsed.

Coming to a moment later, Deborah heard the crowd chanting, "Kill the boy! Kill the boy!"

Qoztobarus stood over her. He brought the end of the blade to her neck, turning it so that the flat, cold iron rested against her skin. "Get up, boy," he said. "I want to make your head fly off nicely."

Still dizzy, Deborah pushed against the warm sand, sitting up.

"Kill the boy! Kill the boy!"

"On your knees." He took a step back. "Yahweh is waiting for you, if He exists."

She got up on her knees.

"Hold your head up," Qoztobarus brought the sword to her neck again. "That's perfect."

"Kill the boy! Kill the boy!"

Qoztobarus swung the blade sideways, ready to strike across. "You should have killed me when you had the chance."

It was the end, Deborah knew. No way out. Would it hurt when the blade cut her neck? It hurt already to know that Seesya was about to win as his sword would now kill the girl he had sworn to destroy. She wanted to see the eagle once more, to ask her how this could happen, why had Yahweh abandoned His devoted servant—

"What's this?" Qoztobarus pointed down with the blade.

Deborah looked and saw blood trickle from her crotch on the inside of her thighs, down to her knees, pooling in the white sand.

Bending forward, the high priest stared closely.

The crowd, which couldn't see the reason for the holdup, kept chanting, "Kill the boy! Kill the boy!"

She exhaled. Was this a message from Yahweh, a final dose of humiliation before she died? Was this His rebuke for pretending to be a boy, a punishment for bearing men's weapons?

Qoztobarus contorted his face with disgust. "Female blood?"

Why, Deborah wondered, would Yahweh disgrace her after He had already abandoned her to defeat and execution? Was it not enough?

"Kill the boy!" The crowd stomped the benches with each word. "Kill the boy!"

Their eagerness for her death infuriated Deborah, and she wanted to scream for Yahweh that He should save her before it was too late, but then, she remembered the eagle's words at the bottom of the copper mine: "Freedom must be earned, not collected as a gift."

Fueled by her rage, an idea ignited in her mind.

"You're a girl!" Qoztobarus spat on the sand. "A damn girl dressed as a boy."

"I'm sorry," Deborah said in an exaggerated feminine voice while her hands began to gather sand behind her knees. "Lying is a sin."

Up close, the high priest's eyes were as pale as Sallan's, yet radiating dark hostility. "I noticed you were too pretty for a boy."

"Thank you." She ladled more sand into her hands.

The chanting reached a crescendo. "Kill the boy! Kill the boy!"

"Now I understand." He looked towards the balcony. "The healer's son got himself involved with another ill-chosen girl."

"I'm not Sallan's girl."

"Don't lie. I saw how he looked at you."

"As a friend." Deborah balanced the mounds of sand on her palms, getting ready. "He still loves the girl you killed all those years back."

"I didn't kill An."

"Was that his dead-wife's name? An?"

"If she's dead, her blood is on Sallan's hands." Qoztobarus's eyes dropped back to the blood pooling under her crotch. "You, however, I am going to kill."

"Not yet." Deborah threw the sand in his face.

He howled like a wounded jackal, silencing the crowd's chants. The sand in his eyes must have caused terrible pain, but even as he clasped his face with his left hand, he had the presence of mind to raise the sword and hack down on the spot where Deborah had sat, missing her only because she rolled aside.

Shouting in pain and rage, clutching at his eyes, Qoztobarus continued to slice left and right, up and down, blindly chasing after his prey. Deborah rolled again and got up. She considered circling him and trying to take away the sword, but he did not cease slashing in all directions, and the young priests were already running over with buckets of water. Deborah sprinted around the arena to the next exit. Finding it blocked by soldiers, she kept going, and came full circle back to the crane in front of Qoz's statue across from the royal balcony.

She paused, unsure what to do.

The crowd stood on the tiered benches all around, shouting with unbridled agitation. High above, Leola screamed again. And on the balcony, everyone stood at the railing, staring down at her. No one moved, except for Sallan, who did something with his hand. Was he signaling to her, or waving off a fly? Deborah wasn't sure.

He did it again, rotating his hand in small circles.

What was he trying to tell her?

With his other hand, he patted his hip.

She understood. The sling!

Deborah untied it from around her hips.

Some in the crowd shouted at her and pointed. She turned to see Qoztobarus on the move. He was still rubbing his eyes, but he would soon recover enough to use the sword effectively.

There were no stones in the sandy arena, which rendered her sling useless.

Leola screamed again, the pole swayed, and Deborah realized where she could find a stone. She ran to the box at the base of the pole, reached up over the side, and grabbed one of the stones.

Qoztobarus was getting closer.

With the stone fitted in the pouch, Deborah grasped the hook and the tab and let the pouch dangle below her hand.

He started running towards her, gaining speed.

A pang of fear hit Deborah as she remembered Seesya's attack in Ein Gedi, where she had a single chance to hit her target or die—by the same sword!

Rushing at her, his feet throwing up sand, Qoztobarus raised the sword, ready to bring it down on her.

Inhaling deeply, Deborah focused on his face, spun the sling once, twice, and let it go at the top of the third rotation. He tried to dodge, but the distance between them was less than fifteen steps, and the stone hit his left cheek with a loud clap. He swiveled, hit the sand, and rolled over.

The crowd roared.

The memory of his quick recovery earlier made Deborah reach into the box to grab another stone.

Qoztobarus groaned, rose on all four, and looked in her direction. The left side of his face was bashed in, and blood poured from his nose and mouth.

Deborah fitted a stone in the pouch.

He got up, swaying, and looked around for the sword.

She let the sling dangle down by her leg to feel the weight of the stone.

He picked up the sword.

She rotated the sling just as he dashed towards her with surprising speed. There was no time for a full second rotation, and she let go of the tab early, shooting the stone out of the pouch. It flew diagonally downwards and hit his right knee. He went down hard while still gripping the sword. As the blade dug into the ground, it caused his arm to twist back, and his shoulder popped out with a sharp cracking sound.

Deborah quickly tied the sling around her hips while stepping forward, grabbed the sword, and retreated. He got up slowly, his right arm hanging limply by his side, his head tilted forward, his mutilated face oozing blood, and charged towards her, limping badly, yet as quick as a cat. She ran around the base of the crane, and he kept going after her. She ran across the width of the arena to the low wall encircling it and hopped on.

Facing the crowded tiered benches, Deborah raised the sword and slashed left and right, forcing the people to dodge and make room. She put her right boot forward and stepped onto the first bench, but a hand grabbed her left ankle, causing her to fall across the next bench up, the sword slipping from her hand. She twisted around and saw Qoztobarus, bent over the low wall, his hand clasping her left ankle in a tight vise. He pulled her down, growling madly, spewing blood out of his broken mouth. She held on to the bench, but his strength was greater, and she slipped down towards him.

His mouth twisted, and she realized he was grinning. With all his agony and pain, this man rejoiced at the prospect of killing her!

Rage exploded inside Deborah. She raised her right leg, bent it, and kicked with the thick sole of her leather boot into his mangled face. He cried, spraying her with blood, and fell backwards off the low wall into the arena.

Shocked by her own cruelty, Deborah scrambled to her feet, picked up the sword, and stepped down from the bench onto the low wall.

Qoztobarus was lying on his back in the sand below her. He moaned, his left arm pressed across his face. The crowd roared around her in a state of madness, but she ignored the noise, keeping her eyes on her nemesis, and prayed that he would stay down.

He sat up, his bloody face turned up towards her, his eyes creased, focused on her.

"Stay down," Deborah said. "I don't want to kill you."

The lopsided grin flashed again. "You can't do it, girl."

She gripped the hilt with both hands and raised the sword above her head.

He twisted, got up on his left knee, and spat a mouthful of blood on the sand.

The crowd thundered around the arena.

"I will kill you," Deborah said. "Stay down."

Qoztobarus stood up, groaning in pain, and lunged forward.

Deborah brought the sword down.

The blade landed on his bald scalp and sliced his head in half like a piece of fresh fruit, parting it all the way down through the middle of his throat, and lodged in the top edge of his chest bone. The inside of his head wasn't bloody, as she expected, but filled with a gray substance, neither liquid nor firm, resembling a rotten apple. His body remained upright for a brief moment, and collapsed.

The whole amphitheater fell into total silence.

She stepped down from the low wall, bent over, and vomited.

Thousands of eyes bore into her as she twisted the sword to release it from the corpse and walked across the sand to the crane. The wheels screeched as she pushed the base, making it turn until Leola was no longer above Qoz's thunderbolt. Deborah untied the rope from the pole and held it while walking around Qoz's throne to unwind the rope. Leola descended to the sand, and Deborah removed the harness and helped the shaken girl stand.

Up on the balcony, King Esau the Twentieth held out his hand and turned his thumb up.

6

A moment after the king raised his thumb, a group of men ran out through the doors under the balcony, carrying rattles, hand drums, horns, pipes, oboes, flutes, and small harps. They gathered in the arena in front of the royal balcony and began playing a fast-paced tune. The crowd applauded while a dozen acrobats cartwheeled around the arena. Next came jugglers, tossing multi-colored jars in the air between them. Meanwhile, the acrobats formed a human pyramid, with the man at the top doing a handstand, abruptly losing his balance, almost falling, but recovering with a single hand resting on the head of the man below. Even Leola, after all she'd been through, watched with amazement. The crowd clapped to the music, pointed at the performers, and laughed out loud when a trio of jesters struggled to climb onto tall stilts, teetering precariously.

Deborah watched as the grim young priests wrapped Qoztobarus in a white sheet and carried him away. The oldest among them, who bore uncanny resemblance to Qoztobarus, stopped and stared at her darkly.

"I am Qozmadorus." He pointed up at Qoz's thunderbolt. "Prepare to die, Hebrew boy!"

She took Leola's arm and pulled her to the nearest exit, where the soldiers watched the entertainment and ignored them.

The street outside was empty. Deborah headed downhill, the roar of the crowd in her back.

"I want my mother," Leola said.

"Me too."

"Where is your mother?"

Deborah's mother's face briefly appearing in her mind. "She's dead, and we'll be dead, too, if we don't get out of Bozra."

Leola stopped, shaking her arm free. "Out of Bozra?"

Deborah tried to pull her along. "Yes, right now."

"Where to?"

The crowd roared at the amphitheater, and the sound echoed from the nearby houses.

"I have friends near the Sea of Salt, or in Moab—"

"You're not my husband." Leola wouldn't move. "I'm not allowed to be alone with you."

Deborah barely resisted admitting that she, too, was a girl. "Would you rather die with your husband?"

Leola turned and ran back uphill.

Some kind of an explosion sounded, followed by cheers from the crowd, and the noise jolted Deborah. She resumed running downhill. The street switched back and forth, crossing the city from side to side in a moderate descent. She couldn't remember how far down was Sallan's family home. Her chest armor bounced up and down, chafing her breasts, and her leg armor squished with the blood on her inner thighs.

As she turned another corner, Deborah recognized the tall hedges along the front of the large garden. The sight gave her renewed energy, and she ran faster while planning in her mind the next steps: cross the garden, enter the house, collect her sack and spear, back to the garden, into the horse stable, saddle Rogez, and gallop away.

The noise from the amphitheater mixed with another sound – horse hooves drumming the ground somewhere uphill.

Sprinting through the garden, she heard the horses come closer.

At the entrance to the house, she bumped into a servant.

The horses neighed as they halted on the street behind the tall hedges. Deborah was gripped by indecision. What should she do? The eagle's words came to her: "You don't win a fight by fleeing."

The servant bowed.

"Go," she said. "Bring a jug of wine and two goblets. Fast!"

The servant hurried to the kitchen.

The clicking of metal outside told her the dismounting riders were armed. She ran to the dining table under the jujube tree, dropped into Umm-Sallan's chair at the head of the table, and lounged back, her hands behind her head, fingers interwoven.

General Mazabi marched into the garden with a company of soldiers. Deborah didn't move, reminding herself of Sallan's rule about exuding confidence around dogs and men. She inhaled deeply, trying to control her panting. The general paused and looked around the garden as if expecting a trap. He had recovered his copper spear, which he held in his only hand.

Exhaling slowly, Deborah gestured at a chair by the table.

He walked over, pounding his spear on the ground with each step, and sat down.

The servant rushed out of the house with the jug and goblets, but froze when he saw the soldiers. She clicked her fingers and signaled for him to serve them. He placed a goblet in front of her, filled it with wine, then poured one for the general, as well.

With another deep breath, Deborah raised the goblet. "To Princess Needa."

Propping his spear against the table, the general took the goblet and emptied it with a series of loud gulps. Deborah brought the goblet to her lips and feigned a sip, watching him over the lid. He smacked his lips and slammed the goblet down on the table. She put hers down, as well, and the servant refilled the goblets.

General Mazabi raised his goblet. "To Qoztobarus, the unlucky loser."

She feigned another sip. "You think it was luck?"

"The high priest was a formidable man. You're a skinny weed."

"God was on my side."

"Gods. Priests. Kings. They can be fooled. But me?" He beat his chest with his one fist. "I know fighting, and weeds don't beat oaks."

Clasping her hands under the table, she smiled. "If you know fighting, tell me why I won."

"Three reasons," he said. "Agility. Smarts. Tools."

"Tools?"

He touched his spear. "This to trip him. Sand to blind him. Sling to maim him. And the sword to finish him off."

"Smarts?"

General Mazabi glanced at her sword. "It's a heavy one. You waited for high grounds and used the weight of the blade for the final blow. That was smart."

There had been no planning or waiting, only a fight for survival at each moment, but she didn't correct him. "Agility?"

"You were finished, totally defeated several times, but somehow, you sprang back with a new tactic every time."

"Not bad for a weed."

He chuckled. "A capable weed, but not a soldier. I can tell."

Her chest tightened, and she barely managed to speak. "How?"

"Soldiers follow habits. Stand. Fight. Die."

"I wasn't ready to die."

"Or to fight." He chuckled. "Dodging. Begging. Running for the exits. Escaping to the benches."

"Our God forbids killing unless it's necessary to survive."

"Who trained you?"

"Despair. Necessity. Persistence."

"They did well." General Mazabi gestured in the uphill direction, where the crowd was still roaring. "You don't like music? Acrobats? Jesters?"

Inhaling deeply, she shrugged. "Death is no cause for celebration."

He watched her, his creased face doubtful.

"I needed to think," Deborah added. "I have a long journey ahead to find the princess—"

"The girl said otherwise."

"What girl?"

He clicked his fingers, and the soldier stepped in from the street, dragging Leola across the garden to the table. She was whimpering.

Deborah felt panic rise in her chest.

"She said you were planning to escape."

"Why would I escape after victory?" Deborah got up, took her goblet to Leola, and brought it to her lips. When the girl finished the wine, Deborah put the goblet on the table, removed the soldier's hand from Leola's arm, and beckoned the servant. "Take her inside and put her to bed."

General Mazabi watched Leola and the servant disappear inside. "She mentioned Moab. And the Sea of Salt."

Pushing back the panic, Deborah shrugged. "Poor girl. She's confused."

He rubbed his gray beard, watching her.

"Have you ever been tied in a harness over sharp spikes?"

He laughed. "Not yet."

"Imagine the effect of the experience." Deborah filled her goblet from the jug and toasted. "To life!"

His face grew serious. "The king sent me."

She watched him over the rim of the goblet.

"He's suspicious."

Deborah put down the goblet. "My faith is true and honest."

"He offered a reward for rescuing Needa."

"What is it?"

"Fifteen dozen silver coins."

The amount shocked Deborah, but she kept a straight face. "Will I live to spend the reward?"

"The king will guarantee your safe passage."

"Where to?"

"Canaan."

Was he trying to trick her into admitting that she had brought Sallan from Canaan, not from Egypt? "Why Canaan?"

"You're a Hebrew, aren't you?" He rested his fist on the table. "What's your answer?"

It wasn't like she had a choice. "I accept."

"Good." He glanced at the house. "Keep it a secret."

"Why?"

"Silver shines brighter in the dark."

Deborah understood his subtle warning about her hosts. Was he trying to put a wedge between her and the only friends she had in Edom?

"I must tell Sallan," she said.

"Tell him and his mother, but no one else." He stood up. "You leave tomorrow at dawn."

"Will you accompany me on the journey to the Negev Desert?"

General Mazabi adjusted the armor over his right shoulder, where his arm was missing, and picked up his copper spear. "Isn't your God enough?"

Deborah watched him leave, pounding his spear on the ground as he walked. The soldiers, however, stayed behind. Two went to guard the horse stable, two took positions at the front door, and the others spread around the garden and behind the house.

7

Outside the gates of Bozra at sunrise, the loincloth under Deborah's armor was already damp. She shifted in the saddle, seeking a comfortable position. Rogez stomped his front hooves, eager to get going, but Sallan's horse seemed morose, as was the camel shared by his two boy-servants. They had packed sacks of food, jugs of wine, bundles of firewood, and sheets of cloth for tents. Three pack camels were tied behind in a line, bearing sacks of trading goods, such as copper dishes, tools, and ornaments.

General Mazabi arrived with four mounted Edomite soldiers in leather armor and plain leather helmets without rooster combs. The soldiers lined their horses up behind the pack camels, whereas the general rode up to Sallan.

"They're good men," he said. "They'll obey you."

Sallan tilted his head at Deborah. "They should obey the one responsible for this suicidal folly."

The general looked at her. "You too, boy. Obey the Elixirist."

"I obey God alone," she said.

"You wish to meet Him?" General Mazabi pointed the copper spear at her. "Right now?"

Rogez reacted without hesitation, neighing as he reared up and pawed the air at the pointed spear. General Mazabi's horse whinnied and retreated, and the general barely managed to stay mounted. Rogez came down on all four, but continued to sway his head from side to side in agitation. Deborah rubbed his neck and spoke in a hushed voice until he calmed down.

The general got his horse under control.

"Don't take it personally," Sallan said. "Borah's previous horse is buried by the Sea of Salt after taking a bunch of spears in the chest to defend—"

"The Sea of Salt?" General Mazabi's eyes narrowed. "It's in the opposite direction from Egypt."

"I misspoke," Sallan said. "I meant the Sea of Reeds."

"And I meant no disrespect," Deborah said. "God is greater than any man. He will help me find Princess Needa. Sallan and your soldiers can stay here."

General Mazabi ignored her and spoke to Sallan. "Act as a merchant. You'll be safe."

"Safe?" Sallan sneered. "It'll be a miracle if I survive this journey. Umm-Sallan will never forgive you."

"The king sent you against my advice. I'm risking as much, sending them along." The general tilted his head at the four soldiers in the rear. "You have the ingredients?"

Sallan patted a black leather satchel tied to his saddle.

Their conversation made little sense to Deborah, but she held her tongue.

"Follow this trader." The general pointed at a merchant caravan that was departing from the fairgrounds near the gate. "The leader's name is Navad. We paid him well."

Sallan watched the caravan. "Can he be trusted?"

"To navigate the trade routes. Nothing more."

"How much does he know?"

"He knows about him." General Mazabi gestured at Deborah. "Everybody knows."

"That's what I'm afraid of," Sallan said. "News of what happened in the amphitheater yesterday is already halfway to Beersheba."

"Aren't you happy? Your sworn enemy is dead."

"His son will pick up the torch of hate."

"Qozmadorus?" General Mazabi sneered. "Arrogant young fool."

"Doesn't matter. I doubt we'll make it alive to Tamar, let along Beersheba."

"Doubting the Gods? Or your Hebrew boy?"

Sallan wasn't amused. "If we make it by the Gods' grace, I'll report back."

"Find Princess Needa," the general said. "We'll be ready,"

"Ready?" Deborah rubbed Rogez's neck. "Ready for what? Something to do with the ingredients you mentioned?"

The two men looked at each other, neither answering her question.

"Don't keep secrets from me," she said. "I am the one who promised to bring Needa back, and I intend to achieve it peacefully."

"Peaceful?" General Mazabi spat on the ground. "Hebrews are never peaceful."

"That's an understatement," Sallan said. "Even to each other, they're quarrelsome and combative."

"How do you know?" Deborah glared at him. "Have you met many Hebrews in Egypt?"

Sallan's face hardened. "I met you, Borah, have I not?"

"Drop this charade." The general chuckled. "Lies are like fruit – they don't keep long before smelling." He turned his horse and sprinted back to the gate and into the city.

They followed the caravan towards the rising sun. On the road across the valley, the leader of the caravan glanced back over his shoulder occasionally, but his wives and children never looked back. At least two of his sons were old enough to carry spears. Deborah wondered why no one carried bows and arrows like her Moabite friend Zariz, who travelled with his father's caravan.

They left the green fields and fruit orchards behind and started up the meandering road up the eastern hills. At the top, Navad stopped in the shade of a jujube tree, and everyone dismounted. Deborah gave Rogez water in a bowl and drank directly from her waterskin. Sallan shielded his eyes with his hand and gazed back across the long valley at Bozra, whose white walls and copper roofs glittered in the sun. He sniffled. She touched his shoulder, but he shook off her hand and stepped away.

The afternoon brought no relief from the heat. A wind from the west blew sand off the mountain ridges, stinging any exposed skin. Deborah took the blanket out of her sack and covered herself. Later on, she heard the drumming of hooves and peeked from under the blanket. A herd of white antelopes passed barely a hundred steps away from the road. The graceful beasts had long horns and striped cheeks, like the image that graced the flag of Ephraim. She thought of her father, quoting God's blessing to Joseph, father of Ephraim and Manasseh: "And his horns are the antelope's horns, with them he will impale foreign nations."

Shortly before sunset, they stopped at a small oasis nestled at the foothills. Navad and his family set up camp beside a thicket of low trees and shrubbery. Sallan's boy-servants put up a tent nearby, and so did the four soldiers. Deborah started a fire with her father's stones.

While the servants prepared the evening meal, she stepped away from the camp, carrying her sack. Twilight gave the desert a golden sheen, and the air began to cool down. She untied the sling from her hips, picked up a stone, aimed at a rock across a wide crevice, and made the shot, missing the target. She repeated the shot, and missed again. Unplugging her waterskin, she wet her hands and rubbed her face. Feeling refreshed, she selected a medium-sized stone, aimed carefully, and slung it. The stone hit the side of the rock with a sharp whack and bounced off.

"That's better," Deborah said out loud.

She practiced until twilight faded to darkness. Making sure no one was nearby, she loosened her armor, lowered her undergarments, and took off the soiled loincloth. It smelled sourly, and she dropped it on the ground in disgust before crouching to relieve herself. With a few drops from her waterskin into her palm, she cleaned herself, rubbed her grimy hand in the soil, and put on a clean loincloth from her sack. With the tip of her boot she dug into the hard soil, pushed the loincloth into the hole, and covered it.

Back in the camp, under a half moon, the boy-servants put out bread, cheese, figs, and apples. The soldiers went to sit near the horses and camels, where they ate and talked quietly. The two boy-servants went into Sallan's tent.

Deborah poured wine for herself and for Sallan. She raised her cup. "To life."

"What life?" Sallan emptied his cup and put it down. "The new life you gave me and, then, you took it away?"

"I didn't ask the king to send you along. Why are you angry with me?"

He glared at her over the fire. "Sometimes I wonder if, despite your occasional moments of brilliance, you're still the same anxious, ignorant, stupid girl from Emanuel."

She recoiled from his venomous tone. "I'm none of these things."

"You don't even understand why they chose Leola for sacrifice, do you?"

"Offer Qoz that which you ask for," she quoted Qoztobarus.

"You're good at memorizing mindlessly, the way Hebrew boys memorize your Holy Scriptures. Think for yourself. Why Leola?"

Deborah added a piece of wood to the fire. "She's your niece, and she looks like the girl you once took away from Qoztobarus."

"And the king? What was his motivation?"

"To humiliate you."

"Why?"

"To show the people that Qoz no longer likes you?"

"Correct," he said. "That's why Leola was chosen, and that's why you should not have interfered."

"What?"

"You should have stayed on the balcony and shed helpless tears like everybody else."

"And let Leola die?"

"Call me cruel," Sallan said, "but Leola's suffering was necessary. Her death on the thunderbolt, screaming in agony and despair, would have shown the people that the great Elixirist, who, long ago, had saved the old king's life, liberated the nation of Edom from Egypt's army, and won the hand of the most beautiful girl in Bozra, was nothing – a pittiful old man who couldn't save his own niece. Sacrificing Leola would have restored the young king's confidence and satisfied Qoztobarus's burning vengeance. And I would have been able to settle back at home and spend my remaining years unmolested, surrounded by family and friends."

"And Leola would have lost her young life."

"That's a price I was willing to pay – sadly, regretfully, even achingly, yet willingly, because it would have lifted the menace of the king's envy and the high priest's enmity from my head. But you had to leap into the air in another one of your outrageous, reckless, heart stopping stunts and destroy my chance at a good life. You literally forced the king to send me away on a journey from which I'm unlikely to return." Sallan leaned towards her, his face demonized by the dancing flames. "Why did you have to interfere? How was it your business? Who asked you to save that doomed girl?"

"I did," a voice said in the dark.

They turned, startled.

A slim figure dressed in black stepped into the light of the fire.

Sallan scrambled to his feet. "Is it really you?"

"If it's not me," Umm-Sallan said, "then someone who looks like me is very cold."

Deborah wrapped the matriarch in a blanket and sat her down by the fire. A moment later, a young man appeared, grasping the reins of two horses. It was Leola's husband, and he was numb with exhaustion and chill. Deborah summoned the boy-servants to take care of the horses and poured wine for the two arrivals.

Sallan asked, "How did you find us?"

"We knew where you're heading," Leola's husband answered. "I've travelled these with my father to trade with the Hebrews and the Philistines."

Umm-Sallan shivered. "When the sun went down, we had only the moon to guide us."

"And no one to protect you," Sallan said. "Why didn't General Mazabi send soldiers with you?"

"He didn't know I left. Other than my maid, everyone thinks I'm bedridden with worry for you, too upset to receive visitors."

"It's madness." Sallan's voice trembled. "At your age, on the road—"

His mother put a finger to his lips. "I'll go to the Gods in peace, satisfied that I spent my last moments with my son on the road, rather than at home without him, waiting for news, fearing the worst, losing you again."

"You won't lose him again," Deborah said. "We'll be back in Bozra before long."

Umm-Sallan grasped her forearm. "How can you be so certain?"

"When you pursue your True Calling, God provides the shortcuts."

Sallan tossed a pebble into the fire. "There she goes again."

Leola's husband perked up. "She?"

After a moment of awkward silence, Umm-Sallan said, "Borah was quoting a famous Hebrew woman. Now, go find some more wood for the fire, will you?"

He picked a burning stick, got up, and walked into the dark.

"Watch out for snakes," Umm-Sallan called after him, and in a hushed voice said to Sallan, "You must be careful. Exposure will be fatal for her."

"True," Sallan said. "Sooner or later, someone will see through this masquerade. I'm surprised no one has figured it out yet."

"Qoztobarus did," Deborah said.

"When?"

"Yahweh made my female blood come just when Qoztobarus was about to behead me, causing him to bend closer to look, and giving me an opportunity to throw sand in his eyes."

Sallan burst out laughing.

"What's so funny?"

Unable to answer, Sallan laughed on.

"Men." His mother shook her head. "Like little boys."

"I don't understand."

"He's laughing because Qoztobarus died knowing that a girl beat him."

Sallan pantomimed Deborah's sword landing on the high priest's head, making himself laugh even harder.

His mother rested her hand on Deborah's arm. "Did your God actually tell you to go on this journey, or was it just a feeling in your heart?"

Closing her eyes, Deborah recalled the desperate moments in the arena, when the eagle had appeared. "His message was clear," she said. "As clear as the spoken words of a person."

"Nonsense." Sallan got up. "Yours is a false God."

"Then how have I come halfway to realizing my True Calling?"

"Halfway to nowhere." He waved dismissively. "Look around you. Where's your lovely homestead? Where's your great palm tree? Where's your faithful Hebrew audience? You would have been better off staying in Emanuel. Maybe I should have stayed, too."

He stormed off, and they heard him mumble angrily as he got into the tent.

"Don't take offense," Umm-Sallan said. "He'll calm down by morning. His father was the same way."

"He thinks I have a choice," Deborah said. "I don't. Do you believe me?"

The matriarch's teeth glistened in the glow of the fire. "I believe that you believe."

Leola's husband returned with a few dry sticks, which he dropped into the flames, raising a flurry of sparks.

After a while, Umm-Sallan fell asleep. Deborah lay beside the old woman and spread her own blanket over both of them. It smelled of the tiger's tail with which it had shared her sack.

8

When Navad and his family got up and began to pack, Deborah woke up to find herself wedged between Umm-Sallan and Leola's husband, who bolted up and looked around with a bewildered expression. The matriarch needed help to stand, her gaunt figure swaying. Sallan and his boy-servants were up soon, too, as were the soldiers. Crouching to hide what she was doing, Deborah reached into her sack, took out the jar Sallan had given her in Bozra, and smeared a layer of stubble paste on her cheeks and chin.

A burst of howling startled her.

Navad's sons and the four Edomite soldiers grabbed their weapons and took positions around the horses and camels.

A pack of jackals appeared out of a ditch near the camp. They were fighting over something, tearing at it, snapping at each other. Deborah recognized her soiled loincloth. She glanced at Umm-Sallan, who was already looking at her.

The horses neighed and pulled at their reins, shaking the trees to which they were tied. The camels bared their teeth and brayed hoarsely. One of the soldiers stepped forward and hurled his spear at the closest jackal, which dodged it with ease. Navad's oldest son also tried, with the same result. The jackals started to close in, howling with such ferocity that Deborah would have covered her ears had she not been busy untying the sling from her waist.

One of the jackals sprang forward and tried to bite Navad, who managed to hit it with the butt of his spear. The jackals showed no fear, continuing to close in.

Sallan picked up a stone and shoved it into Deborah's hand. She fitted the stone in the pouch and readied the sling to shoot.

The jackals had formed a half-circle that gradually narrowed. Most of them were too close for a slingshot, and Deborah focused on one in the rear. She slung the stone and hit it in the leg, breaking it. The jackal fell over, wailing in pain.

The other jackals, however, continued to advance. One of them sprinted forward, feigned a bite at Umm-Sallan, who fell back into the arms of one of Navad's wives, and came at Deborah. She had no time to find another stone, and instead used the sling as a whip, lashing it on its nose. The jackal twisted its head, locked its teeth, and pulled the sling out of her hand while another jackal attacked. Had they somehow recognized her as the source of the bloody loincloth? Deborah drew her sword and slashed the jackal's head, opening a deep gash. In an instant, the rest of the pack went after it, biting into their injured mate. One of those who couldn't get in a bit noticed the jackal with the broken leg and leapt at its neck.

"Let's go," Navad yelled.

Her sling was lying on the ground not far from the frenzied jackals. With the bloody blade held forward, she stepped in, picked up the sling, and retreated. Running her fingers from the tab, along the strap, to the pouch and down the other strap to the loop, she found a few bite punctures, but nothing worse. She tied it around her hips.

Her soiled loincloth remained in tatters near the ditch.

Within moments, Leola's husband was heading back to Bozra, and the caravan moved on, the rising sun at their backs. Deborah stayed near Umm-Sallan, who rode sideways on a small mare. The road ascended the moderate ridges of the Seir Mountains and descended eastwards into a vast desert of sand dunes and rocky outcrops. She remembered traveling through this wide valley on the way to Bozra.

Near sunset, a cluster of limp Jujube trees and a few short palms appeared in the twilight. They set up camp beside a spring. Deborah found a few ripe dates under the palm trees. She gave one to Rogez, who chewed it quickly and nudged her for more.

Two other caravans arrived later from the opposite direction and set up camp. Deborah found a place to change her loincloth, which wasn't as damp as the previous one. She buried it under a pile of rocks.

The night was uneventful. First to rise at dawn, Deborah washed her face, applied a fresh layer of stubble paste, and stepped away from camp. After a series of practice slingshots, she drew her sword and wielded it up and down, left and right, jabbing the blade at imaginary opponents until her arms ached.

That evening, after slow travel through the hot desert, they arrived at Tamar. The sun was still above the horizon. Ten or twelve caravans camped along the stream. The spot Navad chose for a camp was near where Kassite's Edomite slaves had tried to rape Deborah on the journey south from Canaan. Sallan looked at her, but she couldn't tell if there was glee or sympathy in his gray eyes. She missed his good-natured humor – his friendship, really. The unfairness of his anger towards her and, even worse, his cruelty regarding Leola, had upset Deborah at first, but now she only felt sadness.

Sallan sent the boy-servants to the market for fresh fruit, bread, and cheese. Deborah took Umm-Sallan to show her the mound of stones near the partly collapsed house among the charred ruins at the edge of Tamar.

Umm-Sallan touched the stones. "Whose grave is this?"

"An old healer," Deborah said.

"My husband was a healer, too."

"I buried her here."

"You?"

"On our escape from Canaan, we stopped here for the night and I learned that this used to be a Hebrew town, though only one old woman had remained here. I went to see her, and she called me by my mother's name."

"She knew your mother?"

"Tamar was once a frontier town of the Judah tribe, but when my mother was about my age, the Edomite army attacked. They killed all the Hebrews except for the unmarried maidens, whom they planned to take as plunder. The Edomite commander wanted the healer to treat the wounded soldiers, but she refused unless he sent all the unmarried maidens to the nearest Judah town, Arad, so that they could marry, have babies, and replenish the lives lost in Tamar. The Edomite commander threatened to kill her, but she insisted, and he agreed. According to the old healer, the prettiest of the girls was my mother, Raquellah."

"I'm not surprised. You inherited her beauty."

Deborah blushed. "Her red hair, too, but you wouldn't know it."

Umm-Sallan caressed Deborah's coated cheek. "Your female bleeding is almost over."

"How do you know?"

"I raised five daughters and helped raise their daughters. I can tell when a girl bleeds, when she's ripe for her husband's seed, and when she's pregnant – even before she knows."

"Was your husband as good at seeing hidden facts?"

"Why do you ask?"

"General Mazabi."

"There was nothing between us until my husband died. I always followed the advice my late mother had given me on my wedding day." Umm-Sallan took a deep breath. "A secret in a marriage is like a rotten core in an apple."

"I'll remember that."

The matriarch smiled. "Tell me more about the old healer."

"She had waited many years to find out whether the Edomite commander had kept his promise. My arrival was the answer, and she died that night. The next morning, I buried her and said a prayer." Deborah replaced a stone that had fallen off the mound. "You see, Yahweh had brought me here for a reason."

"To give peace to the old healer?"

"And to teach me an important lesson. When I first came here, I was determined to become a man. Your son and Kassite mixed the Male Elixir for me and helped me learn how to act like a man, be proactive, even-tempered, adventurous, and logical."

"Most men aren't like that."

"True." Deborah smiled. "For me, finding out about the old healer's sacrifice and my mother's painful journey made me realize that being a wife and a mother can also be a True Calling from God."

"When you bring Princess Needa back to Bozra, the king's reward will allow you to return to Canaan, where good men will line up, eager to win your heart, fight your battles, and work the land of your inheritance."

The idea of men queuing up to marry her seemed ludicrous, but tempting. Deborah imagined them, strong and faithful young men of Ephraim, standing one behind the other with their eager faces turned up to her. She easily recognized the first in line: Barac, son of Abinoam.

Back at the camp, the boy-servants had boiled barley and put out bread and cheese for dinner. Sallan wasn't there. One of the boys pointed to a neighboring caravan, where Sallan was sitting with a few men around a fire, a pig roasting above it. He was finishing a story, and the men laughed and raised a toast.

"That's good," Umm-Sallan said. "Melancholy doesn't linger in good company."

He returned later, his face radiant. The men, he explained, had told him about a city called Rekem, whose inhabitants had excavated a vast network of tunnels and rooms into a mountain.

"I've never heard of Rekem," Deborah said. "Are they Moabites?"

"Midianites," he said.

"The descendants of Midian?" She thought for a moment, trying to remember. "Wasn't Midian the son of Abraham from his wife Keturah?"

"We're all Abraham's children." Sallan smiled. "My people's forefather, Esau, was the older brother of your forefather, Jacob. Their father was Isaac, son of Abraham."

Deborah didn't want to spoil Sallan's mood by pointing out that Esau had sold his firstborn rights to Jacob, whose name was later changed by an angel to Israel, whereas Esau skulked off to the desert.

"It's nice," she said. "We're like branches of the same old tree."

The next morning at dawn, Deborah got up, went upstream, and stripped down. She was relieved to find the loincloth clean, as Umm-Sallan had predicted. She immersed in the water, which was invigorating, and stood up to dry, shivering from the cold. While putting the armor pieces back on, it occurred to her that, were she still in Emanuel, she would have had to wear a red robe for the next seven days, whereas here, she wore armor and bore weapons as a young man whose masculinity wasn't questioned by anyone.

On the way back to camp, she stopped at a large rock by the water's edge. It was the rock she had been sitting on when the Edomite slaves had surrounded her with lusty grins and grabby hands. The tree trunk where Rogez had been tied still bore the chafing marks from his struggle to get free and defend her.

She untied her sling and lashed at the air where the Edomite slaves had stood. The straps made a slapping noise, and she imagined them falling backwards, stricken and shamed. She turned to face the tree and practiced lashing the trunk from as far back as possible, only the tab at the end of the strap making contact with the bark. She proceeded to lash at branches, aiming at particular spots, gradually improving her ability to make contact with the exact target she chose. When she missed, and the strap looped around a branch, she pulled hard and broke the branch, shaking it to unspool the strap from the branch.

One of the soldiers whistled and beckoned her from downstream. She returned to camp, where everyone was ready to go.

At first, the air was pleasant, but as the sun cleared the mountains behind them, it beat down with rising intensity. The road meandered as it gradually ascended the southern reaches of the Judean Mountains. The low desert gave way to jagged ridges and rocky slopes.

Deborah maneuvered Rogez next to Umm-Sallan's mare. "Are you feeling well?"

The matriarch nodded.

"Have you ever travelled this road?"

"This is my first journey out of Bozra," Umm-Sallan said.

"It must be nice to stay in your own city, put down roots, spend a lifetime among your family and friends."

"A nice life isn't the same as an exciting life. When I was very young, the son of a merchant wanted to marry me. I dreamt of travelling with his family's caravan to Arabia, Persia, and Egypt, visiting strange lands and meeting fascinating people. My parents, however, did not approve."

Deborah thought of Zariz and his father's caravan – her own chance at exotic travels that would never materialize. "Do you think Princess Needa dreamed of travelling to distant lands?"

"Doesn't everyone have such dreams?" Umm-Sallan thought for a moment. "When the old king died, his feebleminded son couldn't become king, so his grandson was crowned as King Esau the Twentieth, with his beautiful sister, Princess Needa, at his side. Many delegations brought gifts from neighboring kingdoms and tribes, including the Hebrew tribe of Simeon. The tribal leader's son brought jugs of good wine and seeds of hardy barley. He also proposed a treaty of friendship and mutual defense between Edom and his tribe. Our young king, however, declined the offer."

"Why?"

"His advisors warned it would be an affront to the powerful Hebrew tribe of Judah, which shares a long border with us, though I heard that

Princess Needa argued in favor of Simeon's offer."

"What was her reason?"

"She was charmed by the handsome tribal leader's son, who headed the delegation."

Deborah laughed.

"Ironically, he abducted her, which confirmed Simeon's unworthiness as allies."

"Is it possible that she left willingly?"

"Anything is possible, but it's unlikely. Princess Needa gave up marriage and family to stay by her brother's side. She's practically an old maid at twenty-eight, though still very beautiful."

Deborah ruffled Rogez's white mane, and he rocked his head up and down. "Why didn't the king put a siege around Beersheba instead of searching the desert? Surely they would have released the princess to save their main city and its many people."

"General Mazabi explained it to me," Umm-Sallan said. "A siege far from home requires a large army and long supply lines through hostile territory. It also requires slaves to build ramps and engineers to operate wall-piercing machines. Besides, war interrupts trade, and selling copper products is the king's primary source of revenues."

Up ahead, Navad stopped the caravan for rest and water. Deborah was glad to pause the conversation as fear crept into her heart. How could she succeed where the whole kingdom of Edom came short?

9

They spent the next two nights at isolated patches of pale greenery fed by meager springs – too little to sustain permanent farming, but sufficient to refresh weary travellers. Deborah got up every day at dawn and practiced with her sword to strengthen her muscles and sharpen her instincts, and with her sling to improve her long-distance aim and her short-range proficiency at lashing and hooking.

On the road, they encountered a few groups of riders on horses, camels, or donkeys, as well as merchant caravans. Despite the harsh landscape, the road was well trodden and easy to follow. On the afternoon of the third day, they crested a hill and saw a village nestled in a narrow valley below.

From their high vantage point they could see several tunnels and dams, ready to direct flashfloods to a waterhole, which was almost empty. Deborah imagined how wonderful it would be to feel rain on her head and arms, to open her mouth and taste the cool drops on her tongue, the way she had done at the tannery near Aphek. It seemed like a lifetime ago.

Halfway down the hillside, the ruins of a large structure came into view near the path. Its former grandeur was evident by the thickness of the crumbling walls, the craftsmanship of the fallen stone columns, and the prominence of an altar at the far end of the ruins. Deborah saw no statues of false gods, giving her hope that this had been a temple to Yahweh.

As the path switched back and forth downhill, they passed more ruins and traces of streets – remnants of a long-gone city.

The village in the valley below had no defensive walls. Three men stood on the road between the town and a vacant open field across the road, which was dotted with remains of cooking fires. The men carried swords and wooden spears, but wore no armor, only short robes that ended above their knees and white caps on their heads. Deborah noticed a yellow flag with a drawing of a lion perched on a swell of land, gazing into the distance.

"It's the flag of Judah," she said to Sallan.

He grunted.

As Navad approached, one of the men stepped forward. He was tall and wide-shouldered, with bushy hair and a full beard. His short robe revealed lanky yet muscular legs and plain sandals. His posture, Deborah thought, radiated power and confidence that was worth imitating. He spoke with Navad, who gave him a coin and proceeded into the field with his caravan. Sallan urged his horse to follow Navad's family, but the tall man stepped into his path.

"Good day," Sallan said. "We are merchants from Edom. What town is this?"

"Arad," the man said. "This is the land of Judah."

Deborah felt her heart speed up. Her mother had come to Arad as a maiden after surviving the attack on Tamar.

"We're delighted to be here," Sallan said. "Go quickly and tell your leader that Sallan of Edom invites him to share a jar of excellent Bozra wine."

"I'm the leader here." He pressed a fist to his chest. "Goor-Aryeh of Judah."

"An honor," Sallan said, smiling broadly. "My invitation is delivered, then."

"Our God forbids drinking gentiles' wine."

"Bring your own wine." Sallan chuckled. "We'll provide the food."

"Another time, perhaps."

"As you wish."

"Have you seen other travellers along the way?"

"A few caravans, hot and tired like us."

"Any Hebrews bearing arms?"

"Not until we saw you." Sallan maintained his friendly demeanor. "Nightfall isn't far off. We really should set up camp."

Goor-Aryeh looked at Umm-Sallan. "Who's the old woman?"

"My maid. She's not very useful anymore, but I take her along. Better than nothing, right?"

Umm-Sallan lowered her head, and Deborah struggled not to laugh.

Counting with his finger, Goor-Aryeh said, "Five soldiers. Do you expect a battle?"

The smile remained on Sallan's face. "The desert is a dangerous place for a hardworking merchant."

As before, Deborah was amazed at how easily he lied.

Goor-Aryeh paced around Sallan and looked at Rogez. "I've seen this horse, or one identical to it. An Egyptian prince passed through here last year on his way to visit the King of Hazor in Canaan."

"Gorgeous, isn't it?" Sallan gave Deborah a cautionary glance. "I bought it from a Moabite trader and I'm taking it to sell in Gaza. It might even go back to Egypt."

"The sword, too?" Goor-Aryeh reached to touch Deborah's bejeweled silver hilt, but Rogez stepped sideways and rocked his head menacingly.

"Could be," Sallan said. "For a true merchant, everything is for sale."

Goor-Aryeh looked up at Deborah. His eyes were brown, and in them she saw both warmth and strength, or so she imagined.

"We're very tired," Sallan said. "Here's a coin."

Goor-Aryeh held out his hand to accept it while his gaze lingered on Deborah. "You don't need to keep watch tonight," he said. "We patrol the area to keep us and our guests safe from outlaws."

Sallan put his purse back under his robe. "Have you caught any outlaws lately?"

"A few men of Simeon." Goor-Aryeh clenched a fist and pounded it into his other hand. "We taught them a lesson."

Sallan urged his horse towards the field.

"One last question." Goor-Aryeh walked alongside Rogez. "Are any of you Hebrews?"

"I'm a Hebrew," Deborah said.

"But you travel on the Sabbath."

"Is it Sabbath today?"

He nodded.

Deborah climbed down from Rogez, her face flushed. "I've lost count of days."

"What tribe?"

"My father was of Ephraim, but my mother was of Judah." Deborah held Rogez's reins with one hand and pointed at the village with the other. "She came here after the loss of Tamar."

"Your mother was one of the maidens of Tamar? My wife was also one of them."

"She probably knew my mother." Deborah was filled with joy. "May I speak with her?"

Goor-Aryeh's face fell. "My wife died in childbirth last year."

"My mother is dead, too."

"Borah!" Sallan waved her to follow.

As she led Rogez across the field, Deborah glanced back and saw Goor-Aryeh watching her. Meanwhile, the Midianite caravan paid its dues, entered the field, and settled at the far corner.

Umm-Sallan dismounted the mare with Deborah's help. She patted the girl's cheek, her hand lingering for a moment. "Ah, good. Your female bleeding is over."

When they sat for the evening meal, two men approached and said their leader wished to see Borah.

As she was getting up, Sallan whispered, "Say nothing."

Walking into the village, she felt no fear, even though her sword, spear, and sling were left at the camp. They passed by the waterhole, which measured about ten steps across the top and gave off a foul odor. A gate led into a large courtyard full of armed men, who were eating, drinking, and chatting. She immediately spotted Goor-Aryeh, a head taller than anyone else, standing in a corner with two other men.

Noticing her, he told his companions, "This is Borah. He rides a magnificent horse, as white as a priest's robe on the Day of Atonement."

His calm voice resembled that of her late father.

One of the men drew on a pipe, and smoke petered out of his mouth as he spoke. "Earlier today, a traveler told me of a Hebrew boy who beheaded the high priest of Edom in Bozra."

"I didn't behead him," she said, and immediately regretted speaking.

They stared at her. Now, she had no choice but to explain.

"He tried to kill me, and the only way to stop him was to kill him first, so I did."

The man gestured with his pipe. "They say the priest was as big as a bull."

"As a house," the other one said, picking at a fresh scar on his left cheek. "I heard there was blood flowing all over the temple."

Deborah wanted to correct them, but they left her no opening to speak.

"Impressive." Goor-Aryeh looked her up and down. "Were you injured?"

"I'm bruised, nothing serious, and he was large, yes, but not larger than you."

He chuckled, pleased.

The one with the scarred cheek pressed her arm. "You're skin and bones. How did you win the fight, boy?"

"Yahweh won it."

Goor-Aryeh nodded. "Through you as His soldier, but now you serve an Edomite merchant. Why?"

"God ordained that, as well."

"Borah," the scarred one said. "What kind of a name is Borah? I've never heard it before."

"It's the male version of Deborah." She glanced around at the crowded courtyard. "Are you expecting an attack on Arad?"

"The opposite," Goor-Aryeh said. "We're preparing to go on an attack."

"Yahweh ordained it," the smoker said, and the three of them laughed.

She smiled. "Tonight?"

He glanced up at the crescent moon. "In five days, when the night is darker, we'll strike at our depraved brothers."

In her mind, Deborah calculated five days ahead. The attack would take place on Thursday night. But where?

A man in a priest's robe entered the courtyard.

Everyone quieted down.

"And before he died, Jacob blessed each of his sons." The priest closed his eyes and quoted from memory. "Judah, your brothers will praise you, your hand will be on the neck of your enemies, and your father's sons will bow before you."

"Amen," the men yelled in unison, raising their fists. "Amen."

"And Jacob said unto Judah," the priest continued. "The scepter will not depart from Judah, nor the ruler's staff from between his feet, until he to whom it belongs shall come, and the obedience of the nations shall be his."

The men cheered.

"As Jacob blessed our forefather, let me bless you, the brave sons of Judah, as you go to wipe out the wicked, unite the land of the desert, and capture the wells of Abraham and Isaac from the unworthy, disowned descendants."

Deborah committed his words to memory in order to ponder later.

The priest raised his hands over the men's heads, his fingers parted in pairs, and recited the traditional priestly blessing: "May Yahweh bless you and protect you. May He show you kindness and grace. May He illuminate your path and grant you peace." And then, he added a sentence Deborah had not heard before: "May He fortify your hearts and give you victory."

"Amen!"

The priest departed, and the men resumed eating and drinking with heightened vigor.

"Borah." Goor-Aryeh placed both his hands on her shoulders, facing her, his brown eyes bearing down into her eyes. "Join us."

"Me?"

"With your mother's blood of Judah in your veins and true faith in your heart, there courage in you well beyond your years, boy. I can tell. Will you join us?"

Deborah gazed up at his tanned face, framed by his bushy hair and beard, which sparkled in the light of the torches. She inhaled his masculine scent, mixed with the smell of horses and smoke. Her shoulders felt hot under his large hands, and her chest burned with yearning to fall into his arms, bury her face in his neck, and go with him anywhere he wanted her to go.

"I'd like to," she said, barely hiding the tremor in her voice. "If my master allows me."

"Forget your Edomite master." His hands squeezed her shoulders, his broad face up close, his eyes penetrating. "Fetch your horse and weapons and join us. We're leaving tonight."

"Tonight?" She glanced up at the moon. "Not in five days?"

The smoker exhaled audibly like an exasperated parent. "We're going to meet up with other men of Judah first."

"Come with us," Goor-Aryeh said. "Ride your great horse, swing your magnificent sword, and share in our victory and spoils."

Through a fog of confusing emotions, Deborah struggled to speak. "Can I come without the horse and the sword?"

"Why?"

"I didn't pay for them." She patted her chest armor. "I didn't pay for this either. Yahweh forbids stealing."

Goor-Aryeh's hands dropped from her shoulders, and she felt both relieved and deprived.

"We don't have horses," the scarred one said. "Or armor."

The smoker grunted. "I have an old sword you can use."

"Will you teach me how to fight? I've never been in a real battle."

The three men looked at each other, and the smoker said, "Go back to your Edomite master, boy."

Hanging her head in feigned shame, Deborah turned to leave.

"Borah," Goor-Aryeh said. "Come back when you're ready."

She felt her hands shaking as she made her way through the densely crowded courtyard. Nearby, a man raised a goblet and yelled, "To the warriors of Ziklag." His friends repeated the toast and emptied their goblets.

Outside the courtyard, the street was quiet and empty. She wanted to break into a run, but kept a measured pace.

"Borah!"

She turned and saw Goor-Aryeh's tall figure.

"Take an oath," he said, "that you won't repeat what I told you."

Deborah pressed her fist to her chest and took the oath he was asking for – no less, no more: "I swear that I will not repeat what you told me."

"Good," he said. "And you should know that I meant it."

"Meant what?"

"Come back when you're ready."

The urge to press herself to him burned hotly inside her again, but she had to tell him the truth. "God tells me where to go, and I don't think it will be here."

It was dark, and the weak moonlight brought out the contours of his face. "Where, then?"

"First, to Beersheba, and then, back to the Samariah Hills of Ephraim."

10

In the morning, they left Arad with empty waterskins and, at least for Deborah, a heavy heart. The priest's words rang in her mind: "Let me now bless you, the brave sons of Judah, as you go to wipe out the wicked, unite the land of the desert, and capture the wells of Abraham and Isaac from the unworthy, disowned descendants." Who were the wicked men they were going to wipe out? Whose disowned descendants were they? What parts of the desert would be united? She knew the tribe of Simeon was Judah's only Hebrew neighbor in the desert. Did the land of Simeon have enough water to replenish Judah's shortage?

Navad led the way at a fast pace, and the convoy raised a cloud of dust that stayed with them in the absence of wind. The road curved to the west, rising over hills and dropping into dry streams, until it intersected with a gorge and ran alongside it at a moderate descent. They stopped at midday in the shade of a massive rock outcropping. Deborah helped Umm-Sallan down from the saddle. Sallan shared a handful of figs with his mother and Deborah, and the Midianites sent over a girl with palm dates.

During the rest of the afternoon, Navad kept going despite the heavy heat and stifling dust. Deborah noticed Umm-Sallan sway in the saddle, brought Rogez alongside, and handed her a waterskin.

"Thank you." The matriarch drank some and handed it back. "The heat plays tricks with my mind. One moment I'm an old woman riding a mare in the desert, the next I'm a young woman healing a sick customer while my husband is away at war and my boy, Sall, is on a dangerous quest that I encouraged him to take."

"Sall?"

"That was his name then, before the war."

"The war with Egypt?"

"Yes, that horrible war." She sighed. "I shouldn't complain. My husband returned unharmed whereas all the men of Edom died in battle."

"Is that when Sallan turned the women into a new army?"

The matriarch was silent for a long moment, her eyes gazing forward at Sallan, riding ahead of them. "He was barely sixteen, but the Gods chose him to lead us from subjugation to freedom. Many years have passed, but I still can't figure out how he managed to transform six thousand grieving women, devastated by the loss of their fathers, brothers, husbands, and sons, into a disciplined army of soldiers. Within a day, he had them marching in the fairgrounds, wearing makeshift armor, bearing assorted blades, shooting arrows they had carved from planks and sticks."

"His Male Elixir." Deborah touched her chest armor. "It has changed me, too."

Umm-Sallan smiled. "Leola is alive because it."

"Do I resemble the girl Sallan loved?"

"In some ways, yes." Sadness returned to her face. "Poor An, she was unlucky. Why do you ask?"

"When Qoztobarus realized I was a girl, he said something odd." Deborah quoted from memory. "The healer's son got himself involved with another ill-chosen girl."

"How did you respond?"

"Sallan still loves the girl you killed all those years back."

The matriarch's eyes widened. "Did he admit killing her?"

Deborah shook her head and quoted the high priest: "I didn't kill An. If she's dead, her blood is on Sallan's hands."

"That's also true, in a way. An drank his Male Elixir, and it made her brave, like you, but unlike you, her daring resulted in her death."

"How?"

Umm-Sallan reached for the water skin, drank some, paused, and drank some more. "She rode into the desert alone, trying to save a group of maidens. It broke my son's heart."

They rode in silence, the setting sun in their eyes until it disappeared behind the horizon. Twilight gradually darkened, but Navad didn't stop. Deborah was about to speed up and question him when she noticed flickers of fires in the distance. Closer yet, she could make out palm trees, several tent encampments, wooden shacks, and a stone building alongside a mass of reeds that could only grow near water.

The horses and camels stepped up to a pond and began to drink. The men knelt by the edge and slurped noisily. Deborah filled a waterskin, gave it to Umm-Sallan, and filled another for herself.

A young boy came over to summon the leaders of the caravan to the stone building. Navad, Sallan, and the Midianite foreman headed there. Deborah followed, entering behind them into a large room, which was surprisingly cool. Glow from the fires outside filtered through the white cloth curtains over the windows. The boy who had summoned them picked up a bucket and splattered water onto the curtains, which explained the coolness.

As her eyes adjusted to the darkness, Deborah was startled to notice men sitting along the walls. They wore drooping headdresses and long robes in the style of desert dwellers. Swords and clubs rested on the floor by their feet. A second boy was serving wine and food to the men. Some of them smoked pipes with a distinct, sweet scent.

In the middle of the room, a stocky, gray-bearded man lounged in a cushioned chair by a large table, exhaling smoke. His pipe had a silver mouthpiece and a copper beaker for the leaves.

Navad placed a coin in the man's hand. Sallan and the Midianite foreman did the same.

"Welcome to Kabetzel." The man put the coins in a purse, which he slipped under his robe. "I am Ohad of Simeon, judge of this city."

Deborah almost laughed at the word "city," but it dawned on her that he had said, "Simeon," which meant that Barac could be in this room, assuming Seesya had lied about killing him. She glanced around furtively, searching for Barac's young, dark-skinned face, his sparse adolescent goatee, and his muscular build. She thought of the last time she had seen Barac, standing under the night sky by her family's abandoned house at Palm Homestead. His father, Abinoam, had said: "My wife, may she rest in peace, was from the Simeon tribe." And he was certain Simeon would take the two of them in because, "Everyone can use a good blacksmith." To which Barac responded, "And a soldier, as well. That's what I'm going to be. I'll learn to be a soldier and a great warrior so that I can fight Canaanites and Edomites until we restore the glory days of Joshua!" His boyish bravado had made her heart race, and it beat harder now as she peered at the faces around the smoked-filled room. Their features were blurry under the drooping headdresses. Would she be able to recognize Barac without his white cap, bulging over his unruly black curls?

Navad, Sallan, and the Midianite foreman bowed politely and walked out. She followed them.

"Damned Hebrews," Navad whispered, "This place was in Judah's hands when I passed through last year, and in Simeon's hands the year before."

Deborah wondered if this "city" was the place Goor-Aryeh and his men were planning to attack, but the priest had said, "capture the wells of Abraham and Isaac," and this oasis had no wells, only a single spring.

"I prefer Judah," Navad muttered. "The men of Simeon are the wormwood of the Spice Route, more bitter than peganon."

Deborah glanced back over her shoulder. "Why?"

"They steal without hesitation and cheat without regret, almost as bad as the Arabians prowling the road to Persia."

She could not believe his words. Simeon was a Hebrew tribe, its men followers of Yahweh's Ten Commandments, which forbade stealing and cheating. Besides, Barac's father would not take his only son to dwell with a tribe of sinners.

The three groups set up camp together in a tight knot of horses, camels, tents, and sleeping mats. Deborah started four fires around the camp and set a watch rotation with the four Edomite soldiers, Navad's two sons, and three Midianite men. She told them to sleep near the fires with their weapons on hand in case the watchman raised the alarm. No one questioned her orders.

Deborah couldn't sleep, even though her body was aching with exhaustion from days in the saddle under the beating sun. Her mind wandered, thinking of what Umm-Sallan had told her about An, of Goor-Aryeh's calm strength and penetrating eyes, of Barac, who wasn't as tall, powerful, and mature as Goor-Aryeh, but equally strong and fearless, the way he had stood up to Seesya in Emanuel. She realized that a similar tide of heat swelled inside her for each of them with equal intensity. Was it possible for a girl to crave two men who were so different from one another?

When sleep came, it was fitful. Sometime during the night, she heard horses trotting nearby, sat up, and stared into the darkness beyond the fires, seeing nothing. Was it a new caravan, coming in for the night, or was one leaving before dawn, preferring the dangers of the night to the heat of the day? When the sound grew weaker, Deborah went back to sleep.

At dawn, she stepped away to practice with her sling and sword, returning to the camp when everyone was getting up and starting to pack.

Navad came over. "You did well, boy, organizing the watch." He handed her a silver coin.

She accepted it, not wanting to insult him. "Thank you."

"I was at the amphitheater in Bozra," he said. "Never will I forget your fight against Qoztobarus."

"I won't forget it, either."

He chuckled. "How do you plan to find Princess Needa?"

"God will guide me."

"Divine guidance is more effective when you know where you're going."

Deborah laughed. "I have a general idea about the land."

"Show me," he said.

"I once travelled with a Moabite caravan in the Samariah Hills, and a boy drew a map for me." She picked up a stick and marked a line in the sand. "This is the Jordan River, coming down from the Sea of Galilee to the Sea of Salt." She made a circle at each end. "And here, in the west, is the shore of the Great Sea." She drew a straight line from north down to south.

"Not exactly." He took the stick and corrected the line in the sand. "The coast of the Great Sea starts to curve westward at Gaza until it heads straight to the west near the Nile River in Egypt." He marked Gaza by the coastline. "The Philistines control the coast north and south of Gaza. That's where the Spice Route begins its way to Beersheba." He drew a line inland and marked the large city of Simeon. "It continues east to where we are now, Kabetzel." He marked it. "And further east to Arad, where the trade route splits, either up north to Hebron, Bethlehem, and Jerusalem, or south-east to Tamar." He drew the lines and marked the towns. "In Tamar it splits again to Edom, Moab, and Persia."

Deborah looked at the map, orienting herself. "And we just entered the territory of Simeon from Judah, correct?"

He sighed. "These two Hebrew tribes are always at loggerheads, like two aging brothers still angry about some foolish grievance from their youth – in this case, many generations ago, when their tribal forefathers were alive. Your Hebrew scriptures explain it, right?"

"I don't know," Deborah said.

"Doesn't every Hebrew boy learn the scriptures?"

"My father died before he could teach me to read, but he had told me many stories about Jacob and his sons, the long slavery and exodus from Egypt, and how Joshua led the tribes in conquering the land from the Canaanites." She knelt by the map, gazing at it. "Do you know what land Judah and Simeon rule?"

"Judah owns most of the mountains and the desert." He drew a large oval in the sand, encompassing the land from the Sea of Salt in the east to the Philistine strip near Gaza, and from Jerusalem in the north to depth of the Negev Desert. Then, he drew a much smaller oval within Judah's land, with Beersheba at its center. "Simeon is landlocked, like a rotten core to Judah's apple."

"Or a piece of cheese to Judah's flatbread," she said. "Do you know of a place named Ziklag?"

He poked a hole in the sand above Beersheba. "It's about as far from Beersheba to the north as to Arad in the east."

"Two days of walking?"

"Yes."

"And from Arad to Ziklag?"

Navad looked at the map in the sand. "About three days."

Deborah calculated in her head: three days from Arad to Ziklag and two days from Ziklag to Beersheba added up to five days. Was that Judah's target on Thursday night? The name Beersheba in Hebrew meant Seven Wells, but she had assumed it wasn't a literal description.

"Are there actual wells in Beersheba?"

"Yes, several good wells. That's why the trade routes pass through Beersheba – not only for the abundance of drinking water, but also for the wonderful farm produce, oil, and wine."

Deborah had a vague memory of a story her father had told her about Abraham making peace with a mighty king in the desert after they had argued over a well, only to have the same king confront Abraham's son years later about wells that Isaac had dug in the desert. Had both disputes involved the wells of Beersheba? Were the wells of Beersheba the same "wells of Abraham and Isaac" that the priest in Arad had spoken of?

"Is there any other place in the Negev Desert with several wells?"

Navad shook his head. "If there was such a place, it would not have remained a secret. One well, perhaps. Two wells, unlikely. But several wells in one place would have nourished another big city with a market large enough to attract traders like me."

There was Yahweh's hand again, Deborah thought, reaching down to help her solve the riddles that stood as barriers in her path. She thanked Navad and returned to help prepare for the road. Her mind simmered with what she had learned, but the most pressing question remained unanswered: How did God expect her to negotiate Princess Needa's release with the leader of Simeon at the same time Judah was about to attack?

Umm-Sallan had difficulty mounting her mare. Deborah crouched and put her hands together, fingers interwoven, near the ground. Placing her small foot on Deborah's makeshift step and her hands on Deborah's shoulders, Umm-Sallan mounted the mare, sitting sideways.

"Thank you," the matriarch smiled. "Have you learned useful information from Navad?"

"I learned that we might arrive at a time of war between the tribes."

"When your enemies fight each other, they make you stronger."

"They're not my enemies." Deborah rubbed her hands. "They're my brothers."

Umm-Sallan untied the reins from the saddle horn. "A thin line separates close brothers from worst enemies."

As they were leaving Kabetzel, Deborah noticed a green flag hanging from a vertical rope between two small trees. The crude drawing on the flag showed city gates between two masonry guard towers. Was this the flag of Simeon? What did it mean? She glanced again, hoping it would awaken a memory of a story from her father. Was the drawing a depiction of the gates of Beersheba? Tonight, she would see for herself and, perhaps, receive a visit from the eagle and ask her how to free Princess Needa and whether Barac was alive, or not.

Excited and nervous, Deborah rubbed Rogez's neck, and he neighed happily.

A short while after leaving Kabetzel, heading west on the Spice Route, they heard the drumming of horses behind. Deborah looked over her shoulder. A tight pack of riders caught up quickly, galloped by the Midianite caravan, and flew by Deborah and Navad's family ahead, leaving everyone engulfed in dust. The riders stopped in a swirl of dust, turned around, and blocked the road. As the dust settled, Deborah noticed the helmets with rooster combs. A one-armed giant emerged from the pack and rode over, stopping next to Umm-Sallan, whose mare was dwarfed beside the warhorse.

General Mazabi dismounted and took off his helmet.

"Leaving at night?" General Mazabi planted his hand on the mare's back behind the saddle. "Without a word? Without a goodbye?"

"I didn't want to be prevented from leaving."

He scratched his beard, spraying dust. "You're too old for this."

"And you're too old to play the hero."

Deborah dismounted Rogez and stood by Umm-Sallan. "I'll miss your company on the road, but if you stay with us any longer, you'll die."

"The Hebrew boy is right," General Mazabi said. "You're coming back. That's an order."

Umm-Sallan smiled at Deborah. "When a woman captures a powerful man's heart, she risks becoming his captive."

The general leaned closer and spoke in a low voice. "Please return with me. Your family needs you."

"What about my son?"

"The king's plan is good. It's likely to succeed."

Sallan helped his mother down from the mare and hugged her. Umm-Sallan rested her forehead on his shoulder. They remained this way for a long while.

Turning from him, she grasped Deborah's hand. "Promise me that you'll bring him home alive."

"I promise."

One of the soldiers lifted Umm-Sallan and placed her in General Mazabi's saddle. The general mounted behind her, stabbed his heels at the horse's ribs, and took off. His soldiers sprinted after him, galloping down the road towards the morning sun.

Sallan sheltered his eyes with his hand and watched them ride off.

"All those years away, I thought of her as my father's quiet wife, his capable household manager, his stoic pillar of humble support. How I underestimated her!"

Deborah tied the mare behind one of the camels. "The king's plan, what is it?"

"Sending you," he said, "a brave Hebrew boy, backed by the Hebrew God, to negotiate with the Hebrew tribesmen. That's the king's plan."

11

During the morning, they continued west. The hills gradually shrank, and the desert became an endless expanse of sand and rocks. The sun baked the arid earth, and the heat bounced back with transparent fumes that blurred the horizon. The road melted into the flat landscape, only the gorge of the dry Hebron Creek left to keep them on track.

Even Rogez, usually alert and vigorous, hung his head low and followed listlessly behind Sallan's horse. Deborah leaned forward, resting her head on her sack over the saddle horn. Once in a while, she sat up and gazed ahead, searching for signs of vegetation. Glancing back over her shoulder, she saw the boy-servants seated together on the camel, their heads covered over with a cloth. Behind them, the three pack camels ambled along, followed by the four soldiers on their languid horses. She closed her eyes and listened to the shuffle of Rogez's hooves and the whisper of her own breathing.

"Do you miss Umm-Sallan yet?" It was the eagle's voice, coming through a pale haze. "Do you?"

"Yes," Deborah said.

"She would have died in this heat, you know."

"Then I would have missed her even more."

"An orphan girl is condemned to forever seek a new mother."

Orphan. The word sounded helpless, pitiful, and fit for a child. Had she sought Umm-Sallan's closeness for some fleeting maternal comforts?

"Not me," Deborah said. "I don't need a new mother. What I do need are answers: Who should I speak with in Beersheba? How will I manage to convince the judge of Simeon to give up the Edomite princess?"

"Not by sleeping on your horse, that's for sure." The eagle chuckled through the haze.

"What's so funny? If I'm dreaming this, perhaps you don't exist at all."

Flapping her wings, the eagle diffused the haze and became visible. "How about now?"

They were facing each other, not on the ground or in the air, but inside a clear bubble suspended in a sea of haze.

"Yes," Deborah said. "That's better."

"Do I exist because you can see me?"

"It depends. Am I still sleeping?"

"What if you are?"

"Then I'm dreaming and not actually seeing you, which means you might not exist."

"Sleeping. Dreaming. Seeing." The eagle flapped her wings. "Aren't they all various forms of existence?"

"If I'm awake and see you, then you surely exist."

"But the opposite isn't necessarily correct."

"Why not?"

"Let's say that you dream of Palm Homestead while asleep. Would that prove that Palm Homestead doesn't exist?"

Deborah shook her head.

"And what if you're awake in the middle of the desert, does Palm Homestead cease to exist because you can't see it?"

She tried to answer but her throat was parched.

"You'll have water soon," the eagle said. "Every road in the desert leads to an oasis, and every weary traveller dreams of it and keeps going, because he knows it exists further down the road."

Coughing to clear her throat, Deborah asked, "And then? How will I find Princess Needa?"

"The same way you will find your way back to Palm Homestead, and then, find your voice to speak for Yahweh." The eagle faded into the haze. "If you believe that your destination exists and is worthy, your faith will provide the strength to persist."

"Wait—"

"Believe, and be brave."

Deborah tried to give chase, but her legs were running in place, finding no traction in the void of the bubble. "Tell me," she begged. "Is Barac still alive?"

No longer visible, the eagle's voice sounded like Umm-Sallan's. "Be brave as you were in Emanuel, Shiloh, Aphek, Ein Gedi, and Bozra. Be brave, Deborah."

Men's voices woke her up. She sat up in the saddle and saw twenty or thirty bearded men, dressed in long robes and drooping headdresses, wielding swords and clubs. A few blocked the road just ahead of Sallan, separating off Navad's family ahead, while others cut off the Midianite caravan in the rear.

The four Edomite soldiers drew their swords, urged their horses forward, and took positions around Sallan and Deborah, who also drew her sword.

"We are merchants," Sallan yelled. "What do you want?"

One of the men pointed his club at a large tent, which Deborah hadn't noticed as it was the same color as the surrounding desert, except for a green flag with a crude drawing of city gates between masonry towers.

Navad whistled, and his family resumed travelling down the road. The Midianite caravan took a wide bypass and followed Navad's caravan.

The two boy-servants stayed with the horses and camels while Deborah, Sallan, and the Edomite soldiers dismounted and went to the tent.

Thick smoke welcomed them inside. Some of the men came in, too, and sat cross-legged, smoking pipes, their swords and clubs in their laps. At the center of the tent, next to a wooden pitch pole, the stocky, gray-bearded judge from Kabetzel lounged in a cushioned chair at a table. He blew a column of smoke upwards and put down his pipe – the same extra-long one with a silver mouthpiece and a copper beaker. She recalled his words: "I am Ohad of Simeon, judge of this city." The sound of horses riding away from Kabetzel last night must have been this group. She looked around the tent, pausing briefly at each face, but Barac wasn't among them.

Judge Ohad held out his hand.

Sallan reached forward with a coin.

The judge flipped his hand over, palm down, before Sallan could drop the coin in, and laughed heartily. "I have enough coins," he said. "What I don't have is the boy's fancy sword. That's what I'll have."

Sallan put the coin back in his purse.

Deborah stepped forward. "If I give you my sword, what then?"

"What then?" He laughed again. "I'll grant your companions safe passage."

"And me?"

"An easy death."

"Why?"

"My divine duty is to judge people." He sat back, arms folded over his bulging gut. "And I judge you to deserve death."

"A judge should know Yahweh's Commandments." She raised her voice. "Do not kill!"

"A learned boy." Judge Ohad's laughter died down. "If killing is forbidden, why did you come all this way to kill us?"

Deborah felt rage begin to simmer in her chest. "I'm not here to kill you or anyone else."

"We've heard about the boy on a great white horse riding west to attack us on behalf of the Edomite king. Is there another boy like you, coming from Bozra?"

Sallan said something to the Edomite soldiers, who held forth their swords and formed a protective ring.

The old man's belly danced with another bout of laughter. "You want to fight it out, ten men to one?"

Deborah tilted her sword, the blade halfway up. "What have we got to lose?"

"Pain," he said, shaking a stubby finger. "Lots of pain."

"A wise leper woman once told me this." Deborah quoted Miriam. "Pain is the real gift from God, for without pain, there is no life."

"You want pain, you'll have pain." He threw up his arms. "Pity, because either way, in the end, you'll be dead and I'll have your silver sword and your white horse."

"I don't think so," she said.

Her confidence punctured his jubilance. His men sensed it and began to stand up with their weapons. The Edomite soldiers shifted, aiming their swords, ready to fight.

"Pity you," she said. "You won't get to see one of God's most unique creations."

Judge Ohad leaned forward, his gut pressing against the table.

"What's that?"

Gradually tilting up her sword, avoiding sudden movements that would trigger a fight, she held the hilt with both hands, the blade rising vertically in front of her. "The inside of your head," she said. "If it's anything like the head of the Edomite high priest, it will be a fascinating sight, I assure you."

He touched the pipe on the table, his hand showing a slight tremor.

"A clean cut," she said. "From the crown, down the middle, halving your skull. I can do it before any of your soldiers reach me."

He looked up at her, the blade between them, lined up with his head.

She quoted the Holy Scriptures: "He who rises to kill you, rise first and kill him."

"My soldiers will slice you to small pieces."

"I'm not afraid of dying," she said. "God sent me here, and He will receive me with grace when I leave this world. You, on the other hand, He will dunk in boiling water at a place of eternal suffering."

His whole demeanor indicated Judge Ohad wasn't a righteous man, but there was enough faith in him for her animated warning to fracture his glee and puncture his arrogance. "I can't let you walk out of here," he said, his voice low, almost conspiratorial.

"Why not?"

"You told the whole of Edom that you would come here and take away my son's bride, as if the men of Simeon are lowly desert nomads, unworthy of the king's sister. How can I let you live without losing face with my tribe?"

His words explained what she had heard him say back in Kabetzel: "I am Ohad, the judge of this city." He had meant Beersheba, the main city of Simeon, which made him leader of the tribe.

"My son Mamreh descends from Jacob, Isaac, and Abraham. He's superior to any girl of Esau's blood."

Deborah edged her sword towards him.

Sallan raised his hand. "We're not here to fight or kill. We're here to trade."

"Trade?" Judge Ohad sneered. "With what? Copper pots and pans?"

"A trade of signatures," Sallan said. "I speak for King Esau the Twentieth, who authorized me to accept your offer to bind our two people in a treaty."

Deborah turned to him. "What?"

Removing a scroll from under his robe, Sallan declared, "Treaty of Friendship and Mutual Defense, binding us against a common enemy: the men of Judah." He unrolled the scroll on the table and pointed. "Go ahead, read it."

"Wait," Deborah said. "Why haven't you told—"

"Silence, boy." Sallan looked at her coldly. "Or my guards will cut you down as a favor for these good men of Simeon, who are about to become our allies."

"Friendship and Mutual Defense." Judge Ohad rested his hands on the table. "Why didn't you say so right away?"

"There's one condition," Sallan said. "Our royal sister, Princess Needa, must return to Bozra in good health."

Judge Ohad sighed. "I'll notify my son, but I cannot guarantee his consent to this condition."

"I'm sure many noble Hebrew girls will jump at the opportunity to be his bride."

"True, but when a young man falls for a girl, the rapid beating of his swollen heart drowns out the voice of reason, the sense of honor, and the alertness to peril."

"Our condition isn't limited to Princess Needa alone. If your son's love is true, I have the king's authority to grant permission for the marriage, provided the couple will come to Bozra together for a royal visit."

Judge Ohad clapped. "We accept!"

"Marriage?" Deborah lowered her sword. "The princess will never consent to marry the man who abducted her."

"Consent?" Sallan waved dismissively. "A woman does what she's told."

It sounded to Deborah as if his words were directed at her, and she remained quiet, though determined to question him about all this when they were alone again.

The men of Simeon hesitated, looking at their leader.

"We're all friends now," the judge declared. "We're family."

Sallan went around the table, and the two men hugged and kissed the air by their cheeks.

"Let's go to Beersheba." Judge Ohad held Sallan's arm, leading him out of the tent. "You'll stay at my house, and I'll throw a feast in your honor."

The four Edomite soldiers and all the men of Simeon walked out. Deborah remained behind, bewildered by the quick turn of events. She had seen Sallan lie convincingly in the past, but how could she tell whether he had just uttered the biggest lie of all in order to save her life, or had told the truth after keeping such a crucial secret from her? Either way, he had carried the scroll with him, which required advanced planning behind her back. Was it part of the "king's plan" that General Mazabi had mentioned?

As Deborah was standing in the empty tent, a boy came in, tied a rope to the bottom of the wooden pitch pole in the center, and ran out. The rope tightened, causing the pole to flip sideways, and the tent collapsed on her.

Trapped under the heavy cloth, Deborah dropped to her knees and struggled to push her way out. The stiff leather armor hindered her movements, and the long sword anchored in the dirt.

She yelled for help and heard men laughing and a horse neighing. Was it Rogez? She couldn't tell.

Unable to stay upright, Deborah tumbled sideways to the ground, which released the tip of the sword from the soil. She turned to face the ground and clawed the coarse desert earth with her fingers, shuffling forward under the collapsed tent.

Eventually, her head popped out from under the heavy cloth. The glaring sun blinded her. The laughter she'd been hearing came closer, and a hard object struck her head. The helmet blunted the strike, but before she could crawl further out and defend herself, another strike landed, and another.

Daylight dimmed into darkness, and the horse neighed again. It was Rogez, she could tell, before everything went dark and silent.

12

The pain pulsated inside Deborah's head, which was upside down. She groaned and opened her eyes to see a tongue licking her face. It was Rogez, turning his head all the way back to reach her face. She was lying on her belly over the saddle, her head down by his left ribs, her bound legs over the right side. She tried to move her arms, but felt a rope cutting into her wrists. Rogez licked her face again. Craning her head to look around, she saw the men of Simeon packing up the encampment.

Judge Ohad approached, the silver hilt of her sword glinting by his hip, his bearded face grinning. "Soon, we'll reach Beersheba, and my people will see you slumped like a hunted antelope over the hump of this splendid horse."

"Soon, Yahweh will punish you." She filled her lungs and shouted a quote from the Holy Scriptures: "If you violate my laws and break my rules, I shall bring my hand down upon your head and smite you!"

Everyone stopped what they were doing and stared.

Judge Ohad's smile faded. "Who are you to speak for God?"

"Who are you to disobey Him?"

He slapped her hard, grabbed the back of her neck, and hissed into her ear. "The illiterate Edomites may believe your act, boy, but not me. I know what to do with arrogant troublemakers!"

Rogez turned his head back and clamped his teeth on Judge Ohad's shoulder.

He screamed, and his men ran over, clubs held high.

"Release him," Deborah said.

The jaws parted, and Judge Ohad fell back. The men didn't dare come closer to the horse.

She wanted to praise Rogez, but the slapping had rattled her head and jacked up the pain, which got even worse when the convoy moved. She fainted again.

When Deborah came to, the sun was low over the horizon. The road continued along the dry gorge of the Hebron Creek. The desert was dotted with brittle shrubs and faded thorn bushes. A fresh breeze swept aside the dust raised by the convoy and propelled rolls of tumbleweed, which raced over the flat desert like living creatures without legs or heads.

The men urged the animals to go faster. Rogez was tied behind another horse, and the faster pace battered Deborah's stomach on the saddle and caused her head to bang on Rogez's ribs. She held back her tears and remembered Miriam's words about pain as a gift from God, a reminder that she was still alive and closer to her destination.

"There it is," someone called.

Deborah twisted her upper body and turned her head to see Beersheba. The city was built on a what looked like a giant molehill, surrounded by flatland that thrived with fields, orchards, and palm trees.

A crowd had gathered at the entrance to the city, which had a single wooden gate and no masonry guard towers. A defensive wall stretched in both directions from the gate, but appeared to be in disrepair.

As the sun slipped behind the horizon, cheers welcomed the convoy. Half-eaten fruit and scraps of refuse pelted Deborah. Rogez snorted, stomped his hooves, and rocked his head.

Judge Ohad rode back from the head of the convoy and positioned his horse at a safe distance from Rogez.

"People of Simeon!" He held up a burning torch. "Here is the boy from Edom, who promised to humiliate the proudest tribe of Israel! Yahweh delivered him into my hands!"

The crowd applauded.

Deborah twisted her neck to look at them. Was Barac among the men cheering her tormentor, unaware that the captive boy was in fact the girl with the carrot-colored hair from Emanuel?

Waving the torch from side to side above her, the judge continued. "Here is the boy from Edom, who will burn at the stake tomorrow for threatening the men of Simeon!"

Two soldiers pulled Rogez by the reins away from the crowd. Deborah glimpsed Sallan's impassive face in the flickering torches. Inside the city, they proceeded down a narrow street that stunk of rotting garbage. It reminded her of the paupers' tents and shacks at the lower part of Emanuel.

The soldiers stopped in front of a stone building and secured the reins tightly to a wooden bar, leaving no room for Rogez to move his head to either side. One of them grabbed Deborah's bound legs, and the other came around the back of the horse in a wide circle and grasped the straps connecting her chest and back armors over her shoulders. They pulled her down over the rear of the horse and carried her to the building.

A guard was smoking a pipe beside an oil lamp, his spear leaning against the wall. He put down the pipe and lifted a wood crossbeam that barred a heavy door, which he pulled open, grunting with effort.

The soldiers carried Deborah inside and dropped her on the dirt floor. The hard landing knocked the air out of her with a high-pitched yelp. The soldiers left, the door closed behind them, and the crossbeam screeched as it barred the door from the outside. A moment later, she heard Rogez whinny, and a thump, followed by a man's cry.

"Good horse," she said.

There was no lamp in the room and no windows. The only light came from the thin crescent moon through the patchy thatched roof. She could see three figures seated on the ground at the far end of the room. Two of them got up and shuffled towards her. As they came closer, she could tell they were young men with beards and long robes.

One put his face near hers, and his breath was foul when he spoke. "You yelp like a girl."

She coughed. "Clean your ears, stinker."

His friend giggled.

Deborah rolled onto her back, which hurt her bound hands, and again onto her stomach, away from them.

The stinker reached up through the tightly spaced roof planks and plucked patiently at the thatch to let in more moonlight. His slow, methodic manner unnerved Deborah. She jerked her arms and legs to test the ropes binding her wrists and ankles, but the knots were tight and firm.

He crouched, put his hands under her midriff and rolled her onto her back. She felt her right elbow hit the front wall. Her weight pressed on her bent arms, hurting her elbows, shoulders, and the small of her back, poked by her bound wrists.

His friend knelt by her feet and giggled again.

The stinker touched her cheek, paused, and used a fingernail to scrape off some of the stubble paste. "Hiding your smooth cheeks." He unstrapped her helmet, removed it, and caressed her head with eerie gentleness. "Short hair, but soft."

She turned away, but he took her face in his hands, turned it back, and kissed her on the forehead.

The giggler asked, "A girl?"

"Maybe," the stinker said.

"Leave him alone," a man said from the back of the room. "You've sinned enough already."

The stinker crossed the room and pounced on the third man, who cried in pain.

"Stop it." Deborah managed to sit up, her back to the wall. "Yahweh will punish you."

He continued punching.

"Guard!" Deborah tilted her face up to be heard through the roof. "Help!

The guard pounded on the door outside. "Shut up, or I'll come in and break your teeth."

The stinker left his victim, came back, and kicked Deborah, knocking her over. Her head hit the ground, and the explosion of pain dazed her.

He knelt beside her and caressed her head again. "Such a delicate face."

His friend giggled. "A pretty boy?"

"Check between the legs, and we'll know the truth."

Lying on her back, Deborah felt the giggler's hands push her knees apart.

"Hurry up." The stinker fumbled with his robe, pulling it up to his hips. "I'm ready for a little fun."

She felt the giggler's hands between her thighs and held her legs together. He put his teeth over her kneecap and bit down. As she screamed and jerked her knee aside, he pushed in between her thighs. His hair brushed the exposed insides of her knees as he fumbled with her leg armor.

"Grab it," the stinker said. "Anything there?"

At the other side of the room, the beaten man groaned.

With her wrists bound behind her back, her weight forced her elbows apart, her shoulders threatening to dislocate.

Groping her crotch, he giggled. "The loincloth is in the way."

The stinker rubbed his hands. "Baal and Ashtoreth, let it be a girl."

"Dressed like a soldier?" He tugged at the bottom of her chest armor.

"Anyone can put on armor." The stinker sniffed her neck. "Smooth as a pomegranate."

"Tall, too." The giggler's hand squeezed her lower leg. "And strong."

The stinker looked into her eyes in the dim moonlight. "What are you? A boy or a girl?"

She coughed abruptly, startling him. "Neither," she said. "I'm neither."

Giggles came from between her thighs. "Neither. Neither. Neither."

"Can't be neither." The stinker reached down with his own hand to grab her crotch. "A boy or a girl. No one is neither."

"Yahweh is neither," she said.

He clenched a fist and punched her in the forehead.

The punch stunned Deborah, and everything turned dark, yet not completely silent. She continued to hear the third man groaning across the room and feel the two young men's hands fumbling with the leather straps over her shoulders and down by her thighs. Her right leg armor was off, her sweaty skin suddenly chilled by a gust of wind as wings flapped above.

"Smells funny," the giggler said, his hair prickling the inside of her thighs. "Neither. Neither. Neither."

The eagle's appearance filled Deborah with embarrassment. "Please go away," she said. "I don't want you to see this."

"Are you going to lie there and let them rape you?"

Her other leg armor was off, and the stinker's bad breath puffed on her face again, his lips flickering by her cheek.

"I need your help," she said.

"No," the eagle said. "Freedom must be earned, not collected as a gift."

Deborah remembered the eagle saying those words when she had been locked up at the bottom of the abandoned copper mine, but this situation was truly hopeless.

"My wrists and ankles are bound. There's nothing I can do."

A hand forced its way through her loincloth.

"Wrists and ankles," the eagle said. "Arms and legs."

The stinker pressed his lips to hers while the giggler groped under her loincloth, chanting, "Neither. Neither. Neither."

The man at the opposite side of the room stopped groaning.

"Be brave," the eagle said. "And use what you have."

Her question confused Deborah. What did she have?

Teeth!

She opened her eyes.

"Look who's back." The stinker leaned closer to kiss her again. "Give us some love, will you?"

Lifting her head abruptly while tilting it sideways, she got his nose in her mouth and clamped down, locking her teeth firmly behind the bone at the bridge of his nose. He froze, and she felt his nostrils flare against her tongue.

What else did she have?

Legs!

She pressed her knees inward, catching the giggler's head in a vice, her bound ankles providing the leverage she needed to get a firm grip on his head.

The giggler tried to pry open her thighs, yelling, "Neither! Neither! Neither!"

Keeping the pressure inward with her knees, Deborah rolled sideways, taking both of them with her. Pulled by his nose, the stinker fell over, still facing her, and screamed in agony and terror. The giggler, his head locked between her thighs, made a strange sound that reminded her of the sound Patrees had made when the Edomite slaves had closed in on her by the stream in Tamar. The memory fueled her rage, and she knew what to do now.

Her wrists were still tied behind her back, but as she was lying on her side, her elbows were free to flex. She straightened her arms and reached down below her buttocks until her fingers tangled with the giggler's hair. She arched her body backwards, bringing his head up against her buttocks while her fingers ran down his forehead, over his eyebrows, and slipped into his eye sockets. She felt the soft balls of his eyes burst, and warm liquid squirted on her fingers. He shrieked and tore away, rolling on the floor. At the same time, she bit down hard, sinking her teeth deeper into the warm flesh. The stinker wailed, his exhalation hot on her chin. She felt her teeth grind against the bone in the back of his nose until her upper front teeth made contact with her lower ones. She twisted her head left and right, tearing his nose off. He jerked backwards, howling like the wounded jackal at the oasis, his hands pressing at the hole in his face.

Deborah spat out the nose. Her mouth filled with bitter saliva, and she spat again, and again.

The guard pounded the door. "What's going on there?"

Still in the same arched-back position, Deborah bent her legs as far back as she could until her fingers reached her boots.

Her two attackers continued to scream.

Pounding some more, the guard yelled, "Answer me!"

She felt with her fingers for the rope around her ankles, found it, and began to untie the knot.

The crossbeam bumped on the outside of the door as it was lifted.

The stinker was rolling on the floor, now in the middle of the room, his screams reduced to the gargling of a man choking on his own blood. The giggler was on his feet, running blindly into the walls, shrieking.

The knot undone, her ankles drew apart, free at last.

The door opened, letting yellow light in.

Deborah crawled on the floor and, with her bound wrists behind her back, managed to grab hold of her helmet and the two leg-armor pieces. She stayed down and watched the guard enter, carrying the small oil lamp.

With Deborah lying motionless on the floor by the front wall, he ignored her and proceeded into the center of the room, where the stinker was writhing violently on the ground.

As soon as the guard faced the other way, Deborah got to her feet, holding the helmet and armor pieces behind her back, and stepped outside.

"Calm down," the guard yelled. "What happened to you?"

The giggler screamed, "Neither! Neither! Neither!"

She heard the guard tell the stinker to remove his hands from his face.

In the bleak light of the moon, she looked around for the crossbeam. It was propped vertically against the wall behind the open door, next to the guard's spear. She dropped her helmet and armor pieces, turned her back to the crossbeam, and bent sideways until she managed to grab hold of it. Straightening up, she balanced the crossbeam horizontally behind her back, which wasn't easy to do with bound wrists, and stepped backwards into the door, putting her weight against it. The door moved slowly, and the crossbeam threatened to slip from her grip.

The guard shouted, "Stop!"

Desperate, Deborah pushed backwards until the door met the frame. Letting go of the crossbeam, she felt it slip into place just as the guard threw himself against the door inside.

The commotion attracted attention from the paupers' hovels nearby, but they stayed back, watching from a safe distance. Deborah ignored them. She stepped backwards to the guard's spear, felt up the rod with her fingers for the sharp flint tip, and began to grind it against the rope that bound her wrists.

The guard's shouting came clear through the thatched roof. The more curious among the paupers stepped closer. How long before they raised the alarm and attracted Judge Ohad's soldiers?

Grinding the rope faster against the flint, Deborah was panting while stabs of pain shot inside her head.

She heard horse hooves approaching.

The guard continued to yell.

"Shut up," she said, "or I'll go back in and bite off your nose, too."

He stopped yelling.

The sound of horses was getting closer.

As hard as she tried, the rope wouldn't budge.

Horses appeared in the dark end of the street. She knelt, grabbed the helmet and armor pieces behind her back, and ran along the wall, away from the street, into the dark space behind the houses. She ran uphill for a while, until an animal corral blocked her way. She bent forward and rolled over the fence, falling inside, scattering several goats. When she sat up, her wrists were free, the last few threads of the rope finally broken by the fall.

A man yelled nearby.

Deborah instinctively reached for her sword, but her hand found nothing by her hip. The sling was still tied around her waist. She collected her armor pieces, climbed over the wooden fence, and resumed running uphill behind the rear walls of houses and courtyards, which grew larger with the elevation. Thorns scraped her shins, exposed above the boots, and rolls of tumbleweed tripped her several times, but she kept going uphill behind the houses and the animal corrals. The higher she reached, the quieter it became.

As she crossed a garden behind a house with no burning fires or lamps, Deborah tripped over a rock. A snake slithered away. She stayed down, crawled under a bush, and curled up, panting hard. As her breathing slowed, she listened, but heard no pursuers.

While strapping on her helmet and leg armor pieces, she wondered whether the snake would come back to bite her. She thought of the snake on the blue flag of the tribe of Dan, whose men had massacred the villagers in the hills near Bethel, the snake that struck the mice in the vendor's cage at the fairgrounds in Aphek, and the snake that left its traces in the sand on the morning after her escape from Emanuel, when Zariz had told her: "A snake reserves its venom for things it can eat."

With her head resting on her bent arm, Deborah tried to calm down. The cool night air carried scents of smoke, animal waste, and cooking. As her panting slowed, she listened to the sounds of the city – dogs barking, people talking, and babies crying. She recalled spitting the severed nose and wiping the liquefied eyes from her fingers while the two men screamed in horrified agony. She could still taste the bitter blood on her tongue. Out of nowhere, a sob burst from her chest, then another, and her whole body convulsed as she wept into her soiled hands.

13

Deborah woke up at dawn, shivering from the cold and achy from the hard ground. Her head was sore, the scalp tender to the touch. She crawled out from under the bush and stood up. God's reasons for what had happened were still a mystery to her, but she was beginning to understand that He had sent her to Beersheba for a higher purpose than to rescue an Edomite princess. She was here to stop her fellow Hebrews from shedding each other's blood.

But how?

The answer wasn't clear, but first, she had to reclaim her horse and sword from the wily Judge Ohad. As the most important man in the city, his house was likely at the top of the hill. That's where she headed. Sure enough, in a large stable behind a stately home, a great white horse pushed through several black, brown, and spotted horses to welcome her.

Rogez shifted about and rocked his head, spreading unrest among the other horses. Deborah scratched his neck while he nuzzled her. The saddle had not been removed from his back, and her sack was still attached to it. She reached in for the jar of stubble paste and applied a fresh layer. They had also left her spear in the sheath attached to the other side of the saddle. Deborah pulled it out. She would try to avoid a fight, but if one ensued, a weapon would be handy.

The big house was dark and quiet. She sniffed the air for pipe smoke, but all she could smell was the plain smoke of embers, left overnight in fire pits to be rekindled in the morning.

"Keep quiet," she whispered to Rogez.

A wall surrounded the large courtyard. She tried the rear gate, but it was barred from the inside. The red glow of dawn grew in the east. Time was running out. She had to find a way to enter the house unnoticed and slip into the judge's room, grab her sword, and force him to have a frank conversation about God and His will.

A few steps back gave her a better view of the house, which reminded her of Judge Zifron's house in Emanuel, where he resided in the rear room on the second floor, farthest from the noise and dust of the street. Gazing up at the last room on the second floor, she noticed it had windows on three sides – over the courtyard, back towards the horse stable, and in the downhill direction, overlooking the city all the way down to the gate and the fairgrounds. The three windows were blocked with curtains, another clue to the dweller's importance.

She reentered the horse stable, patted Rogez to keep him calm, and reached inside her sack for her father's fire starters – a thin flint stone, about as long as her forefinger, and a coarse, veiny quartz rock, almost as big as her fist. In direct sun, the second stone had a glistening orange-yellow vein that her father had called "fool's gold." She also took out the plain robe, slipped it on over the armor and pulled the hood over her helmet.

A roll of tumbleweed she found in the open area caught a spark from her father's fire starters. She blew on it until the flame began to spread, grasped the top carefully to avoid the thorns, and flung it over the wall into the courtyard near the house under the judge's room.

The horses were the first to raise the alarm, neighing and stomping, but as the flames caught the wooden planks of the first floor, a woman screamed. The quiet courtyard exploded with activity. Hiding behind the horses, Deborah shook the robe loose over her armor and made sure the hood was low over her face.

Through the yelling and running behind the wall, she could hear water splashing. The curtains in a window on the second floor shifted aside, and Judge Ohad's bearded face appeared through the smoke. He leaned over the windowsill and looked down into the courtyard. Deborah crouched low and listened to his gruff voice shouting orders. Meanwhile, the door in the rear wall opened, and a man ran out to sooth the agitated horses. She picked up her spear and proceeded quickly around the other side of the stable, where the horses hid her from the man, and entered the busy courtyard.

With her head down, she propped her spear against the wall and ran to the well in the middle of the courtyard, where men and women lined up with jars and buckets. She grabbed a bucket and joined the line. Two slaves handled the pulley with speed and efficiency, bringing up water from the well and pouring it into each container. When her turn came, Deborah held forth her bucket to be filled and ran to empty it on the burning wall. She noticed a pale girl about her own age, whose long black locks rippled around her shoulders down to her waist as she ran with a small jar.

By Deborah's third trip, the flames were out, leaving charred planks and few remnants of tumbleweed, which no one seemed to notice. A faint dawn glowed over the back wall.

Judge Ohad leaned out the window, said something to one of the men in the courtyard below, and withdrew into his room, shutting the curtains.

Below the window was an entrance that, Deborah assumed, led to a stairwell. Walking casually, she went to collect her spear. More than a dozen men and women were milling about the courtyard, but no one paid attention as she headed for the entrance under the judge's quarters. She slipped behind the wooden staircase and knelt in the tight space to wait for things to quiet down. Her eyes adjusted to the dark, and she heard the floor above creak a couple of times. The sweet smell of a pipe drifted through the walls.

A woman cried outside, and a man admonished her as he entered, clutching the thin arm of the girl with the long black hair, whose white face stood out in the dark.

The woman followed behind. "Please, she's too young!"

"Be quiet, wife," he said in a low voice. "You'll upset him."

"Let me talk to him."

They spoke with an accent that Deborah didn't recognize.

The girl reached back with her free hand for the woman, who clasped it.

"Have mercy for our daughter, I beg you."

"Is she really my daughter?"

The woman sucked air sharply.

He pulled the girl halfway up the set of stairs. "The judge asked for her, and if she bear him a child, we'll be safe here—"

"A child?" The woman didn't let go of the girl's hand. "She hasn't had her blood yet."

Pulled on opposite sides, the girl whimpered, and Deborah rose, ready to step out from behind the staircase and intervene.

"Please," the woman begged. "She's not ready."

"You were younger when you started."

"Let me go to him."

"He didn't ask for you."

"I can still satisfy him."

The man kicked the woman, who lost her grip on the girl's hand and fell backwards through the entrance to the courtyard. Deborah was halfway out, but paused when two younger children knelt by the woman, clutching her while she wept.

The man was already near the top, dragging the girl up the stairs, murmuring incoherently.

A door opened above, letting out lamplight, and Deborah heard Judge Ohad's voice.

"Shush that whiny wife of yours, or I'll banish your clan from Beersheba."

"I'm sorry," the man said. "She's upset because the girl hasn't had her—"

"Here's your coin, Cainite. Go."

The door closed. The man sighed and came downstairs. Deborah seethed, her hands locked on the spear. He paused at the entrance, his figure dark against the dim light outside. She barely controlled the urge to get out from behind the stairs and kick him twice as hard as he had kicked his distraught wife a moment earlier.

When the man was gone and the children led the weeping mother away, Deborah listened for noises upstairs. She had hoped that, in the calm after the fire was put out, Judge Ohad would go back to sleep, and she could slip into his room unnoticed. Her plan, however, had to change as the old judge gave up sleep for the company of a girl young enough to be his granddaughter.

A loud bang sounded above, followed by the raspy sound of tearing cloth, a girl's yelp, and Judge Ohad's laughter, which Deborah recognized from the tent on the road from Kabetzel.

She ran up the stairs and burst in through the door.

He was facing the other way, bent over the girl, who sat on the edge of a bed. Her robe was torn at the front, revealing a milky white chest and delicate breasts, but Deborah's gaze was drawn to the girl's eyes, which were large and unusually colored – a rich turquoise, like gems Deborah had seen at a merchant's stall in Aphek. The judge wore only undergarments, his uncovered head was bald on top, with matted gray hair over his ears. His shoulders were soft and hairy. He didn't bother to turn, but said irritably, "Whip your stupid wife, Cainite, or I will."

"I don't have a wife," Deborah said as she stepped forward, raising the spear sideways, both hands clenching it near the flinthead.

As he began to turn, she swang the spear as a club and hit him on the side of the head, producing a dull thud. He toppled over, but blocked his fall with a hand and opened his mouth to yell. She swung the spear the other way and landed it on the bald crown of his head. This time, he dropped to the floor and remained motionless.

The girl pulled a blanket from the bed, covered her chest, and moved backwards, away from Deborah, until the wall blocked her way. Her turquoise eyes, which contrasted starkly with her black hair, stated at the fainted judge. Deborah grabbed his headdress from the floor, rolled it up, and muzzled him, tying the ends behind his head. She found a used loincloth and bound his wrists behind his back. His body odor sickened her, but fleeing was not an option, considering the risk to the girl.

The bejeweled sword, still sheathed and attached to her leather belt, rested on the floor by the bed. Deborah took off the robe she had worn over her armor, put on the belt, and adjusted the sword at an angle against her hip. On a shelf above the bed she noticed a line of small effigies of various false gods. She knocked them to the floor and stomped with her boot, crushing each one to pieces.

The girl began to move along the wall towards the door.

"It's not safe for you," Deborah said.

Though her eyes were still wide with apprehension, the girl paused.

"Your father will drag you back here. Do you understand?"

She nodded.

Deborah found a leather belt on the floor and handed it to the girl. "Strap it on over your torn robe."

On the floor, Judge Ohad shifted and groaned.

The girl dropped the blanket, gathered her torn robe tightly around her, and strapped on the belt.

"What's your name?"

"I am Yael," the girl said. "Yael of the Cainite Clan."

Deborah leaned close and whispered, "I am Deborah, a maiden of Ephraim."

Yael drew back, her eyes on Deborah's cheek.

"It's not real." She scraped a bit of the stubble paste off. "Can we trust each other now?"

Yael nodded.

"People know me as Borah." Deborah stepped behind Yael and quickly separated the long locks of her hair, braided them, and pushed the braid under the robe down her back, before pulling the hood over Yael's head. "The less men see, the better."

For the first time, Yael smiled. "Yes, Borah."

14

The courtyard below the window grew busier with sunrise. On the floor, Judge Ohad shifted. Deborah found a jar of water in the corner and emptied it over his head. He groaned and trembled. She grabbed one of his elbows, Yael took the other, and together they turned him over and made him sit up on the floor with his back to the foot of the bed.

He looked up, saw Deborah, and struggled to free his bound arms.

Picking up her spear, Deborah placed the flint point against his chest. He froze.

"Good morning," she said. "Yahweh would like to know why a Hebrew judge violated three of the Ten Commandments in less than a day." She pointed to the crushed effigies and quoted from memory. "Do not worship false gods over me!" She patted her sword. "Do not steal!" She gestured at the girl. "Do not covet!"

His eyes went up and down, from the tip of the spear to her face, and back.

"Do you repent?"

He nodded.

"Are you willing to pay due compensation?"

He grunted, nodding again.

"Good," Deborah said. "In addition to returning my sword and horse, you'll grant this girl freedom from you and from her father. Agreed?"

He shrugged.

"I'm going to remove the headdress from your mouth. Don't yell, or I'll run the spear through your gut."

Getting on the bed behind him, Yael untied the rolled-up headdress, pulled it out of his mouth, and scurried away.

Judge Ohad looked up at Deborah. "Assaulting a judge is also a sin."

"A God-fearing judge, maybe."

"Nice trick with the fire." He smirked. "I had a man once before me for starting a fire as a diversion to stealing. I sentenced him to burned at the stake, which he did."

"You were going to burn me at the stake, too. How's that working out for you?"

"I mistakenly assumed you escaped into the desert last night."

"I don't do what's expected of me."

"And how do you expect to get out of here alive?"

"By making a bargain with you."

He glanced down at the tip of the spear.

"I want a full pardon, publicly."

"Fine. You can go in peace, together with this little Cainite whore."

"And Princess Needa."

"Why? The Edomite king consented to the marriage."

"Not if your son treats girls the way you do." Deborah gestured at Yael.

Judge Ohad waved dismissively. "My poor son worships that princess. If only I could free him of her bewitchment."

"Threaten to disown him."

"You haven't yet fallen for a girl, have you?"

Deborah shook her head.

Judge Ohad sighed. "When a woman steals a man's heart, she also steals his mind. My son would rather live in a desert cave with her than be the next Judge of Simeon without her."

Considering his words for a moment, Deborah said, "Then promise me this: before the ceremony, you'll grant Princess Needa the right to decide whether she agrees to the marriage, or not."

"What do you offer in exchange? My life?"

"And the lives of all the people in Beersheba."

"You're in no position to threaten my tribe."

"Not me," Deborah said. "The men of Judah."

"Judah isn't our friend. Everybody knows that."

"But only I know their actual plan to attack Beersheba very soon."

He looked at her doubtfully.

"Do we have a deal?"

He glanced at the curtained window, which brought in light and sounds of men and women from below. "I agree. When will they attack?"

"I'm young," Deborah said. "Not stupid."

He couldn't hold back a grin.

"Before I tell you anything, you'll stand with me at the window and pronounce that you pardon me because I came here to help defend Beersheba from an attack, that you give the girl Yael her freedom, and that every man of Simeon must provide me with all the privileges and protections afforded to an honored guest."

"You drive a hard bargain, boy."

"The slave master in the holy city of Shiloh once told me that, in business, good information is better than silver shekels." Deborah also remembered something Zariz's father had said, but she didn't repeat it out loud: "A successful trade is always based on a fair balance of mutually assured exaggerations and understatements."

With Yael's help, Deborah got him up by the window. She noticed the swelling bruise on the bald top of his head from the second spear strike. The first strike was probably as bad, but the hair on the side of his head hid the bruise.

She set aside the curtains.

The courtyard below was bustling, but his appearance drew everyone's attention. They gathered closer, looking up at the unusual sight. As she had done repeatedly since arriving in the territory of Simeon, Deborah scanned their faces, but Barac wasn't among them.

"The boy Borah is pardoned." Judge Ohad's voice was hoarse but clear. "He was falsely accused of intending to harm us. In fact, he came here to help us defend Beersheba from an attack. As a token of my gratitude, I've given him this girl of the Cainite Clan as a gift, to do with her as he wishes."

He glanced at Deborah and smirked.

"From this day on," he continued, "Borah may bear his sword and ride his horse among us and enjoy all the privileges and protections afforded to honored guests of Simeon."

Stepping back from the window, he sat heavily on the bed.

Yael left the room while Deborah untied him.

He exhaled with relief, flexing his short, thick arms. "When will the attack take place?"

Deborah took a deep breath. Was she breaking her vow to Goor-

Aryeh? He had told her of an attack, but all the other details, which helped her figure out when, where, and how the attack would take place, she heard from others – the priest and soldiers in Arad, Navad, Sallan, and even this undignified judge and his men. Every detail she had learned added up to provide the full picture of the coming attack. No, she decided, her disclosure would not break her vow, and even if it would, didn't saving lives take precedent over everything else?

"In three nights," she said. "That's when the attack will come."

"The night after tomorrow night?"

"Yes, on Thursday night, they'll come down from Ziklag."

He rubbed his hands. "We'll set a trap by the road from Ziklag and harvest them like ripe wheat, not one will be spared."

"I don't think they'll travel by road."

His eyes narrowed. "Do you know more than you're telling?"

"Once I go around the area and make a map in my head, God will help me foresee their plans more clearly."

"You're a presumptuous boy. No one has heard Yahweh's voice since Joshua many generations ago."

"Sinners' ears are deaf to His message."

"Why would God speak to you rather than to priests, or judges?"

"Stop sinning and repent, and He may speak to you, too." Deborah saw the anger on his face and added, "The men of Judah have a righteous leader in Arad."

"You speak of Goor-Aryeh?"

She nodded. "He wanted me to join them. My mother was of Judah, but my father was of Ephraim."

"Ephraim be cursed." Judge Ohad clenched his fists. "Joshua promised to Simeon the city of Shechem and all her environs, but Ephraim grabbed all of the Samariah Hills, and we ended up in this desert, landlocked by Judah – an injustice wrapped in an insult!"

She was startled by his rant, but it explained the image of the gates and masonry guard towers on Simeon's flag. It was the city of Shechem, the jewel of their pilfered tribal territory.

"It's all Judah's fault," he continued, his voice rising. "But this time, we'll exact our revenge and go north to take what's ours from your tribe of Ephraim."

"I think Shechem is in the land of Manasseh, not Ephraim."

"They're both the sons of Joseph." He sneered. "Arrogant pretenders like their forefather, sowing discord among the rest of Israel."

Deborah didn't argue. She remembered two women of Ephraim with a dead baby, fleeing a burning village in the hills, describing their attackers: "They carried the banner of King Javin of Hazor and the effigy of Ra, the sun god of the Canaanites, but when they thought we were all dead, they cheered, "Manasseh's birthright is redeemed!" That's how we knew their true identity." Deborah could not understand why men of Manasseh, Judah, Simeon, or Dan, thought that ancient grievances justify violating the divine order, "Do not kill!"

"Dreaming, boy?"

"I was wondering," she said. "Why do the tribes of Israel hate each other? Aren't we all Hebrews, chosen by God above all other nations?"

"It's the nature of men. Where in Ephraim do you come from?"

"Emanuel," she said. "It's a small town."

"We have a new blacksmith from Emanuel. He talks of an oppressive judge. Have you fled the same judge?"

Deborah couldn't speak. A new blacksmith from Emanuel! Who else could it be, but Abinoam? Was Barac alive, too, or was his head rolling in the dust where Seesya had cut it off? She coughed to mask the internal turmoil of fears and hopes while remembering Barac's face, his bright smile, and his words on the night he escaped from Emanuel: "Deborah, don't despair. Yahweh will show you kindness again. He will." She pleaded silently with God to show her kindness now and reveal that Barac was alive."

Judge Ohad was looking at her. "What's wrong with you, boy? Have you drunk too much wine?"

"I'm thinking about our unjust judge," Deborah said. She wanted to ask whether Barac had come here with his father, but knew not to reveal anything this crafty judge could use against her. "As unjust as you were yesterday, locking me in your jail with evil men who attacked me."

"You don't seem harmed, which cannot be said for your cellmates. Two are dead and the third is blind."

Deborah shuddered. Do not kill!

"You were bound hand and foot. How did you do it?"

"God saved me."

"An all-powerful God could have plucked you out through the door, the roof, or the wall without killing and maiming those men."

The argument made Deborah pause, but the answer came to her with the eagle's words, which she repeated out loud. "Freedom must be earned, not collected as a gift. God made me brave—"

"And bloody." Judge Ohad pointed at her sword. "Is this the blade you used to cut open the Edomite high priest's head?"

She nodded while the image of the halved skull flashed before her.

The judge touched the bruises on his head. "I guess I should consider myself lucky."

Yael returned with two male servants, carrying clean clothes and a bowl of warm water.

"Go, boy," Judge Ohad told Deborah. "Look around the city and figure out how the men of Judah will attack us. I'll speak with you tonight at our celebratory dinner." He lay back on the bed with a sigh. "Your Edomite master promised to spice up our wine with a magical elixir of joy and merriment."

15

The sun was up when Deborah exited the stairwell with Yael and crossed the busy courtyard. Yael's father approached, bearing a jug of wine and a goblet. The mother, her lips painted bright red, followed him with a plate of sliced pomegranates and honey cakes.

"Welcome to Beersheba," he said to Deborah, holding forth the goblet. "A drink?"

Deborah gestured at Yael. "Serve your daughter first."

He held on to the goblet, his face flushed.

"Do it." She rested her hand on the silver hilt of her sword. "Now."

He gave Yael the goblet.

"And tell her how sorry you are for what you did."

"Listen, my young friend." He lowered his voice in feigned intimacy. "When you get older, you'll learn that a man never apologizes to a woman. The whip is how you deal with them."

Deborah nodded thoughtfully. "Is that right?"

"I'm telling you, boy. A good lashing is the only language these stupid creatures understand."

She grinned at Yael, who burst out laughing, spraying the wine from her mouth. Her father grunted in anger and raised his hand to slap her.

"You touch her," Deborah said, "and I'll cut off your hand."

He glanced at the judge's window on the second floor and stepped back.

"Beg for her forgiveness."

"Forgive me," he said to Yael, his voice flat. "I thought you're old enough to earn your bread."

"Her sustenance is no longer your concern," Deborah said. "You heard the judge."

"She's not his to give away."

"She's not yours, either. A father who whores his daughter is not a father."

He sighed, deflated. "Our people are strangers among the Hebrews. We bear the mark of Cain and the shame of his crime. And we're poor."

"Now you have one less mouth to feed." Deborah turned to Yael. "How is the wine?"

"Very good."

Taking the goblet, Deborah drank the rest and held the goblet out for him to refill, which he did. She drank a little more, but stopped, feeling the warmth build up inside her.

The mother, whose painted face was now lined with tears, held out the plate for them.

"Thank you." Deborah took a slice of pomegranate, bit into it, and wiped her lips on her sleeve. She threw the skin in the gutter and ate a piece of honey cake, followed by another. "I haven't eaten since yesterday morning," she said.

The mother picked a piece of honey cake and held it to Yael's lips, which the girl obediently parted as a nest-bound baby sparrow accepting a treat from its mother. The husband grunted with disapproval, but as he looked at Yael, his eyes softened, and he said nothing when his wife hugged the girl, pressing her tightly to her bosom. Watching this, Deborah remembered what Umm-Sallan said: "Good and evil always compete for man's heart."

At the stable, Deborah saddled Umm-Sallan's mare and helped Yael mount it. The girl's hands trembled as she clasped the reins. Deborah remembered her own first ride, sitting on a horse in front of the Moabite boy, Zariz, his dark hands resting on top of her freckled hands, his chest pressed to her back, his sweet breath on her neck.

"A boy taught me a simple rule," she said. "Keep your doubts from showing. You must pretend to be confident, or the horse will not respect you."

"How?"

Deborah kept rubbing the mare's neck. "Let the horse know what you want. Pull back on the reins to stop, tug the left side to go left, and the right to go right."

"And forward?"

The question made Deborah smile, because it was a question that a girl who lacked courage would not have asked. "Kick in with both heels

– gently to go slow, harder to go faster. Ready to try?"

Yael nodded.

Mounting Rogez gave Deborah a powerful jolt of joy. She was free again, back in the saddle, having overcome Sallan's treachery and Judge Ohad's cruelty – the collapsing tent, the clubbed head, the pelting at Beersheba's gates, the death sentence, the foul lockup, the two would-be rapists, and the unspeakable things she had to do for freedom.

Her head still hurt, but she held it high while riding across the courtyard.

Everyone stepped aside to make way.

Out the front gate, she turned left on the wide street and trotted downhill. Yael followed on the mare. From this high vantage point, Deborah could see that Beersheba was divided into sections. Well-appointed houses occupied the higher part of the city. Down below, the left side was a dense jumble of tents and huts, where the poor lived. In the center, near the gates, were larger storage structures for produce and other goods, as well as animal corrals and several wells. On the right, columns of smoke in various shades and plumes of dust from many feet indicated a busy marketplace and craftsmen's workshops. That's where she was going.

At the bottom of the hill, Deborah turned right and rode down a street busy with many merchants hawking their goods. Shoppers touched the merchandise and haggled over prices. The local men were dressed in the same desert outfits as Judge Ohad and his men – long robes, flowing headdresses, and untrimmed beards. The women wore long-sleeved dresses, which went down to their ankles, and colorful scarves over their hair. The slaves were easy to recognize with their sleeveless long shirts, bare feet and, for the male slaves, shaved heads.

Word of the judge's pardon must have spread quickly, for not one person failed to move aside at the sight of the great white horse.

Near the end of the street, she saw Abinoam in an open-air workshop between a baker and a potter. All three workshops had fire pits burning, and the radiated heat chased away the freshness of the morning air. In the rear of Abinoam's workshop was a crudely built wooden shed, about ten steps wide, with a thatched roof and a narrow doorway. She wondered if Barac was inside the shed.

His hands wrapped in rags, Abinoam was hammering a red-hot piece of iron.

Deborah tied Rogez to a wooden bar at the front.

He paused and looked up. "Good day, soldier. What can I do for you?"

She hesitated, peering at the dark interior of the shed in the rear.

He stepped closer to her and eyed the bejeweled hilt of her sheathed sword. "That's a beautiful piece of work."

Drawing her sword, Deborah held it up to give him a better look.

His eyes narrowed. "I know this weapon."

"You should," Deborah said.

He retreated and wielded the hammer.

She sheathed the sword, smiling. "I'm no threat to you."

"Did Seesya send you?"

"Don't you recognize me?"

Abinoam stared at her.

"Look at my face."

"I don't have time for games, boy."

"You and Barac saw me last at Palm Homestead."

His eyes creased, then widened, and the hammer fell from his hand. "Deborah?"

She nodded.

The shock on his face turned to dread. He glanced at the neighboring workshops, but no one was paying attention. Pointing at Yael, he asked in a hushed voice. "Does she know?"

"She can keep a secret."

"They'll burn you." He grabbed Deborah's arm and pulled her towards the shed. "Hide here, and I'll go and buy a woman's robe for you."

Deborah shook free from his grip. "Don't worry."

"I shouldn't worry?" He looked around. "You're wearing men's clothes and bearing men's weapons. If anyone notices, God have mercy on us."

"You didn't notice, did you?"

He pointed at Yael. "Why did you tell her?"

"In a man's world, every woman needs a friend – even a woman who pretends to be a man."

"Pretending is lying." Abinoam gestured impatiently. "And lying is a sin, because lies beget lies like mice in a baker's shop."

"Lying isn't a sin when it's necessary to save one's life." Deborah pointed at herself. "I shortened my name to Borah."

"I heard that name. Wasn't it the boy who slayed the Edomite High Priest in their temple?"

"News travels fast," she said.

"I'm confused." He picked up the hammer and put it on the workbench. "We saw Seesya and his soldiers take you that night. We assumed he made you his wife. How did you get away?"

Deborah told him about her nighttime escape from Emanuel, Seesya's chase and deadly confrontation with the Moabite caravan, and her attempt to seek the protection of Shatz Ha'Cohen, one of the high priests at Yahweh's temple in Shiloh, who instead forced her to marry Seesya.

Abinoam sighed. "How could a priest hand a girl over to that murderous young man?"

"He told me it was God's will."

"Based on what?"

"On what God told Eve after she fed Adam the forbidden fruit in the Garden of Eden." Deborah quoted. "And to the woman God said: I shall multiply your pain and agony; in anguish you shall bear children; always you shall lust after your husband, and he shall reign over you."

"Sometimes," Abinoam said, "I'm ashamed to be a Hebrew."

She didn't know what to say to that.

"How did you escape the marriage?"

"Seesya couldn't consummate our union. They put me on trial to have me executed like my sister, but a friend of Sallan advocated for me and tricked Seesya into admitting that the same thing had happened to him with my sister, too."

"No wonder he's so angry all the time. Who was the clever friend of Sallan?"

"Do you remember the story Barac told me that night at Palm Homestead."

"The Elixirist who had turned the women of Edom into men to beat back an Egyptian army."

She nodded. "Sallan told me where to look for him."

"Is that why you're dressed as a man?"

"Yes."

His eyes rested on her cheeks.

"It's fake," she said. "Sallan made stubble paste for me. Under it, I'm still a girl, but stronger. Much stronger."

"That's obvious." He also smiled, suddenly resembling Barac. "Tell me the rest."

Her burning question—whether Barac was alive or not—was at the tip of her tongue, but she was too nervous to ask it, in case the answer was the one she dreaded. Instead, she told him about the lepers who risked their lives to hide her on the way to Aphek in search of Kassite, the man Sallan had falsely told her was the Elixirist. She described how Kassite perpetuated the lie and made her do hard labor in the tannery in order to build masculine physical strength, resilience, and tolerance for pain, as well as transforming her character from the female "passive, temperamental, small-minded, and anxious" to the superior male's "proactive, even-tempered, adventurous, and logical." She chronicled the mass escape of the slaves from the tannery, the arrival in Emanuel under masquerade, the ingenious way Kassite managed to convince Judge Zifron to release the supposedly dying Sallan—who was the real Elixirist—and how Vardit inadvertently caused Seesya to recognize Deborah just before leaving Emanuel. Abinoam listened with rapt fascination to the description of her trial, which ended not with her being stoned to death, but with Seesya releasing her from his betrothal and suffering lashes for the murders of her parents and sister. The deadly ambush in Ein Gedi shocked Abinoam, but he laughed out loud when she described Seesya wading away in the Sea of Salt with a shattered jaw.

"And that's how I got this," Deborah patted Seesya's sword, sheathed at her hip. "And his horse, as well." She pointed at Rogez.

"Are you still hoping to change into a man?"

She answered by telling him how, after arriving in Bozra, Sallan and Kassite had locked her up at the bottom of the abandoned copper mine.

"I never liked that conniving Edomite slave."

"Sallan is an exceptional man," she said. "Exceptional in both his good and evil sides."

"Sides? What sides?"

"It's an old Edomite saying, which his mother told me—maybe to explain her son's behavior." Deborah shrugged. "Greed and spite dwell like wicked brothers in every man's heart, constantly fighting their good sisters, charity and sympathy."

"It's true."

"I'm grateful for what happened because, down at the bottom of the copper mine, I found the answer to my doubts over the transformation into a man."

"And?"

"I'm determined to succeed as a woman in answering my True Calling – go back to the land of Ephraim, take ownership of Palm Homestead, and deliver God's word to the Hebrews."

He gazed at her, saying nothing.

Deborah felt her heart race. It was time to ask the question. "I've missed Barac," she said with a quiver in her voice.

Abinoam exhaled with a long sigh.

"Is he here, too?"

"No."

"Why?"

"I lost him." Abinoam hung his head. "I lost my son forever."

The words hit Deborah with a physical force.

Lost!

Forever!

She stumbled back, her knees folded under her, and she dropped to the ground. Barac's face came to her as he was in Emanuel, smiling with white teeth against his dark skin, eyes glinting with joy as he carried the bales of straw for her up the hill to the basket factory, then waved goodbye with both hands and ran back to his father's workshop.

Lost forever.

She buried her face in her hands and wept.

16

Abinoam pulled Deborah up and hustled her to the shed while murmuring words she couldn't discern through her bitter sobs.

Barac. Lost forever.

She dropped to the floor inside the dark shed, and he stood over her, shaking a finger in her face. "Quiet, or you'll get us both killed!"

A shadow flew through the door as Yael ran at full speed and knocked Abinoam down, landing on top of him, punching him with small fists. Shocked by the sudden attack, he recovered and shoved the girl aside with a swipe of his arm. She rushed back, her fists up.

"Stop," Deborah cried. "Leave him alone."

Abinoam got up, went to the doorway, and glanced outside.

Yael stood next to her, ready to fight.

"His son." Deborah sat up, hugging her knees, rocking back and forth. "He's dead."

"You're crazy," he said over his shoulder. "Both of you."

Yael knelt on the ground, embracing her.

"Why?" Deborah wept. "I don't understand. Why?"

A donkey brayed in the corner of the shed, revealing its existence for the first time.

Satisfied that the noise alerted no one, Abinoam turned. "Silly girl. Barac is not dead."

She looked up at him. "But you said—"

"I lost him, because he's an ungrateful, insolent, hardheaded boy, who'd rather run around playing soldier in the desert than honor his father and learn the respectable trade of his forefathers."

The fog of grief began to lift, but she dared not hope yet. "Barac is alive?"

"I assume so. Haven't seen him in many weeks."

Deborah wiped her tears. "Why?"

Abinoam sat in the only chair. "For the same reason I had to flee Emanuel. His stubborn and selfish behavior. Who in their right mind would defy the rulers of his town and refuse to cast a stone at a girl who's already dead? And when we finally arrived here safely by the grace of God and won permission to open a shop, he directed his selfish stubbornness at me."

She watched him, waiting for more.

"At first, he helped me set up the shop and build this shed so that we wouldn't have to sleep under the stars. He met other young men, who fancied themselves great warriors." Abinoam sighed. "Boys think that playing with swords turns them into men. I allowed it. What could be wrong with forming bonds of friendship in a new city? We're not of this tribe, you know, our only connection being through my late wife, who was of Simeon."

She nodded.

"I put my foot down, though, when he wanted to travel with the judge's son to Bozra. I have only Barac to continue my name. How could I allow him to go into the red heathens' den of false gods and human sacrifice?"

"But he went anyway?"

"Against my wishes." Abinoam raised his voice, the risk of attracting attention now forgotten. "I reminded him of God's commandment: "Honor your father!" But he argued that he's honoring God by becoming a soldier in order to liberate the Promised Land from the Canaanites. I told him: "A good blacksmith can make swords for a hundred soldiers, but he shut his eyes to my pleas and told me that I'd be proud of him one day. Proud? What father feels pride in an insolent son?"

The last words he shouted, and sure enough, men were gathering up front.

Deborah stood up, wiped her eyes, and stepped out of the shed, shielding her face from the sun.

A man asked, "What's all the yelling?"

"A donkey," she said. "It won't come out."

As soon as her eyes adjusted to the light, Deborah realized the men were not curious shoppers or merchants, drawn by the noise. Rather, they were armed with swords and clubs, and their young leader was mounted on a good horse. She recognized him from the tent by the road to Kabetzel.

"Where is Abinoam the blacksmith?"

"Good morning, Tsruyah." Abinoam came out of the shed.

"And to you. Donkey problems, I hear?"

"Only a stupid animal would chew on the planks that hold a roof over its head."

"Only a stupid man would bother to yell at a donkey."

Abinoam chuckled as if the joke wasn't meant as an insult. "What can I do for you?"

"The judge wants you to drop everything and start making swords."

"I'm making one for a customer right now. When I finish—"

"We require fifty swords."

"Fifty?" Abinoam was taken aback. "That's a lot. I'll need copper, lead, and iron, as well as a firewood – a lot of it."

Tsruyah snapped his fingers, and a horse-drawn wagon approached. The men put down their weapons and unloaded large buckets of red and gray soil. Judging by their flushed faces and panting, the buckets were heavy. Next came bundles of fire logs, several jugs of wine, baskets with fruit, cloth-wrapped chunks of cheese, and a sack of flatbreads.

"Please thank Judge Ohad for his generosity." Abinoam poked the fire with a long rod. "I'll start working on it tomorrow morning."

"Start now," Tsruyah said. "We need everything ready in three days."

"That's impossible. It takes me three days to make one sword. Fifty will take me until Passover."

"The night after tomorrow, men of Judah are coming to destroy Beersheba."

"What?" Abinoam stepped back, shocked. "How do you know?"

Tsruyah pointed his club at Deborah. "He told us."

Abinoam looked at her, and she nodded.

"We need a sword for every able man in Beersheba." Tsruyah tapped his club against his headdress. "If your head is dear to you, make the weapons."

"I'll start immediately," Abinoam said. "What about the other blacksmiths?"

"They got similar orders."

"Then they must have also told you it's not enough time."

"They did, as did the carpenters who will make hundreds of clubs for all the farmers in the area." Tsruyah was already turning away. "Recruit men to help you. That's what the food is for. Three days. Get it done."

After they left, Yael emerged from the shed. Abinoam spread a sheet of cloth on the ground and put out bread, slices of cheese, and some fruit. He poured wine in wooden cups. They sat on the ground, thanked God for the food, and ate.

While eating, Deborah told him everything she knew about the attack.

"Beersheba is doomed," he said.

"Why?"

"The tribe of Judah is ten times bigger than Simeon. Worse yet, Judge Ohad's son, Mamreh, is loitering in the desert with all the young men who accompanied him to Bozra, which leaves the judge with only twenty or thirty armed men under Tsruyah."

"That's why he wants to arm more men."

"Beersheba is a city of merchants, artisans, laborers, and paupers, with a ring of homestead farmers in the surrounding land. If Judge Ohad sends these men to battle, they'll be cut down like wheat under the scythe."

Standing up, Deborah tightened the sling around her hips, adjusted the sheathed sword, and checked her helmet, armor, and boots. Yahweh hadn't sent her here to watch a whole Hebrew city get slaughtered by other Hebrews. It was her duty to prevent the killing, but how?

"There must be a way," she said. "What would you do to defend Beersheba from the men of Judah?"

"There's nothing anyone can do." Abinoam tossed several logs of wood into the fire. "It'll be the end of Simeon and its tiresome grievances. They had it coming for generations." He put food and tools into a sack and pulled the donkey out of the shed. "You should leave Beersheba, too. The sooner the better."

"Me?" Deborah ruffled the hair between the donkey's ears. "I must stay to prevent this bloodshed."

He tied the sack with a rope. "The tribes of Israel have been fighting each other since our namesake ancestors bickered in the sibling rivalries that the Holy Scriptures describes."

"I have to try."

"Have to?"

"My father dreamt that I would deliver God's word to all the Hebrew tribes, not only to Ephraim." Deborah kept her voice even, free of contention or quarrel, knowing that her aspirations to realize her father's dream as a woman seemed blasphemous, even to a good man like Abinoam. "It's my True Calling."

"May God watch over you." Abinoam sighed. "I'm going back north, if I can get away from Beersheba without being detected by Tsruyah and his men."

"And then?"

"I would have liked to return to Emanuel. Judge Zifron needs my skills and likes my tax payments, but if Seesya survived the Sea of Salt and the Mountains of Moab, he will take revenge on me for what Barac did."

The thought of Seesya being alive sent a shudder through Deborah. "Wait here a few moments," she said. "I'll find Tsruyah and ask him to show me the area to the west. It will give you time to sneak out of the city."

Abinoam tightened the sack over the donkey. "Be careful with him, not only today, but as long as you are in Beersheba. Tsruyah has a nasty reputation."

The concern in his voice touched her, and she hugged him, taking in the familiar smell of smoke and melting iron.

He hugged her back and whispered, "Is it true, Deborah?"

"What?"

"That Yahweh speaks to you?"

She hesitated. "I hear His message, yes."

"Will you give me your blessing?"

In a soft voice, Deborah recited the words: "May Yahweh bless you and protect you. May He show you kindness and grace. May He illuminate your path and grant you peace." She paused, and said, "Now, will you grant me a favor?"

"Anything," he said, his voice hoarse with emotions.

"Forgive Barac."

He took a deep breath and exhaled at length. "If he apologizes."

Deborah smiled. "I'll make sure he does."

"And tell him that I'll be waiting in Kadesh Naphtali, near the Sea of

Galilee. We have distant family there."

As she mounted Rogez, Deborah prayed silently for Barac, too. With Yael in tow, she rode through the crowded market. At the other blacksmith shops, which were larger than Abinoam's, the fires burned higher, and at a carpenter shop, men were unloading large quantities of wood from a wagon. Signaling to Yael to catch up, Deborah watched her tug on the reins and kick in her heels. The mare quickened its pace and came up beside Rogez.

"Well done," Deborah said. "Tell me, was Tsruyah the reason you stayed inside the shed?"

The smile faded from Yael's face. "When my mother goes to serve him, she always comes back with bruises. He is a bad man."

"Unfortunately, most men are capable of both good and evil."

"That's how my father is."

Deborah thought about Sallan, who had been both her champion and her tormentor, and remembered his advice. "Here is a good rule," she said. "With dogs and with men, if you cower and show weakness, they will abuse you, but if you stand proud and exude confidence, they will seek your approval."

Yael sat up straight in the saddle, feigning haughtiness, which made Deborah laugh.

Tsruyah was on his horse near the gate, watching his men pile up rolls of tumbleweed and dry twigs around an upright wooden stake.

Deborah rode over to him. "The judge asked me to tour the area."

"What do you want from us, boy?"

"Show me around the city."

"Your little whore, too?"

Yael's mare retreated a few steps, but Deborah stabbed her heels into Rogez's ribs, urging him forward and around to line up with Tsruyah's horse so that she faced him up close, her hand on the hilt of her sword.

He struggled to control his horse.

"She's still a maiden," Deborah said. "Apologize to her."

He sneered, and his hand clutched the hilt of his sword

She kept her glare steady. "Two men forced me to kill them recently. One was a high priest, the second a criminal. What are you?"

After a brief pause, Tsruyah removed his hand from the hilt. "I was joking. No offense. What do you want to see?"

Deborah tilted her head in the opposite direction from where they had arrived the night before. "Let's start on the west."

He gestured with exaggerated politeness to let her go first.

Rogez took off, and Yael's mare stayed abreast, showing unexpected vitality. Tsruyah followed behind.

Approximately a quarter of the way around the city to the west, the defensive wall was in disrepair, with whole sections reduced to mounds of rocks. The surrounding land was cultivated and lush, contrasting with the barren desert further out. They stopped at the edge of a gorge, as deep as a two-story house, which ran north-south along the western edge of Beersheba.

Tsruyah caught up with them. "This is the Beersheba Creek. Two other creeks feed into it. I'll show you."

He took off at a fast pace, heading north along the bank of the Beersheba Creek, all the way along the western wall of the city and further north, until they reached a fork.

"That's the Hebron Creek." He pointed to the right at the gorge that came from the east along the northern wall of the city.

"I've seen it on the way from Kabetzel. And this one?" She gestured at the gorge coming down from the north.

"Betarim Creek," he said. "It comes from the hills near Ziklag."

"Is there a road from Ziklag to Beersheba?"

"The road from Ziklag goes a bit to the east, connecting to the Spice Route from Kabetzel and Arad."

Deborah imagined the map in her head and committed it to memory. "Let's ride up the Betarim Creek. I want to see more of it."

She directed Rogez down a steep goat path into the Hebron Creek, crossed the gorge, and went up the opposite bank. Continuing north alongside the Betarim Creek, she rode beyond the cultivated fields into a rocky desert dotted with thorny bushes and tumbleweeds. In her mind, Deborah considered the possibilities this landscape offered for a stealth attack under the cover of darkness.

Tsruyah rode up next to her. "Have you seen enough?"

"For now." She hoped Abinoam had slipped out of the city safely. "Take us to a well. The horses are thirsty."

17

They stopped at a well and used a bucket to bring up water, which was clear and fresh. When they returned to the main gate, the sun was beginning its afternoon descent. The stake was ready with packed tumbleweeds and twigs, and a wooden platform had been erected across from it. A large crowd had gathered, with more people arriving. There were no dividing ropes or marked sections, but Deborah could see that the people fell into three groups: the well-dressed merchants and artisans, who lived in the upper city, the ragged poor from the tents and shacks inside the wall at the bottom of the hill, and the sunburnt farmers from the surrounding area. Vendors walked through the crowd, offering wine and treats, and beggars worked the crowd with their hands held out. Deborah didn't need to ask what was about to take place. She had seen three trials already, neither of them fair, or just.

Her arrival drew curious glances, pointed fingers, and hushed chattering.

She turned to Tsruyah. "I'd like to speak with the judge now."

"After the trial."

"Why hold a trial at a time like this, instead of preparing—"

"This is part of the preparations." Tsruyah gestured at the crowd. "Do you think they would come here if we summoned them to fight the army of Judah?"

He left her and assigned his men to positions around the fairgrounds, facing inward, ready to prevent the people from leaving after the trial.

A priest emerged from the gate in a white robe with blue fringes, holding a ram's horn. He climbed the stairs to the platform and turned to face the people. Next, seven elders appeared in their white Sabbath robes and took their seats on a bench beside the platform. The priest blew the ram's horn in a series of sharp bleats while Judge Ohad rode out through the gate on a dark horse, carrying the flag of Simeon on a short pole. He glanced at Deborah from under the low edge of his headdress. Sallan rode behind him, followed by the soldiers who had taken Deborah to jail the night before, tossing her on the floor like a sack of trash.

Sallan saw her and rode over, turning his horse to line up with Rogez. "It's good to see you in good health."

"Not thanks to you."

He chuckled. "I'm due some gratitude for helping you transform from the ignorant and anxious girl you were in Emanuel into a one capable of what it took to free yourself and gain such importance in a strange city."

She had to admit that the innocent girl she had been on the day of Tamar's stoning would not have managed to defeat the two men at the jail, outsmart the guard, and regain her freedom as an honored guest in this city.

"I'm grateful for everything you've taught me," she said. "None of it, though, gives you the right to betray me."

"Are you upset about the treaty?"

"And the marriage permission."

The soldiers helped the judge dismount and took the flagpole. He climbed up to the platform unaided. The crowd clapped.

Sallan made his horse step closer to Rogez. "I made it all up," he whispered. "King Esau would never enter a treaty with these savages, or give his sister to one of them."

Deborah turned to him. "What?"

"Did I have a choice? They were about to kill you."

"But you carried a parchment with you."

"Don't you know me already?" He smirked. "I play the long game."

"Life is not a game."

"To the contrary. Life is a game of prediction in which the winner prepares for every possibility with an effective countermove."

"You wrote a fake treaty?"

"I had a feeling that we might need it and, sure enough, we did."

"But if this is your doing, what's the king's plan?"

"Don't worry about that. I already sent one of the soldiers back to inform the general of our impressive progress."

"And the other three?"

"They set up camp with my boy-servants." He gestured towards at area where several merchant caravans were camped. "I'll send another messenger when we find out where the judge's son is hiding."

Deborah peered into his gray eyes, but found neither a glint of trickery, nor a sparkle of sincerity, leaving her in doubt.

On the platform, she expected to see the effigy of Mott, the Canaanite God of Death, but unlike Judge Zifron of Emanuel, Judge Ohad did not bring Mott or any other false god. She wondered if he had replaced the effigies she had smashed in his bedroom that morning.

"I'll never betray you," Sallan said. "It would be like betraying myself."

"Why did you say nothing when the judge announced my forthcoming execution last night? And why did you let them throw me in jail?"

"I was going to bargain for your life in the morning, but you surprised me again, setting yourself free against all odds." He chuckled. "How in Qoz's name did you manage it? Wait, let me guess. Yahweh saved you, right?"

Judge Ohad raised his hand. "Bring forth the accused."

A mounted soldier rode out of the gate, pulling a rope. At the other end of the rope was a young man with bound wrists and a bloodstained cloth over his eyes. He walked barefoot, and every time he tripped, he giggled.

Deborah let out an involuntary groan, and Yael looked at her, but said nothing.

The soldier dismounted and tied the end of the rope to the elders' bench. The giggler turned left and right, mumbling incoherently, and tried to walk away until the rope ran out, making him fall.

The crowd laughed.

Judge Ohad raised his hand for silence. "Who among you wishes to accuse this man?"

"I accuse him," Tsruyah called from the back of the crowd. "This man is named Summin, son of Alav. He was locked up after getting caught copulating with a goat in another man's corral."

The audience burst out laughing again, but the elders looked down, embarrassed.

"The accusation was made," Judge Ohad said. "Now, let us hear the law."

The priest pulled a scroll from under his white robe. "This is the law that God gave to Moses on Mount Sinai." He unrolled the parchment and read from it. "And a man who copulates with livestock, both he and the animal shall be put to death."

"Death it is." The judge said. "In what manner?"

"The method of execution is not specified," the priest said. "The previous entry in the Holy Scriptures, which refers to the sin of a man copulating with his wife's mother, decrees that both of them shall be burned at the stake. Copulating with livestock is worse."

The judge smirked. "Obviously, you haven't met my mother-in-law."

The crowd roared with laughter.

Even the priest smiled briefly. "Where is the animal?"

A farmer stepped forward with a goat on a string. "Here she is."

"Did you witness the accused copulate with your goat?"

"She cried for help." His voice trembled. "It was heartbreaking."

The crowd hooted, and the giggler looked around, mumbling to himself.

The owner looked around with a wounded expression.

"We've heard the accusations," the judge said. "We learned the law and received the evidence against the accused. Now, the elders shall pronounce his guilt, and I'll declare his punishment." He glanced at the stake.

Deborah couldn't believe it. Were they really going to burn him alive? It was even worse than stoning.

The elders looked at each other, nodding, and one of them declared, "Guilty."

Sallan reached over and put a restraining hand on Deborah's forearm.

She shook off his hand and urged Rogez forward. "Where is the evidence?"

The giggler turned in her direction and yelled, "Neither!"

Judge Ohad gestured dismissively. "You're a guest here, boy, not of our tribe."

Rogez shifted and rocked his big head, and the people nearby moved back.

Deborah patted his neck. "The laws of Yahweh require solid evidence against the accused."

"The accused is an idiot, in case you haven't noticed."

The crowd laughed.

She dismounted Rogez, handed the reins to Yael, and made her way to the platform. "His idiocy is a reason to treat him with compassion."

Summin tried to run away, shouting "Neither! Neither! Neither!"

A soldier came over and hit him with a club, knocking him to the ground.

Judge Ohad turned to the priest. "What says the law?"

The priest contemplated for a long moment. "Punishing an innocent man is worse than letting a guilty one go unpunished."

"Fine," the judge said. "The boy Borah will speak for the idiot's defense."

"Thank you," Deborah said. "First, I'd like to ask the witness a few questions."

"Neither!" Summin raised his head, his bloody bandage facing her. "Neither!"

The soldier raised his club, but Deborah stopped him, knelt beside Summin, and whispered in his ear. "I'm not going to hurt you."

He lurched away. "Neither!"

She pulled the rope to keep him close and repeated more slowly. "No more pain, I promise."

"Neither," he said, shaking his head. "Neither."

"You need to stay quiet so I can help you."

"Be quiet," he said.

"That's it." She patted his shoulder. "Be quiet."

"Be quiet," he repeated.

She addressed the goat owner. "What do you know about Summin?"

"He came to this area with survivors from Kabetzel after the men of Judah captured it last year. I heard that his family was killed while he watched from a hiding place."

Confused, Deborah turned to the judge. "Don't you control Kabetzel?"

"We took it back, and don't worry, we cut down the men of Judah who had killed our people the year before."

The thought of all that blood soaking the ground in that small oasis sickened Deborah, but she forced herself to focus, turning back to the goat owner. "Who told you?"

"His no-good cousin. He's the real sinner."

"Where is that cousin now?"

"Dead," Judge Ohad answered for him. "Last night in the jailhouse, he stuck his nose where it didn't belong."

"Neither," Summin said.

Her face flushed, Deborah struggled to concentrate.

"He deserved to die," the goat owner said. "Copulating with my poor goat."

His plaintive voice made the crowd laugh again, but Deborah saw an opening.

"When you heard your goat cry, did you run out to help her?"

"Of course."

"And who did you see copulating with her?"

"His cousin."

"Not Summin?"

"He did it before his cousin, I'm sure of it."

"Why?"

"The way he was standing there, touching himself, you know where, and giggling." The goat owner was shouting now. "My poor goat was crying, and he was giggling!"

"Be quiet," Summin said. "Be quiet."

People around her were laughing to tears, and Deborah also smiled, because she suddenly saw how to help the man she had blinded.

Once the raucous quieted down, she faced the judge. "The witness didn't actually see the accused committing the crime, only behaving in a manner that fits his feeble mind. Most likely, the accused didn't even understand what his cousin was doing—"

The crowd booed.

"Be quiet," Summin yelled. "Be quiet!"

"The evidence is sufficient," the judge said. "The accused and the goat shall be burned to death."

The goat owner stepped back. "But she didn't do anything."

"Are you challenging the laws of Yahweh?"

"She's the victim."

Laughter erupted again, and people imitated him. "She's the victim! She didn't do anything!"

A soldier came over and reached for the rope, and when the owner resisted, hit him with the club. The owner cried and let go. The soldier led the goat to the stake and tied the end of the string to the pole. The goat began to nibble at the tumbleweed. The soldier returned, untied the rope from the elders' bench, and pulled Summin to the stake.

Deborah approached the platform and beckoned Judge Ohad, who bent forward in his chair.

"Will you pardon him?" She kept her voice low. "He didn't do it, he doesn't understand it, and he's already suffered enough for it."

"His suffering will be over soon."

She took a deep breath, keeping her frustration in check. "To execute one who's innocent is equal to murder."

"I can't disappoint the people," the judge said. "Some of them walked half a day in the hot sun to see him burn. I have to give them what they came for, before I tell them they must stay here to fight."

His deceit was revolting, but his words gave her an idea. "Tell them he'll burn in three days to thank God for the victory over the men of Judah."

Narrowing his eyes, Judge Ohad looked at her for a long moment.

"If you burn him now, they'll have nothing to stay for. They'll run, rather than fight for you. How many soldiers does Tsruyah have here? Twenty?" She waved around. "Can they stop all these people?"

Behind her, there was a sound of fire crackling, and Summin yelled, "Be quiet!"

The crowd cheered.

Deborah turned and saw him on top of the pressed tumbleweeds and twigs, his back to the stake with his arms tied behind it. The goat jumped repeatedly as the fire nipped at its hooves.

"Let him burn," Judge Ohad said. "It'll be over soon."

"Be quiet," Summin cried, stomping his feet at the rising fire. "Be quiet!"

The crowd was laughing and clapping.

Deborah circled the stake to the back, where the fire hadn't reached, climbed on top of the tumbleweeds and twigs, and started to untie the knot by his wrists. He was in full panic now, hopping in place, which caused the knot to tighten and slip from her hands.

"Stand still," she said.

"Neither!" He was panting. "Be quiet!"

The crowd saw what she was trying to do and protested loudly.

"Almost there." She struggled with the knot while smoke burned her eyes. "I'm trying."

Projectiles hit her from all directions, but she continued undoing the knot until it broke free. She pulled him down from the pile of fuel, away from the burning stake. The front of his robe was already on fire. She grabbed the lapels by his neck, tore the robe in half, and stripped him. Behind her, the goat cried in short shrieks reminiscent of a feverish baby.

The pelting continued. Summin stood shaking in his sandals, loincloth, and bloody headband. She led him to the platform, up the steps, and to the front between the priest and Judge Ohad, who had risen from his armchair.

"People of Simeon," she shouted. "Yahweh sent me here—"

Those sitting closer heard her and started shushing the others.

"Yahweh sent me to you—"

As the crowd quieted down, the fire grew, and the goat stopped shrieking.

The silence of the goat made Deborah look around for the owner. She saw him near the elders' bench, his face buried in his hands, his shoulders trembling.

Summin tried to walk away, but Deborah held him firmly by the arm.

"Yahweh is our creator," she declared. "And our protector."

Hundreds of eyes looked back at her. The judge grunted, but did not interfere. The fire engulfed the stake, crackling and hissing.

Summin dropped to his knees and mumbled, "Be quiet."

"People of Simeon," she said. "Let this blameless goat serve as a burnt offering to our God, because on the night after tomorrow, we'll need Him to save us from the sword of Judah."

They all started talking at the same time.

She raised her arms to silence them. "Judah has more men and more weapons."

Again, the crowd erupted with questions and, this time, wails of fear.

"But we're not alone."

They were harder to quell now, and she had to yell.

"God is with us!"

Their tense faces told her they were ready to bolt and run away.

"He sent me here to unite you, all the men and women of Simeon."

She paused, looking around. "Yes, the women also, because the coming battle will require every man and woman of Simeon to stand together and repel the men of Judah."

They listened.

Deborah put her hand on Summin's head. "After our victory, we'll come back here, build a new stake, and make a new offering in gratitude!"

They looked at each other, hesitating.

She pointed at Tsruyah. "This young man leads the judge's soldiers, who will serve as the tip of Simeon's spear against the men of Judah."

Mounted on his horse at the rear of the crowd, Tsruyah raised his club in acknowledgment.

"For the rest of this day," she continued, "those of you who live inside the city shall take in those who live outside, feed them, and give them a place to sleep tonight. Tomorrow morning, we'll meet here again and prepare for victory."

No one moved, their eyes wide and fearful, and she realized they might still choose to run. She turned to the priest and muttered, "Bless them, quick!"

The priest stared back at her, his mouth slightly open, his trembling hands locked on the ram's horn, pressing it to his chest.

"Be quiet," Summin said. "Neither."

Judge Ohad reached over, tapped her shoulder, and whispered, "You bless them, Borah."

With her fingers parted in pairs in the manner of priests, Deborah recited the blessing: "May Yahweh bless you and protect you. May He show you kindness and grace. May He illuminate your path and grant you peace."

The crowd chorused, "Amen!"

Walking in groups, engaged in intense discussions, the people entered Beersheba. Deborah remained on the platform, her heart beating hard. Was this the realization of her father's dream? There was no palm tree for her to sit under, and she was very far from Palm Homestead, yet she had spoken for God, and they listened, believed, and obeyed.

"Impressive," Judge Ohad said. "Now we have to whip this mob into an army capable of killing the men of Judah."

His crude words felt like a slap on her face. Deborah looked away, lest he noticed her disgust.

Tsruyah and his men gathered, their eyes shifting between Deborah and the judge as if they weren't sure who was in charge.

"Judah has many soldiers," she said. "Simeon has shopkeepers and farmers, who will not become soldiers in two days."

"Men fight when they have to," Judge Ohad said.

"A mouse will fight a tiger when there's no way out, but who's likely to win?" She whistled, and Rogez trotted over. Yael followed on the mare, with Sallan behind her. When Rogez came to the platform, Deborah put her boot into the stirrup and hopped onto the saddle. "In a battle with Judah, Simon is the mouse."

"Neither!" Summin stood up, his loincloth came undone, and he grabbed it before it fell. "Neither!"

Tsruyah and his men laughed.

"Listen to me, Summin," Deborah said. "My friends will take you to get dressed and put medicine on your eyes. Do you understand?"

He nodded.

Sallan and Yael dismounted, took the steps up to the platform, and led Summin away with comforting words, while he turned his head to look blindly over his shoulder and kept saying, "Neither? Neither? Neither?"

The judge watched them go. "Why does he keep saying it?"

"The idiot thinks it's Borah's name," Tsruyah said. "Neither."

The soldiers sniggered, but Judge Ohad looked at her thoughtfully.

"About Judah," she said. "You've fought many battles. How do you expect them to attack?"

"From the east at sunset," Tsruyah said, drawing a sharp glance from the judge, who turned and gazed into the eastern horizon in contemplation.

They waited.

"Here's what Goor-Aryeh will do." Judge Ohad pointed north. "He'll march his army down from Ziklag and set up camp near the Spice Route, between Kabetzel and Beersheba. He'll send a small force ahead to kill our roadside watchers. Long before dawn, he'll start going west towards us on the Spice Route, timing it to get near here before the sun clears the mountains. At sunrise, he'll attack at full speed while the sun blinds our sleepy guards. The bloodthirsty men of Judah will storm the gate and get over the walls and pounce on us while we're still rubbing our sleepy eyes."

"They spoke of attacking at night," Deborah said.

"No one attacks a city at night."

"Why?"

"A large army is unruly at night." He waved at the open view from the gate eastward, where the rocky desert was cut by shallow crevices, swollen by mounds of sand, and dotted with thorn bushes and tumbleweeds. "Look at this land."

"They'll trip and fall," Tsruyah said. "They might spear themselves or slash their fellow soldiers in the dark, or even get lost in the desert before finding an enemy."

"Or run away," Judge Ohad said.

Deborah considered their arguments. "What if he gives them torches?"

The judge shook his head.

"Why not?"

"Three reasons," Tsruyah said. "One, if they carry burning torches, our guards would see them from a distance and have enough time to organize a strong defense. Two, if they carry only one or two torches and stop nearby to light up all the other torches and distribute them to the forces, our guards would still have enough time to sound the alarm. And three, even if they manage to get here, they would have to fight with one hand while holding a torch with the other."

Deborah shut her eyes and imagined a visit from the eagle. What would she say?

Instead of the eagle, however, Sallan's words came to her mind. "Strategy is what men of power and wealth use for self-preservation. When a situation comes up, they look at all the facts, figure out what they can use to their advantage, and come up with solutions that promote three things: their safety, their fortune, and their power."

Opening her eyes, she said, "We need to look at all the facts."

"Facts?" The judge seemed confused. "What facts?"

"The facts Judge Goor-Aryeh had considered before making his plans. Only then can we guess what he'll do." She turned Rogez around. "Let's take another ride around the city."

18

Judge Ohad and Tsruyah followed Deborah to the gorge, where she turned right and rode along the western edge of Beersheba all the way up to the intersection of the three creeks. She let Rogez find his footing as he climbed down into the dry Hebron Creek, crossed it, and went up the opposite side. From there, she continued further north along the dry gorge of the Betarim Creek to the point where she had stopped at in the morning.

The others caught up with her.

"I'm wondering," she said. "How could Goor-Aryeh use this gorge to his advantage at night?"

The judge scratched his head and winced in pain, giving her an angry look.

"The gorge can lead them in," Tsruyah said. "Even with a small moon, the stars would be enough to keep the men between the banks."

"It would fit Judah," the judge said. "Sneaking in like rats in the dark."

Deborah dismounted Rogez, pulled the spear from the saddle attachment, and used it to draw a circle in the sand. "That's Beersheba. Ziklag is up north." She marked it, too, and drew a line between them. "Betarim Creek comes down to Beersheba and meets the Hebron Creek." She added a horizontal line just above Beersheba, going east. "Together, they become the Beersheba Creek, which goes down along the western edge of the city to the south." She ran a line to show it, as well, and looked up at Tsruyah and the judge. "If you were in Goor-Aryeh's boots, with plenty of soldiers and a determination to attack Beersheba in the middle of the night, wouldn't you use all three gorges to approach in stealth?"

"No," the judge said. "I'd wait for morning."

"Indulge me," Deborah said.

"Listen, boy, you'll understand if you ever dare to walk on a dark night, far from any town or farm, with no lights to guide you."

"I have dared," she said. "And I was alone. Goor-Aryeh will have an army."

Judge Ohad tugged at his beard, while Tsruyah sheltered his eyes and gazed up the Betarim Creek in the direction of Ziklag, two days away, then back over his shoulder at Beersheba's crumbling walls.

Getting back in the saddle, Deborah urged Rogez down the steep bank into the dry creek and back towards the city. The two men followed her. The creek bed was rocky and rough, with patches of sand and pieces of wood brought down by flash floods. The horses picked their steps carefully.

Back at the intersection of the creeks, Deborah stopped. "He'll divide his army into three: one column will march down the Betarim Creek, a second column will come in from the east through the Hebron Creek, and a third column will circle around the west and come up from the south through the Beersheba Creek."

"Coordinate three separate forces in the dark?" Judge Ohad sneered. "Even the arrogant Goor-Aryeh won't try such a folly."

"He will, because it's the best way to attack Beersheba, and because you're not expecting it." She looked at the city. "How will you defend against such an attack?"

"Like any other attack," Tsruyah said. "We need hundreds of armed men ready to kill the attackers. Whoever is still alive at the end is the victor."

In Deborah's mind, the streets of Beersheba ran with blood, bodies strewn everywhere, a handful of victors walking about, covered in gore from the killing. She felt sick. Why had Yahweh involved her in this terrible situation, which was certain to end up in a spectacle of violence, carnage, and death?

Back at Judge Ohad's house, she was shown to a clean room on the second floor. A servant brought in a bowl of water, as well as a jug of wine and a plate with fruit and honey cakes. After taking off the helmet, armor pieces, and boots, she washed, ate, and lay down on a cot of soft linen, which felt cool against her skin.

As soon as Deborah closed her eyes, she was asleep, dreaming of the Betarim Creek. She heard the flapping of the eagle's broad wings as the giant bird soared over the gorge, her wings spread out against the blue sky, casting a shadow as dark as the night. She glided to a soft landing in front of Deborah, her yellow eyes alight like small oil lamps.

"Tame me from here," Deborah said. "I don't care where to, only that it's far away."

"Didn't you come to Beersheba for a reason?"

"Whatever I do, many Hebrew men are going to die."

The eagle watched her, not responding, until the silence became uncomfortable.

"Please," Deborah said. "I want no part in it."

"Isn't it too late?"

"Why?"

"You've already interfered a great deal."

"Me? I've done nothing."

"You illuminated new facts and possibilities to the judge and his loathsome deputy."

"They're both loathsome."

The eagle chuckled, leaning forward to rub her white head against Deborah's shoulder in a gesture of familiarity.

"Do you think I was right about Judah's likely plan?"

"The facts support it," the eagle said. "Now you need to figure out the best strategy of defense."

"How?"

"Consider all the facts – the three creeks leading to the city, the gaps in the walls, and the number of soldiers available to defend against Judah."

"These facts point to a bloody disaster. Nothing I can do."

"Running away is not an honorable strategy," the eagle said. "Do you remember discussing fear with the Moabite boy, the one who gave you flowers at the gates of Shiloh?"

"Zariz." Deborah smiled. "He was delightful."

"What did he say about fear?"

"Fear is good if it makes you careful and watchful, but it's bad if it turns you into a coward who runs from hard duties and fails to pursue good opportunities."

"And what did you ask him?"

"How could I tell the difference between situations in which duty requires staying and situations in which opportunity requires pursuing?"

The eagle joined Deborah as they quoted Zariz's response together: "Listen to your fear, but don't let it control you."

They laughed, and the eagle said, "Fear, duty, and opportunity are often intertwined."

Deborah thought about it. "It's true. I fear failing in my duty to prevent a bloodbath, but I have an opportunity to defend Beersheba and earn Judge Ohad's gratitude so that he would release the princess and help me find Barac."

"Do you want to marry that boy?"

Blushing, Deborah nodded.

"Why? For his friendship, courage, and good looks? Or because you need a husband to facilitate inheriting Palm Homestead?"

"All of it."

The eagle sighed. "The prospect of marriage presents a whole new set of fears, duties, and opportunities, which you must weigh carefully to make sure you are acting based on correct assumptions, or your brief moment of happiness would turn into lifelong misery."

Eager to change the subject, Deborah said, "How can I prevent a bloodshed? Most of the people of Simeon are farmers, merchants, and artisans, not soldiers."

"Men and women can defend a city in many ways beside fighting. What else did you see at the trial?"

"Injustice."

"That's not unusual." The yellow glow in the eagle's eyes dimmed. "Unfortunately, laws are to justice as logs are to fire – helpful either to build it up, or to smother it down."

"They almost executed a blind man, and they might still burn him after the battle, if the city survives."

"He recognized your voice despite all the noise around."

"And almost exposed me as a girl."

"Yahweh gives blind people the gift of exceptional hearing."

"I think the judge suspects something."

"An experienced judge can see a lie behind an innocent face, hear a lie from under a slick tongue, and sense a lie beneath a thick disguise."

"He sent a goat to burn at the stake. What's the point of punishing a goat?"

"It's not about the goat. It's about making people nervous."

"How?"

"Fire frightens men because it is a living force that can spread and kill by itself."

"I used fire this morning to gain entry into the judge's house."

"That was clever." The eagle clapped her wings, creating a cool breeze on Deborah's hot face. "What gave you the idea?"

"It was available." She took a deep breath, exhaling slowly. "A lot of tumbleweeds around here."

"That's a useful fact to consider."

Deborah's eyelids felt heavy. "Tumbleweeds?"

"Indeed. And what else is in abundance around here?"

"Rocks." Deborah's eyes closed. "Rocks and tumbleweeds everywhere."

"And many men and women, right?"

"Yes," she mumbled. "I'm so tired."

"Sweet dreams," the eagle said, and her wings fluttered, generating a final gust of wind.

19

The noise in the courtyard woke Deborah up. She went to the window. Burning torches lit up the courtyard below, where a large group of men sat around a long table, chatting and laughing. The table was loaded with food and drinks. At one end, Judge Ohad lounged in an armchair, and at the other end was Sallan, who noticed her and beckoned.

Deborah washed, put on her armor, boots, and helmet, strapped on her sword, and tied the sling around her hips. She applied the stubble paste and went downstairs.

Judge Ohad pointed at a vacant chair to his right, across the table from Tsruyah.

She recognized the priest and some of the elders from the trial. The other guests had the appearance of well-to-do merchants. Everyone cheered her arrival with raised goblets and greetings that sounded too jolly for the occasion. The reason became apparent when they all emptied their goblets and held them out for refilling by the servants. Her goblet was also filled, and she brought it to her lips, but paused at the sharp odor that came from it.

The judge pointed at Sallan. "The great Elixirist of Edom improved our wine with a magical elixir that will make you happy."

"And smart," Sallan said, emptying his goblet. "The more you drink, the smarter you become."

"And who needs it most?" Tsruyah slammed his goblet on the table. "Neither!"

Everyone laughed.

"Drink, boy." The judge reached over and tilted Deborah's goblet, forcing the wine into her mouth until it was finished. "That's better."

The men around the table watched her reaction.

She burped.

They roared.

The courtyard began to spin around Deborah, slow at first, then faster, and faster. She shut her eyes, and a black carpet with tiny stars in various colors moved across her field of vision. She grabbed the table.

"He's knocked out," Tsruyah yelled. "We lost Neither!"

She opened her eyes, relieved that the courtyard was spinning more slowly. "Why are you yelling?"

Her question made everyone holler.

"Tell us, boy," Tsruyah yelled. "Has your mighty Yahweh whispered something new in your ear?"

A servant refilled her goblet. Deborah held it up, leaned forward over the table, and emptied it in Tsruyah's grinning face.

The wine dripped down his dark beard while his grin froze in place like a wooden mask.

Everyone became silent.

Tsruyah wiped his face on his sleeve and rose slowly to his feet, his hand reaching for his club, which leaned against the table by his side.

The men seated near him moved away, as did those near Deborah.

At the head of the table between them, the judge lounged back, his hands folded on his gut. "That's it," he said to Deborah with a smirk. "You've gone too far, boy."

Tsruyah gripped the end of his club. He was able and strong, but she noticed that he swayed on his feet. Without lowering her eyes under his glare, she surreptitiously undid the knot on her sling and slipped it off her hips.

Tsruyah raised his club.

"Young man," Sallan called from the opposite end of the table. "I wouldn't recommend it."

Tsruyah didn't acknowledge him.

Pressing with her legs, Deborah pushed her chair slowly back from the table. The middle finger of her right hand slipped into the loop of the sling, and she let the tab end drop down. The sling dangled by the side of her chair, unnoticed by anyone, the tab-end coiled on the ground.

Without breaking eye contact with her, Tsruyah asked, "Judge?"

Judge Ohad sneered. "The boy brought it on himself."

"Don't do it." Sallan shook a finger. "It'll end badly."

The grin on Tsruyah's face returned to life. He leaned slightly forward, poised to swing the club above the table and land it on her head.

With the speed of a striking snake, Deborah raised her right hand, spun the long strap of the sling in a hissing circle and, leaning forward, looped it around Tsruyah's club. His eyes followed the lashing sling in bewilderment, and before he had time to comprehend what she was doing, Deborah yanked hard on the sling, snatching the club out of his grip. She swiveled the club in the air above her head and brought it back at high speed, slamming the side of Tsruyah's head with a hollow thud.

His eyes rolled back in his head, and he collapsed. The sling unspooled from the club, which dropped to the floor.

"I warned him," Sallan said. "Didn't I?"

A group of soldiers rushed over. Two knelt by Tsruyah, the others approached Deborah, gripping their clubs.

Sallan raised his goblet. "Let's drink."

Tsruyah's men looked at Judge Ohad for permission to attack Deborah. His expression was a mix of shock and dismay. He adjusted his headdress and patted it on the side of his head, where she had clubbed him with the spear in the morning. He leaned sideways to look down at Tsruyah, lying on the ground by the table.

"To our treaty!" Sallan raised his goblet even higher. "To friendship and mutual defense!"

The judge peered at Deborah, tugging at his beard for a long moment.

A storm was roaring inside her, but she kept a lid on it, maintaining eye contact with him, remembering Sallan's advice about standing proud and exuding confidence.

With a grunt, Judge Ohad reached for his goblet and raised it.

The soldiers retreated, staring at Deborah, who retied the sling around her hips with an air of indifference.

"Splendid," Sallan said. "To life!"

While the soldiers carried Tsruyah away, the guests emptied their cups, thanked the judge, and departed with barely concealed rush. Deborah, however, filled a plate with food and ate without haste. The two men, one at each end of the table, sipped wine quietly, watching her. When she pushed her plate away, Sallan chuckled and stood up.

"May I suggest," he said, "a get-well visit to the poor young man?"

Judge Ohad raised his eyebrows, shrugged, and gestured for them to follow.

The soldiers slept in a smoke-filled room near the gate to the street. Several oil lamps hung from the walls. Lines of cots filled the room, about half of them occupied by young men sleeping or smoking pipes. Deborah wondered whether Barac had spent time in this room.

Tsruyah was lying on a cot in the corner, a strip of wet cloth on his forehead. When he saw them, he pulled off the cloth, sat up, and covered his tangled hair with a headdress.

Sallan smiled. "How are you, young man?"

Tsruyah grunted and glanced at the other soldiers.

"This isn't the time for quarrel," Judge said. "Make peace with one another."

A few of the soldiers got up from their cots and started to move closer.

Deborah gripped the hilt of her sword.

"I may be able to assist," Sallan said. "Having survived multiple armed confrontations and violent skirmishes with Borah, I think his actions in this particular instance were not about a personal grievance."

Tsruyah and the judge looked at him.

"He's right," Deborah said. "I threw the wine in your face for insulting God."

Pointing a finger at her, Tsruyah said, "I asked you a question, that was all."

Imitating his tone, she quoted his question word for word: "Tell us, boy. Has your mighty Yahweh whispered something new in your ear?"

The judge chuckled. "Fair enough."

Sallan put a hand on Tsruyah's shoulder and the other hand on Deborah's shoulder. "The two of you ought to submit now to the wisdom of Hebrew law. Judge?"

Deborah noticed Tsruyah glancing in disgust at Sallan's hand, which was missing the little finger.

Judge Ohad shut his eyes as he quoted. "He who admits his sin and corrects his ways shall be forgiven."

Tsruyah snorted. "If my question insulted Yahweh, I ask for His forgiveness."

"And I pray He grants it," Deborah said. "And that He heals your injury."

"Excellent." Sallan patted their shoulders. "Let us now leave all our differences behind and join forces to save this ancient city of your forefathers."

"Agreed," Judge Ohad said. "We'll talk in the morning."

As Deborah and Sallan headed to the door, the judge stayed behind with Tsruyah.

Outside, the courtyard was empty, the fire pit reduced to smoky embers. A baby cried in one of the rooms.

"Crafty old judge." Sallan glanced back at the door to the soldiers' quarters. "I wonder what he's telling Tsruyah."

She made her voice hoarse like the judge's. "We need Borah to help us beat Judah, but afterwards, that strange boy is yours to kill—"

"—any bloody way you want," Sallan continued the sentence, brandishing his four-fingered hand. "As long as that crippled Edomite sorcerer doesn't suspect it."

They laughed and, for the first time since leaving Bozra, she felt their former kinship rekindled. Sallan rested his arm around her shoulder, which was awkward as she had grown taller recently, and limped beside her across the courtyard to the stairwell.

For safety reasons, Deborah relocated to the room Sallan shared with his boy-servants, Yael, and Summin, who were already asleep. She propped her spear against the door to make it harder to open from the outside. As she settled down on her cot, Yael woke up.

"How is he?" Deborah pointed at Summin.

"Better." Yael smiled. "Sallan dressed the wounds and gave him something to sleep."

"Did you visit your parents?"

The smile faded. "They're preparing to leave Beersheba."

"Why?"

"Our clan is banished from the land of Judah, and my father is certain Simeon will lose the battle."

"Where will they go?"

The girl's eyes filled with tears. "Some members of our clan are allowed to live in the territory of Javin, King of Canaan, near Hazor of the Galilee."

"Do you want to go with your parents?"

"No."

"If you change your mind later on, I'll help you find them."
Turning away on her cot, Yael covered her head with the blanket.

20

Deborah did not wake up until sunrise brightened the window. She got dressed quickly and left with Sallan to meet Judge Ohad.

Sallan stopped in the hallway and whispered, "What is your goal today?"

His question was odd, but she answered it anyway. "Find a way to defend Beersheba and prevent bloodshed."

"Our bloodshed." He knuckled her chest armor. "Your goal today should be to keep us alive."

"Us and everyone else."

"Sparing your enemy's life is a favor he's unlikely to reciprocate if given the chance."

"Only the judge and Tsruyah are my enemies. All the others are my fellow Hebrew people, and my duty is to find a way to repel the attack without bloodshed."

"Then make sure the people know that you saved them, not the judge and his henchman."

"God will save them, not me."

He groaned, took her in his arms, and embraced her as a loving father would a precocious child. "Your God is lucky to have you."

They went down to the courtyard and were directed to the rear of the house, where a terrace overlooked the rest of the city. A table was set for four, and Judge Ohad was already there, smoking his pipe while examining a parchment.

He rolled it up and added it to a bundle of parchments in a sack. "Nobody wants to pay their taxes, but they're generous with excuses, regrets, and denials. How does your king keep his people straight?"

Sallan sat down. "Our king doesn't rely on tax revenues to sustain the kingdom."

"What, then?"

"Copper mines."

"I heard about it. Some of the Edomite merchants travelling through Beersheba complained of losing the copper mines their families had owned for centuries. Now they plow the trade routes with plenty of time to contemplate that grave injustice."

"A wise leader puts the needs of the many before the needs of the few."

Judge Ohad sneered. "If I tried to confiscate people's property, they would replace me with a new judge before sunset."

"Tell them God made you king and, therefore, owner of all the land of Simeon."

"God banned kings," Deborah said, quoting, "Do not anoint a king over yourselves, for I am your king, the creator of the world."

"He's right," Sallan said. "The Hebrew tribes would never agree to be ruled by a king who's not of their particular tribe."

Tsruyah appeared, his robe and headdress clean, his beard wet and brushed, and his eyes bloodshot. He put his club on the table, sat down, and plucked a grape from a bunch in a bowl, popping it into his mouth.

"Good morning," Judge Ohad said. "Are you feeling better?"

Tsruyah chewed the grape slowly and swallowed. "Our new blacksmith disappeared, right after Borah had visited him."

"Are you surprised he fled?" She took a piece of cheese and nibbled at it. "You gave him an impossible task and threatened to kill him if he failed. I'm surprised the other blacksmiths and carpenters haven't bolted."

"Two of them have," he said. "And one claims a sudden illness, but I'm going to drag him out of bed and whip him by the gate to make an example."

"An example of what? Injustice? Brutality?"

"Borah is right," the judge said. "Time is short. We need a plan to defend the city from Judah."

Popping in another grape, Tsruyah said, "Kill them, or be killed. That's the plan."

"No killing," Deborah said. "God wants us to save Beersheba without any bloodshed."

"That's impossible," Judge Ohad said. "Either we survive, or Judah. Who do you stand with? Us or them?"

"Neither." Tsruyah spat a pit over the terrace railing, put two fingers in his mouth, and whistled.

A few whistles came in response, followed by voices of men yelling. The streets below filled with people heading downhill to the gate.

"I'll get them ready." Tsruyah got up. "If we have enough bodies to throw at the enemy, we'll win the battle by the numbers."

"That's not a plan," Deborah said. "It's a massacre. They're farmers and tradesmen. They don't know how to fight."

Tsruyah collected his sword and club. "A farmer can fight with a pruning hook, a sickle, or a scythe, and a tradesman with his hammer or chisel."

"Wait." Judge Ohad sat down. "We should hear what Borah has in mind."

Tsruyah shrugged.

Deborah knew she had to come up with something. "Assuming the men of Judah will split into three columns and approach Beersheba from three directions inside the gorges—"

"We'll ambush them," Tsruyah said. "Slash and kill."

"Goor-Aryeh will attack from three directions, each with a force of six hundred, maybe seven hundred soldiers. We have a total of thirty soldiers and a bunch of untrained farmers and city people. See the problem?"

Judge Ohad cleared his throat. "Has God told you what to do?"

"To look at all the facts," she said. "And then, devise a plan."

"Any plan is better than no plan." Tsruyah headed for the connecting door to the house. "We'll fight the men of Judah until the better of us is left standing."

When he was gone, Judge Ohad said, "The men of Judah will cut us down like weeds."

Sallan got up. "Let's go down to the gate before Tsruyah can announce his foolish plan."

21

The crowd parted, giving the three horses a path to the platform. The elders were already sitting at their bench as if a trial was about to begin, and Tsruyah stood at the foot of the platform, conferring with his soldiers. The priest sat on the platform steps, his face in his hands.

Judge Ohad dismounted and took the steps to the platform, startling the priest, who got up quickly. The ram's horn, which rested in his lap, fell down the steps. The priest yelped and hurried to pick it up and kiss it.

Sallan whispered to Deborah, "Go up there and take over."

She hesitated.

He nudged her. "You must speak to the people. Now!"

Mounting the platform, she could see that the crowd was smaller than the previous day. The poor residents of Beersheba had not come out from their tents and shacks. When she looked to the right, she saw some of them peeking over the wall from inside the city.

The crowd became completely quiet.

Deborah glanced at the judge, who nodded.

"Men and women of Simeon," she said. "Yahweh sent me to Beersheba to prevent bloodshed among His children. I promised you to meet here this morning to prepare for Judah's attack with the help our mighty God, creator of the world—"

A horn blew into her ear, causing her to dodge sideways into Judge Ohad, who began to fall, but was caught by Tsruyah. The priest came after her, blowing the long, serpentine horn again, his face red, his eyes bulging. He paused to inhale and blew again. The sound was deafening, and Deborah felt a puff of warm air with flecks of spittle from the open end of the horn. She grabbed the horn and ripped it out of his hands.

The priest's mouth remained curled for a moment, before he inhaled deeply and shouted, "Do not raise Yahweh's name in vain!"

Deborah recognized the third of the Ten Commandments, but could not understand what had angered him. Was it her claim that Yahweh had sent her here?

Turning to face the crowd, the priest pointed at her and shouted again, "Do not raise Yahweh's name in vain!"

The people stood motionless, their faces grim.

The priest stepped to the edge of the platform, his finger still pointing sideways at her, his shrill voice cutting through the silent air. "Do not raise Yahweh's name in vain!"

Deborah raised the ram's horn, put her lips to the narrow opening, which was moist from his spit, aimed it at his ear, and blew as hard as she could.

The noise cut him off in the middle of another repetition of the commandment. His hand shot to his ear while he jumped away, lost his balance, and fell off the platform.

The crowd roared in laughter.

The priest got up and climbed back onto the platform, screaming in rage.

Tsruyah signaled to his soldiers, who ran up to the platform, grabbed the priest, and led him to the steps. Halfway there, he slipped out of their hold and ran back, shouting at Deborah.

"Do not raise Yahweh's name in vain! Do not raise—"

Tsruyah stepped over and delivered a quick strike with the side of his hand at the front of the priest's neck under his beard. The strike silenced the priest mid-sentence. He tried to breathe, but couldn't. His eyes widened in terror as the soldiers carried him away.

Deborah stepped to the edge the platform. "The poor man," she said with a forced smile. "He must be confused. How could we not invoke Yahweh's name at a time like this?"

Her question didn't elicit any response from the people.

"When I travelled to the Holy Temple in Shiloh, a wise priest told me something to remember."

The mention of the Holy Temple, which the tribesman of Simeon could only dream of visiting, brought curiosity to their faces.

"Faith frequently falters under fear." She paused, her gaze travelling over the crowd, and repeated it. "Faith frequently falters under fear."

Some of the people nodded, others sighed.

"Isn't it true?" She pressed a hand to her chest. "When we're afraid, our confidence in God falters – at the very time when we need it most. I think that's what happened to the poor priest, don't you?"

A few yelled, "Yes!"

"Let us put our trust in God as we prepare to defend this ancient city and honor our forefathers Abraham and Isaac for the abundant wells they bequeathed us."

Many of the men cheered, and the women smiled. On the platform beside Deborah, Judge Ohad clapped, but Tsruyah watched her coldly.

The crowd quieted down.

"We have several advantages," she said. "First, we know the area well, whereas the men of Judah do not."

Murmurs of agreement passed through the crowd.

"Second, we know that the men of Judah will come at night in three columns. From the east, the Hebron Creek." She pointed while speaking. "From the north, the Betarim Creek. And from the south, the Beersheba Creek."

People looked at each other nervously.

"Our third advantage is that we are many men and women, ready to defend Beersheba. Yes, I include women, because our victory over Judah will not require wielding a sword, hurling a spear, or slugging a club."

Tsruyah sneered. "Destroy the men of Judah without weapons?"

"We don't need to destroy them. We only need to scare them away." She quoted something Zariz had told her. "A snake reserves its venom for things it can eat."

Judge Ohad turned to her. "A snake?"

Deborah saw Sallan below the platform, standing among the people, watching her. He clenched a fist and beat it to his chest, reminding her of his advice not to show doubts, but to stand proud and exude confidence.

"Let me recount our advantages," she said. "First, we know our land better. Second, we know their plans. Third, we are more numerous. And the fourth, the greatest advantage we have, is our access to unlimited quantities of stones, tumbleweeds, and twigs." She raised a hand to stop any interruptions. "How can we use those things?"

"Fire," a man yelled.

"That's right," she said. "Tumbleweeds and twigs can fuel fires."

"We can throw stones," a woman said, her voice hesitant, glancing up at a man beside her.

"Imagine that," he said, smiling at her. "A shower of stones on their cursed heads."

"Exactly," Deborah said. "A hundred people can throw three hundred stones in the time it takes me to finish this sentence, and do it again and again, thousands of stones in a short time. Imagine the men of Judah walking for hours in the dark under a sliver of a moon, tripping on boulders, sloshing through sand, when suddenly, it's raining stones!" She paused, lifting both arms, looking up at the sky. "Stones coming down on their heads as if God had unleashed His divine fury at their sinful attack, determined to quash them like flies!" Shielding her head with her arms, Deborah cowered under the imaginary attack.

People imitated her, pantomiming throwing stones, getting hit, and bending under a barrage.

"And then," she continued, "while the stones rain down, balls of fire start to ignite along the steep banks and roll down into the gorges, flames raging, an inferno closing in, about to burn each and every one of them unless they turn and flee back the way they came, never to attack the tribe of Simeon again!"

Some in the crowd resumed cheering, but quieted down as Tsruyah stepped forward.

"It won't work," he said. "They'll notice us ahead of time."

"They won't," she said.

The people strained to hear.

"Do you expect the men of Judah to be blind and deaf?"

"We'll hide quietly until the right moment."

"How could hundreds of people sit quietly along a gorge for half the night?" Tsruyah gestured at Deborah. "This boy speaks of God, of sins, and of punishment. His tongue is slick, but he knows nothing of fighting battles. I do, and the only way to win tomorrow night is for each of you to grab the sharpest blade you own, a hammer, or a plank of wood, if that's all you have, and spend every moment between now and tomorrow night learning how to kill."

"Or be killed," Deborah said. "I saw the men of Judah three nights ago. Each one of them has a good sword and knows how to use it."

"But we're many," Tsruyah said. "We can overwhelm them, three, four, or five to one."

"Five to one?" She paused for effect. "Five of Simeon to one of Judah will die."

He waved a fist. "Whatever it takes!"

Deborah turned to him. "How many of us will die tomorrow? A thousand?"

"It doesn't matter," he shouted.

"Two thousand?"

"So what? It's a price worth paying!"

His words were left hanging over the silent crowd. The judge sighed, and Tsruyah glared at Deborah, realizing she had goaded him into revealing his disdain for their lives.

"No," she said. "There's no need for such bloodshed."

He pointed his club at her. "We heard enough from you, boy!"

Deborah grasped the end of his club. "Imagine this is one of the gorges. Let me show you why no one has to die tomorrow night."

He tried to pull the club free, but she held on, keeping it horizontal between them.

The crowd watched, mesmerized.

"Listen to this complete silence," she said. "That's the silence we'll use tomorrow night to surprise the men of Judah."

People looked at each other, but made no sound.

"Today and tomorrow," she continued, "we'll collect thousands of stones and set up mounds along both sides of each gorge some distance from the city, and continuing for a thousand steps." She used the horizontal club to demonstrate where the stones would go. "We'll also collect many rolls of tumbleweed and secure them against the wind next to the mounds of stones. We'll light small oil lamps and shelter them behind the piles of stones. All of you, men and women of Beersheba and the farmers who came yesterday to watch the trial, will work together to set up everything before sunset tomorrow night. To keep order, we will use the method that Moses himself used."

Deborah couldn't remember exactly what her father had taught her, but the general idea had stuck in her mind.

"Moses led the Hebrews through the exodus from Egypt by dividing them into groups of ten, fifty, a hundred, and so on. We will follow a similar system. You'll choose your leaders from among you – every ten will choose a leader, every ten leaders will choose their leader, and so on. The top three leaders will report to me, Tsruyah, and Judge Ohad for instructions."

No longer pulling on his club, Tsruyah looked at her with a mix of resentment and awe.

"Before sunset tomorrow night," Deborah continued, pointing at the horizontal club, "each group will take its position, spreading evenly along both sides of the creeks by the mounds of stones and piles of tumbleweeds. I'll wait with our blind man, whose hearing is sharp, at a far point up the Betarim Creek, where the main force of Judah will probably arrive. The leaders of the other two forces will find a blind person to assist them. When the men of Judah approach, word will pass down to alert everyone. We'll lie down quietly along the sides above the gorges while the men of Judah come through, oblivious to our presence. We'll wait until they're close in in, then rise as one and shower them with thousands of stones while lighting up tumbleweeds and rolling them down the sides into the creeks."

"A stampede," Sallan said from the front of the silent crowd.

Tsruyah looked down at him. "What's that?"

"When I travelled with my father many years ago, we saw a herd of antelopes get spooked in a crevice near the Sea of Reeds. They ran as fast as they could, all of them as one, oblivious to anything ahead, and leapt over a cliff, piling up at the bottom, writhing with broken legs and puncture wounds from their antlers." Sallan sighed. "I still feel ill at the memory."

"That's what we should do." Tsruyah's eyes glinted. "When the men of Judah start running back, we'll block their escape in each creek and slaughter them, except for their leader, Goor-Aryeh. He will burn at the stake right here at the gates of Beersheba!"

Shouts of support sounded from crowd.

Judge Ohad pounded his fist into his hand as if crushing his lifelong enemy.

Deborah waited for the crowd to quiet down and asked, "Are you suggesting that we trap a herd of mighty lions with their backs to the wall?"

"Yes," Tsruyah said. "And fight them to the death."

"To our death," she said.

There was a long silence, and everyone looked at the judge for his decision.

"We cannot beat Judah by force." Judge Ohad's tone was tinged with disappointment. "Borah's plan aims to cause a complete surprise, a total panic, an overwhelming terror that will make the men of Judah forget how strong they are and run away – run without stopping, not only up the creeks, but all the way back to their land. They might return for another attack one day, but by then, my son and his men will be back to defend Beersheba with honor."

22

While Tsruyah brooded, Deborah and the judge watched from the platform as the men and women of Simeon talked and argued in small groups until order began to emerge. Eventually, three men approached the platform and introduced themselves as the top leaders of the groups, each numbering more than a thousand men and women. Deborah picked the youngest among them, whose name was Taanach, and headed to the Betarim Creek, followed by the men and women under Taanach's leadership. The judge took responsibility for the Hebron Creek, and Tsruyah was left with the Beersheba Creek.

Deborah rode up and down the gorge to give instructions. The men and women worked in units of ten, each responsible for a section on either side. They worked hard despite the heat, collecting fist-sized stones from the nearby desert, making piles thirty steps apart along the edge of the creek. As a guideline, Deborah determined that each pile must reach the height of a man's hip and measure three steps across. Several men brought their donkeys from the city and went further into the desert to collect rolls of tumbleweed. In the afternoon, someone brought a camel and two horses, fitted with large baskets to help transport stones from greater distances, as the land nearby had cleared out. Once in a while, Deborah would hear yelling as someone encountered a snake or a scorpion. Taanach collected the dead snakes in a sack for fear of attracting hungry jackals, coyotes, or even the rare tiger or lion.

Shortly before sunset, Deborah rode east to check on the progress at the Hebron Creek, finding an equally diligent effort there under their leader, though Judge Ohad had departed much earlier back to the city. She rode on to the Beersheba Creek, where work had not progressed as well. The group leader's robe was slashed in the back and stained by blood from whipping. Tsruyah and a few of his soldiers were sitting in the shade of a tree, smoking pipes.

Deborah rode up and beckoned Tsruyah.

He blew smoke in her direction and stayed seated.

Pointing at the men and women working along the gorge, she said, "If you whip anyone again, I'll have the judge replace you."

More smoke, and a terse comment that made the others laugh.

She dismounted, untied the sling, found a stone, and slung it, hitting the tree trunk above their heads, causing a shower of dry leaves. They scrambled away, cursing.

Her point made, Deborah mounted Rogez and trotted off at a slow pace, lest they thought she was running away.

Back at the Betarim Creek, with the sun gone, she asked Taanach to summon everyone and have them sit down while twilight turned to darkness, so that they experienced the night and practiced being quiet in the company of others. They cooperated, passing around waterskins and dried figs without exchanging a word. When Deborah was satisfied, Taanach released them for the night.

Back at the house, Deborah went upstairs and knocked on Judge Ohad's door.

"It's me, Borah," she said.

There was shuffling behind the door, and he said, "It's not a good time."

"Tsruyah is abusing the people instead of guiding them."

A woman giggled inside.

"I heard you," the judge said.

"If the men of Judah get through the Beersheba Creek, the city will be lost"

"I'll talk to him. Go away, boy."

Yael prepared food and drink, which they ate in the room. The night was uneventful. At sunrise, Deborah rode out to the desert and practiced with her sling and sword until the people arrived to continue working. She spent the morning between the three creeks, as Judge Ohad and Tsruyah didn't show up. The people worked hard, and by noon, mounds of stones had reached the desired size, rolls of tumbleweed were piled up and secured, and small oil lamps were set up at each interval.

Taanach summoned the whole group at the Betarim Creek. After a light meal of figs and cheese, they conducted a drill. Units of ten people took positions along both sides of the gorge behind the mounds of stones and tumbleweeds. Deborah rode further up to a spot where she would wait with Summin to listen for the attackers. After a short wait, she stepped down into the creek and ran south, warning the people that they should lie flat on the ground in silence, grasping a stone in each hand while the attackers walked through the gorge. When she reached the two groups, one on each side, nearest to the city, she waited for a few moments, cupped her mouth, and imitated the howl of a jackal. The men and women rose up, threw the stones they were holding, and reached for the pile, throwing more stones into the gorge, shouting and cursing at the imaginary men of Judah below.

Sallan, who was observing the drill, beckoned Deborah over. "It's very impressive," he said. "Your plan might work. My only suggestion is to tell them not to yell or curse."

"The yelling helps them," she said. "And it will scare the attackers, don't you think?"

"To the contrary," he said. "Unarmed people throwing stones are of little threat to soldiers, but a barrage of stones coming out of silent darkness would terrify even the bravest man. Imagine if Seesya's ambush at Ein Gedi took place at night."

She shuddered. "We would be dead now."

"I would be dead," he said, chuckling. "You, on the other hand, would've been saved by your God, or your horse."

The memory of Soosie saddened her.

"It was a good lesson," Sallan said. "A well-concealed ambush causes confusion and terror, which the target's wild imagination turns into feverish panic."

She assembled the people again and explained the advantages of throwing the stones in silence.

A man raised his hand. "What if some of them come out of the gorge and attack us?"

Many nodded and voiced similar fears.

"I can't promise you that it won't happen," Deborah said. "A few might try, but they'll have to climb a steep bank while being hit with stones and burning tumbleweeds. The men of Judah are not cowards, but they're not gods, either."

Another man asked, "May we bring knives or tools to use as

weapons?"

"Our goal is to prevent any bloodshed, but bring a weapon to use if necessary."

Her answer satisfied them. She conducted a few more drills to make sure they recognized the jackal's howl and were able to aim at the middle of the gorge and not over to the opposite side, where they would hit their fellow defenders.

While the people went down into the gorge to collect all the stones from the drills, Deborah rode to the other two gorges to conduct similar drills. The absence of the judge and Tsruyah did not diminish the people's enthusiasm, and the system of staggered leadership worked well to pass down instructions and bring up good suggestions.

In the late afternoon, she released everyone to go back into the city for food and rest until sunset.

At Judge Ohad's house, Summin heard Deborah's voice and perked up, turning in her direction. He had slept since the trial, and his eyes no longer bled through the bandage, which Yael had changed every few hours while applying a potion Sallan had mixed.

Deborah held his hand. "Are you feeling pain or discomfort?"

"Neither."

Yael laughed, caressing his head.

"From now on," Deborah said, "I'd like you to call me Borah."

"Borah," he said. "I was bad to Borah. My cousin was also bad to Borah."

"I forgive you," Deborah said. "Do you forgive me?"

He nodded. "Borah saved me from the fire."

She sighed. He wasn't saved yet, but how could she explain that to him?

"Come, Summin." Yael led him by the arm. "We'll ride on my horse. She's a nice horse."

They rode up the Betarim Creek to a spot Deborah had chosen, about three hundred steps north of the last pile of stones. She explained how Summin's acute hearing should give them advance warning when the men of Judah approached. At that time, Deborah would ride down the creek to alert the people, whereas Yael and Summin would go to hide in a small crevice nearby.

"You'll stay here and wait," Deborah said. "Once the ambush is over and the men of Judah run away, I'll come to fetch you."

"Be quiet," Summin said.

"That's right." Yael patted his arm. "We'll be quiet until Borah comes back."

The possibility of failure had preyed on Deborah's mind intermittently, kept at bay only by the intense preparations. What if Goor-Aryeh and his men braved the barrage of stones and the onslaught of burning tumbleweeds, rushed to the sides of the gorges, climbed out, and attacked the men and women of Simeon. She tried to rationalize that no one, not even a brave man, was foolish enough to run into flying rocks and tumbling fires, but Goor-Aryeh was different, with his physical might and his intense confidence in defeating Simeon: "In five days, when the night is darker, we will prevail over our depraved brothers."

Deborah held Yael's hand. "I believe we'll be successful, but if you see Beersheba begin to burn, get Summin and walk away. As long as you don't cross either the Betarim Creek on the left or the Hebron Creek on the right, you'll be traveling north-east. When the sun rises, keep it on your right and ride on. You'll eventually reach the land of Judah, and when you find a homestead or a town, ask for their mercy."

"Mercy?" Yael's voice had an edge of fear. "Why would they show mercy, seeing us alone, a boy and a girl?"

"Borah is neither," Summin said.

They laughed, and it gave Deborah an idea.

"Tell them that you're betrothed to him," she said. "Since he is a Hebrew man, betrothal would make you forbidden to all."

Yael seemed pleased with the idea.

They rode back to the Betarim Creek, making sure Yael remembered the way to the hidden crevice, and returned to the city.

Yael, Summin, Sallan, and the boy-servants took a nap, but Deborah stayed up, unable to silence her worries. What would she do if the ambush failed and a real battle ensued? Would she draw her sword and fight for Simeon? Would she spill Hebrew blood? The answer came to her with surprising simplicity. She had once been racked with guilt over violating the Sixth Commandment—Do not kill!—for stabbing a young soldier to death in Ein Gedi. The eagle, however, lifted that burden off her shoulders, saying, "It's an important prohibition, no doubt about that, but it's not absolute. There's an exception for unavoidable situations. When a person rises to kill you, rise first and kill him." The eagle had explained that any action she took to save herself or her companions from death or from rape would be justified. Tonight, on the other hand, the men of Judah were not coming to kill her. Their attack was merely another link in a long chain of battles over generations of sibling rivalry. She was doing her best to prevent bloodshed, but if her efforts failed, she would not participate in the fighting.

As the evening drew near, people headed downhill. Deborah walked with Judge Ohad, followed by Tsruyah and his men, as well as Yael and Summin. Sallan stayed in the judge's house and promised to care for Rogez until she returned.

On the way down the hill, Deborah saw people lingering at house doors, hugging their children and their elders. Evidently, they shared her doubts about tonight's outcome. Near the gate, on the left, the poor of Beersheba stood outside their tents and shacks, watching the activity.

Outside the gate, she mounted the platform with the judge and waited as the area before them filled up. The crowd divided into three groups, with their leaders standing at the front, each carrying a pole with Simeon's green flag.

The sun touched the hazy horizon.

Deborah held forward her hands, fingers parted in pairs, and recited the priestly blessing: "May Yahweh bless you and protect you. May He show you kindness and grace. May He illuminate your path and grant you peace." Remembering the priest who had blessed the men of Judah in Arad, she added: "May He fortify your hearts and give you victory."

The whole crowd chorused a roaring "Amen!"

As the people left for the three creeks, Judge Ohad said to Deborah, "You did well, boy, but I hope your plan will not be tested."

"No one will be happier than me if the men of Judah don't attack."

The judge beckoned Tsruyah over. The young commander said something to the soldiers, who laughed and stayed put while he came over.

"I'm counting on you." Judge Ohad put an arm around his shoulder. "Beersheba is counting on you, and the whole of Simeon is counting on you."

Tsruyah gestured at Deborah. "On him, not on me. We'll see how it goes. Men die in battles. Boys, too."

Deborah gripped the hilt of her sword. "Are you threatening me?"

"Calm down." Judge Ohad held up his hands to keep them apart. "No one should get hurt tonight, and the treaty with Edom will keep us safe in the future."

"The Edomites?" Tsruyah sneered. "They'll be happy to see Borah dead. He slayed their high priest."

The judge pointed uphill at the direction of his house. "The emissary of the king of Edom warned me a few moments ago that Edom would switch its allegiance to Judah if anything happens to Borah in the land of Simeon. Do you understand?"

"No," Tsruyah said. "It makes no sense. Maybe Borah can explain it?"

"I can," she said. "But I won't."

"It doesn't matter," the judge said. "Send the soldiers to guard the wall around the city and attend to the people assigned to the Beersheba Creek. Don't fool yourself with delusions of battlefield glory. Our only hope tonight is to scare off the men of Judah before they realize how weak we are."

"Don't worry," Tsruyah said. "I won't abandon our people like Mamreh."

Judge Ohad's face flushed. "My son did not abandon us."

Smirking, Tsruyah went back to his soldiers. He sent most of them to guard the walls, except for three who accompanied him to the Beersheba creek.

"My son will come back," the judge said to Deborah. "You'll see."

23

The thin crescent of the moon looked down at her, either a smile or a scowl, Deborah wasn't sure. She assumed that Goor-Aryeh and his men would not arrive early in the night, when people were awake and the guards still alert. The ideal time for an attack on an unsuspecting city, she thought, would be after people went to sleep, but before early risers began milking goats or cows, kneading dough for morning bread, or packing up horses for an early departure on the trade routes.

Deborah left Yael and Summin and walked back down to check on the people. In the dark, her only markers were the small oil lamps, which burned behind makeshift stone shelters. The men and women sat on the ground. Some conversed in whispers, others watched the dark sky, perhaps praying to see another sunrise. The night was getting chilly, and the women took out blankets they had brought with them. The men were comfortable in their long robes and headdresses. Every time Deborah approached a group, everyone got up and surrounded her, eager for her words of faith and encouragement. She reminded them to remain silent while the men of Judah passed by in the creek, and what to do when the time came.

After visiting with the last unit, nearest to the city, Deborah crossed the gorge and began to check on the people along the other side, all the way to the northern-most position. She crossed back and proceeded quietly through the last hundred steps to the watch spot, but had to laugh when she heard Summin say, "Neither, be quiet," and Yael giggling.

The three of them shared bread with cheese, which Yael had brought. Deborah gazed up at the sky, where the thin moon allowed the countless stars to shine brighter. She noted the northern star, which Obadiah of Levi, the priest in Emanuel, had pointed out to her on the night of her escape. That, in turn, reminded her of watching the Dance of the

Maidens in Shiloh on her arrival at the holy city. She whispered about it to Yael.

The girl reflected for a long moment and asked, "Do the maidens sing, too?"

Deborah nodded.

"That's good."

It took Deborah a moment to understand that Yael was thinking of young men like Summin, who were unable to choose a girl by her looks, yet could still participate in the courting through the maidens' singing. Yael's concern touched Deborah's heart. Most girls would not consider marrying a blind man, who couldn't support a family or provide security in times of trouble. Summin was even more limited, having only a child's grasp of the world around him.

Yael leaned closer and whispered in Deborah's ear, "He's kind."

Deborah nodded.

"He'll get better," Yael added, probably responding to Deborah's muted doubts. "And I can be his eyes."

"Be quiet," Summin said.

Yael covered her mouth to muzzle her laughter.

The night wasn't as silent as Deborah had expected. Dogs barked in Beersheba, jackals and coyotes howled in the distance, and an occasional staccato of paws sounded across the rocky landscape nearby.

Summin leaned forward, his face to the north, listening intently, then relaxed, shaking his head.

Yael unfurled a blanket, wrapped it around both of them, and rested her head on his shoulder. Deborah's mind drifted back to her happy childhood at Palm Homestead, playing with Tamar while fire crackled in the stove, mother cooking the evening meal, and father coming with a sack of grapes or figs slung over his shoulder, taking the girls in his arms, hard with muscles and dusty from a day's work, tickling them with his beard, speckled with grains of wheat. She thought of the similarity between her father and Goor-Aryeh, who shared a robust presence, physical strength, and quiet confidence fueled by deep faith in Yahweh and obedience to His laws. She wondered if Goor-Aryeh's wife had children before she died, or did he need a new wife to give him a son to continue his name. He would be a wonderful father, she could tell, as good as her late father.

"Men coming," Summin said, pointing north. "Many men."

Deborah got up. "Go and hide. Now."

Yael collected the blanket and led Summin by the arm into the night.

Deborah slid down into the gorge and ran south, counting her steps. At three hundred, she slowed down to a walk and whispered, "They're coming!"

Someone whispered back, "We're ready."

She continued to whisper to the left and to the right while advancing south. The dark figures of the men and women disappeared as they lay flat on the ground by the piles of stones.

With the last two units warned, she climbed the left bank and dropped to the ground. Beside her, the people stayed perfectly still, making no sound.

They waited.

And waited.

Had Summin been wrong? Deborah regretted rushing him and Yael off before giving him a chance to listen a bit longer.

More time passed.

All she could hear was her own panting. She raised her head and peeked into the gorge, trying to penetrate the darkness.

Nothing.

A woman crawled closer on the ground and whispered, "Is this a drill?"

Deborah shook her head, but the women either didn't see it or didn't believe it. She got on all four and looked for herself. That's when Deborah heard a soft thud of a boot or the butt of a spear against a rock. She pulled the woman down and placed a hand on her mouth.

The men of Judah materialized out of the dark, walking three abreast, not fast, but in a measured pace that would allow a solider to regain his balance if he tripped on a rock or stepped into soft sand. The darkness hid most of the details, but as they got closer, she saw the man in the middle of the leading trio. He was tall and broad-shouldered.

Turning her head away from the gorge, she cupped her mouth and let out her best imitation of a jackal's howl.

Beside her, the men and women raised their arms and hurled the stones they were holding, then picked up more stones and threw them at the gorge below. Two women turned to light the tumbleweeds, which burst into flames as they rolled down the bank. The flames illuminated the men of Judah, who cowered and shielded their heads from the raining stones.

They were not running away!

Deborah's chest tightened.

Up the creek, the other groups hurled stones and rolled down burning tumbleweeds. In the gorge, the burning tumbleweeds illuminated a long column of men in short robes. Her chest tightened until she could barely breathe. The enormity of the power imbalance between the army of Judah and the stone-throwing people of Simeon filled her mind with terrifying images of Judah's men leaping on the banks of the gorge, plowing up to the top, and butchering the men and women she had naively brought here to die.

She wanted to yell, but her breath was too shallow to produce anything more than a whisper. "Run!"

No one heard her as they continued to throw stones and light up tumbleweeds.

The pile of stones grew smaller.

The men of Judah still cowered.

Or did they?

Deborah ran up along the creek, passing the second group, which was as busy as the first throwing stones and lighting tumbleweeds.

Behind the leading few, the men of Judah were running away!

In her excitement, Deborah grabbed a stone and threw it at the remaining soldiers, hitting the man to the right of the tall leader. He lowered both arms that shielded his head and grabbed his elbow in pain. At that moment, another stone flew from the opposite side of the creek and hit his head. He fell back, knocking down another soldier, and both of them scrambled to their feet and ran north at full speed. This injected new enthusiasm into the men and women of Simeon, who now had only four remaining targets to terrorize. Another solider ran away, then another. The man to the left of the tall leader tried to run, but couldn't, his arm gripped by his commander. As he struggled to set himself free, a large stone hit the back of his head and he collapsed, no longer moving.

In the light of the fires, she recognized Goor-Aryeh, his arm raised to protect his head. Tumbleweeds burned around him, and stones hit him from all directions, but none brought him down. He drew his sword and sprinted to the west bank of the creek – the opposite side from her. He didn't slow near the bank but put a leg forward and kicked the wall of dirt, which propelled him upward. In the light of the flames, she saw him rushing at the group of men and women on the other side. They were slow to react, and only one or two managed to throw stones at him before he reached them, slashing with his sword from side to side. Deborah saw blood bursting from a man's arm, while the others spread out, running away, screaming in fear, except for one woman who stayed by the injured man.

Goor-Aryeh turned north and shouted, "Men of Judah!"

The woman tried to stem the blood from the man's injured arm.

Deborah untied the sling from her hips.

"Come back, men of Judah!" Goor-Aryeh noticed the woman and stepped towards her.

Deborah grabbed a stone from the pile and shoved it in the pouch.

He reached the woman.

"Stop!" Deborah began to rotate the stone. "Stop!"

His head turned in her direction, his sword raised. The flames in the creek between them painted his face red, his eyes glowing like embers.

Her arm continued to rotate the sling with the stone in the pouch, cutting through the air with a whistle, and she yelled, "Do not kill!"

Goor-Aryeh's face twisted, and he quoted the Third Commandment. "Do not raise Yahweh's name in vain!"

"I didn't break my vow."

He waved his sword around as if saying, "What's all this, then?"

"I vowed not to disclose what you told me, but I learned everything from your priest and your men."

His head began to turn down to look at the woman, who was sobbing over her fallen man.

Deborah slung the stone across the creek. It hit the side of his head with a glancing blow, and he fell. She jumped down and ran across the gorge.

Shouting drew her attention.

Up the creek, fifty or sixty steps away, three of Goor-Aryeh's soldiers were running down towards her at full gallop. They must have heard his call to return. She drew her sword with both hands, but at that moment, a heavy barrage of stones pelted the men from both sides. One man stumbled, changing direction, and tripped the man to his left. The third man stopped to help them. In an instant, men in long robes jumped into the gorge and rushed at the three men of Judah. She saw the flickers of blades from short knives and curved scythes.

"No," Deborah yelled. "Do not kill!"

Like a swarm of angry bees, the men of Simeon descended on the three soldiers, stabbing and slashing.

Deborah turned away, sheathed her sword, and climbed out of the gorge. She put her ear to Goor-Aryeh's nose. He was breathing. The stone had scraped some skin off his temple, but his bushy hair had protected him from a worse injury.

He groaned and sat up.

Down in the gorge, other men attacked the soldier who had fallen next to Goor-Aryeh and slaughtered him, too.

"Get up," she said.

Goor-Aryeh rubbed his head.

Men of Simeon began to gather around, some with knives and scythes that dripped blood. Their faces flickered with reflections of the flames. They glared at Goor-Aryeh. One of the men raised a scythe.

Deborah blocked him. "Do not kill!"

"He came to kill us," the man said.

The others voiced their support, stepping closer, raising weapons.

"He's no longer a threat," she said.

"But he deserves it," the man said. "Let us kill him, Borah."

"That's right," said the woman on the ground. "He killed my husband."

The one with the scythe tried to go around Deborah. "An eye for an eye!"

Pointing at the gorge, Deborah commanded with a thickened voice, "Go back to your positions, now!"

They hesitated.

"The men of Judah may come back for him." She pointed at Goor-Aryeh. "He's their judge."

That impressed them. It was one thing to kill a common soldier, but a judge? Most of them had never seen a judge other than Ohad, and they all feared him.

"Go back to your stone piles and stay there!" Deborah drew her sword and used it to point. "Now!"

They obeyed her.

She helped the woman up and pushed her towards the city. "Go home to your children. The priest will take care of your husband's body."

When everyone was out of earshot, Goor-Aryeh chuckled.

"Not bad," he said. "Not bad at all – for a girl."

She was too stunned to respond.

"You're making a name for yourself, Deborah."

"Borah," she said. "My name is Borah."

"I know who you are." Groaning as he got up, Goor-Aryeh glanced at his sword, lying nearby on the ground, but didn't reach for it. "Your father was Harutz of Ephraim."

"My name is Borah," she repeated.

"I heard all about you."

"From whom?"

"My soldiers. Many of them came from the north – Hebron, Bethlehem, Jerusalem – where people have been talking about a girl named Deborah, who stood trial for trying to kill the son of Judge Zifron of Ephraim, but won acquittal and caused the whipping of the judge's son for murdering her family. After she left Emanuel with an Edomite prince, the judge's son raced ahead of her to Ein Gedi and set an ambush. They say she was dressed in men's armor, carried men's weapons, and fought as well as an army of men, killing all of his soldiers."

"Not all," she said. "One soldier was spared to go back and tell the people what had really happened in Ein Gedi."

"The judge's son went back, too."

"He's alive?" She regretted the fearful tone of her voice, but it was too late.

Goor-Aryeh's face was barely visible now, as the flames had consumed most of the tumbleweeds. "Yes, he survived, but people say he returned home with a shattered jaw, and his father summoned a famous Canaanite healer to fix it. And there's another story going around about an earlier event at a tannery near Aphek, where all the slaves vanished shortly after the son of Judge Zifron came looking for his rebellious wife, the same Deborah, who was supposedly hiding in the tannery. How did you make hundreds of slaves disappear into thin air?"

"The tannery owner was like Seesya," she said. "They're evil men, whom Yahweh rightly punished."

"And you believe God sent you to deliver their punishment?"

Voices of men came from the direction of Beersheba. The battles in the other creeks must have ended, as well. She wondered who had prevailed there."

Goor-Aryeh picked up his sword.

Deborah stepped back and drew own sword.

He smiled. "Don't be ridiculous. You're safe with me."

"You aren't safe here."

"The men of Simeon are sinful. Yahweh has abandoned them."

"It looks like He has abandoned Judah."

"This was only a third of my army. The rest attacked through the other creeks. Our victory is certain. You can hear it."

She glanced in the direction of the voices. Were those men of Judah, or of Simeon?

He reached into a pocket in his short robe, pulled something out, and offered it to her.

Deborah looked closely. It was a ring.

The men's voices were coming closer. Was it Tsruyah's voice she was hearing?

"Be my wife," Goor-Aryeh said.

Her face burned, and she was grateful for the meek light. "You carry a ring with you everywhere?"

"Not since my wife died. I had no desire to marry another until I heard the stories about you and realized why, back in Arad, I was drawn to you, which at the time was terribly confusing." He smiled, his teeth white against his dark face. "Borah, Deborah, the connection was obvious, and I knew you're the girl I want to marry, which is why God brought us together again tonight."

Deborah touched the ring with the tip of her forefinger, and a flood of longing and desire came over her, same as she had felt in Arad, but more powerful.

"I'll treat you well," he said. "I'll protect you and give you healthy children."

The men were shouting now, very close.

"You're a great man," she said, her heart heavy. "But I can't."

"Why not?"

"Only a husband of Ephraim can help me inherit my father's homestead." She pushed him. "Run before they kill you."

"I own a good homestead," he said.

Men were running at them.

"Accept it." Goor-Aryeh held out the ring. "I feel that you want to."

Several soldiers came at full sprint and rammed into him, sending him down. They beat him and bound his arms and legs. A moment later, Tsruyah appeared on his horse, a burning torch in his hand. He looked down at the captive's face, grinned, and turned to Deborah.

"Your crazy plan worked," he said. "You even caught their judge. I didn't expect it."

"Neither did I." She sheathed her sword. "God has been generous to me."

He laughed.

The soldiers threw Goor-Aryeh over the back of Tsruyah's horse.

After they left, Deborah crossed the creek to the other side and headed north-east in the direction of the crevice where Yael and Summin were hiding. The remnants of flames along the creek guided her in the dark. Groups of men and women were walking back towards the city, and their cheerful banter contrasted with her heavy heart. The bloodshed could have been worse, but still, four soldiers of Judah and a man of Simeon were dead, and Goor-Aryeh's capture would surely result in his death.

She reached the crevice and called Yael's name.

There was no reply.

She yelled louder.

Nothing.

Stepping deeper into the crevice, she stumbled on a blanket, which she picked up.

Now worried, Deborah yelled at the top of her voice, "Yael? Summin?"

A distant voice yelled back, "Neither!"

From inside the crevice, she couldn't tell where his voice was coming from. "Where are you?"

A woman screamed. It sounded like Yael, somewhere in the direction of the creek.

Deborah ran.

Another scream, closer now, definitely Yael's voice, followed by men hollering, and Summin yelling, "Be quiet!"

Ascending a swell of sand, Deborah's boots sank, slowing her down. She kept going, and as she cleared the top, the desert ahead was lit up by a large bonfire. A few dozen men milled about, feeding the fire with leftover tumbleweeds.

Yael screamed again, and Deborah saw men holding her while others were pushing Summin towards the fire.

"Stop!" Deborah ran. "Stop!"

With a final shove, they drove him into the flames. He screamed and kicked and plowed through the fire, throwing up a fountain of sparks, and came out the other side, the bottom of his robe burning. Other men, laughing hard, pushed him back into the flames just as Deborah arrived. She grabbed his arm, pulled him out, and he fell. Unfurling the blanket, she used it to douse the flames around his legs.

The men's laughter died out, replaced by protests.

Yael wriggled free and ran over. She dropped by Summin's side, crying.

A man confronted Deborah. "It's the law. He who copulates with an animal shall be put to death."

His quote earned a round of supportive voices from the others. "Throw him back in!"

The man grabbed Yael's arm, pulled her away from Summin, and grasped the front of his robe to pick him up.

"Be quiet," Summin cried. "Be quiet!"

The man pushed Summin back towards the fire while the others started cheering.

Blinded with rage, Deborah untied the sling from around her hips, slipped two fingers into the hook, and lashed the man across the back. He wailed and let go of Summin. She lashed him again on the back and, as he turned to her, continued to whip him across the chest and face and arms, again and again, from the left and from the right, with swiftness and accuracy and a blazing determination to decimate him, destroy him, kill him!

The man collapsed, crying in fear and pain. The others stepped in to stop her, but Deborah turned on them, lashing their arms and faces and backs until they fled.

24

Beersheba was alight with fire pits and torches. Men and women drank and sang in the streets and courtyards. The victory over the men of Judah with the loss of only one man was considered a miracle, and effigies of various false idols were abundantly displayed and bowed to. Deborah barely restrained her tongue while sitting at a place of honor by Judge Ohad as he presided over a celebratory dinner in the courtyard.

Sallan came later and sat at a chair that awaited him next to Deborah. He leaned over and spoke in her ear. "I treated Summin's legs for the burns. He'll be left with severe scars."

"Is he in pain?"

"He must be, though the shock has rendered him mute." Sallan shook his head. "I gave him wine mixed with a sleep elixir."

Deborah felt the heat of fury rising inside her again. How cruel men were!

The singing stopped as soldiers shoved Goor-Aryeh into the courtyard, a rope tied around his neck. Tsruyah, who was holding the other end of the rope, yanked it hard, forcing the prisoner to kneel before Judge Ohad. Deborah could hardly recognize the proud, dignified leader of men she had seen only a short time earlier. His short robe was torn and bloodied, his face was bruised, and his hair was wet.

"Do you hear?" Judge Ohad waved his hand at the noisy city. "The tribe of Simeon rejoices while the tribe of Judah retreats."

His eyes on the ground, Goor-Aryeh didn't respond.

The judge leaned forward, raising his voice. "The tribe of Simeon is triumphant while the tribe of Judah is trounced."

"Bring his weapons." Tsruyah beckoned a soldier, who ran over carrying a spear and a sword, laying them on the table among the plates of food.

Judge Ohad picked up both weapons and held them high up with a big smile.

Slowly, Goor-Aryeh raised his head.

Up close, Deborah was shocked to see his bloodshot eyes and the swelling around his nose and mouth – the result, no doubt, of beatings.

"As you keel before me," Judge Ohad said, "so shall the whole tribe of Judah."

A hint of a smile appeared on Goor-Aryeh's face.

"You won't be smiling for long." Judge Ohad poked him with the spear. "Nor shall your people, when the tribe of Simeon regains the hills of Jerusalem while the tribe of Judah repays the debts of theft, betrayal, and arrogance."

"We also found this on him." Tsruyah tossed a ring on the table.

Judge Ohad picked it up between a thumb and a finger. "Is it gold?"

"Copper," Tsruyah said.

"Borah can have it," the judge said. "A reward for capturing the leader of Judah."

Deborah accepted the ring and put it in a pocket under her armor.

"Use it to betroth a wife," Tsruyah said, smirking. "We have many healthy maidens in Simeon."

The men around the table hooted and clapped. Deborah did her best to look pleased the way she imagined a strapping young man would, though Tsruyah's dark eyes made her want to strike him and proclaim her womanhood.

"Thank you," she said to the judge. "There's a small favor I'd like to ask. The blind youth, Summin, helped us with his acute hearing, but after the victory, some men pushed him into a fire. Will you pardon him?"

Everyone was silent, watching the judge.

Tsruyah spoke first. "We promised the people to burn him after the victory."

"Not exactly," Deborah said. "And the people would appreciate their leader's compassion after Yahweh has shown us His kindness."

Beside her, Sallan coughed to hide a chuckle.

"Why not?" Judge Ohad clapped. "The people will enjoy a better show tomorrow, when we burn this murderer."

"I'm a judge," Goor-Aryeh said. "A leader of my people."

"Not here." Judge Ohad shook his finger. "Not a leader, not a judge, not even a soldier. Here, you're a murderer."

"Give me a fair trial, before you beat me with sticks, hang me with ropes, and drown me in water."

"Our water," Tsruyah said. "The same water for which you came to kill us."

The men around laughed, but Judge Ohad did not, and his gaze made Tsruyah explain.

"We wanted to know where his men were going, where their camp was, and other important questions, but he wouldn't answer, no matter what we did to him."

Goor-Aryeh glanced at Deborah, and she understood. Tsruyah's questions were about her or, more likely, about the boy Borah, who had claimed to have met Goor-Aryeh in Arad. She felt deep gratitude to him, for if he had told Tsruyah the truth about her, she would be kneeling beside him now with a rope around her neck.

"Take him," Judge Ohad said. "Walk him down to the gate and tie him to the stake, where he will be judged and burned in the morning."

"Jacob spoke of your tribe," Goor-Aryeh said. "Do you remember what the Holy Scriptures say?"

Judge Ohad waved in dismissal.

"And of Simeon, his father Jacob said this." Goor-Aryeh raised his voice. "Keep my soul from their company, my honor from dwelling among them, for in malevolence they kill men, on a whim they castrate cattle."

Tsruyah yanked on the rope again, causing Goor-Aryeh to gag, but as they dragged him across the courtyard, he continued quoting. "Damn their malice, for it's fierce, and their wrath, for it's cruel. I shall cut Simeon off from Jacob and scatter them among Israel!"

The words cast a bleak mood on the judge and his guests. The meal was finished quickly, and everyone departed.

A small oil lamp burned in the room. Sallan's two boy-servants slept on the floor, Yael and Summin slept in adjacent cots, and two empty cots awaited her and Sallan.

He lay down with a sigh. "Not much left of this night."

The sight of her cot was almost beyond resistance, but Deborah shut her eyes and imagined the stake by the gate, flames leaping up around Goor-Aryeh, his eyes looking back at her through the blaze.

"I need your help," she said.

Sallan groaned. "Don't tell me you're going to risk our lives again."

"It's my duty."

"To save a murderer?"

"He's not a murderer. He's a faithful judge, a leader whose army ran away."

"From your brilliant ambush. Do you feel sorry for him?"

"I feel for him what a girl sometimes feels for a man."

Sallan's eyes widened.

Blushing, she added, "And I feel gratitude for his silence."

Gazing at her in the light of the oil lamp, Sallan said, "I keep forgetting that, behind your proactive, even-tempered, adventurous, and logical Borah character, there hides a girl as feminine as any other temperamental, small-minded, and anxious female."

Unlike his past insults, this time his words bounced off without denting Deborah's confidence and resolve. "I know a few men who are often as temperamental, small-minded, and anxious as any woman. In fact, one of them is in this very room, looking back at me."

His face was blank for a moment, and then, he chuckled. "Fair enough. I can't deny it. We're similar in other ways, as well. I also tried to save a great city without causing bloodshed, but only succeeded in the first goal, whereas you succeeded both in saving this city and preventing terrible bloodshed."

"Some men died tonight."

He waved dismissively. "A negligible loss considering the magnitude of the event."

"Will you help me prevent one more death."

He made a faux bow. "At your service."

Deborah gestured at Yael and Summin, who slept through the noise. "Whatever you gave them, do you have any left? I want to put the guards to sleep."

Reaching under his cot, Sallan pulled out the black leather satchel he had carried since Bozra.

The house was quiet. They went through the kitchen into a storage room. She uncorked two wine jugs while Sallan unbuckled his black leather satchel, took out a cloth bag, and untied a string from around its opening.

He poured a small quantity of fine powder from the cloth bag into each of the wine jugs. "What will you do after the guards fall asleep?"

"I'll set him free," she said.

"That's it?" He plugged the jugs and shook each one vigorously. "He runs away, and you come back to sleep?"

"Yes." She searched the storage room and picked up a torch and a waterskin, which she filled from a large jar of water. "What else can I do?"

"Create a cover up." Sallan led her to a workroom off the kitchen. "They would never believe he escaped by himself."

In the workroom, they found a pile of dirty robes and headdresses. She took two of each and picked up a rope, as well, while her mind devised a plan.

The courtyard was empty, and the city had quieted down. She hurried to the rear door and unlocked it. Sallan followed with the two wine jugs. The horse stable was full. She rubbed Rogez's neck and whispered calm words in his ear, but saddled another horse, which had no distinguishing marks and seemed healthy. Sallan secured the wine jugs, one on each side, as well as the unlit torch, the waterskin, the rope, and the bundle of clothes.

Leading the horse, Deborah walked downhill through the unkempt area behind the houses, whereas Sallan went back to the courtyard, leaving the door unlocked. Halfway downhill, she mounted the horse. It snorted and swayed its head at the unfamiliar rider, but she spoke calmly, and the horse relented and trotted on.

The people had gone to sleep, and she managed to reach the bottom of the hill without running into anyone. Avoiding the gate area, she took the market street west, past Abinoam's abandoned shop, all the way to the perimeter wall. She lit the torch in a fire pit near one of the houses, headed north along the crumbling wall, and found a place to ride through. Continuing north, she reached the three-way split of the gorges and crossed over to the Betarim Creek. Holding up the torch, she found what was left of the first pile of stones, dismounted, and tied the end of the rope to the saddle horn. With the torch in one hand and the unfurling rope in the other, she climbed down into the gorge and walked north.

Howling startled her.

She raised the torch and saw two jackals feeding on the corpse of the man who had stood beside Goor-Aryeh earlier. Continuing to advance, she yelled and waved the torch, which trailed a flurry of sparks. The jackals bared their bloody teeth, but when she came within a few steps, they fled.

A quick glance at the mutilated body was enough to sicken her. Laying the torch down on the sand, she quickly tied the end of the rope around the soldier's legs, picked up the torch, and ran back to the horse.

The jackals howled while Deborah led the horse away from the creek. The rope tightened and pulled the corpse up over the side of the gorge. She turned the horse and went back.

Hefting him onto the back of the horse took a great effort. Back in the saddle, panting, she rode south. Crossing the Hebron Creek at the split required strong nerves, both hers and the horse's, but they went through and kept going south along the Beersheba creek, around the wall, and east towards the gate. She stopped just out of sight to put on a robe and a headdress, which fell down over her forehead to her eyes, tied the horse to a small tree, and propped the burning torch against a rock.

With a wine jug in each hand, she walked the rest of the way. At the fairgrounds across the road, everything was dark and quiet, no one awake yet at any of the caravans. Passing by the platform, she saw a dark figure tied to the stake.

Two guards sat on the ground near the gate, smoking pipes. Deborah swayed in the manner of a drunk and crouched beside the guards.

"We beat them." She spoke slowly with a vacillating drunken voice. "The cowards of Judah."

They grunted, puffing smoke.

She pointed at the stake. "Is that their leader?"

"Their judge," one of the soldiers said.

"We should burn him now." She uncorked one of the wine jugs and pretended to drink from it.

They eyed the jug.

"Have some," she said. "It's the best."

One of them took the jug and drank directly from the neck.

The other one elbowed him.

"Here, take this one." Deborah uncorked the other jug and gave it to him. "Drink and be happy."

He took the jug and gulped from it.

Within moments, they slumped and began to snore.

Deborah poked them. "What's wrong with you? Can you hear me?"

They didn't respond.

Sallan's potion was shockingly effective.

Getting up, she collected the half-empty wine jugs, looked around to make sure no one was watching, and emptied the jugs on the guards, soaking their robes. She ran to fetch the horse, and rode back.

A hint of dawn glowed along the dark horizon.

Goor-Aryeh stood atop a mound of tumbleweeds and twigs, his arms bound behind the solid wooden stake. Deborah dismounted, went behind him, and untied the rope. He fell forward, groaning in pain. She got the waterskin, wet her hands, and patted his face.

"You're here," he said hoarsely. "I prayed that you come."

Deborah helped him drink some water. "There isn't much time. Can you stand?"

With her help, he stood, swaying.

She gave him the long robe and headdress. He put them on, groaning in pain, while she pulled the dead man off the horse and hooked her arms under his armpits. Turning her face away from the torn flesh, she stepped backwards, dragging the corpse to the stake and up onto the pile of tumbleweeds and twigs, which cracked under her boots.

"His name is Teffen." Goor-Aryeh helped her prop up the corpse and loop the rope around several times to keep it upright like a live prisoner awaiting execution at the stake. "He was my second cousin."

"I didn't want anyone to die," Deborah said.

"I know." Goor-Aryeh knelt by the stake and murmured the prayer for the dead.

She reached into her pocket, took out the ring, and handed it to him. "May Yahweh help you find a good wife."

"He helped me find you. Come with me, Deborah."

She took his hand and slipped the ring on his little finger. "Get on the horse and go."

In the east, the red line over the horizon grew brighter.

"Be my wife," he said. "I'll treat you as a queen."

Inhaling deeply, she struggled to keep her voice even. "If you don't leave now, we'll both die here."

"I'm serious," he said. "Yahweh has called me to rise up and lead my tribe. You'll help me."

"Help you kill others?"

Goor-Aryeh took her hand. "I'm not an evil man."

She pulled her hand free before he could feel the tremor caused by his touch. "Tell that to the wife of the man you killed at the creek."

He sighed. "We didn't come here to kill the people of Simeon. I ordered my men to subdue the guards and hurt no man unless he raised a weapon. Our plan was to conquer Beersheba by stealth while everyone was asleep and force Simeon to surrender without a fight."

If what he said was true, Deborah thought, then several men had died only because she had informed Simeon of the coming attack and set up the ambush.

"No," she said. "Unrealistic good intentions aren't really good intentions."

"Unrealistic? Why?"

"Because you should have known that the men of Simeon would fight."

"Some would have died, it's true. There's no battle without bloodshed."

She touched the torch to the fuel around the stake. "You must go now."

"Shalom, Deborah." Goor-Aryeh mounted the horse. "We shall meet again."

She watched him gallop away. "Perhaps we will," she said quietly.

The flames leapt high around the stake and the dead man tied to it. Deborah ran to the gate. As she passed by the sleeping guards, dawn splashed a red hue on the flag of Simeon at the top of the pole. She took the path behind the houses, all the way up the hill. Back at Judge Ohad's house, everyone was still asleep, except for Sallan, who sat up in his cot as she entered the room.

"All good," she whispered. "It's done."

"Thank you, Qoz." Sallan took a deep breath and exhaled. "I was sure you'd get caught."

Deborah lay down, rested her head on her sack, and closed her eyes. The tension and exhaustion combined into an ache that went from her neck all the way to her ankles, and as her body unwound, the pain spiked in different spots. She breathed steadily and thought of Goor-Aryeh riding through the desert, pushing the horse hard, gripping the reins with his right hand, the ring glistening on his little finger. Was she wrong to reject his proposal? He was a great man, and his faith was as strong as hers, but he would never be what she needed—a man of Ephraim, eligible to claim her inheritance by law and support her in answering her True Calling.

A rowdy commotion erupted in the courtyard outside their window. Men talked excitedly, horses whinnied, and doors banged. Someone yelled, "Where's Judge Ohad? Wake him up!"

"That's it." Sallan clutched his chest. "You went too far this time. We're doomed."

Deborah couldn't move. Had the guards only pretended not to recognize her? Had they woken up and called for help? Had they caught Goor-Aryeh? She recounted her steps frantically, trying to figure out where she had erred. Had she left any evidence behind? Had there been a third guard out of sight, who saw what she'd done?

The noises grew louder, invading the room through the curtained window, as more men filled the courtyard, more voices, more shouting, and then, as Sallan had feared, the door to their room shook under violent banging.

Yael sat up. "What's happening?"

Sallan attempted to speak, his mouth open like a gasping fish.

The door flew open, and Tsruyah appeared, his head uncovered, his feet bare, his long robe disheveled. "Get up, Borah. The judge wants you and the old Edomite in the courtyard. Right now."

25

Deborah helped Sallan get up. His hands shook, his lips trembled, and his eyelids fluttered rapidly.

"Calm down." She brushed his hair with her fingers and straightened his robe. "You're the personal emissary of King Esau the Twentieth. The men of Simeon won't dare harm you."

The noise outside subsided. Was that a bad sign? She wasn't sure.

On the way downstairs, Sallan mumbled prayers to Qoz and to other, less powerful Gods. When they stepped out of the house, Deborah saw more armed men in the courtyard than she'd seen before. Had Tsruyah recruited new soldiers?

Judge Ohad stood by the fire pit, also wearing only a night robe and no headdress. He saw her and yelled, "Borah, come over here!"

Her hand on the hilt of her sword, Deborah approached him. She had no chance against all these men at once, but she could get behind the judge, put the blade to his neck, and demand they bring Rogez."

She glanced around at the soldiers' faces, which were young and tired, but not hostile. What was going on?

"You see, Borah?" The judge smiled broadly. "Didn't I tell you my son would not abandon us?"

Deborah turned to him. "Your son is here?"

"Mamreh sent his deputy." Judge Ohad patted the shoulder of the man beside him. "The blacksmith's son."

The courtyard, the surrounding men, the sounds and the smells, all melted away into a distant, pale, muffled background, while Barac's face filled the void. It was him, very much alive, yet transformed. His skin was darker, his jaw wider and clenched in resolve, his brown eyes not wide with excitement, but calm and serious. Familiar, yet so different, his face wasn't framed by the wild mane of black curls, but by the flowing headdress of a desert dweller. And as her eyes dropped to his chin, she was relieved to see that his goatee had remained sparsely adolescent.

Judge Ohad knuckled Deborah's chest armor. "This is Borah, the boy who scared Judah away."

Barac looked at her. "This is not a boy."

Deborah heard his words and, in an instant, the courtyard, the armed men, the sounds and the smells, all rushed back into her consciousness with the realization that this moment of utter joy, of having all her prayers answered, was about to become a deadly disaster. She wanted to warn Barac, but couldn't find the right words.

"What?" The judge seemed confused. "What did you say?"

Barac's lips parted to clarify the damning words, but a hand rested on Deborah's shoulder, and Sallan's voice came booming. "Borah isn't a boy, that's true. He's a man – a brilliant young man who saved a whole city!"

"Exactly," Deborah blurted. "That's right. Yes. I've grown and changed. Yahweh has made me a man to help my people."

Barac's gaze went from Sallan to her and back, his face almost comical with confusion.

"A boy, a man, doesn't matter." Judge Ohad rubbed his hands. "The important thing is that we've scattered our enemy and reconciled with Mamreh, who sent this delegation to deliver his love and beg my forgiveness."

"Wonderful," Sallan said. "Perfect timing."

The judge rubbed his hands. "Let's drink to it."

A man ran into the courtyard and yelled. "The judge of Judah has burned!"

"We saw the stake burning," Barac said. "And your guards were asleep at the gate, smelling of wine, oblivious to our arrival."

Tsruyah sent a few soldiers to investigate and replace the guards.

Everyone looked at the judge.

Deborah pointed at the pale sky. "God punishes those who sin."

The men turned to her.

"He reaches down from above," she said, "and ignites fires to smite sinners."

Barac stared at her with a bewildered expression.

"Borah is right," Judge Ohad said. "Let it be a lesson to all our enemies. Whoever raises a sword against Simeon shall die in agony."

The men in the courtyard voiced their agreement. Behind her, Sallan exhaled with a muted sigh.

Servants brought out food and wine, and Judge Ohad invited Barac, Deborah, Sallan, and Tsruyah to sit at the table with him. He toasted his son, his son's men, his son's future bride, and his son's future brother-in-law, the Edomite king. It was obvious that the judge had feared he'd never see his son again, and with Barac's arrival, that fear had been lifted. He outlined his plans for Mamreh's return to Beersheba and the lavish celebration they would hold for the couple's wedding and the treaty's signing. Meanwhile Tsruyah's men and the dozen or so men who had come with Barac sat together on the ground, drank wine, and caught up on each other's experiences during the time of division.

Throughout this impromptu gathering, Barac drank very little and said nothing. Deborah smiled at him occasionally, but he never returned the smile. Sallan, who was sitting beside Deborah, grew talkative and cheerful in what she recognized was an effort to divert attention away from Barac's brooding.

The judge raised his goblet for yet another toast. "To my son's return home with Princess Needa!"

They drank.

Barac stood. "With your permission, judge, I'd like to pay my father a visit."

"Don't bother," Tsruyah said. "Your father fled before the attack — a coward and a traitor."

"Not true," Deborah said. "He fled from you, not from the enemy. I was there when you threatened to kill him if he didn't make fifty swords in three days — an impossible task."

"Kill him?" Barac leaned over the table, glaring at Tsruyah. "How dare you threaten my father?"

"Nothing personal." Tsruyah sipped from his goblet. "I said the same to every blacksmith and carpenter. We needed those weapons."

"Calm down, boys," Judge Ohad said. "This is a time for coming together, not for fighting."

With visible effort, Barac turned away from Tsruyah. "I'll prepare my men to leave immediately. We'll need fresh horses, food, and water."

"I was thinking," Sallan said. "How long will it take you to deliver the news of the treaty with Edom and return here with Mamreh?"

Barac hesitated.

Tsruyah pounded the table. "Answer, boy."

His disrespect for Barac made Deborah wonder whether Tsruyah had hoped to take Mamreh's place as the judge's heir – a foolish aspiration for someone with Tsruyah's crude ignorance of anything but brutish fighting.

"I cannot speak for Mamreh," Barac said. "My mission was only to deliver his message of loyalty and affection for his father, our judge."

"And you did it well," Sallan said. "Where is he staying now?"

"I don't know. Mamreh moves the camp often. He told me where to wait for him when I return to the area."

"Good," the judge said. "Tell him to come home as soon as possible."

"I'll deliver the message," Barac said. "Mamreh will decide when to return."

"A son must obey his father. Go back and tell him what I said."

Barac bowed, Tsruyah sneered, and the judge's face turned red.

"This is most unfortunate," Sallan said. "King Esau the Twentieth instructed me to return to Bozra without undue delay and report about the response for the treaty and the safety of his beloved sister. My king will be most unhappy if I am unable to attest firsthand to Princess Needa's good health."

Barac looked at Sallan with the same bewildered expression, and Deborah almost laughed, imagining the utter confusion in Barac's mind. Last he knew, Sallan had been a slave, managing a basket-weaving factory at Judge Zifron's house in Emanuel, far north in Canaan. And now, only a few months later, the same Sallan was a guest of Judge Ohad in Beersheba, honored as a personal emissary of the king of Edom, travelling in close companionship with Deborah, the orphan girl who had somehow morphed into a soldier, credited with saving Beersheba. Deborah felt a gushing admiration for his fortitude in holding back the questions that must have been burning at the tip of his tongue.

"There's another issue," she said. "The men of Judah might come back for another attempt."

"No." Judge Ohad shook his finger in the air. "Not after they hear how their judge was burned at the stake. They'll be terrified of us for years."

"Fear won't quell their thirst for revenge," Deborah said and quoted the Holy Scriptures. "Evil dominates man's heart from his youth."

It was the last thing Judge Ohad wanted to hear, but she was glad to have spoken, if only for the new expression of utter dismay on Barac's face. Was he impressed by her command of the Holy Scriptures?

The judge rested his elbows on the table, cradling his chin in his hands.

"Borah is right," Tsruyah said, surprising her. "The men of Judah might return to avenge their judge's blood."

Or worse, Deborah thought. Their judge himself might return to avenge his own torture and humiliation.

Judge Ohad sighed. "What can we do?"

"In Edom," Sallan said, "the king would take drastic steps."

"Such as?"

Sallan counted on his fingers. "Draft every citizen to work. Rebuild the walls and erect guard towers. Require every carpenter and blacksmith to do nothing but produce weapons. Train every able man to defend the walls."

"Yes." Judge Ohad slammed the table before him and pointed at Tsruyah. "That's what we shall do. That's my command. Start immediately!"

Tsruyah smirked. "The people won't be happy."

"Tell them it's temporary," the judge said. "Soon, the princess of Edom will be living among us and her brother's army will be ready to defend us. Judah will never again dare to attack Beersheba."

"That's true," Sallan said. "Provided there are no more delays. In fact, why don't we all go to Mamreh? We'll celebrate the marriage at his desert camp, sign the treaty that day, and immediately send word to Bozra with the news."

The judge hesitated. "I'd like nothing more than to see my son again, but how can I leave the people of Beersheba at a time like this?"

"You can go," Tsruyah said. "I'll stay to defend the city."

"Time is of the essence," Sallan said. "The sooner your son marries the princess, the sooner we finalize the treaty. You'll return here with the backing of Edom – a formidable guarantee of this city's safety from Judah."

Again, Deborah could not tell whether Sallan was lying to the men of Simeon or to her about the treaty and the marriage permission. Either way, travelling with Barac would keep her close to him and bring her closer to Princess Needa.

"It's a good idea," she told the judge. "Mamreh will only trust words that he can hear directly from your mouth."

"I'm not young anymore," Judge Ohad said. "It's a dangerous journey."

"God will watch over you." She pressed his forearm. "Believe in Him. Be brave."

Watching her display of audacity, Barac finally smiled.

26

The preparations for the journey fired up the house. The servants ran about with food, blankets, and other supplies. The horses neighed as men pulled them into the courtyard, saddled them, and checked their hooves. Barac's soldiers reunited briefly with their families, only to say quick, tearful goodbyes.

Back in the room, Yael asked to stay in Beersheba with Summin, but Sallan insisted they'd be safer on the road than under Tsruyah's temporary rule. He took Deborah aside to speak in private.

"I need to know where Mamreh is hiding,"

"It can't be more than a few days' ride," she said. "The territory of Simeon is completely surrounded by Judah's land."

"But where? West towards Gaza? South in the Negev Desert?"

"We'll find out when we get there."

Sallan groaned. "Only a death-wishing fool embarks on a journey without knowing its destination. Go and ask Barac."

"He won't tell me what he refused to tell Judge Ohad himself – you heard it."

"Find out without asking."

"How?"

"A direct question reveals what you desperately want to find out, whereas a veneer of indifference entices your opponent to show off his knowledge."

"Barac is not my opponent."

"That's why it would be natural for you to saddle up to him, reminisce about the old days, catch up on what's happened since you separated, and talk about the journey ahead. Tell him how curious you are about the sights awaiting your eyes, the aromas awaiting your nose, the sounds—"

"I get it," she said. "You want me to trick him."

"He would be grateful. Men love to talk, especially with a beautiful girl who interrupts them only with brief, earnest questions."

"You talk to him." Deborah's anger flared up. "Go and talk, man to man, reminisce about how you used him to pass the story of the Elixirist to me, and how you convinced me to go and search for Kassite, risking my life many times because of your lies."

Sallan stepped back from her, raising his hands defensively. "Calm down. I'm only asking you to—"

"To do to Barac what you always do to me – play mind games, tell half-truths, and throw off diversions."

He groaned, pressing a fist to his heart. "Everything I do is for your sake."

"For me?"

"Yes, for you, even when I deceived you, the way I sent you from Emanuel on a false pretense, but only because I saw myself in you. Many years before, when I had been your age, I left home on an equally dangerous quest, suffered injuries, cruelty, and despair, as you have suffered, only to grow stronger, wiser, and braver. My harrowing journey had made me capable of saving a whole city and its people, and I knew that your journey would turn you into a hero, as well."

"I don't feel like a hero."

"Why not? Have you not saved Beersheba and its people? Are you not due to receive fifteen-dozen silver coins from the king when we return with Princess Needa? Will you not have the means to travel to Canaan and answer your True Calling? My heart aches at the prospect of your departure, yet I do everything possible to help you succeed."

"Then tell me everything. What is the king's plan?"

He exhaled loudly. "I told you. It's nothing to worry about."

Groaning in frustration, Deborah turned away from him. She helped Yael change Summin's bandages and dress him for the journey. He said nothing and didn't respond when spoken to.

Out in the courtyard, Deborah gave Rogez water and brushed him, especially his mane and tail, resulting in a splendid luster that drew a circle of admiring soldiers.

"Get back to work," Tsruyah yelled at them.

They dispersed.

Barac was readying his own horse nearby. He glanced at Deborah and continued working. She tied her sack to Rogez's saddle, secured the spear and two waterskins, and mounted. Sallan got on his horse, while Yael shared her mare with Summin. The boy-servants rode a horse together out of the courtyard ahead of everyone in order to collect the Edomite soldiers and the three camels from the fairgrounds.

Judge Ohad came out last. The servants helped him onto his horse, and he led the way. Riding down the main street of Beersheba, he waved at the people, who had gathered along the sides as word had spread about his departure and the planned defense work.

Outside the gate, the caravan assembled between the platform and the smoldering skeletal remains of Teffen at the singed stake. Barac advanced along the caravan towards the front to lead the way. Deborah hoped he would stop to greet her, but his eyes avoided her.

Tsruyah sprinted from the gate and blocked Barac near Deborah.

"Hold on," Tsruyah said. "Don't you two know one another?"

Rogez snorted and stomped the ground. Deborah tugged on the reins, signaling him to stay put, though her heart was racing.

"I saw you at his father's workshop," Tsruyah said. "You're both from Emanuel, two boys about the same age. You must know each another."

They didn't respond.

"Answer me!"

Deborah pointed at a man poking with a stick in the ashes by the stake. "See that man over there?"

He turned to look.

"Do you know him?"

"No," Tsruyah said. "What's that got to do—"

"Aren't you both from Beersheba?" Deborah colored her voice with sarcasm. "Two men about the same age. You must know one another."

Behind her, Sallan laughed.

Barac urged his horse around Tsruyah and joined the judge at the front of the caravan, which began to move.

They rode east through flourishing homesteads that grew wheat and barley, held spacious corrals with goats, sheep, and cattle, and tended to orchards of pomegranates, figs, olives, and palm trees. Deborah thought of Palm Homestead.

Further east, the land grew barren. When the sun was halfway up,

Barac turned right onto a narrow road heading south. They crossed stretches of sand flats that slowed the horses. The sun kept rising until it was directly above, beating down on their heads. Despite her growing discomfort, Deborah kept her eyes wide and memorized the way, imagining it as a map with notable land features as markers.

Barac stopped near a mound of boulders for a rest. While everyone stayed in the shade, he climbed on the boulders and gazed ahead. Deborah assumed he was figuring where to go from here.

Later, they passed by a hill with a serrated ridge. Barac seemed relieved to see it and quickened the pace. Near sunset, they arrived at an oasis. Deborah noticed skeletal remains of a large predator, perhaps a lion or a tiger. She wondered how it had died.

Several roads intersected near the oasis. They were narrow and not well maintained. She gave Rogez water and food, started a fire, and sat with Sallan and the three Edomite soldiers, who stared at Yael while she served the food. Deborah hoped for an opportunity to speak with Barac in private after dark, but he shared a light meal with his men and lay down to sleep among them, leaving one awake to guard the encampment and keep a fire burning to ward off animals.

The first glow of dawn woke Deborah up. She stretched to loosen her aching muscles and rose on her elbows to look around. A man was standing guard nearby, his face in the dark. He wore no headdress, and a profusion of black curls framed his head. His hand moved in the dark, beckoning her.

Barac!

Had he taken the last watch of the night hoping she would be up early?

Rising slowly to avoid disturbing Yael and Summin, who slept beside her, Deborah followed Barac around a few jujube trees and behind a cluster of reeds to a small pond by the spring. She dipped her hands in the water and wiped the stubble paste from her cheeks and chin until her skin was smooth.

They faced each other in the dark.

Deborah spoke first. "I was afraid that you were dead and I'd never see you—"

He leaned forward and pressed his lips to hers.

She froze as a cascade of emotions washed over her – shock, surprise, delight, terror, bewilderment – all gushing at once with a paralyzing roar. And then, like a flashflood, the emotional torrent passed through and drained away, leaving her with simple joy. She kissed him back, tasting his warm lips and his sweet breath.

His lips quivered over her cheeks and nose, her eyebrows and forehead, while she slid her fingers into his mass of curls, soft and thick as sheep's wool before the shearing. He held her, his face close, his eyes glistening. She felt her knees grow weak. He caressed her neck, her ears, and the side of her head, where her hair was still short.

He smiled, his teeth white in the dark. "I've dreamt of your beautiful hair."

"You'll have to dream a bit longer."

They laughed, kissing again.

She had never kissed a man, though Seesya had pressed his mouth to hers once, making her convulse. Now she understood why women whispered praiseful stories about the pleasures of a loving man's kiss.

Barac gestured at the glow of dawn. "The others will be up soon."

"I have to put that stuff back on." She patted her cheeks. "Sallan made it for me. Do you know who he really is?"

"The Elixirist from Edom. They were all talking about him at the judge's house. I don't understand why he told me the story about the Elixirist who had turned the women of Edom into men to fight the Egyptians, but didn't say that, actually, he was that Elixirist."

"Because he wanted someone to go and search for his old friend, Kassite, who had been sold to a tanner in Manasseh."

"Devious old man."

She chuckled. "It's a strange thing, but his lies are often well-intended. I owe him a lot, though it hasn't been easy."

"Tell me what happened after we parted ways. I want to know everything you've been through."

Speaking rapidly, Deborah recounted her experiences since she had last seen Barac and his father at Palm Homestead on the night of Tamar's stoning. As Barac listened to her harrowing experiences, he kept shaking his head. She finished with her joy at finding Abinoam in Beersheba and learning that Barac was alive.

"Your father asked me to tell you that he will wait for you at Kadesh Naphtali, near the Sea of Galilee."

"When I'm capable of fighting the Canaanites, I'll go north and gather brave men of Naphtali, as well as Asher, Zebulon, and Issachar, and liberate the land that Yahweh had promised to the children of Israel."

"I believe it," she said.

He smiled. "You alone understand my heart."

"And you, mine."

They kissed once more and headed back to the camp.

He pointed at the brightening dawn. "A new beginning for us, Deborah."

At the camp, Sallan alone was up. He opened his arms to embrace Barac.

Barac held back. "How could you send a girl alone to chase a fictional Elixirist around Canaan, while you were the man she was seeking?"

Sallan hushed him with a finger across his lips and gestured at the men sleeping nearby.

"You used her." Barac lowered his voice. "Shame on you."

"I had good reasons for everything," Sallan whispered. "And here she is, safe and free, not strung up on the Weeping Tree in Emanuel beside her dead sister. You should thank me."

Glancing at her, Barac said nothing.

"Right now," Sallan continued, "you're the one placing her at mortal risk."

"Me? How?"

"Traveling with a small force through a barren land among belligerent tribesmen."

"There's no fighting this far south."

"There are wild animals, poisonous snakes, high cliffs, and flash floods."

"It's safer here than in Beersheba."

"Here, maybe, but what about our destination?"

"You'll see." Barac looked to the south. "We'll be there in three days."

"Where? Another city?"

Barac chuckled. "Nothing but wild animals and a hole in the ground."

Sallan's eyes creased. "A hole?"

The men began to rise, and the horses shifted and snorted.

"A big hole," Barac said. "Vast enough to build a hundred cities side-by-side, if only there was water to sustain them."

"Ah," Sallan said. "You speak of the Ramon Crater. It's a marvel, isn't it?"

"It is," Barac said. "God's creation at its grandest."

Deborah followed the brief exchange with amazement at how Sallan had managed to make Barac reveal their destination.

She smeared the stubble paste on her cheeks before anyone noticed. Soon, the camp was packed up, and they moved on, the sun still half-hidden under the horizon. A while later, when Barac stopped to orient himself, Deborah noticed that only two Edomite soldiers followed behind.

Sallan came closer and spoke in a low voice. "I sent one of them to Bozra with an update. The king will be delighted with your progress."

There was more to his actions than reporting on their progress, she was certain. Would the king lead his army across the harsh Negev Desert on the basis of such threadbare information? It was unlikely. Whatever Sallan was planning, Deborah was determined to stick to her mission, which was to bring the princess back home safely, not to give her away to a husband who was one of those the king had called "roving Hebrew outlaws." She imagined arriving at Bozra with the king's lost sister, watching the royal reunion while a huge crowd cheered, and receiving the promised reward from the king, which would enable her to return to Canaan.

With the sweet taste of Barac's lips on hers, Deborah remembered Umm-Sallan's wise advice to find a good man of Ephraim who would secure her inheritance, defend Palm Homestead from Judge Zifron and Seesya, and help her deliver God's word to the Hebrews.

27

By mid-day, as the air grew hot, they stopped at a village surrounded by well-tended fields and orchards. The houses were quiet, and no smoke emerged from any of them. Everyone dismounted in the shade of the trees near a well. It had a waist-high circular well and a roped bucket. Sallan's boy-servants lowered the bucket down and drew water.

A bearded man came out of one of the houses. "It's the Sabbath today," he said. "Drawing water is forbidden."

Deborah realized the man was right. Sabbath had commenced the previous night at sunset.

More men emerged. They wore white caps and prayer shawls with blue fringes.

Sallan got up and addressed the bearded man. "Please forgive us. We're Edomite travellers, not accustomed to observing the Hebrew laws. May we draw water from your well."

"Yes, you may," the leader said. "In fact, it's not a well, but an ancient cistern. It's quite low because there hasn't been rain around here for two full moons."

"We'll pray for rain." Sallan motioned his boy-servants to resumed drawing water. "What is the name of this village?"

Judge Ohad answered from where he was sitting. "This is Revivim, isn't it?"

Deborah smiled, because the name meant drops of rain or dew, which were obviously scarce here.

One of the men asked, "Aren't you a Hebrew?"

"Yes. I'm Judge Ohad of Beersheba."

The men ogled him while women and children peeked out from the doors of the houses.

Nearby, a donkey brayed.

Deborah stepped forward. "We are on a journey of great importance.

The survival of the whole tribe of Simeon may depend on it."

"We are of Simeon, too," the leader said, "and we don't travel on the Sabbath."

"But you may travel if you have to," she said, hiding her self-doubts with an air of confidence. "The commandments are not absolute. Do not kill, for example, does not forbid killing a man who comes to kill you. Shouldn't a person be allowed to violate the Sabbath if a life depends on it?"

His eyes dropped to her sword. "I don't know."

"I do," Judge Ohad said. "Under the laws of our God, the sanctity of life supersedes all other sanctities."

Several women brought out food and wine, and all the men of the village, as well as Barac and his young soldiers, sat on the ground before Judge Ohad. He thanked Yahweh for the food and took the first bite. Everyone ate and drank, while he launched into an embellished recounting of the attack on Beersheba, how the men of Judah had fled in panic, as planned by the clever Hebrew boy, who had slain the high priest of Edom.

The locals looked at her in awe.

When the meal was over, the judge said, "You have treated us with hospitality as generous as our forefather Abraham had treated the angels. May God bless you as He blessed Abraham with abundant offspring, wealth, and long years."

The local men murmured their thanks.

Barac was the first to stand up. "We should continue our journey."

"Stay with us," the leader said. "It's the Sabbath, and the day is half over."

"I agree," Sallan said before the judge could decline. "Having seen the power of the Hebrew God during my travels with Borah, I'd rather not risk His wrath."

Deborah knew he was lying, having heard him mock her faith many times.

"My home is yours," the bearded man told the judge. "Rest in my bed and recover from the road."

Judge Ohad accepted the invitation. The neighbors took in Sallan, his boy-servants, and the Edomite soldiers, as well as Barac and his men, but Deborah declined and stayed under a tree with Yael and Summin, who lay down, curled up as an infant. Yael caressed his head, chanting a soft tune in her native language.

The afternoon and evening passed quietly, and the night was uneventful, as well. Deborah was up at dawn. She washed her face, applied the stubble paste, and walked a short distance away to find a tree fitting to stand-in for an adversary. Unsheathing her sword, she swung, thrust, lunged, parried, deflected, feigned, and stabbed her imaginary opponent, continuing despite the burning muscles in her arms, shoulders, and legs.

Catching a movement in the corner of her eyes, she turned to see Sallan arrive from the desert. He was carrying an oil lamp in one hand and, in the other, a bunch of plant cuttings with narrow, pale-green leaves and tiny fruit that seemed purple in the weak light. He was startled to see her, but recovered quickly with a smile and kept walking to the village.

When the sun was up, Deborah went back and found Yael kneeling by Summin, sobbing bitterly. He had died during the night.

The locals directed them to a patch of land behind a grove of olive trees, where Revivim buried its dead. Barac and his soldiers dug a grave, and Deborah stood by Yael while Summin was lowered in and covered with soil, pebbles, and a mound of rocks.

Everyone stepped back, looking at Judge Ohad, who gestured at Deborah. She extended her hands above the fresh grave and recited the blessing over the dead.

"Amen," everyone mumbled and went to the horses.

Sallan's boy-servants helped the weeping Yael mount her mare.

Alone by the grave, Deborah knelt and touched the rocks. The thought of his body pressed down under the soil, pebbles, and rocks made Deborah shudder. She thought of Vardit, the first wife of Judge Zifron and the mother of Seesya, her back lacerated from the flogging she had received on her son's orders after Deborah's escape from Emanuel. Vardit had been in great pain, yet comforted by the words of the priest, Obadiah of Levi, who had told her: "After death, sinners go to a place of fire and torture, but the righteous go to a place as wonderful as the Garden of Eden." Closing her eyes, Deborah imagined Summin arrive at a place where everything was lush, colorful, and serene, a place where his eyes could see again and allow him to enjoy the surrounding beauty, where Yahweh Himself walked among the trees and greeted the righteous. She hoped Obadiah had been right about the contrasting fates of sinners and the righteous, though she wasn't sure about her own place after death. Would God welcome her among the righteous, or send her to spend eternity with sinners in fire and torture? She assumed that her efforts to answer His calling should weigh in her favor on the scales of sin and virtue, but along the way she had killed and maimed others, including the young man lying under these rocks. Would the blood she had spilled be justified as self-defense when her time came to lie dead beneath a pile of rocks and face divine judgment?

"Forgive me for taking your eyesight." She coughed to clear the lump in her throat. "And for failing to protect you from others. Rest in peace, Summin."

Before mounting Rogez, she stopped by Yael on her mare. "Our God is merciful. He collects the righteous after death and brings them to a place as wonderful as the Garden of Eden. That's where Summin is going, I'm sure of it."

The girl nodded, sniffling.

South of Revivim, they crossed a wide expanse of flat desert. The horses and camels followed Barac's horse, requiring no input from the riders. At midday, he stopped briefly so that the horses could drink and rest. No one spoke much, either due to the heat, or the effect of watching a burial that reminded everyone of their own mortality.

In the afternoon, the hills grew taller and more rugged. Barac stopped frequently to determine the way ahead. On the descent, though, his confidence returned as another flat expense of desert stretched ahead. At the foothills, as the sweltering sun finally set behind the horizon, he pointed to a clutch of greenery in a rocky crevice and announced it would be their camp for the night.

The spring was pitiful, but with patience one could refill a waterskin and drink cool water that washed away the taste of dust.

Sallan sent the two Edomite soldiers to hunt. They returned after sunset with a fox and a jackal, which they skinned and gutted. The boy-servants took out wood logs from a bundle tied to one of the camels and collected twigs and tumbleweeds. Deborah used her father's fire starters to get a flame going, the soldiers built a contraption of spears, and Sallan supervised the roasting.

The meal started with wine and storytelling, especially by Judge Ohad, who was animated and happy as he recounted Mamreh's brilliance in memorizing the Holy Scriptures as a young boy, though his real passion had been the trapping of rodents to serve as bait for venomous snakes, which he collected in clay jars, terrifying his mother and sisters until, one day, a slave girl knocked over a jar, and the snakes slithered all over the house while the bitten girl ran around the courtyard screaming until she dropped. The men laughed to tears and tore into the meat with relish, including the judge, who stuffed his mouth while talking. Only Deborah and Barac did not touch the meat in observance of Yahweh's dietary laws against eating carnivorous animals. Instead, they ate bread with cheese and olive oil, as well as figs and dates, which their hosts in Revivim had given them for the road. Yael, who had spoken little since Summin's burial, ate nothing.

During the night, everyone became violently ill, except for Barac, Deborah, and Yael. It started with vomiting and progressed to uncontrollable diarrhea, which sent the men stumbling from the camp to relieve themselves with loud moans and groans. Deborah and Yael refilled the men's waterskins at the spring, wiped their faces with wet rags, and supported those who struggled to get away from camp before soiling themselves. Barac took on the care of Judge Ohad.

Sallan seemed the least ill, and Deborah had the impression that he exaggerated his suffering with theatrics. When she examined a spot where he had stepped over and retched loudly, she could find nothing on the ground. Back at camp, he was lying down, breathing heavily, seemingly faint and oblivious to her presence. She had a nagging suspicion. Had he smeared some potion on the meat to cause this illness?

A search of his saddle and sack produced no sign of the plant cuttings she had seen him carry in from the desert. The only place she couldn't search was the black satchel, which he used as a pillow under his head. Looking around at the miserable men curled on their cots, she found it hard to believe he could be so cruel. Yet, after all she had experienced with Sallan, Deborah knew he would do anything to serve his goals — and come up with the most plausible justification afterwards. The question was, what purpose could possibly be served by sickening everyone?

By nighttime, the vomiting and diarrhea had slowed down. The men were either asleep, or lying on the ground, too weak to move. Deborah and Yael went from man to man with waterskins, helping each one take small sips. No one wanted to eat, except for Sallan, who ate a few dates, sighing repeatedly. Deborah started a fire and took turns with Barac guarding the camp until dawn, when she applied the dark-speckled stubble paste and practiced with her sword and sling. Her weary body ached, but the total concentration required by the sword and the sling — and the deep satisfaction when she succeeded — took her mind off the unpleasant reality of the journey.

Sunrise brought a faint breeze from the east, which cleared the stale air from the camp and breathed new life into the men. They were still pale and weak, but their appetites started to recover. Barac helped the judge sit up, his back supported by a horse saddle, and fed him morsels as one would feed a child. Riding was out of the question, and the day passed in rest, allowing Barac and Deborah to take turns catching up on sleep before another night of guard duty. Even when they woke each other at night to stand watch, the risk that one of the men might be awake prevented them from showing any affection or speaking more than a few words.

By the next morning, the men were up on their feet, and the judge ordered to resume the journey, having lost two and a half days between the Sabbath at the village and the unexpected illness. As Deborah was helping him onto his horse, he spoke meekly.

"Borah, your righteousness saved you. I'll never again allow forbidden meat to be served in my domain."

"It's a good start." She guided his boots into the stirrups.

"Yahweh spared us for a reason."

"He is merciful." Deborah handed him the reins. "Maybe that's the reason."

28

They travelled at a slow pace, stopped often, and made camp early in a barren stretch of desert with nothing in sight but pale rocks and sand. Deborah built a fire while Sallan's boy-servants and Yael put out bread, honey cakes, and pomegranate slices. Sallan was asleep before she found an opportunity to question him in private. Barac took the first shift, and Deborah lay down with her sack under her head and fell asleep.

In her dream, she was standing on a riverbank, the sand soft and cool under her bare feet. The river was wide, flowing lazily. Birds chirped in the nearby trees. A gentle breeze carried the fresh scent of a recent rain, mixed with the acrid odors of the tannery. She recognized Kassite's house, propped up on pylons over the water a short distance upstream. The tannery was deserted, not a single slave working, no sign of Kassite or the group leaders. Cowhides soaked in the tubs, more were draped over working tables, and some were drying over the wooden fence.

Deborah heard sloshing in the water and turned back to the river.

"It's been a while." The eagle floated like a giant duck. "How are you?"

"I'm not sure," Deborah said. "Where have you been all this time?"

"Here and there." The eagle's eyes twinkled. "And here again now, like you."

"Why are we back at this smelly place? I risked my life to get away from here."

"Perhaps we're curious to know what has happened since the great escape."

She looked around. "Seems the same."

"You're different."

"I'm happy. Barac is alive, and we've grown close to one another."

"Not too close, I hope." The eagle winked.

Her face flushed. "We're never alone."

"Sin always lurks in the shadows for an opportunity to tempt the righteous."

"I didn't even have a chance to tell Barac about Sallan's new machinations."

"The Edomite potionist?"

"Elixirist." Deborah took a deep breath. "I think he's up to something."

"Something?"

"He was anxious to find out where we're going."

"Do you know where you're going?"

"A big hole," Deborah said. "According to Barac, it's big enough to hold a hundred cities side by side, but there is no water to sustain settlements. Sallan said it's the Ramon Crater. He sent a messenger to Bozra, and then, he encouraged us to stay for the Sabbath at a small village. The next day, after he prepared the meat for dinner, everyone got sick, and we lost two more days. He might have put something in the food."

"Did you see him do it?"

"No, but he wasn't as sick as the others, and he sent a second Edomite soldier away. I'm waiting for a chance to question him in private."

The eagle tilted her head. "How will you know if his answers are truthful?"

"I'm not sure yet."

"When someone engages in subterfuge, exposing it requires counter-subterfuge."

"Counter-subterfuge was exactly how Sallan tricked Barac into revealing our destination." Deborah quoted Sallan's advice. "A direct question reveals what you want to find out, whereas a mask of indifference entices your opponent to show off his knowledge."

"Beautifully put. I'll use it myself from now on."

Deborah didn't like it. "Faking indifference is lying, which would make me as bad as Sallan."

The eagle chuckled. "You can never become bad. It's an impossibility."

"Why?"

"You're filled to the brim with goodness, no room for badness at all."

"What about my anger? I often get furious until I can't see straight."

"That's because your young soul is fighting with itself."

"Fighting over what?"

"Ambitious goals require proportionally painful moral compromises. It's an uncomfortable truth. A person cannot do only good in this world."

"Don't I become a bad person when I do bad things?"

"To do a lot of good, you must do a little bad along the way."

Deborah took a moment to contemplate. "It's like paying a small price for something much more valuable, or adding a pinch of bitter herb to enrich the taste of delicious stew."

"That's the spirit, girl."

The eagle's wings splashed the water with powerful strokes as she took off, soaring into the clouds, which absorbed her.

Dawn tickled Deborah's eyelids, waking her up. She applied the stubble paste and walked some distance from camp for her daily swordfight with an imaginary opponent.

The men were up with sunrise, and the convoy got ready and moved on before the heat began to build up.

At the end of a stretch of barren lowland, a tall mountain with a pointy summit appeared ahead. Barac called it Ovdat and led them south alongside the mountain and across a well-trodden east-west road. He said it was a new spice route used by the Nabateans, who lived in a city carved into the belly of a red mountain. Deborah wondered whether he was speaking of Rekem, the city Sallan had heard about from the Midianite merchants in Arad. She imagined it as a network of tunnels, dark and damp like Kassite's abandoned copper mine. Why would men choose to dig into solid rock and live in the dark like moles when they could build a city above ground and defend it with a wall?

After an uneventful night by a small oasis, they continued along a dry stream, which Barac called the Aricha Creek. At midday, he veered off the streambed and started up an ascent, which wasn't steep, but treacherous, strewn with rocks and lined with fissures, making for a tiring slog.

By the afternoon, everyone was exhausted, thirsty, and hungry. Deborah could barely think straight, but she continued to memorize all the notable landmarks they were passing in order to create a map in her head, in case she would have to retrace the journey on her own.

Late in the day, the land leveled out, and they reached the edge of a high cliff overlooking a vast cavity in the desert landscape. It looked like a giant clay bowl with a rough bottom and vertical sidewalls. Deborah dismounted and held Rogez by the reins. She peeked over the edge at the rugged face of the cliff, which dropped straight down all the way to a distant bottom.

Barac appeared beside her. "Makes you want to fly like a bird, doesn't it?"

If only she could tell him that she had actually flown – on an eagle, no less – and that the flight had changed her life.

The judge stayed mounted. "Is this the Ramon Crater? No wonder people don't want to settle here."

"There is a hidden spring nearby," Barac said.

"Is that where my son is?"

"Mamreh moves his camp often. He'll find us when he's ready."

"I am ready," the judge said.

"It's too late in the day."

Barac rode a short distance along the cliff to a wooden pole that was fixed in a crack between rocks. He pulled a piece of fabric from his sack and unfurled it, revealing the pale-green flag of Simeon with the drawing of masonry guard towers. Standing in the stirrups, he reached the top of the pole to secure the flag, turned his horse, and headed back the way they had come.

As she mounted Rogez, Deborah noticed that Sallan was wiping tears.

"What's wrong?"

"The sweet ache of fond memories," he said.

"You have memories from here?"

He gestured back at the cliff's edge. "My father brought me to see this place. I was half your age, a mere child, but who can forget this?"

"Why didn't you tell me?"

He wiped his eyes again. "I'm telling you now."

They caught up with the convoy.

"You should have told me," she said. "I didn't realize that you knew this area."

"I know a lot of things," Sallan said. "It's one of the few advantages of old age."

She recognized that he was avoiding a direct answer, but perhaps she could learn more indirectly. "Why did your father bring you here?"

"He travelled far and wide to collect plants for his potions. I loved going with him, learning from him, and having him to myself. Before that particular trip, he had told me to expect to see a divine hand, and when we arrived, he waved at the view and said, "Look, son, at the imprint of Qoz's fist, where he punched the land of the Hebrews in anger over their blasphemy."

"You don't really believe that, do you?"

Sallan looked at her, his gray eyes moist. "I believe my father was speaking of the past as a hint of things to come – a confrontation with the Hebrews here, at the Ramon Crater, which is forthcoming."

Deborah wanted to ask what he meant, but at that moment, Barac turned right, dropping into a dry crevice, which forced everyone to ride single file. The crevice circled back towards the cliff at a lower elevation. Halfway down, in a narrow ravine to the right, she noticed greenery around a small pond.

Barac continued down the crevice to a wide, flat area and selected a site to camp near a few thorny trees, about a hundred steps back from the edge of the cliff. The view was similar to what they had seen from the higher point, yet different as the colors were changing with the approach of sunset.

They set up camp, lit a few fires, and ate bread, cheese, and figs. The Edomite soldiers' eyes followed Yael with a craving that reminded Deborah of the slaves' attack by the stream in Tamar. After the meal, when Yael walked up the crevice with the empty waterskins, the two men followed her. Deborah grabbed a burning branch and hurried after them.

The soldiers were talking with Yael in hushed tones while she filled the waterskins from the spring in the ravine. One of them caressed her black hair, which was no longer covered by her hood, but flowed loosely around her shoulders and down to her hips.

Yael was the first to see Deborah. "I'm fine, Borah," she said. "It's nothing."

Deborah clenched the hilt of her sword.

"They aren't bothering me," Yael said.

"Are you sure?"

Yael nodded, shook her hair, and smiled in a manner that reminded Deborah of the girl's mother.

"You two," Deborah said to the Edomite soldiers. "Go back in the camp,"

They walked away, glancing back at Yael.

When they were gone, Deborah said, "You're playing with fire, girl."

"I'm not a girl anymore." Yael gestured down at her crotch. "The morning Summin died, I had my first blood."

Deborah sighed, remembering the fright and despair she had felt when her first blood came.

"My mother prepared me for womanhood," Yael said. "She taught me how a woman can have her way with men and warned me not to take a husband who might sell my services and keep the coins for his drinking and smoking."

The change in her was dramatic, and Deborah suspected it had more to do with Summin's tragic last days than with the arrival of her female blood. "You don't have to adopt your mother's trade."

Yael held the neck of a waterskin under the spring. "It's what I know."

Deborah braided the girl's hair and slipped it under her robe in the back. "It's a sin to lie with a man other than your husband."

Yael plugged the waterskin. "A sin for a Hebrew girl may be an opportunity for a girl of the Cainite Clan."

"You have a choice." Frustration sharpened Deborah's voice, and she regretted it immediately. "Besides, what you're doing is dangerous."

"Not as dangerous as what you're doing."

Deborah sighed. "I have no choice."

"If I could choose, I'd be like you – fearless and decisive. Sadly, I'm neither."

The last word made them smile, sharing the memory of Summin. Yael carried the oil lamp in one hand and the waterskins in the other as they headed down the path. At the camp, everyone had gone to sleep, except for one guard. Yael went to join Sallan's boy-servants, while Deborah stoked the fire and lay near it, her sack under her head. She thought of Barac, of his smile and of the sweet taste of his kiss. Her breath quickened as she imagined him lying beside her.

The moon was down to a thin crescent. Looking up at the sky, Deborah marveled at the brightness of the stars, free from the interfering glow of a moon. She was surprised, however, to see no stars in the west part of the sky, and became alarmed when more stars disappeared from view. She stared at the western sky, trying to decipher this strange, dark divide. The bleak, solid darkness continued to spread, covering a third, then half of the sky. Deborah was about to wake Sallan up to show him, when a drop of water landed on her arm. Another tickled her cheek.

Deborah lay back, opened her arms wide, and laughed.

Rain clouds!

It poured as if the clouds where basins full of water. Moments later, the crevice began to run with a heavy flow, which grew in volume and pace until it was roaring past the camp and over the cliff. Everyone woke up. The rarity of rainfall made it an experience they wanted to feel from head to toe. They walked in circles, taking great pleasure in getting wet, until the clouds moved on and the stars reappeared.

29

The rare drenching left behind temperate air, free of the arid dryness that parched the throat and crusted the nostrils. Having woken up during the night, everyone slept through the breaking dawn. Deborah, however, got up and found Barac standing watch. She quickly washed her face, rinsed her mouth, and tiptoed between her sleeping neighbors. The eastern horizon glowed with a golden hue, free of the usual red tinge caused by the dusty desert air.

Barac followed her to a spot behind the horses and, without a word, took her in his arms and kissed her. She kissed him back openly, taking in his sweet taste and manly scent. The horses shifted, and Rogez glanced back, rocking his head. Barac caressed her back and kissed her neck, tenderly at first, then with growing urgency and hunger, pressing his body firmly against hers. Startled, she pulled away, only to press back against him, at once nervous and awed by this masculine, physical manifestation of his fiery feelings for her, so different from the memory of Seesya's failure.

Men's voices drew them apart. Sallan approached with the two Edomite soldiers. "Good morning," he said. "Up early?"

"The rain produced a beautiful dawn." She gestured. "We were admiring it."

"Ah." He smiled. "Childhood friends, becoming adults."

Barac mumbled something about waking up the men and left. The two Edomite soldiers saddled their horses and tied up waterskins and spears. They already had their armor on.

"Where are they going?" Deborah asked.

"Only he's going," Sallan said.

One of the Edomite soldiers took his horse by the reins and walked along the cliff's edge towards the new dawn. Once he gained some distance, he mounted the horse and galloped away. The man and horse shrunk to a moving speck along the edge of the cliff, which curved gently to give the Ramon Crater its bowl shape.

The other Edomite soldier, the last of the four who had left Bozra with them, sat on the ground and chewed on a piece of bread.

Deborah spoke softly so that only Sallan could hear. "Do you expect to learn new information soon?"

"It's a good day for reunions."

His cryptic answer irritated her. "What reunions?"

"You and Barac. Mamreh and his father."

"How do you know he'll come here today? Maybe he doesn't even know we're here yet."

"He does."

"How can you be certain of that?"

"I'll show you, but first, go and put on the stubble paste I made for you, before your fellow Hebrews wake up, figure out what you are, and burn you at the stake."

Deborah went back to her sack, took out the jar, and applied the paste to her cheeks and chin.

Sallan was waiting for her at the edge of the cliff. "I'm having a reunion, too."

"How so?"

"With my father's memory. A whole week we spent here together. While he collected rare plants and critters, we saw the most fascinating things." Sallan pointed down to the middle of the vast crater. "There are huge rocks that look as if Qoz reached down and cut them from the earth in perfect shapes, ready to build a giant house. And over there is a multicolor wall." He pointed in a different direction. "Huge, solid rock of vivid colors, as if a cloth dyer had tested his skills with a whole rainbow of dyes. We also spent a moonlit night by a hidden pond, larger than you'd ever expect to find in such a barren place, and watched animals come to drink, not only deer, antelopes, and wild goats, but also predators that never show themselves during the day – wolves, bobcats, foxes, tigers, and even a pair of lions with their two cubs, prancing out of the shadows to the water's edge with suddenness that would have made me yelp, if not for my father's ready hand over my mouth. The next day, to amplify my astonishment, he took me to a different place where the rocks were etched with the skeletons of sea creatures such as fish, snails, and crabs, right here in the middle of this barren crater, far from any sea. Can you believe it?"

Deborah shook her head.

"I couldn't, either, but there they were, perfectly preserved remains of sea creatures, as real as the rocks in which they were resting forever." Sallan waved at the view. "I haven't seen a greater marvel than this crater in the Negev Desert, and the most fun I had was at a narrow canyon with a sandy bottom and fresh water, where we bathed—"

"Bathed?"

"The water was cold, because the tall walls blocked the sun inside the canyon, which was curved like a colossal horseshoe. I named it Horseshoe Canyon, and when I praised Qoz for making such a magical canyon, my father explained how the horizontal lines along the walls showed the stages of deepening as water and winds carved the canyon out of solid rock over thousands of years, more than we could count." He wiped a tear. "My father was a wonderful teacher."

They stood in silence for a few moments, gazing out at the deep crater below as it slowly changed colors with the progress of sunrise.

"I'd like to see those marvels," Deborah said.

"Sightseeing has to wait while we concentrate our efforts on staying alive."

"The judge and his men came here to make peace and celebrate. Don't you trust them?"

"Trust?" He sneered. "Why should I trust those who don't trust each other?"

"I trust the agreement I made with the judge: if Princess Needa says she doesn't want to marry his son, the marriage will not take place and we can take her home, and if the princess says yes, we can have the wedding, sign the treaty you wrote, and accompany Mamreh and the princess to Bozra. The king will be happy to see his sister married to the man she loves, and the treaty with her husband's tribe will make sense."

Sallan burst out laughing.

"Why are you laughing?" She hoped he would finally reveal his intentions.

"Come, girl," he said, still laughing. "Let's do a bit of sightseeing."

Rogez followed Sallan's horse across the shallow valley, not directly east along the edge of the cliff as the soldier had ridden earlier, but diagonally to the left in a north-easterly direction. The middle of the valley was muddy, and the horses' hooves sunk in, slowing them down. At the opposite side, a few thousand steps away from camp, the land swelled upward. It was rocky and rough, but the horses managed to climb to the top of the slope, where Sallan turned left and rode slowly along the ridgeline, peering at the ground.

Deborah caught up with him. "What are you looking for?"

"Evidence to support my assumption of distrust among your fellow Hebrews." He dismounted and continued to search while the sun rose higher. "Here it is."

She saw several date pits and pieces of pomegranate skin.

"That's the spot," he said. "Mamreh's scouts spied on us from here yesterday evening."

Looking towards the encampment across the shallow valley, Deborah could see Barac and his men tending to their horses, the judge sitting on a rock with a wine jar in his hand, and the boy-servants and Yael preparing food by the fire.

Sallan walked down the eastern slope facing the early sun. At the bottom were several piles of horse manure.

"Look closely," he said. "Horses produce different-looking waste, depending on their size and manner of chewing and digesting."

Gazing at each pile, Deborah found that three lumps looked similar, while the other two shared a different appearance. "Two horses."

"Correct. How long do you think they stayed here?"

"About half a day."

"I agree." Sallan started back up the slope. "The judge's son sent two men to spy on his fellow tribesmen. Do you think he did it out of trust?"

"How did you know to look here?"

Sallan paused halfway up, catching his breath. "Always watch people carefully, because they have good reasons for what they do, and if you can figure out those reasons, you'll know what to expect next."

"What did you see that made you expect this?"

"Your friend Barac took us yesterday to the highest point on the cliff and flew a flag from a waiting pole. He wasn't doing it to please Judge Ohad's territorial delusions. It was a signal that could be seen from every direction, even from a distance."

"Why bother with signals and spying? Barac could have left one of his soldiers with a message that all was safe."

"A messenger could be lying."

"You're using messengers to communicate with Bozra."

He chuckled. "They won't lie to their grandfather."

"Grandfather?"

"General Mazabi. There's no doubt about their loyalty."

"Loyalty to the general, to the king, or to you?"

"To the general, of course, and the general is loyal to the king, but also to my mother." Sallan chuckled. "Anyhow, that's why Barac flew the flag and took us to an open area, where Mamreh had told him to set up camp so that it could be spied on easily. And it worked as planned. Mamreh saw the flag at the high point, sent his spies, and by late last night he received a report that Barac was here with Judge Ohad."

"What was Mamreh afraid of?"

"Betrayal. His man could have switched sides to a new judge of Simeon, to Goor-Aryeh, or to the king of Edom."

"Barac would never become a traitor."

"The finest man could be turned traitor by greed, fear, or trickery."

"Not Barac."

"What if our king had you tied to the stake, ready to burn, unless Barac betrayed Mamreh?"

There were two possible outcomes, and Deborah didn't like either of them. "I remember something Kassite had told me," she said. "He who assumes the worst about his opponent wins the conquest."

"And about his ally, too," Sallan said.

30

Back at the camp, Deborah and Sallan joined Judge Ohad, Barac, and the young soldiers around the fire for the morning meal. Soon after, the drumming of distant hooves startled everyone. Barac and his men got up and pulled their weapons. Deborah remained seated by the fire with Judge Ohad and Sallan, her hand resting on the hilt of her sword.

The riders came from the east, cloaked by the blinding glare of the morning sun. The small force, which Deborah estimated at about twenty men, rode in an arrowhead formation. At the point of the arrow, a rider in a long robe and flowing headdress made his horse rear up, the front hooves stomping the air. When the horse came down, the rider jumped off with boyish agility. He was about nineteen or twenty and had Judge Ohad's wide face and shrewd dark eyes.

The judge sipped wine from his goblet with an air of indifference. Mamreh handed the reins to one of his men and sat by the fire. Unlike his aging father, Mamreh radiated boundless health and vigor, and Deborah imagined how his body would feel in a woman's arms – as firm and as powerful as Barac when he had pressed himself to her in passion. The thought made her face hot.

"Shalom, father," Mamreh said. "How are you?"

Judge Ohad put down the goblet. "How should I be, when I'm forced to leave my home and my people and travel across the desert to beg my only son to do what every son should do without being asked?" His voice was rising. "Honor your father! Do you remember the Ten Commandments? Do you?"

Mamreh bowed his head.

"Ten times we almost died on this journey," the judge continued. "Treacherous roads, predatory animals, dangerous bandits, zealous villagers, a stomach ailment that brought us to the gates of death!"

Sallan sighed, nodding gravely.

"And here we are." Judge Ohad gestured at the surrounding desert.

"A place even God has forgotten, without a roof over our heads or a woman to keep us warm at night. Will we even see Beersheba again, or have you drawn us here to finish us off and take over the judgeship of Simeon?"

"Father, please." Mamreh suppressed a smile. "I'm as ready to be the judge of Simeon as a goat-kid is ready to give milk."

Deborah understood he was alluding to the parable of kindness from Holy Scripture: "Do not cook a goat-kid in its mother's milk."

The judge grunted.

"I respect you with every bone in my body," Mamreh said. "It was never my intention that you travel here in person."

"What choice did I have?"

"To trust me and give me time to solve the situation with Edom while I'm safely hidden in the desert."

"You feel safer here than in Beersheba?"

"I have won Princess Needa's heart," Mamreh said. "I would not risk her head."

"In other words, you didn't trust me to protect her in Beersheba." Judge Ohad groaned as if in pain. "Distrust is the worst form of disrespect."

"It's not a matter of—"

"Don't you trust me to negotiate with the King of Edom? Don't you trust me to achieve a compromise with our red cousins of the east?"

Sallan held forth a parchment.

Judge Ohad pointed. "Here is the proof that you should have trusted me."

Mamreh looked at the parchment. "What is this?"

"A Treaty of Friendship and Mutual Defense between our ancient tribe of Simeon and the great nation of Edom."

All the soldiers, including those who came with Mamreh and those who accompanied Barac, burst into cheers.

Mamreh raised his hand to hush them. "Why now? What has changed since my offer was rejected in Bozra?"

"The king of Edom must have realized the benefits of joining forces against the arrogant tribe of Judah, our common enemy."

"What about Princess Needa?"

Deborah remembered what Judge Ohad had said in the tent on the road from Kabetzel to Beersheba: "When a young man falls for a girl, the rapid beating of his swollen heart drowns out the voice of reason, the sense of honor, and the alertness to peril." She could see the first two in Mamreh and wondered whether he would also fail to notice the peril he was in.

The judge pointed at Sallan. "The honorable emissary from Edom will tell you."

Sallan gesture to the east. "King Esau the Twentieth authorized me to deliver his royal permission for the marriage of Princess Needa to Mamreh, son of Judge Ohad of Simeon, on the condition that the couple shall present themselves in person at the royal palace in Bozra for the king's personal blessing of their union."

Not waiting for his son, Judge Ohad repeated what he had already said in the roadside tent: "We accept!"

The soldiers cheered again, and this time, Mamreh didn't hush them, which confirmed to Deborah that he was indeed too excited to sense the danger. She recalled Sallan's whisper at the gate of Beersheba: "I made it all up. The king would never enter a treaty with these savages." Had he lied to her, or to Judge Ohad?

Mamreh bowed and kissed the tips of his father's boots, a gesture of complete submission and appeal for forgiveness.

Finally, Judge Ohad relented and opened his arms, crying, "My son! My son!"

They hugged and wept in each other's arms while the soldiers clapped.

As fascinating as all this was, Deborah took her eyes off the Hebrews and watched what Sallan was doing, as he had taught her to do when trying to figure out someone's plans and intentions. She saw him smile and join in the clapping, but his eyes turned to the lone Edomite soldier standing by his saddled horse. She was puzzled. Was Sallan about to send this one, as well, to report on the last developments? It would leave him with no soldiers, completely at the mercy of the Hebrew men controlling this desolate, faraway place. What was his plan?

With one arm still around his father, Mamreh said to Barac. "You've done well, my friend."

Smiling, Barac bowed.

"It's time," Mamreh said. "Bring the princess."

Leading a group of mounted soldiers, Barac took off. He didn't ride east, where Mamreh had come from, but up the crevice, disappearing around the craggy hillside. Another indication, Deborah realized, of the distrust Sallan had talked about.

Judge Ohad pointed at Deborah. "This is Borah of Ephraim. He's young, but clever. He helped me save Beersheba from the men of Judah, who came at night to murder us in our beds."

Mamreh reclined his head in a greeting, but his eyes were narrow with suspicion.

She raised her goblet. "Yahweh's grace upon you, the future judge of Simeon."

Sallan chuckled, raising his own goblet. "Better drink to that, because in my experience, Borah and your mighty God have each other's ear."

The four of them drank, and Judge Ohad recounted the people's enthusiastic participation in setting up the ambush, and how the men of Judah had fled in terror. When hearing of how Borah had captured Judge Goor-Aryeh, who was later burned at the stake, Mamreh smiled and gave Deborah an appreciative nod, but when he heard that Tsruyah was now in charge of the city, his smile disappeared, his jaw tightened, and his face darkened.

"Tsruyah cannot be trusted," he said.

"He is heavy handed," the judge said. "The people will never trust him as a judge in our place."

"Not yet," Mamreh said.

Deborah exchanged glances with Sallan. He had been right, she thought. They didn't trust each other and, therefore, wouldn't trust anyone else, including Sallan and her.

Mamreh turned to Sallan. "Not to appear ungrateful, but I can't help but wonder about your king's generous change of heart about his sister's hand."

Sallan smiled. "Our king is wise beyond his years."

"Could you elaborate?"

"Who am I to presume knowledge of royal considerations?"

"Try," Mamreh said.

"If you insist," Sallan said, taking a moment to contemplate. "Perhaps the king has reflected more about the deep ancestral roots in antiquity that we both share, and your people's national reputation for persistence."

"You call us stubborn?"

Fearing open hostilities, Deborah said, "Yahweh himself called us a stiff-necked people."

"That, we are," the judge said cheerfully. "Hebrew men are worse than donkeys when it comes to hardheadedness. The king of Edom must have realized my son would hide in the desert for years rather than give up the girl he loves."

Everyone laughed.

"It's true," Mamreh said. "I'm still wondering, though, why would the king permit me to marry his sister after scouring the desert for weeks with his chariots?"

"An excellent question." Sallan cradled his cheek in his hand. "Tell me, when you visited Bozra, did the king see you in person?"

"I had audience with him several times, as well as dinner with him and his sister, the princess. But then, his one-armed general came to deliver a summary dismissal."

"The king saw you, then." Sallan nodded slowly. "That must be it."

They looked at him, waiting.

"Our king, as I said, is wise beyond his years." Sallan chuckled. "He asked you to leave because he was deeply impressed and worried that his sister would become irresistibly enamored with you. And who could blame her?"

The flattery was so blatant that Deborah expected Mamreh to see through it and react with outrage, but to her surprise, the young man accepted the explanation as plausible. Seeing this, she remembered what Mamreh had told his father earlier: "I have won Princess Needa's heart. I would not risk her head." Had Mamreh actually won Princess Needa's heart? If the princess confirmed it before the wedding, the mission Deborah had taken upon herself would no longer be about rescuing the princess from abduction, but the opposite, helping her marry the man she loved and accompanying her back to Bozra with him.

"It's all about Princess Needa's happiness," Deborah said. "The king chased you as an abductor, but if she wishes to stay with you, her loving brother will delight in her happiness."

"Exactly," Sallan said. "Borah is right."

Mamreh looked at her. "I've never heard the name Borah before."

"It's short for Deborah," she said.

"Why would a father give his son a short version of a woman's name?"

She was tempted to lower her eyes under his intense gaze, but persisted and said, "Why would a father give his son a name that means disobedience?"

"Hold on," Judge Ohad said. "I can answer that. Mamreh was named after the homestead of Abraham, Elonei Mamreh, near the city of Hebron, where he hosted three strangers, serving them tender calf's meat with butter and milk. His generosity moved them to reveal themselves as Yahweh's angels and promise him that his old wife, Sarah, whose female blood had long stopped coming, would soon be with a baby boy whose seed would become a powerful nation inhabiting all of Canaan and its environs. When my firstborn son arrived, I named him Mamreh in hopes that our forefather's blessing would apply to him."

Sallan raised his goblet. "May our two nations flourish side by side and fulfill the divine promises given to our forefather Abraham."

Mamreh took a quick sip and got up. He summoned the remaining soldiers and had them clear the rocks from an area near camp. He measured it by walking the perimeter and ordered them to expand the area several times until he was satisfied. Next, they dug holes and fixed their spears into the ground around the cleared area, with the dull ends in the dirt, and used the stones they had collected to secure the base of each spear, as well as a taller pole in the middle. They untied packages from the back of their saddles, unfurled them into sheets of cloth, and secured them to the spears in a prearranged order to erect a tent over the perimeter with a pitched center pole.

Deborah was impressed with Mamreh's handling of the soldiers, who were about his age or younger, some not older than her. When one of them ran into difficulty with a spear or a knot, Mamreh did not yell, but came over and demonstrated how the task should be done. He treated them in the manner of an older brother, and they sought his approval.

When the tent was complete, Mamreh walked up the crevice to the small ravine. He returned a while later, his face cleaned of the dust, his beard and hair wet and brushed.

"I'm ready," he said to his father. "She'll be here shortly. Will you officiate?"

"With joy," the judge said.

Sallan glanced at Deborah, and she realized it was time for her to enforce the judge's promise to ask the princess what she wanted. Discussing it in front of Mamreh, Deborah realized, was likely to cause open conflict. Instead, she decided to try and delay the marriage ceremony to give her time for a private conversation with Judge Ohad.

"God's laws," she said, "must be obeyed."

Mamreh and his father turned to her.

She thought about her own painful experience. "Your bride has to dip in a ritual bath, and there's none here."

"There will be one soon." Mamreh pointed in the direction of the ravine. "My soldiers are digging it right now."

Judge Ohad clapped. "My son thinks of everything."

"That's good," Deborah said. "What about a sacrificial goat?"

"It's coming," Mamreh said.

"And a priest," she said. "You cannot marry without a priest's blessing."

Mamreh turned and yelled, "Gershon!"

A young soldier ran over.

"Tell them," Mamreh said. "Who was your father?"

"Yehoshafat of Levi. He was a priest in Gezer until he died of the fever."

"Gezer is the largest city of the tribe of Dan," Deborah said. "Surely they needed a priest. Why didn't you take your father's place?"

"My eldest brother inherited our father's position. He didn't want to share the offerings with the rest of us."

"Have you conducted wedding ceremonies?"

"Whenever the families were too poor to make worthy offerings, the task fell to me."

"Are you ready to conduct one here?"

"Yes."

Mamreh looked at Deborah. "In case you're wondering, we also have more cloth sheets to close the front of the tent and provide the required privacy for the consummation of the marriage."

The men laughed.

Sallan shook a finger in the air in mocked warning. "Not before the great feast and the signing of the Treaty of Friendship and Mutual

Defense, ushering a new era of brotherhood between Edom and Simeon."

"Amen," Judge Ohad said.

31

The sun was high and the heat was heavy when the sound of an approaching rider drew everyone's attention. He was coming from the east, and Deborah soon recognized him as the Edomite soldier Sallan had sent off at dawn. He slowed down and waved as he came closer. Across the back of his horse, a young antelope was tied down, its neck sliced across, the blood dry. Behind it was a smaller animal, also dead, which Deborah recognized as a gazelle.

"Wonderful," Sallan said. "Just in time."

While the boy-servants and Yael unloaded the carcasses, Sallan walked with both of the Edomite soldiers—the one who had just returned and the one who had been waiting—to the edge of the cliff, their heads together. Deborah saw Sallan turn and point out to them the distant slope at the opposite side of the flat expanse, where Mamreh's men had spied on the encampment the previous day. Sallan then pointed to the sun, explaining something, and the two soldiers nodded. With that, they went to their horses, mounted, and rode off.

Sallan came back to sit by the fire. "They'll hunt for more game. I told them which animals your God allows you to eat."

"That's thoughtful," Mamreh said. "How do you know which animals we may eat?"

"Borah told me," Sallan said.

Mamreh looked at Deborah. "A soldier and a scholar. What other surprises are you hiding, boy?"

Her heart pounded, but the words came easily to her lips. "I'm not hiding any princesses, if you're worried about competition."

Sallan and the judge laughed. After a pause, Mamreh joined them, though she could see that his suspicion of her had not diminished.

Moments later, Princess Needa arrived in a caravan that, despite its obvious dearth of luxury, managed to attain a royal flair. Barac led the way down the crevice with six mounted soldiers, followed by the princess, who was covered from head to toe in a copper-colored outfit with only a slit for her eyes. The canopy over her side-facing saddle matched the color of her outfit and the robes worn by her two maids, who rode a donkey. A group of soldiers followed behind, large packages secured to their horses, as well as several camels, donkeys, and goats.

The convoy crossed the level area from the bottom of the crevice and stopped in front of the large tent. Mamreh rushed to help the princess down from the horse. He spoke to her, gesturing excitedly towards the men by the fire, then led her over by the hand while the maids and the soldiers carried cushions, waterskins, and food into the tent.

Judge Ohad stood up, straightened his robe, and smoothed his headdress.

"Father," Mamreh said. "Please meet my bride, Princess Needa of Edom."

With a hand over his heart, the judge said, "We are honored to meet you."

The vailed princess nodded.

Pointing to Sallan, Mamreh said, "And you probably know the honorable emissary your brother has sent from Bozra with the good news."

"Blessed be Qoz." Sallan bowed. "It's been many years, and you were a little girl when I—"

Sneering loudly, Princess Needa turned and walked into the tent.

Mamreh hurried after her, with Judge Ohad in tow. Sallan and Deborah followed, but the soldiers blocked their way.

"Move aside," Sallan said. "I am the personal emissary of King Esau of Edom."

Mamreh came out of the tent. "The princess wishes to rest. When the ritual bath is ready up at the ravine, her maids will help her to dip, and we'll hold the ceremony."

"I am pleased," Sallan said. "You have obviously sustained our beloved princess in comfort and safety, even in this wilderness."

"Are you surprised?" Mamreh glared at him. "Do you think we're barbaric nomads?"

Sallan chuckled. "I didn't mean to—"

"We're an ancient people," Mamreh said, raising his voice. "We descend from glorious ancestry, our laws are just and divine, and our land is rich with milk and honey, bequeathed to us by the one true God!"

Deborah wanted to cheer him and, at that moment, understood how a princess could fall for this handsome, well spoken, and passionate young leader.

Judge Ohad emerged from the tent with an alarmed expression. "Why the raised voices?"

"I meant no disrespect," Sallan said. "My words expressed only admiration and gratitude for the honor you have shown our royal sister and the extensive preparations you have made for a ceremony before there was any certainty that it would happen."

"Very well." Judge Ohad clapped. "We're all friends now."

"Family, almost," Sallan said. "With your permission, I wish to greet Princess Needa in person and deliver best wishes from her brother, King Esau the Twentieth of Edom."

"No," Mamreh said. "The princess clearly doesn't like you."

"You mean, the sneering?" Sallan waved dismissively. "When she was six-years old, her grandfather, the old king, asked her jokingly if she wanted to marry me. She said yes, and I – a foolish sixteen-year-old boy – said that I was in love with another girl. And you know what? Princess Needa kicked me!"

Judge Ohad burst out laughing and pounded Sallan's shoulder. "You deserved it!"

Deborah didn't laugh, because Sallan's story, amusing as it was, implied that the princess was much older than Mamreh. Judging by his expression, Mamreh drew the same conclusion.

"All is in the past," the judge said, still chuckling. "After the ceremony, during the feast, we'll sign the Treaty of Friendship and Mutual Defense, and the newlyweds will receive well-wishers. You'll be the first."

Sallan reclined his head. "As you wish."

Judge Ohad left them and headed up the crevice. The soldiers started several fires while Sallan and his boy-servants skinned and butchered the animals, which were put up to roast. More sheets of cloth were set up as lean-to shade from the beating sun over bowls of dry fruit, bread, and honey cakes.

It occurred to Deborah that she hadn't seen Yael in sometime. Unable to find her in the camp, she walked up the crevice and into the narrow ravine.

A group of soldiers were finishing the excavation of a deep hole in the ground. She recognized the rectangular shape as a ritual bath. They had also dug a narrow channel from the spring to the ritual bath.

Yael appeared from behind a large boulder in the far end of the ravine. Judge Ohad was right behind her. His face was red, his breathing heavy, and his robe misshapen. He straightened it, grinned at Deborah, and stopped by the spring to wash his hands.

The soldiers sniggered.

Deborah took Yael's arm and pulled her back behind the boulder

Yael rolled up her hair and covered it. "Please don't be angry with me."

"What did he do to you?"

"He didn't hurt me."

"It's not pain I'm worried about."

"I know what I'm doing." Yael showed her a silver coin and a shining copper tent peg. "He gave me two gifts. Which one do you want?"

"Neither," Deborah said. "I should stop using this word."

"I like it."

"Summin wasn't the only good man in Canaan. Once your heart heals from losing him, you can find a kind husband who will take care of you. Why sell yourself, if you can have a family, children, and a virtuous life?"

Yael laughed as if Deborah were joking. "Have you forgotten what I am? Girls of the Cainite Clan can only marry men of our kind, men who are marked with perpetual shame like our forefather, men who sell their wives and daughters to other men. I rather do the selling myself and not have any daughters, who would suffer the same fate."

Deborah was taken aback by the harshness of Yael's words, and even more, by her deliberate choice to whore herself.

They walked in silence down the crevice.

"The truth hurts," Yael said. "Do you think lesser of me now?"

"I don't like your choice."

"It's the only choice available to me."

"You could choose to become a Hebrew woman," Deborah said. "When we return to the Samariah Hills, we'll tell no one about your roots."

"How does one become a Hebrew?"

"Accept the truth of the one true God, the almighty Yahweh, and obey his laws."

Yael sighed. "I can't do that."

"Why not?"

"Because there are no true gods."

Stunned, Deborah turned to her. "What?"

"If even one almighty god existed, the world would not be filled with so much pain and injustice. Summin would not have suffered such horrors, my mother would not be forced to whore every day, and my little sisters would not be next."

They reached the bottom of the crevice. Walking towards the camp, Deborah saw Sallan and his boy-servants unpack wine jars from the camels, line them up, and unplug them. Sallan kneeled by the open jars. His back was to her, and all Deborah could see was that he shook each jar before moving on to the next one.

When he was done, Sallan stood and looked around. The black leather satchel slung from a strap around his neck. Noticing her, he waved. Deborah waved back, but her heart beat faster. What was he up to? Had he put something in the wine jars to cause another epidemic of loose bowels?

Yael cleared her throat. "Are you still upset with me?"

"I have bigger worries."

"What about?"

"I took a vow to rescue Princess Needa, but now I'm not sure she wants to be rescued."

"Why would a princess stay with the rough tribesmen of Simeon, if she could return to her palace and servants?"

"Mamreh has the makings of a great man." Deborah said. "And she may prefer to be a wife and a mother, rather than remain a royal sister

At that moment, Princess Needa emerged from the tent with her maids, Mamreh, and several soldiers. He helped the princess onto her horse, and they headed to the crevice.

"Get me near her," Yael said. "Maybe I can find out what she really wants."

They walked quickly to intercept the group halfway to the spring.

"One thing," Deborah said, covering her mouth as they got closer. "If there's any threat to the princess, you must defend her."

"How?"

"Use the tent peg as a weapon."

Mamreh saw Deborah approach and paused, the rest of the group stopped with him.

"Greetings," Deborah said. "I'd like to offer my servant girl to help the maids. I'm sure the princess could use another female maid today."

He turned to the princess.

She nodded, and one of her maids said, "We accept."

As they continued up the crevice, Princess Needa glanced back at Deborah through the narrow slit in the veil. Her eyes, as blue as her brother's, were cryptic. Was it a desperate plea for help? An indifferent peek of mild curiosity? Or a haughty dismissal?

Deborah went to the tent and looked inside. Judge Ohad was lounging on large pillows.

"Come in, Borah." He beckoned. "I have good news. Princess Needa assured me that she truly wants to marry my son."

"What did she say exactly?"

"The princess expressed her fervent love for Mamreh and her utmost joy at the prospect of joining our tribe. I couldn't be more pleased with her response."

The jubilation in his voice sounded hollow to Deborah. "I prefer that you ask her in public."

"That would be redundant." Judge Ohad sipped from a goblet. "Rejoice, Borah. It's a great day for the Chosen People."

She didn't respond.

"What's wrong?" He put down the goblet. "Don't you trust me?"

Again, she didn't answer.

"Have you forgotten which side you belong to?"

"I belong on Yahweh's side."

The smile faded from his face. "He is the God of the Hebrews, not of the Edomites."

She nodded.

"You must decide, Borah." Judge Ohad poked his finger at her chest armor. "Will you treat me with respect, or with distrust?"

"I'll treat you with honesty," Deborah said. "As to respect and trust,

those must be earned, but your actions have caused me only confusion."
He laughed as if she had spoken in jest.

32

While Princess Needa was at the ritual bath, Mamreh returned to the tent, and everyone else gathered at the bottom of the crevice. Gershon of Levi, wearing a priestly white robe with blue fringes, walked up the crevice to where the narrow ravine split off and stood beside the princess's horse.

She reappeared dressed in a long white dress. A sheer face veil was secured with a string around her mass of wavy hair, which was now exposed, sparkling in the sun with an orange hue that was brighter than ripe carrots and almost as radiant as a burning fire. Deborah could barely breathe at the sight of this abundant hair, which resembled her own, before Kassite had cut it.

A soldier began beating a handheld drum.

Aided by her maids and Yael, the princess mounted her horse, sitting sideways in the saddle under the four-posted canopy.

Everyone commenced singing the traditional Hebrew wedding hymn. The lyrics described the marriages of Jacob and his two wives – the older and wiser Leah and the younger and prettier Rachel. The men sang with deep voices, which brought up Deborah's painful memory of her own wedding procession in Shiloh.

Descending the crevice, the procession advanced across the flat area towards the cliff and stopped in front of the great tent. The maids and Yael helped the princess down from the horse. Deborah tried to catch Yael's eye, but the girl was focused on the princess.

A large rock served as an altar. Gershon approached it, glancing at his fellow-soldiers with an embarrassed smile.

The singing ended.

Judge Ohad emerged from the tent, his arm interlocked with Mamreh's. The young man had replaced his robe and headdress with a woolen coat and a white cap, and his sandals with boots. He bowed before the princess, reached around to the back of her head, and untied the string holding the veil.

For the first time, Deborah saw Princess Needa's face. Her regal features were a feminine version of the king, but while his face expressed anger or joy with explicit bluntness, her countenance was impregnable, showing neither delight nor dread of the impending marriage. Deborah wanted to point it out to Sallan. She looked around, searching for him, and noticed his bushy gray hair among the men preparing the food near the fires.

A soldier brought a goat, its front and rear legs bound together, and placed it on the altar, lying on its side. The goat bleated and jerked its legs in a futile effort to escape, causing a few twigs to fall off the altar.

"Men of Simeon," Judge Ohad said. "Honored guests."

Sallan came over, wiping his hands on his robe.

Princess Needa glanced at him, her gaze lingering.

He bowed. "It warms my heart to see you, Princess Needa, all grown up."

Her eyes narrowed and her lips pursed as she looked away.

Judge Ohad put his arm around Sallan's shoulder. "We're delighted to seal a bond of family and friendship with the great nation of Edom. Let us proceed."

Gershon stepped forward. "Under the laws of our God, this man, Mamreh, son of Ohad, Judge of Simeon, takes as his betrothed bride Needa, princess of Edom, who from this day on shall be named Needa, wife of Mamreh.

Mamreh smiled and smoothed down the front of his coat. Her face remained blank.

"With this offering," Gershon continued, "we ask Yahweh to sanctify this marriage, make this bride's womb fertile, and give her many sons to continue her husband's name."

Everyone chorused, "Amen."

Raising a knife over the goat's neck, Gershon recited the traditional marriage blessing: "Blessed be Yahweh, our God, king of the world, who created man in His own image and made the woman to lust after her husband and obey him in all matters until death."

The goat bleated breathlessly as the soldier pulled its bound legs up. Gershon brought down the blade and sliced across with a single motion that opened the goat's neck from side to side. The bleating stopped, and blood pulsated out of the severed neck while the goat writhed.

Deborah looked away, remembering how she had fainted at her own wedding in Shiloh.

Singing broke out.

Mamreh took Needa's hands and smiled at her. She looked at him, her blue eyes inscrutable. He kissed her on the lips – a brief kiss, which she didn't resist. The soldiers circled the couple, singing and clapping. Barac was in the middle, his face glowing with joy, while the whole throng moved together into the tent.

Meanwhile, Gershon cut open the goat's underside and removed the internal organs. A soldier brought over a burning torch to ignite the twigs and wood on the altar.

Yael and the two maids carried bowls of steaming food and jugs of wine into the tent. Deborah stayed outside with a nagging feeling that something was wrong. She saw Sallan leave the cooking fires and walk to where the horses were tied. He was holding the black leather satchel. She wondered whether the Edomite soldiers had gone to hunt for more meat, as he had said, or were on the way to Bozra to report, which made little sense considering the distance.

Another possibility occurred to her. The king could have sent an army as soon as Sallan's second messenger had reported Barac's disclosure that Mamreh was hiding near the Ramon Crater. Had there been enough time for the messenger to reach Bozra and for an army to march all the way here? A rider on a horse could move very fast, but how quickly could an army of steel chariots travel?

This possibility explained Sallan's efforts to slow the convoy on the way south. Was he trying to slow things down now? The wedding ceremony was over, but Mamreh had not yet possessed his bride to consummate the marriage. Was Sallan planning to somehow take Princess Needa away before the feast was over? To do it, he would have to poison all the men, including Barac.

Peeking into the tent, Deborah saw the revelers begin to drink and eat. Barac was holding up a goblet and singing. She stepped in and shouted at the top of her voice. "Stop! Stop! Stop!"

The singing ceased, and everyone turned to her.

At that moment, Sallan entered, came behind her, and whispered,

"Don't interfere."

She had to interfere, but what should she say? The danger was real in her mind, but it was merely a guess, and if she spelled it out, the consequences could be fatal – for Sallan and for her.

"Yahweh has spoken," she said. "I will bless this union."

Judge Ohad smiled, nodding.

Deborah extended her hands forward, fingers parted in pairs, and recited the priestly blessing: "May Yahweh bless you and protect you. May He show you kindness and grace. May He illuminate your path and grant you peace."

"Amen," everyone shouted in unison, raising their goblets to resume drinking.

"Hold on." She kept her hands forward. "For the blessing to materialize, God requires us to fast until sunset. No food or drink."

They looked at each other, and the judge stepped towards her, his lips pursed in displeasure.

"Where's Gershon?" Deborah turned to the open end of the tent, where the soldier-priest was finishing up with the goat. "Come here, priest."

Gershon entered, his white robe stained with the goat's blood.

"Yahweh commands you," she said. "Recite the story of our ancestor Abraham and the three wise men who came to his tent – their plight, their blessing, and their promises for the future of Abraham's descendants. And when the sun sets behind the horizon, this marriage shall be blessed, and the revelers may hold a feast, but if you eat or drink before sunset, this marriage shall be cursed. So says Yahweh!"

It was only midday, and the men were visibly disappointed. Leaving no room for argument, Deborah marched out of the tent and turned towards the horses. Rogez saw her coming and neighed, rocking his white head up and down.

"Wait." Sallan followed her. "What are you doing?"

Deborah turned to face him. "What am I doing? I'm trying to prevent you from poisoning them."

Barac came out of the tent and approached them.

"Say nothing," Sallan said.

"Don't hush me when you're about to—"

He put a hand on her mouth.

Rushing forward, Barac slapped Sallan's hand away.

Sallan reached under his robe, drew a short knife, and held it at Barac.

Deborah stepped between them. "Stop it, both of you."

Sallan lowered the knife.

"Please go back," she said to Barac. "Make sure no one eats or drinks."

"Is it true?" Barac stared at her intently. "Did Yahweh speak to you?"

Gershon's voice came from the tent, telling the story of Abraham and the three angels.

"I can't explain now," Deborah said to Barac. "Don't ask me to."

Barac hesitated.

"You have to trust me," she said. "The food and drink are not safe to consume."

"Not safe?"

"I'll explain later. Please go inside."

He relented and went.

"Deborah," Sallan said. "You made a terrible mistake."

"Stopping you from committing mass murder?"

"There's no poison. Would I risk harming the princess?"

"Then what did you put in their meat and wine?"

"A harmless sleep potion. Once they're asleep, we could put the princess on the back of your horse and take her to safety, as you promised the king, who'll pay your reward. Aren't you eager to regain your little homestead in Canaan?"

Stunned by his forthright admission, Deborah said, "Is that all, or is the Edomite army coming to slaughter them."

"In their sleep?" He clutched his chest as if in sudden pain. "Is this the kind of a man you think I am?"

"I'm too confused to know what to think, but it doesn't matter. Judge Ohad told me that he asked the princess, and she wants to marry Mamreh."

"He's lying."

"What if he isn't? I watched Princess Needa's face during the ceremony and saw no resentment or distress. And when Mamreh kissed her, she didn't push him away, as a princess would to a man she didn't want."

"You're speculating with no facts."

"It's a fact that Princess Needa did not resist his kiss. I think she may actually love him."

"It doesn't matter what Princess Needa wants or doesn't want. She's a woman."

"You loved a woman once."

Sallan's face paled. "Don't—"

"Did it matter to you what An wanted?"

He bent over, resting his hands on his knees, and groaned.

Deborah touched his shoulder. "It hurts to remember, but you're about to inflict the same pain on them."

He shook off her hand and spoke in a weak voice. "It's not the same. Not even close."

Recalling the words of Qoztobarus, she nodded. "Grief and guilt are a terrible mix, I understand, but you know that even the separation itself, the loss of the person you love more than—"

"Enough, please, I have no choice."

"Why?"

"The king wants his sister back. Your life and mine depend on it. Nothing else matter. If the Hebrews fall asleep, we'll take her peacefully. If they don't, Edom's army will take her by force."

Glancing to the east, Deborah understood. "The soldier came back with a message from General Mazabi. The hunting was only a cover."

Sallan straightened up, but didn't look at her. "The king sent General Mazabi to escort Princess Needa home safely. His chariots got stuck in mud after last night's rain, but nothing will stop him from following the king's orders, and the same goes for us."

The mention of chariots changed everything, because Deborah knew that chariots were the ultimate attack weapons. The king didn't send his chariots merely to escort the princess back home, but to make war on her Hebrew abductors.

She ran to Rogez and mounted him.

Sallan followed her and stood before Rogez, raising his arms to stop the horse. "Where are you going?"

"To speak with General Mazabi – to beg him, if I have to."

"You don't know where he is."

Pointing to the east, Deborah said, "There, somewhere."

Rogez advanced, bumping his nose at Sallan's chest, pushing him backwards.

"Be reasonable," Sallan pleaded. "You'll get lost and die of thirst."

"Where there's mud, there's water."

"You'll never find it."

She pulled the reins sideways, bypassing Sallan. "Didn't you tell me about water at Horseshoe Canyon?"

The expression on his face made her realize she had hit the target. "My horse will find it."

Rogez took off at high speed across the open area, racing along the edge of the cliff. Deborah glanced back, shielding her eyes from the sun, and saw Sallan standing near the horses. Behind him, men were coming out of the tent, some bent over, others sitting down on rocks.

33

Once across the flat area, the path went up a rocky slope and down another, remaining within a stone throw of the edge of the cliff. Deborah kept the reins loose, and Rogez galloped without any guidance from her. His confidence gave her hope that he was chasing the scent of the Edomite soldiers' horses, which had been tied beside him every night since leaving Bozra. She didn't interfere even when he veered off the path and took a narrow trail that was hard to make out in the rough desert landscape.

Unlike the confidence she had in Rogez, grave doubts assaulted her faith in her own ability to handle what was coming. How would she dissuade General Mazabi from his plans? She remembered his mockery of her fighting methods: "Dodging. Begging. Running for the exits. Escaping to the benches." And later, on the morning before she departed Bozra, he had been outright hostile. Would he even listen to what she had to say, or order his soldiers to dispose of her summarily?

The heat was oppressive, but in her haste, Deborah had not taken a waterskin. As Rogez kept galloping, her eyes fogged and her muscles began to ache. After a while, she leaned forward in the saddle, rested her head against his neck, and fell asleep.

The sound of wings flapping came from behind, and the eagle caught up with them, flying next to Rogez. From the side, the curved beak appeared long, the head massive, the right eye yellow and bright.

Deborah had only one question, which she yelled over the noise of the wings and the hooves. "Will I die today?"

"That's up to you."

"It's up to General Mazabi."

"I wouldn't worry too much about him. The louder a man threatens, the softer his will to act."

"General Mazabi is a man of action."

The eagle's eye glowed like a miniature sun. "He's intrigued by you. Intrigue him further."

"How—"

A rough jolt tossed Deborah upward, and as she grabbed the saddle horn and opened her eyes, Rogez came to an abrupt stop, tilting forward, his head to the ground. He recovered his balance, raised his front hooves, and reared up on his hind legs. She struggled to hold on, but her fingers slipped off the saddle horn, and she rolled backwards over his rear end, landing facedown on the ground, which was muddy and soft. Before she could rise, her head was pushed down into the mud, her arms were grabbed and twisted back, and a rope bound her wrists. All that was done without words, but the roughness of the rope sent searing pain through her arms, which jolted her out of the initial shock.

Twisting sharply, she pulled one arm free while yelling, "Rogez! Help!"

He whinnied, the ground shook under his hooves, and a man cried in pain behind her. Someone pushed her hard, and she swung her arm around, fist clenched, colliding with a hairy cheek. She felt Rogez's warm fur against her face, smelled his breath, and heard a crunch as his teeth bit down on someone's bones. Another man screamed and let go of her arm. She shook off the rope, which had not been tied properly yet, wiped the mud from her eyes, and got up.

She was standing in a narrow canyon, its tall walls blocking the sun. Three soldiers with red-horsehair rooster helmets lay on the ground behind her, groaning in pain, while a highly agitated Rogez pranced back and forth between her and more soldiers, who stood further down the canyon in front of several chariots hooked up to horses.

The soldiers drew their swords and began to advance at her.

Deborah showed them both her hands. "I'm not here to fight. Don't you recognize me?"

The soldiers stopped, and one of them said, "It's the boy who slayed Qoztobarus."

She reached down to one of the downed soldiers and helped him up. He was covered in mud, as she was. The second soldier managed to get up unaided, and the two of them helped the third, who could barely stand. Clasping Rogez's reins, she drew him closer and rubbed his neck to calm him down. A stream flowed in the middle of the canyon. She

AVRAHAM AZRIELI

went over and washed her face. Back in the saddle, she sat straight, placing her hand on the bejeweled hilt of her sword.

"Where is General Mazabi?"

One of the soldiers turned and walked past the chariots and down the canyon, around the curved walls, which gave the canyon the shape of a horseshoe. Deborah urged Rogez forward. He stayed near the canyon wall, where the ground was firm. Further down, the canyon was blocked by dozens of chariots whose wheels were stuck in deep mud. A group of soldiers struggled to pull out one of the chariots, while others pushed from behind. The horses, which had been released from the chariots, stood on the firm soil along the canyon walls.

General Mazabi watched the soldiers' efforts with his four grandsons.

She dismounted Rogez and stepped over to him. "Princess Needa married the son of the judge of Simeon willingly. She is fine."

His craggy face showed a hint of surprise. "Has the marriage been consummated?"

"Not yet."

"Good."

"There's no need to attack the Hebrews. The princess needs no rescuing."

"The Elixirist agrees?"

"Sallan doesn't care what she wants, only what the king ordered, but I disagree, because the facts have changed—"

"He's right."

"All I'm asking is that you go there in peace and speak with Princess Needa before making any decisions."

"I don't make decisions. I receive orders and execute."

"But the king doesn't know about her feelings."

The general shrugged, his attention back on the stuck chariots.

Frustration threatened to overwhelm her, but Deborah knew that raising her voice would only cause him to shut her out. She recalled the eagle's advice, but how could she intrigue this old warrior?

The soldiers' efforts made the chariot advance slightly, but the wheels were submerged too deeply in the mud.

"It's too heavy," she said. "Why don't you use the horses?"

"They'll slip, break their legs." He grunted. "You like horse meat?"

"They won't slip near the walls, where the soil is firm."

General Mazabi looked at her, his eyes creased. "Go on."

"Do you have ropes?"

He beckoned the soldier in charge and pointed at her. "Do what Borah say."

Under her supervision, they tied a long rope from each front corner of the chariot to a horse, one at each side of the canyon. The horses stepped forward, the ropes tightened, and the chariot moved, its wheels slushing in the mud, turning very slowly.

Another idea occurred to her. She ordered several soldiers to take off their chest and back armor pieces and lay them in front of the wheels. With a mighty heave, the horses pulled the chariot wheels onto the flat pieces of leather. More soldiers stripped their armor pieces, laying them down in straight lines in front of the wheels while the chariot rolled the rest of the way out of the deep mud.

The soldiers cheered, and General Mazabi raised his copper spear to toast her.

With Deborah directing the work, each chariot was pulled out, reattached to a horse, and driven around the curve up the canyon to drier grounds. When the last chariot was out, General Mazabi mounted his horse. She followed him on Rogez.

Bypassing the column of chariots, she was impressed by the organization and discipline. Each chariot had a driver holding the horse's reins and a soldier armed with a long sword and a spear. The chariots themselves had a curved bar across the front that stuck out sideways to mow down anyone standing in the way.

Reaching the head of the column, General Mazabi didn't stop. The chariot drivers whipped the horses, and the column moved. The pace grew to a steady trot as they left the canyon. His four grandsons took the lead, navigating the way westward. The sun was a quarter of the way down. Deborah sped up to ride next to the general.

"You should know," she said. "Sallan failed. The men of Simeon aren't sleeping."

He didn't slow down, but turned his head to look at her. Did he sense her uncertainty? She had seen some of the men come out of the tent looking ready to collapse, but others could have avoided the food and wine and stayed awake.

"I told them God forbade eating or drinking wine until sunset."

"Sunset isn't far off," he said.

"The marriage will be consummated by then."

"She's been his captive. He's raped her already."

"It's not like that," Deborah said. "He waited to be married under our God's laws. He loves and respects her too much to violate her before marriage. If you saw them together, you'd know."

General Mazabi kicked inward, making his horse go faster, and the chariot drivers followed suit. Rogez needed no prodding and kept up with them. The general glanced aside, his gray beard fluttering in the wind, his lips curled, hinting at a smile. She smiled back.

He roared over the noise, "What's Qoz telling you?"

She couldn't help but laugh.

He laughed, too, which revived her hopes. General Mazabi was an old soldier, and soldiers didn't grow old by rushing into needless battles. Her argument against attacking must have taken root. He had to realize the awful ramifications of killing the new husband of the king's sister — no matter what the king's original orders had been.

When they reached the path along the cliff. The sun was low on the western horizon, blinding them. The ground wasn't completely dry from last night's rain, and the horses' hooves didn't raise a lot of dust, which diminished the risk of being noticed by the men of Simeon. About halfway around the crater, the leading soldiers turned right, away from the cliff.

It was twilight when they stopped in a low-laying area behind a hill. The chariots rearranged in a columned formation of five abreast. She counted ten rows, which added to fifty chariots. General Mazabi and his four grandsons dismounted, tied the horses together, and headed up the slope.

She dismounted and hurried after them. At the top of the slope, they got down on the ground, only their heads above the crest. It was the spot where Sallan had shown her traces of Mamreh's spies. She remembered how he later pointed the place out to the last two Edomite soldiers. Now they were here with their grandfather, using the spot to spy on Mamreh and his men.

The sun had already set behind the opposite mountains. Across the shallow valley, all the way to the left by the cliff, the cooking fires had shrunk to red embers. The large tent was visible against the twilight sky.

It was open all around, though, as the sheets of cloth had been removed from all sides. No torches or oil lamps burned under the tent top, leaving it too dark to see if anyone was there. She stared hard, praying to see men walk near the camp or where the crevice led up to the spring in the ravine. There were none. Had she been too late with her warning to stop the feast? Had Barac and the others already consumed enough wine or food to fall asleep?

"The Elixirist succeeded," General Mazabi said. "You shouldn't have lied to me, boy."

"I didn't," Deborah said. "The encampment looks too quiet. Even if all the men of Simeon ignored my warning, Sallan and his boy-servants wouldn't have eaten or drunk the wine. He would have loaded the princess on a horse and met us here, or signaled to us from there."

"He had to participate," one of the grandsons said. "The Hebrew judge and his son would have noticed if our king's emissary didn't eat and drink like everyone else."

"I agree." Another grandson said. "It's as quiet as the Elixirist told us it would be. He did his magic, and now, we'll do our job."

"That's right," a third one said, gazing at the distant view, shrouded in the approaching darkness. "He put them to sleep for the evening, and we'll put them to sleep forever."

A tremor passed through Deborah. "What do you mean, sleep forever?"

Leaning on his spear, General Mazabi rose to his feet. "Tell the men to be careful not to hurt Princess Needa, Sallan, and his boy-servants."

"Wait." Deborah got up. "How can you kill sleeping men? It's a sin."

"It's war, boy." The general headed back downhill. "Get used to it."

His four grandsons ran ahead and started giving orders to the chariot drivers and fighters.

She followed him down the slope. "The king sent me to find Princess Needa and bring her home. That's what I agreed to do in order to prevent bloodshed, not to cause it. That's why I came looking for you."

"You came for absolution."

"What?"

"To rinse yourself clean."

"Clean from what?"

"The blood of battle."

"Slaughtering helpless men isn't a battle."

"Don't worry, boy." General Mazabi placed a hand on her shoulder. "Their blood won't stain you."

"It'll stain you."

"I serve the king. I'm his long hand."

She understood. King Esau had ordered this attack. This was the king's plan.

"It's my duty," the general said. "Qoz knows it."

"Please," she begged. "Take Princess Needa and leave. There's no need for a single death tonight."

"And tomorrow?"

"We'll be halfway back to Bozra."

"And the Hebrews?"

"They'll wake up, realize it's over, and go back to Beersheba."

"And then? Peace for forty years?"

"I hope so."

General Mazabi chuckled, shaking his head. "Imagine you're him. You wake up. You look around. Where's your bride? Where's your honor? Where's your revenge?"

She wanted to argue, but couldn't. Mamreh may go back to Beersheba tomorrow, but he would not forget. Rather, he'd become obsessed with finding a way to win back his bride and his honor until, one day, he would exact a bloody revenge on Edom.

"This would be worse," she argued. "Instead of one young man angry over losing a woman, you'll cause the whole tribe of Simeon to hate Edom and seek revenge for killing its judge, his son, and so many young men."

Reaching the bottom of the slope, General Mazabi mounted his horse. "A headless snake is harmless. That's Simeon after tonight."

Twilight was rapidly turning into darkness.

The first row of five chariots started up the slope.

An image flashed through her mind of Barac, sleeping under the tent top among his soldiers, unaware of the army of chariots heading his way, reaching him, running over him, stabbing him with spears, smashing his head with—

"No!" She ran to General Mazabi. "Don't do this! Yahweh will punish you for killing the Hebrews!"

The old warrior looked down at her. "Perhaps the opposite."

"How?"

"The Hebrews have sinned. Their God is angry. I'm their punishment. It's possible, right?"

The idea baffled her. Did she have it all wrong? Were these chariots of death the manifestation of Yahweh's wrath at his Chosen People? Had her attempts to stop the Edomites' attack been a sinful interference with a divinely ordained punishment of the sinful men of Simeon?

"God is not dishonorable." She reached up and grabbed his left hand, which was holding the reins "Who kills sleeping men but a coward?"

General Mazabi's horse stepped forward while she continued to clasp his hand tightly. He lost his balance, tilted sideways in the saddle, and fell towards her. She managed to cushion his fall, but his huge bulk took her to the ground with him.

He cursed, scrambled back to his feet with agility belying his age, and kicked her in the ribs, aiming for the narrow space between the chest and back armor pieces. The pain was paralyzing, and she couldn't breathe.

"Stay down," he roared. "Or die!"

34

General Mazabi's grandsons galloped over, but he waved them off and mounted his horse. One of them grabbed Rogez's reins and pulled him along, following the chariots.

Unable to move, Deborah watched helplessly from the ground as the rows of chariots rolled up the slope, the dark figures of the drivers and warriors outlined against the night sky. Her head was pounding, and she shut her eyes to stem the pain. The ground trembled from the rolling chariots.

She imagined Barac again, bleeding from his wounds, crying for her.

Rising on all four, she started up the slope.

The first five chariots reached the top and went over the crest, then the second row, and the third, until the whole force was rolling down the western slope in a deafening racket. She managed to stand, started running uphill, and stumbled on a rock, falling flat. Another glimpse of Barac's bloody face sent her going again. She reached the top and looked down.

The formation of chariots was gaining speed down the slope with a deep rumble that was getting stronger and more frightening. She felt small and powerless, as if a great storm had gathered, growing mightier with every moment, rapidly approaching, unstoppable, about to destroy everything she held dear.

"Rogez!" Deborah fell to her knees. "Come back to me, Rogez!"

The first row of chariots reached the bottom of the slope, followed by the rest in rapid succession. They raced diagonally across the wide valley like a dark cloud over a pale land, covering a third of the way to the Hebrew camp, then half.

Raising her hands to the starry sky, Deborah cried, "God, help me!"

When her eyes descended, the dark cloud of speeding chariots was two-thirds of the way to the camp, closing in quickly. It would soon be over, the men of Simeon all dead, and Barac—

She touched her lips, remembering his sweet taste, and wailed, "Yahweh!"

A light blinked in the darkness across the valley, then another, and a few more. One burst into a flame, then the others. The fires were not random, but appeared in small intervals creating two strings. One string of lights ran at the foothills under the crevice, and the other came to life on a parallel line to the first, so that the two strings of flames created a path through which General Mazabi's chariots were racing ahead.

For an instant, in the glow of the fires, she saw a pallid shadow break away from the dark cloud of chariots and head back in her direction.

"Rogez!" She cupped her mouth. "Rogez!"

As the chariots raced down the path between the flames, the strings moved, curving in towards each other at the rear, closing behind the last of the chariots. At the same time, the flames grew and swirled with flurries of sparks that chased the chariots.

With a chill shooting through her chest, Deborah understood what she was seeing. The men of Simeon were not asleep. They had lain in wait for the attack, ready with the sheets of cloth they had removed from the sides of the tent and other flammable materials. They must have kept oil lamps burning in secret, ready to ignite bundles of cloth while the chariots were racing across the open area. It was reminiscent of the panic-inducing fireworks she had devised for defending Beersheba from the men of Judah.

How had the men of Simeon known about the Edomites' coming attack? Had Sallan cracked under pressure and confessed?

It didn't matter now, because the Edomites' merciless drive to destroy a camp of sleeping, defenseless Hebrew men had just turned into a spectacle of self-destruction. The terrified horses, spooked from the sides and the rear by the swirling flames, thundered ahead with their chariots at top speed, trampled the tent, and continued onward. Illuminated from behind by the chasing fires, row after row of chariots flew off the edge of the cliff into the air.

Rogez appeared as a white ghost out of the night, running up the slope. His breath was hot and heavy as he licked her face. Over at the camp, men were shouting, some in gleeful victory, but others in anger and fear. Had General Mazabi and his four grandsons avoided the fate of the chariots? Had some of the chariots escaped doom, or had their drivers and warriors jumped off before reaching the cliff's edge?

As soon as Deborah got in the saddle, Rogez took off, galloping down the slope. Within moments, they were charging towards the camp. She saw small fires dot the ground. They were the remains of burning cloth sheets the men of Simeon had used to terrify the horses, drive them in a mad stampede over the cliff.

In the flickering lights of the dying flames, she saw shadows of men fighting with swords, spears, and clubs. Shouts of rage and cries of pain intermingled, but in the darkness she couldn't tell Edomites from Hebrews.

"Deborah!" Barac's voice came from the dark on her left. "Deborah!"

She turned Rogez in that direction, realizing that Barac must have spotted the white horse.

He appeared out of the darkness, a sword in one hand, a club in the other, his robe soaked in blood, his eyes wild as a man gone mad. "Run," he shouted. "Run away!"

She stopped Rogez next to him. "Where's Princess Needa?"

He pointed with the club, which had pieces of skin and hair stuck to it.

Deborah felt sick. "At the ravine?"

"Yes."

"Alone?"

"With her maids and Yael." He poked Rogez with the club. "Go!"

Riding off, Deborah glanced back and saw Barac watching her, his sword and club lowered as if he had tired of the killing. Behind him, in a flash from a nearby flame, she saw a bearded giant on a great horse, an arm raised with a glistening spear that was aimed downward at Barac's back. She pulled hard on Rogez's reins and swung him around, shouting, "Behind you!"

Barac turned just as General Mazabi reached close enough to deliver a deadly blow, but her cry drew the general's eyes, distracting him before he stabbed down with the spear. That brief delay allowed Barac to dodge, roll on the ground, and swipe his club at the horse's leg, causing it to neigh in pain and stumble. The general slipped off the saddle with ease, went around the rear of the horse, and faced Barac. With about seven or eight steps between them, Barac's sword and club were out of range, useless against the general's spear, which he raised.

As if reading her mind, Rogez leaped ahead, closed the remaining distance within a blink of an eye, and rammed General Mazabi on the right side of his body, where his missing arm used to be. The massive old man flew in the air like a straw doll, landing hard on the ground. The spear, however, did not leave his grip, and when Rogez caught up with him and reared, ready to stomp him with his front hooves, the general tilted the sharp end of the spear up to impale Rogez as he came down. At that moment, however, Barac reached them and sunk the blade of his sword under the general's chest armor. Rogez twisted on his rear legs and lowered his front hooves safely beside General Mazabi, whose eyes were on Deborah as blood frothed up in his mouth.

Deborah was stunned at the sight of this seemingly indestructible man exhaling his last breath, but Barac wasted no time. He pulled the copper spear from General Mazabi's hand and gave it to Deborah. She took it with both hands, ready for its weight.

"Leave," Barac said. "Now."

"Don't die," Deborah said. "I forbid it!"

She turned Rogez and sprinted away, charged by the terrible noise of men killing each other. Glancing over her shoulder, she saw Barac run back into the battle, his weapons up and ready.

She rode to the crevice and up the incline. Rogez found his footing in the dark while she kept her eyes to the left, searching for the small ravine. She didn't have to look hard, because someone had left a burning torch by the spring at the far end of the ravine.

Dismounting Rogez, she tied him beside Yael's mare and Princess Needa's horse. With the copper spear in her hand, she verified that her sword was in its sheath and the sling tied around her hips, and proceeded cautiously into the ravine.

At first, she saw no one, but the reeds near the spring rustled, and Yael came out. She ran to Deborah and hugged her, murmuring thanks to her Gods. In her right hand, Yael clutched the copper tent peg Judge Ohad had given her.

The reeds rustled again, and the maids helped Princess Needa out. She still wore white, but had covered her head and face, with only a slit for her eyes.

"Your brother sent his army to kill the Hebrews," Deborah said. "And your husband set up an ambush to drive the attackers over the cliff. They're still fighting."

The princess didn't respond.

A man groaned behind Deborah. She swiveled around, tilting the spear with both heads, ready to stab. She saw no one. The groan sounded again, deep and painful. It came from the rectangular hole in the ground, which Mamreh's soldiers had dug earlier for a ritual bath. The channel they had created to direct water from the spring had been dammed up, and she stepped over it to reach the end of the ravine, grabbed the torch from a rock fissure that propped it up, and held it above the hole.

Most of the water had seeped into the ground below, and a person was lying in what was left at the bottom. His head was twisted up against the rough wall, eyes squeezed shut by a swollen face, hair pasted to a lacerated skull, the ear missing.

"Sallan!"

Deborah handed the torch to Yael and climbed down into the hole. Her boots sank in the shallow water. She pulled him up to a sitting position, and he cried in pain.

"It's me," she said. "Try to stand up."

One of his eyes cracked open, and he mumbled, "You came back."

"Yes." She touched his ravaged face. "Who did this to you?"

"Mamreh." He winced, turning away. "What happened?"

"The battle is still on."

He took a few shallow breaths. "And your friend, Barac?"

She choked with dread, unable to respond.

"You must escape." He tried to push her away. "Leave me here and take the princess."

Deborah knelt, pulled him over her shoulders, and pushed up enough for Yael and the two maids to get him off her back to flat ground. He was groaning and shaking. One of the maids unfurled a blanket and covered him while Deborah climbed out of the hole.

His one eye searched around until it found Princess Needa. He mumbled something.

Deborah bent over him, her ear to his lips.

"Take her," he said hoarsely. "East. Go east."

She smoothed down his wet hair. "We'll all go."

He shook his head, twisting in pain. "No time. Go now. You must survive."

"Not without you." She looked up at Yael. "We'll put him on your mare. Do you have a rope?"

"I don't want to go to Edom."

"Edom?" It was a man's voice. "Who's going to Edom?"

They turned and saw Mamreh. He held a club in one hand and a sword in the other, both weapons wet with blood. Judge Ohad was right behind him, carrying no weapons, his face pale and his robe splattered with blood. Behind the two men, the distant noise of fighting had declined, but not completely.

"I asked a question." Mamreh voice rose. "Who's going to Edom?"

Sallan groaned.

"How did he get out?" Mamreh noticed Deborah. "You!"

"Yahweh's blessings on you," she said.

He stepped forward. "You betrayed us."

"The opposite," Deborah said. "I discovered the Edomites' plan and went to plead with General Mazabi not to attack you."

"Lies," he said, raising both weapons as he came closer. "All lies."

Deborah retreated, holding the copper spear with both hands.

"Your sorcerer is a coward." Mamreh kicked Sallan. "He told us everything."

She felt a pang of fear. Had Sallan told them she wasn't a boy? "Then he must have told you that I spoiled his plans—"

"He tried to protect you, but I know the truth. You conspired with him against your fellow Hebrew men."

Thinking of Barac, her fury flared up. "And you? Where are your fellow Hebrew men? They fight on while their leader is deserting?"

"The battle is lost," he said. "My brave soldiers are fighting to give us time to escape safely."

"You're fleeing to Beersheba while your men are dying?"

His face twisted in anger. "They're dying so that the tribe of Simeon doesn't lose its judge and I don't lose my wife before I even possessed her once!"

Mamreh shouted these last words and, raising his sword, rushed at Deborah. She was ready for him and dodged sideways while swinging

General Mazabi's heavy copper spear, hitting Mamreh on his lower back, accelerating his forward movement, making it impossible for him to stop before he fell into the ritual bath, the bottom water splashing up to the surface. She wasn't ready, however, for Judge Ohad, who charged her as a bull ramming a competitor. She flew backwards and fell on the muddy ground by the spring. In the jittery light from the torch, she saw his stocky figure come down, his knee landing on her chest.

"You thought I forgot what you did?" Judge Ohad panted, his gray beard quivering, his hand slipping under his robe. "Invading my room, clubbing me over the head to save that little whore, extorting a pardon from in front of my people – humiliating me!"

His hand emerged, clasping the handle of a knife. She grabbed his wrist with both hands. The point of the blade approached her neck, just above the chest armor.

He leaned forward, using his weight to press down. "It's over, boy."

Behind him, Deborah saw Yael.

"Greet Yahweh for me." The judge smirked and pushed down harder.

Her arms trembling from the effort, she felt the blade poke her skin.

Yael swung her hand and plunged the copper tent peg into the side of his head.

Judge Ohad's gleeful expression changed into surprise. He fell forward, his bulk bearing down on the knife. With whatever power she had left, Deborah pushed him aside, and he rolled off of her, dropping the knife.

The maids screamed.

Deborah grabbed his knife and sat up.

Mamreh climbed out of the ritual bath. He didn't bother to get up but, like a lizard lunging at a prey, sprinted on all fours and pounced on her, his hands closing around her neck, pinning her to the ground. Deborah tried to inhale, but no air could pass through his powerful grip. Judge Ohad's knife was in her left hand, but Mamreh had his elbow on her forearm, jamming it to the ground. She twisted her body, trying to throw him off, but he was too heavy.

Yael stared at Deborah. The flickering torch lit the girl's pale face, her eyes wide with shock. Deborah wanted to scream at her: "Do something! He's choking me to death!" No words, however, could pass through her compressed neck.

A change in Yael's face was followed by a tremor through her whole body. Her eyes blinked rapidly and turned to Mamreh, to his hands on Deborah's neck, and to his father, lying dead with the tent peg in his head.

As her vision narrowed and fogged up, Deborah knew death was coming. She gazed desperately at Yael, who finally bent down to pull out the tent peg. Mamreh noticed and, without letting go of Deborah's neck, lifted his leg and kicked Yael's shin. She screamed, bent over to clasp her lower leg, and fell to the ground, wailing in pain.

For Deborah, dazed and about to faint, this seemed like the end, but then, she felt her left hand move, freed when Mamreh had shifted his weight to kick Yael. Through a fog of incoherence, she clasped the handle of the knife, tilted it to point at him, and stabbed. He jerked and cried, but didn't release his grip on her neck. She pulled her hand back and stabbed again, and again. He let go with his right hand and tried to grab her arm, but she stabbed the palm of his hand. He shouted, released her neck, and punched her.

The air whizzed as Deborah filled her starving lungs. Mamreh fumbled to pry the knife out of her hand. She let go of it, folded her arm while clenching her fist, and punched upward at the front of his neck at the same spot where Tsruyah had hit the priest on the platform in Beersheba. She felt her knuckles collide with the male protrusion under Mamreh's beard, and something crunched inside. His hands shot to his throat, and he made a gagging sound.

She wriggled from under him and scooted back, away, still on her back.

Mamreh's face turned to her, his eyes wide with the realization that he was about to suffocate to death.

Deborah's hand felt something cold. It was General Mazabi's spear, which had flown out of her hands when the judge had rammed her.

Picking his father's knife, Mamreh got up and came at her with his last breath.

Reacting instinctively the way General Mazabi had done under Rogez's raised hooves, Deborah tilted up the spear, the butt anchored on the ground, the tip aimed at Mamreh as he fell on her, impaling himself on the spear, which passed through his abdomen. The knife stabbed into her armor and prickled her right breast before his hand went limp, leaving the knife imbedded in her armor.

Princess Needa uttered a chilling shriek of agonized grief, finally removing all doubts about her love for Mamreh.

Deborah pushed his corpse off and got up. The realization of what had just happened hit her with dizzying ferocity. Judge Ohad and his son, both alive only moments ago, were dead and gone. They would never walk, talk, or lead the tribe of Simeon again.

Princess Needa's shriek echoed from the walls of the ravine.

"They left me no choice," Deborah said, speaking more to herself than to anyone else. "It was either them killing me, or the other way."

The copper spear made a squishy sound as Deborah pulled it out of Mamreh's abdomen. She convulsed, retching, and turned away from the two bodies.

The two maids sobbed while they held Princess Needa, who was silent again.

Yael stepped forward and threw her arms around Deborah. The girl was shaking.

Silence descended, not only in the ravine, but all around them. It told Deborah that the battle was over. Had they all died? Was Barac lying there, as she had feared, covered in blood and whispering her name?

She nudged Yael away. "I must go down to the battlefield and find Barac. He might be injured."

"What about us?"

"I'll be back soon. We'll leave for Bozra at first light."

"Not me," Yael said. "The Edomites hate our clan."

"You're with me, and I'll be in the king's favor. Can I rely on you?"

Yael shrugged. "Fine."

"Good. Now, find Mamreh's sword and stand guard."

"Wait." Yael went into the reeds and came out with a waterskin. "Take this. Wounded men are always thirsty."

As Deborah turned to go, Sallan said, "Wait."

She knelt beside him.

He spoke with difficulty. "Don't go."

"Why?"

"Whoever won the battle, they will kill you."

It was a statement that took her a moment to digest, but she realized

Sallan was right. Both sides had reasons to suspect her of helping the other side.

"I must look for Barac."

"You have her." He gestured at the princess. "Thank your God and escape to Bozra."

"I can't."

He grasped her forearm. "You won. Collect your reward and go home. To Canaan."

"What if Barac isn't dead?"

"Then he'll follow you."

It was a hopeful thought, and for a moment she considered accepting Yahweh's gift and racing off with Princess Needa to Bozra, before any surviving soldiers arrived to avenge their leaders and brothers. With the Edomite king's reward, she would be able to return to the Samariah Hills. If Barac followed her, she'd marry him, and if he were dead, she'd marry another man of Ephraim, one of the many good men who would line up to marry her, as Umm-Sallan had predicted. Either way, she would recover her inheritance by the force of God's law and fulfill her True Calling. She imagined settling back on her family's lush land and building a new life, but then, in a jarring flash, the image returned of Barac lying on the ground, helpless, crushed, and bloodied, calling her name. She struggled to peel Sallan's fingers from her forearm, but his grip was surprisingly tight.

"Let go," she said. "Barac needs me."

With his other hand, Sallan grabbed her chest armor and pulled her closer. "Deborah," he whispered. "Don't be a stupid girl."

35

Tearing away from Sallan, Deborah ran out of the ravine. It was dark, only the thin crescent of the moon starting to rise up. Rogez headed down the crevice slowly, picking his steps. At the bottom, she directed him to the area near the flattened tent and stared into the surrounding darkness, softened only by the thin moon and remnants of burning cloth and red embers. Dark figures lay on the pale ground, inert and silent.

A shadow appeared. It was a man, she could tell, but he didn't have Barac's confident stride, wide shoulders, and proud posture. The man approached her with a heavy gait, his shoulders slumped, and his bearing hunched over.

"Stop!" She gripped the copper spear. "Don't come any closer!"

The figure slowed down, but kept coming.

Raising the spear with both hands, she yelled, "Stop!"

To her dismay, Rogez turned sideways, which made it impossible for him to protect her by stomping with his front hooves, or by kicking with his rear legs.

The man grunted, now only a few steps away. Deborah tried to make Rogez turn, but he wouldn't. She aimed the heavy spear, ready to stab down.

"It's me," the man said.

"Barac?"

He collapsed.

Deborah slipped the spear into the saddle sheath, grabbed the waterskin, and jumped off the horse. Kneeling by Barac, she poured water into her hand and moistened his face. His breathing was fast and shallow, and his skin felt hot. She helped him drink, her hands trembling with dread. Where was he wounded? Was it fatal? The darkness made it impossible to see.

"Our ambush worked." He shuddered. "We thought they were

doomed."

Deborah gave him more water.

"Some jumped off the chariots. Riders veered off the cliff. We didn't expect it. We didn't."

She brushed his hair away from his eyes.

"They were outnumbered, but fierce. Slashing. Spearing. Cutting us down. My friends fell. One after another."

"Don't blame yourself." She caressed his cheek, which felt cooler.

"Like demons, those Edomites. They could see in the dark. They read our minds."

"Their old leader trained them well." Deborah poured water on her hands and wiped off the stubble paste from her face. "He was a formidable general."

"His death broke their spirit." A long moment passed before Barac spoke again. "Will I ever be a formidable general?"

"You will." Deborah kissed his forehead, her lips tasting blood. "I know it."

"Like ripe wheat," he whispered. "They cut us down."

She kissed his eyebrows, his cheeks and nose, her lips finding no open wounds.

"We fought hard. Brought them down. Man after man."

Her hands found the hooks of his robe, undid them, and pulled the rough cloth off his shoulders and down to his hips.

Barac looked up at her, the whites of his eyes like little moons. "You came back for me."

Deborah ran her hands over his neck and bare back, searching his warm skin for wounds, finding none. "God answered my prayers. He kept you alive."

His lips found her mouth, sending a fiery jolt through her. She pulled back, but he held her close, and his tongue flickered over her lips, making her quiver. She stroked his chest slowly from side to side over the curvatures of his firm muscles and the plume of hair in the center, which her hand followed down over his stomach, flat and unharmed.

He lifted the strap of the helmet, breaking off their kiss, removed the helmet from her head, and brought his lips back to hers. While they kissed, she searched his lower back, her hand travelling over skin that was slick with sweat and blood. The tips of her fingers sought gashes, slashes, or stab wounds. There were none. Relief made her eyes well up while her hands continued down to his thighs.

He tilted his head back from her and looked around. "They're dead," he said.

"Everyone?"

He nodded, his eyes glistening in the dark. "At least Mamreh and the judge got away."

Deborah hesitated. "They died, too. Up by the spring."

He groaned and turned away, covering his face.

She smoothed down his thick curls, crusted with dry blood.

"I failed." He was shaking badly. "All this killing, for nothing."

Pressing her cheek to the side of his head, she hugged him.

"So much blood," he murmured. "I'm a sinner."

"No, no, no. You're a good man."

"A terrible sinner."

"Fighting is a duty," she paraphrased what General Mazabi had said earlier. "A soldier kills for his master. Yahweh knows it."

"But I killed for myself," he cried. "I wanted to live. To be with you."

His words hit her hard and, at the same time, delighted her. "That's how I felt, too, thinking of you all the time, worrying about you, imagining you—"

"I killed so many." Barac's voice broke.

Deborah held him tightly. "It was God's will."

"All that blood, on my hands."

"You were only His instrument to deliver punishment to those who deserved it."

He shook his head, no longer able to speak, and lay down on the ground.

Deborah stretched out beside Barac and cradled his head in her arms while he wept. Around them, in the dark, a few meek sighs sounded as someone drew a last breath.

Barac quieted down. His breathing slowed. Was he injured inside, under his skin, a fatal blow that had damaged his heart or stomach? She held her breath, listening to his slow breathing. Each time he exhaled, there was a long pause before he inhaled again, giving her a temporary relief, until the next time.

Moments passed, and Barac breathed on, falling into deep sleep.

Deborah gazed up and thanked God for letting him live, one young man among the many who now lay dead about the battlefield. She was overwhelmed with gratitude, but dared not rejoice, because her own twin fortunes – liberating Princess Needa and reuniting with Barac – contrasted with the twin misfortunes suffered by the tribe of Simeon and the nation of Edom tonight, evident by all the death and destruction that surrounded her.

After a while, Barac shifted and turned to face her. His hands edged up over her shorn hair and brought her head down to him. Their lips came together in a gentle kiss – probing, savoring, and halting. He held her away for a moment, his hands caressing her cheeks, tracing her ears, stroking her nape. Then, he pulled her back to him, and it was a different kiss—hungry, urgent, and desperate. She responded with a craving as vital as a parched traveler in the desert, arriving at a green oasis, gulping mouthfuls of sweet water.

His hands tugged on her armor, found the knots over her shoulders, and untied them.

A flare of fear chilled her chest, and she retreated.

"Deborah," he whispered. "Be my wife."

His words rang in her ears. *Be my wife!*

He fumbled in his pocket. "My father wrought a ring out of copper for my mother. It's the only thing I have left of hers. I've carried it in my pocket for the day I can betroth you."

She held up her finger.

"With this ring," he said, putting it on her finger, "I betroth you to be my wife."

In awe, Deborah touched the ring. It wasn't perfectly round, but in the darkness, she couldn't make out why.

"It's a star," he said. "With six points for the six days God took to create the world."

She couldn't speak as her heart swelled with happiness, her lips showered his face with kisses, and her mind flashed with images from the flight of the eagle over Palm Homestead. She could see the flowery slopes descending to the verdant valley of her childhood – the tidy fields, thick with wheat and barley, the copious orchards, heavy with fruit, and the lush pasture dotted with cattle – all surrounding the house and its livestock corral, where a boy rode a pony, led around by a man whose wide-brimmed hat cast a shadow over his face, hiding it from above. Except that now, she recognized Barac's confident gait and strong arms, and the way he paused to gaze up at the low hill where she stood under the palm tree, wielding her bejeweled sword, addressing thousands of Hebrew men and women, who repeated after her with a thundering roar: "Hear, O Israel! Yahweh is our God! Yahweh is one!"

While she continued to shower him with kisses, Barac removed Deborah's armor pieces, undergarments, and loincloth. Taking her in his arms, he embraced her firmly, pressing their hot, moist bodies together, merging the two of them into one flesh as he entered her, consummating their marriage. A surge of searing pain and thrilling pleasure washed over Deborah, chased by crashing waves of joy as his thrusts grew in force and urgency until he froze and shook violently, and she cried out, "Barac!"

To Be Continued

A NOTE TO THE READER

Deborah's quest will continue in *Deborah Striking*, the fourth novel in the Book of Deborah series.

While the *Book of Judges* describes Deborah's stunning success as a prophet, a judge and a military leader, who liberated her people from Canaanite oppression, it says nothing about her youth and upbringing. How could a girl, growing up in a world controlled by men, rise to rule over them? What hardships fueled her tenacity? What setbacks steeled her resilience? What battles transformed her into a formidable leader? These are the fascinating mysteries we aspire to unravel in this novel series, which began with *Deborah Rising* (HarperCollins, 2016).

To ensure accuracy in describing how people lived in the ancient Mideast, I consulted countless books and articles. They are too many to list here, but I am particularly indebted to the scholarly works of William F. Albright, Yigael Yadin, Avraham Biran, Israel Finkelstein, Benjamin Mazar, Amihai Mazar, William G. Dever, Joyce Salisbury, Carol Meyers, Thomas E. Levi, George Hart, Bruce Routledge, Richard Elliot Friedman, Geraldine Harris, Richard Wilkinson, Boyd Seevers, Gale A. Yee, Brian Schmidt, Alan Dickin, Monroe Rosenthal, Isaac Mozenson, Diana Vikander Edelman, Hershel Shanks and Claudia Valentino.

We are blessed with wonderful friends and family members, who read my manuscripts at various stages, provide insightful observations, and offer enthusiastic support. They include (in alphabetical order) Margie and Arie Adler, Sarai Azrieli, Talya, Ben, and Elan Azrieli, Hagit and Michael David, Rabbi Dr. Israel Dreisin, Don Eddins, Monica and Prof. Michael Finkelthal, Risa and Dr. Opher Ganel, Rachel and Joel Glazer, Prof. Sharon Glazer and Tamas Karpati, Julie and Hanan Gur, Dr. Jennifer and Nir Margalit, Linda and Dr. Bernard Rosenbaum, Glenna Salisbury, Wendy and Avner Skolnik, Stephen J. Wall, Stephanie and Ernie Wechsler, and Carol Wilner.

As always, this novel would not have come to life without the tireless support of my wife, Fiona, a dedicated physician who finds time to read the first draft of every new novel and provides astute critique, perceptive comments, and inspiring encouragement. Fiona and our children fill my life with love and laughter, which sustain me daily.

Last but not least, I owe a debt of gratitude to you, my readers, for choosing to spend your precious time with my books, for recommending the books to your friends, and for posting thoughtful insights and reviews on social media. There is no greater joy for a writer than a supportive community of readers. Thank you!

ABOUT THE AUTHOR

Avraham Azrieli is the author of books and screenplays. His first novel was *The Masada Complex* (a political thriller), followed by Israeli spy novels *The Jerusalem Inception* and *The Jerusalem Assassin*, as well as *Christmas for Joshua* (an interfaith family drama), *The Mormon Candidate* (a political thriller), *Thump* (a courtroom drama featuring sexual harassment and racism), and *The Bootstrap Ultimatum* (a mystery involving the commercialization of Memorial Day). Most recently, he has written a series of novels inspired by the true story of the first woman to lead a nation in human history, starting with *Deborah Rising* (HarperCollins, 2016), and continuing with *Deborah Calling*, *Deborah Slaying*, and *Deborah Striking*.

Beside fiction, he has also authored *Your Lawyer on a Short Leash - a guide to dealing with lawyers* and *One Step Ahead – A Mother of Seven Escaping Hitler's Claws* (an acclaimed WWII true story, which inspired the musical By Wheel and by Wing).

While growing up in Israel, Avraham received extensive Talmudic education, before attending law school and serving as a law clerk at the Israeli Supreme Court in Jerusalem. He later earned an advanced law degree from Columbia University in New York City, served as a law clerk for the Federal District Court, and started his legal career with Davis Polk & Wardwell. He has represented clients in numerous complex court cases before trial and appellate courts, including the United States Supreme Court. He currently lives near Washington DC with his wife and children. Like Ben Teller, the protagonist in *The Mormon Candidate* and *The Bootstrap Ultimatum*, Avraham often rides his motorcycle in the mountainous forests of western Maryland. To learn more, please visit www.AzrieliBooks.com

ALSO BY AVRAHAM AZRIELI

Fiction:

The Masada Complex
The Jerusalem Inception
The Jerusalem Assassin
Christmas for Joshua
The Mormon Candidate
The Bootstrap Ultimatum
Thump
The Elixirist
Deborah Rising
Deborah Calling
Deborah Slaying
Deborah Striking

Nonfiction:

Your Lawyer on a Short Leash – A Guide to Dealing with Lawyers
One Step Ahead – A Mother of Seven Escaping Hitler's Claws

Author Website:

www.AzrieliBooks.com